Kabuki
Dancer

Kabuki Dancer

Sawako Ariyoshi

Translated by
James R. Brandon

KODANSHA INTERNATIONAL
Tokyo • New York • London

First published in 1972 in Japanese under the title *Izumo no Okuni*, by Chuokoron-sha, Tokyo.

Distributed in the United States by Kodansha America, Inc. 114 Fifth Avenue, New York, 10011, and in the United Kingdom and continental Europe by Kodansha Europe Ltd., 95 Aldwych, London WC2B 4JF. Published by Kodansha International Ltd., 17-14, Otowa 1-chome, Bunkyo-ku, Tokyo 112 and Kodansha America Inc.

First Edition 1994
94 95 96 10 9 8 7 6 5 4 3 2 1

ISBN 4-7700-1783-9

Library of Congress Cataloging-in-Publication Data

Ariyoshi, Sawako, 1931-1984
[Izumo no Okuni. English]
Kabuki Dancer / Sawako Ariyoshi; translated by James R. Brandon.
    p.   cm.
   ISBN 4-7700-1783-9
1. Izumo no Okuni, fl. 1600-1607—Fiction.   I. Title.
PL845.R5I913 1994
895.6'35—dc20

Translator's Note

Okuni may or may not have been a priestess-dancer, a *miko*, at the Grand Shrine in Izumo. That part of her life remains a legend, but late sixteenth- and early seventeenth-century historical accounts provide firm evidence that one woman almost single-handedly founded Kabuki theater. Okuni's dances and scenes of town life were the first to be named "Kabuki." Nearly four centuries later, the comic-erotic flavor of Okuni's performance continues to resonate in the sophisticated Kabuki that we see on the stage today.

Kabuki Dancer is Sawako Ariyoshi's recreation of Okuni's life between 1588 and 1609, the period in which historical records describe her performances. Her novel imparts Okuni's sense of discovery when she secularizes the old Buddhist prayer dances, dares to do male impersonation, introduces European dress on stage, devises a comic "prostitute-buying" scene, and creates genre dancing out of folk performance. Above all, Okuni brought characters of daily life onto the stage for popular urban audiences. Her companions in the theater, and her lovers, were also historical figures: Nagoya Sanza, the city dandy who popularized Southern Barbarian fashions, the Noh drummer Sankuro, and, less certain, the comedian Densuke. Little is known about the men in Okuni's life and the author has fleshed them out in her imagination. The lyrics Okuni sings, taken from song books of the time, carry the delicate flavor of an open, expansive, remarkably free society.

Like performers in many cultures, Okuni and the dancers, actors, and musicians in her troupe were despised. They were "riverbed beggars." At the same time, Okuni was admired and famous among the ruling elite—she was summoned to give command performances before the emperor in Kyoto and the son of the shogun in Edo (modern-day Tokyo). Being an artist, Okuni could cross traditional gender and class divisions to give us a commoner's view of an exceptionally colorful and turbulent era of Japanese history. In the novel, Okuni's life and art intersect with Hideyoshi's megalomaniacal invasion of Korea and China, the slaughter of defeated generals after the Battle of Sekigahara, the founding of the city of Edo, and the expulsion of the *Kirishitan*, or Christian, religion.

This is a romantic novel in the sense that the raw power of human emotions dominates the characters, especially Okuni. Okuni is driven by the irresistible need to dance, but Ariyoshi asks, "Does something grow from singing? After dancing, is something left? Is a *kabuki* woman a plant without roots in the earth?" The author is persuasive in showing that Okuni abhorred prostitution—countering the usual equation of female performers with whores. The novel honors a woman whose accomplishments have been largely discounted since men appropriated Kabuki. It is not insignificant that the author of a novel about a determined, independent, and creative woman should possess these qualities herself. Sawako Ariyoshi loved the theater. Her deep knowledge of Kabuki history strongly anchors this work of fiction. She was also an irrepressible playwright, and her talent in writing dialogue is apparent in the novel's scenes of theatrical performance. My interest in the novel lies in its moving account of the creation of Kabuki theater. I was delighted when the author called the novel to my attention and suggested its translation some years past.

Kabuki Dancer (*Izumo no Okuni*) was researched and written over a period of four years, coinciding with serial publication in the magazine *Women's Topics* (*Fujin Koron*), one chapter per month for thirty-six consecutive issues (January 1967 through December 1969). The translation is of that text, subsequently published in three volumes by Chuokoron-sha (1972). Some tangential incidents which the serial publication format encouraged were not considered essential by the author, and these were not included in the translation. I have not translated the second, third, or fourth recapitulations of incidents, which helped serial readers remember events they had read in early chapters, perhaps two or three years previously. In consultation with the author, the order of some sequences was transposed for clarity, a few scenes that essentially restate the context of earlier scenes have been cut, some minor events and secondary characters have been eliminated, and a number of historical sequences have been condensed. I have converted lunar dates used in the Japanese text to Gregorian dates.

Honolulu, July 1993
JRB

PUBLISHER'S NOTE ON PRONUNCIATION: When Japanese names end with the vowel *e*, that vowel becomes a syllable, so that the proper pronunciation of Abe is Ab-*eh*, Mame is Mam-*eh*, etc.

One

Omura Yuko Hogen Baian left Hoshi Temple on the grounds of Tenmangu Shrine in Osaka just before noon. Although he was a priest of the Shinto shrine, nonetheless he considered the Buddhist Tenmangu temple his home. The two religions, one native and one foreign, mingled in the man as easily as they did in these holy precincts. Baian was tall and heavyset. On any other day he would have attracted attention, for over his priest's black habit he was wearing a brilliant crimson robe topped by a bizarre Chinese cowl. But this was not a usual day. Hordes of people raced excitedly past him into the shrine located on Sanjo Street in the southern part of the city. No one noticed that he was Baian, personal attendant to Toyotomi Hideyoshi, Regent to the Emperor and Lord of the Realm.

Baian was happy to be ignored, for today, February 25, 1588, was the day of the Plum Blossom Festival of Tenmangu Shrine. Baian was responsible for reconstructing the shrine buildings to their full splendor after they had been burned to the ground by Oda Nobunaga in 1570 during the civil wars. The new festival's enormous popularity was also solely Baian's doing. Through two clever moves he had succeeded in transforming an ordinary occasion into a major national festival. Tenmangu Shrine's Plum Blossom Festival had long been overshadowed by the nearly simultaneous festival held in late March at the ancient Kitano Shrine in Kyoto. So Baian moved Tenmangu's festival forward, so it would precede Kyoto's festival by nearly a month. The new festival date was highly felicitous, for it occurred shortly after New Year on the old lunar calendar and marked the beginning of spring. Of course, plum blossoms come out a month earlier in Osaka because Kyoto lies in a basin where the cold lingers long into the spring. But Baian was also impelled by a personal motive. He burned with a desire to challenge Kitano Shrine's ancient imperial prerogatives. He would do this by using Regent Hideyoshi's new power.

Baian also gave the festival its unique character. From the venerable Dazaifu Shrine on the island of Kyushu, Baian imported the old belief that one could exchange lies for truth through Buddha's mercy at the time of the New Year. He invented a festival based on this belief. At dawn, shrine priests threw into the air thousands of finches, or *uso*, that had been carved from willow branches and painted deep crimson touched with gilt. *Uso* also means "lie." Today, people were pouring into the shrine in a human avalanche, each person intent on catching one of the finches and then passing it, and a year of lies, to another person. Hands explored neighbors' breasts and sleeves as lies were exchanged for truth. As if intoxicated by the fragrance of the lush pink-white plum blossoms, cheeks aflame like the finches' breasts, men and women were aroused as their closely pressed bodies rubbed against each other. Exactly as Baian had planned, the four-acre expanse that comprised the grounds of Tenmangu Shrine was the scene of an orgy of passionate communal sexuality, cleverly disguised as a religious festival. Perhaps the exchange of finches was a serious ceremony at Dazaifu. But here in Osaka at this historical moment, a quiet festival was inconceivable: Hideyoshi now ruled the whole nation from Osaka Castle and the feeling was rampant that a new era, centering on the city, was beginning.

Baian had already demonstrated a unique usefulness to Hideyoshi. In June 1582, Oda Nobunaga was murdered by Akechi Mitsuhide at Honno Temple in Kyoto. Nobunaga was the first samurai general in a century to wrest national power from Japan's provincial warlords, and he was Hideyoshi's lord. Hideyoshi instantly assumed power by tracking down and killing Mitsuhide. That October, Baian composed a laudatory account of Hideyoshi's bravery,

A Chronicle of Mitsuhide's Mutiny, and presented it to Hideyoshi. It is easy to imagine that Hideyoshi was pleased by the quickness of both Baian's pen and wit. Three years later, in 1585, Hideyoshi dispatched an army to conquer Shikoku Island. Baian could easily have stayed behind in Osaka, but he chose to join the hundred-thousand horsemen and foot soldiers in the thick of the fighting. Writing from a succession of battle camps, Baian penned a detailed history of the campaign and dedicated it to Hideyoshi. Such behavior earned him Hideyoshi's special favor.

Hideyoshi gained unprecedented military victories one after the other. In their aftermath the Lord of the Realm was surrounded by wealthy merchants, masters of the tea ceremony, and even samurai whom he had defeated, dancing attendance at Osaka Castle. Among all those people, no one was more useful to Hideyoshi than Omura Yuko Hogen Baian. Not the least of Baian's talents was his astonishing skill at transforming a lie into truth. For example, Baian did not hesitate for an instant to state in his *Saga of the Rise of Hideyoshi* that Hideyoshi was the emperor's son and that his mother was the granddaughter of an imperial noble when, in truth, Hideyoshi was a farmer's son.

Baian was still recovering from an illness he had contracted the previous year during the campaign to subdue Kyushu. But today he walked through the grounds of Tenmangu Shrine with his body stiffly erect. Glowing in the favor of Hideyoshi, who loved color and brilliance more than anything, Baian noted the bursting plum blossoms and the milling, excited crowd. Though he was rudely jostled by the surging mass and hands boldly groped through his wide sleeves to his breast, nothing dampened his good spirits. Baian's old wrinkled face seemed ready to break into a thousand smiles of satisfaction. It was a new age. Old traditions were dying, and thanks to Hideyoshi's patronage Baian was part of the changing times. Hideyoshi, who people said looked like a monkey, enjoyed calling out to everyone around him, "Wrinkled Baian looks more like a monkey than I do." It was Hideyoshi's special joke to summon the priest before him and loudly proclaim, "They call me prune face, but compared to Baian, I look positively human." And he gave Baian the nickname Great Prune Face.

In an eddy in the moving crowd, Baian heard the rhythmic throbbing of drums and the sharp ringing of shrine hand bells. He found himself pushed toward the worship hall. Here in the backwater of the crowd, groups of entertainers performed on crude stages and straw mats thrown on the ground. Outside the shrine entrance vendors were doing a rush business selling food and souvenirs at their stalls. But here near the worship hall, the performers were failing miserably. The crowds surging past them were too rapturously absorbed in exchanging lies for truth to hear the singing or see the dancing.

"Pitiful," Baian muttered under his breath. Yet he didn't feel pity, he felt elated as he deliberately paced, hands clasped behind his back, before these creatures. In Baian's opinion they didn't deserve to be called artists. They were hardly better than carnival freaks or sideshow performers. They weren't like the troupes of refined actors and musicians who congregated in Kyoto for the great festivals, or even like the traveling Noh troupes who came to Kyoto from time to time and performed at street corners to earn extra income. People who lived in raw, unfinished Osaka, dominated by Hideyoshi's towering new castle, hadn't acquired any appreciation for culture as yet. Baian saw a trained dog do one or two tricks, a top-spinner who couldn't keep his top going, and an acrobat who hopped about on a single stilt. Stupid, childish tricks, Baian thought. Hideyoshi has stopped a hundred years of brutal warfare. His talent and energy are making a new society. Baian felt nothing but loathing for these ignorant creatures and their out-of-date performances. Yet a few times, one or another of the rough stages drew his attention.

He first paused in front of a puppet show. A puppeteer held two old and filthy glove puppets, one on each hand, and moved them about as he sang an antiquated religious tune. The dolls drooped. The words of the song were turgid. The crude simplicity of the performance bored him.

"Rubbish," Baian snorted.

Next, he stopped in front of a blind balladeer. Since medieval times such men had attached themselves to temples, calling themselves priests, though they had no formal connection with Buddhism. They specialized in chanting episodes from the moralistic epic, *The Tale of the Heike*, accenting their quavering phrases by plucking the dull strings of the *biwa*, a thick-toned lute. They wandered from city to city, hardly better than beggars, performing on street corners and wherever crowds gathered. Baian knew the epic, of course, and instantly recognized the verses. Yet, their doleful recitation gave him no pleasure.

"Old-fashioned!" Spitting out the words, Baian turned away. Baian fully shared Hideyoshi's love of new and colorful things. The blind minstrel-monk, wrapped in a filthy hemp robe, was utterly repulsive. Instinctively, Baian knew there would be no room in Hideyoshi's new Japan for the pessimism that permeated *The Tale of the Heike*. The epic's cautionary moral that "the mighty shall fall and the brave shall be blown as dust before the wind" was no harbinger for Hideyoshi's vigorous age. I'll have an attendant beat the man with a broom and sweep him out of the shrine, Baian thought.

He was about to conclude his perfunctory inspection when, above the noise, he heard the clear note of a bell and the voices of young girls singing. He paused for the last time.

> Lord Buddha,
> Man desires goodness
> Which cannot be preserved.
> Man fears hell's tortures
> Which are easily received.
> Praise Amida Buddha. Praise Merciful Buddha.

Again Baian snorted, but this time his tone indicated interest. Baian thought it was natural to hear a Buddhist song at a Shinto festival.

A glance at their rough kimonos told him the girls were from the provinces. From the way the sleeves had been hastily lengthened, he guessed they had passed through Kyoto. Their rude attempt to copy the latest fashion of the capital was laughable. A tall dancer in the center struck a bell with a small wooden hammer. A monk's black robe was draped over the solid body and the face was covered by a large bamboo hat from which the lacquer was beginning to peel. The dancer sang and moved in unison with the five girls. A man, sitting in a small dressing room attached to the stage and unmistakably a farmer, was striking a bell in unison with the dancer in the center, sometimes joining the refrain, "*Namu Amida Butsu,* Praise Amida Buddha."

Baian snorted. The dancer in the center seemed to be a girl.

> Buddha's Way,
> The law of Mercy,
> Leads man to enlightenment.
> Quell carnal desire,
> The circle of birth and death,
> The curse of never-ending rebirth.
> Praise Amida Buddha. Praise Merciful Buddha.

The two bells sounded a different note. Gradually the rhythm of their beating increased. White calves and attractive ankles appeared from behind kimono hems and quickly disappeared. Baian was entranced. He stood without moving.

Baian had not been captured by sexual desire. Although a religious man and more than sixty years old, Baian was still capable of sexual passion, and he served Hideyoshi, a highly sensuous man. Yet at that moment it was not the sight of the girls' legs that held him enthralled. It was the steps they were dancing.

He snorted loudly, then folded his arms and gazed at their dance intently. Hideyoshi avidly patronized the Komparu family of Noh actors, and so naturally Baian had made a point of becoming thoroughly versed in Noh performance himself. In time Baian would compose Noh plays about Hideyoshi's life, such as *The Destruction of Mitsuhide, Shibata's Defeat,* and *Cherry Blossom Viewing in the Mountains,* and present them to his lord. Hideyoshi then chose to play himself in the plays, before hundreds of invited guests, a remarkable event in the long history of Noh. Baian knew the Noh actor's simple sliding step from seeing it a hundred times over. And he was familiar with the steps of Kyoto's popular Wind and Stream circle dances that groups of commoners loved to perform in the streets of the capital. But he had never seen this delightful, buoyant step before. With one foot lifted from the ground, the dancer leaped lightly, her body floating in the air. Legs flashed into view and then into hiding like clumps of white clover blossoms swaying on a mountaintop. For the merest instant, a sole would touch the coarse straw matting and then the young bodies would float into the air again.

Who in the world are these girls? Where are they from, who taught them, where did the steps themselves come from? Baian sensed a fragrant voluptuousness in the dancing of the girl wearing the monk's robe that was utterly alluring, quite unlike the dancing of the other girls whose kimonos so casually opened to expose naked flesh. Her fiercely sensuous movements could certainly arouse a man sexually. Yet Baian thought her dance called out to a man's heart more than to his body.

> Buddha vows: speak my name on your lips,
> Its sound is greater than any other,
> Extending beyond this world,
> Extinguishing birth-and-death.
> Buddha lights the Ten Directions in this world.
> To all who say his name
> Buddha grants his mercy.
> Praise Amida Buddha. Praise Merciful Buddha.

"You there! You, over there! Stop!" Baian bellowed. Without warning he strode forward, planting himself in the center of the stage. At times like this, Baian was exactly like Hideyoshi in his overbearing manner. Terrified, the girls fell to their knees. Baian had been the first person to stop and watch them. They couldn't imagine why he was yelling at them in the middle of their dance.

"Where are you from?" he demanded.

"Izumo, Excellency," answered the farmer, who hurried onto the stage from the dressing room, knelt, and bowed low.

"Izumo, you say?" Baian was impatient, for the farmer's provincial accent was muffled and indistinct.

"Yes, Excellency."

"Which Izumo?" There was Izumo Point in Etchu Province and the ruins of Izumo village north of Kyoto. Sanemon, a farmer, looked up blankly. He couldn't imagine an Izumo other than where he lived.

"Izumo at Izumo," was all he could foolishly reply.

"Izumo of the Grand Shrine?"

"Yes, Excellency, that's it."

Baian snorted contentedly. At the moment he was puffed up like a peacock over the success of his festival. Suddenly he boomed, "I am Omura Yuko Hogen Baian!" as if to a large audience. He was immensely proud of his powerful voice, which he had disciplined by chanting prayers outdoors at Sokoku Temple. Whether he was dedicating some new writing to Hideyoshi, speaking to a gathering of aristocrats, or standing before a ragtag group of performers, he loved to impress others through the power of his voice. Baian felt deeply satisfied when he saw the farmer's eyes pop open as if a millet dumpling were being jammed down his throat.

"I am the priest responsible for Tenmangu Shrine. People often call me Baian the Curate. When you are finished here, mention my name and you will be fed."

Sanemon had little experience with words and none with people of importance. He could not absorb the flowing cadences that danced off Baian's tongue like waving flower petals. He certainly couldn't remember that long name. But he knew the person was important, so he touched his head to the floor and mumbled in his country dialect, "Much obliged, Excellency."

Baian turned to go, then stopped. "That woman. Let me see her face. Take off the hat."

The only person wearing a hat was the dancer in the center. When Baian had leapt on the stage, she had stopped dancing and knelt where she was. Now she unfastened the cords and laid the hat to one side.

Baian sucked in his breath. Staring at the face of the girl, his eyes widened until the wrinkles around them disappeared. Her face was much whiter than he had expected. He was amazed. Her broad forehead, her large and wide-spaced eyes with their glistening pupils, her generous cheeks, and her full, sensuous lips bore an uncanny resemblance to the image of Buddha that Baian secretly kept in his room in Hoshi Temple.

"Who is she?" he asked abruptly. In Baian's eyes, the girl before him was no ordinary person.

"A miner's daughter, sir. I am 'Kuni."

"Okuni? Where does your father work?"

"He dug iron ore in the mountains behind Izumo. He's dead now, sir."

An idea occurred to Baian, and he nodded with resolve. He looked at Okuni and spoke more gently than before, "Do come to see me. You should ask for Baian the Curate."

Sanemon, Okuni, and the girls watched, speechless and dazed, as Baian clasped his hands behind his back and strode away. They could not imagine who he was. Trying to understand what he had said was like trying to grasp a cloud.

Sanemon jumped up. "I'm going to ask. Pack the cart. Get everything ready so we can escape if we have to." Sanemon had seen peasants slaughtered like dumb animals during the terrible civil wars that preceded Hideyoshi's rule. Even in far-off Izumo, farmers helplessly watched their houses burned to the ground simply because they were in the way of a marching army. Sanemon's bitter experience as a peasant told him to flee at the first hint of danger. He took the bell from around his neck and ran off.

"Okuni!" The smallest of the girls ran to Okuni, crying in a frightened voice, "Where did Papa go? When will he be back?"

"Be patient, Okaga. He'll be back soon." Okuni was the oldest of the six girls accompanying Sanemon on the tour. She had never been out of Izumo before, but at seventeen she had a natural confidence the younger girls lacked. She took charge of packing everything into the two-wheeled cart.

When Sanemon did not quickly return, Okaga began to cry, "I want to go home. Yokichi is waiting for me. I didn't want to dance, I want to marry Yokichi." From the time they had left Izumo three months ago, Okaga had done nothing but complain. She was Sanemon's youngest daughter and still a child. She hadn't wanted to leave home, and she thought constantly about Yokichi. But there weren't enough girls without her and Sanemon was desperate to bring money back to Nakamura village in Izumo, so Okaga had had to come. Okuni felt sorry for the child, but Okaga's incessant whining irritated her. Okuni was still in a state of excitement from dancing, and she resented being taken out of.

At last Sanemon came running back, red-faced and waving his arms. His clothes were disheveled, one arm out of his sleeve. Had he been beaten? The girls cried out in fright. He tried to calm them. "It's all right. The man. . .who was here," and then he stammered, almost incoherently, "is a friend. . .a friend of the Lord of the Realm."

"Lord of the Realm?" The girls were reassured but confused. They did not know that Lord of the Realm was the grandiose title Hideyoshi had given himself. Hideyoshi was deeply dissatisfied when Emperor Goyozei had appointed him Imperial Regent. He commanded the allegiance of all other samurai lords and he coveted the title of Sei Tai Shogun—Great Barbarian-Subduing General. But no one born into the peasant class could become shogun. That, of course, was why Baian had claimed imperial birth for Hideyoshi. As was his way, Hideyoshi created his own title, Lord of the Realm.

"Do we have to run away?" Okaga whined.

"No. They said that man serves the Lord of the Realm. He does anything he wants. He likes Noh plays and dancing. That's why he told us to stay."

"What happened to your clothes, father?" Okuni asked. In deference to Sanemon's age Okuni called him "father".

"I was mixed up in the crowd outside. They're playing a funny game, trying to catch wooden finches and pass them on."

The crude stage was packed up and there was nothing to do now but wait for evening and dinner. Sanemon worried, for there is both a good side and a bad side to an invitation from someone as important as Baian. He tried to be cheerful for the girls' sake. "All of you go to the front of the shrine. Join in the game. Maybe you can find a finch, too. They say a finch brings good fortune."

The girls did as they were told. They left Sanemon beside the packed cart and went around to the shrine entrance. When they saw the crowd of people whirling in a frenzy, the others hesitated but Okuni, her cheeks flushed, instantly said, "I'm going to do it." Okaga whimpered, but Okuni plunged into the churning mass of men and women as if she were leaping into the sea. Okuni was large for a woman, but she was nearly swept off her feet by the waves of people pushing and shoving. As she was jostled, she became excited. The regular booming of the shrine drum reached her ears and she was possessed by an urge to dance. She closed her eyes and let her body meld into the mass of people pressing against her. She felt hands grope inside her kimono and touch her breasts. Instinctively she pulled away, and then was startled when she realized it gave her pleasure. Okuni's breasts were large, and some men, when they felt her smooth, soft flesh, tried to probe more deeply. Okuni did not encourage the exploring hands, but she didn't consider the men's playfulness to be obscene or disgusting. As she was jostled, hands touched every part of her body, brushing her breasts and searching inside her clothes. She was reminded of the first time a man had touched her, the day Kyuzo had made love to her amid the flowers on Hono Mountain in Izumo. She remembered that his rough touch had been distasteful and that he had aroused no feeling in her at all. Now, her whole body seemed intoxicated by the spirit of the crowd. She had no desire to stop. She abandoned herself to the sound of the drum and to the rhythm of her body. She felt glorious.

Her granny had raised her after her parents had died. Do not grow up to be *kabuki*, she warned the child. *Kabuki* was a word used in Izumo to mean strange, indecent, improper. Was this what Granny meant? Was it *kabuki* to like something strange and exciting like this? Okuni's heart shivered as the old woman's words came back to her.

"Be patient with me, Granny. If I'm a woman who likes to dance, does that make me a *kabuki* woman? Can this bright, happy feeling be bad? Don't be angry, Granny. Perhaps I *am* a *kabuki* woman."

Two

Densuke squatted before the fire and blew on the small blaze through a bamboo tube. He felt someone's presence behind him and, turning with a friendly smile, said, "Okuni. What are you doing here?"

"Watching you make a fire."

"Come warm yourself if you're cold."

Densuke was the kindest and most generous of all the servants in Baian's household. His small eyes sparkled winsomely in a perfectly round face. And everything he did was naturally comic. He was Baian's favorite. Okuni heard that he used to be an actor with a traveling troupe of comedians, but no one knew what circumstances had brought him to Baian's house to live. Densuke seemed to be a few years older than Okuni, and she noticed that he always spoke to her in a gentle voice.

"Is fire a special thing?" Okuni was thinking of the stories about her father that her granny loved to tell. He had worked as a miner, digging ore that went into the blast furnaces at Iron Mountain. The smelted steel from Iron Mountain made warriors' swords. The fire went into his blood and it made him as hard as steel. And she was his child. Was the fire in her blood, too?

"Oh, it's a luxurious thing," Densuke beamed mischievously. "This fire is cooking rice gruel for special guests." He rose lightly to his feet and lifted the lid with a stick. He began to sing softly to himself.

One night, two nights,
We made love.
Now, our hair is white,
Our hair is white.

It was a popular Short Song that had been in fashion for many years. Usually the singer accompanied himself by beating a fan. Densuke sang in a lively, humorous style, striking two sticks of kindling together to keep time. His voice was beautiful and buoyantly light. It was impossible for Okuni to hold still. Clapping her hands, she sang along with Densuke, the rhythm moving her body.

"You're good. You learn quickly."

"I. . .I like songs." Confused by his praise, she stammered.

"That's why you learn fast. Master Baian is impressed."

"Really? He scolds me every day."

The day after Baian brought Sanemon's troupe into the shrine-temple compound, he started their daily singing and dancing rehearsals. He was very strict. Often Baian could not understand the heavy Izumo dialect of Sanemon and the girls, and they in turn found it hard to follow his Kyoto speech. Irritated, Baian would scold them in his favorite bellowing voice. "Relax. Move gracefully," he would shout. And of course Okaga and the younger girls would freeze in fear. No matter how much he commanded them to flutter their long kimono sleeves, their bodies stiffened at the sound of his powerful voice. At least at first. Gradually, they became used to his ways and learned the special songs and movements he taught them.

On this day the girls were ordered to rise early and dress with special care. As Okuni turned away from Densuke to go back to the temple, Baian's wife was already finishing up her arrangement of Okaga's and the other girls' hair. In a new Kyoto fashion called Chinese curls, the long strands of hair were fastened in back and allowed to fall in swirls to the shoulders. To protect the collars of the girls' new kimonos, Baian's wife tied back the trailing ends of hair with pieces of red cloth. Once the girls had changed into the new kimonos Baian had bought them, the agonies of rehearsal were forgotten.

They were excited by the gorgeous colors of the flowing sleeves and they could not keep their feet from trying out a few dance steps in their new kimonos.

But Okuni was unhappy. She didn't want to wear the dull monk's habit. Even though the robe was made of shiny black silk and the straw hat was new, she was seventeen and she wanted to wear a pretty, long-sleeved kimono like the other girls. Okuni showed her discontent when she put on her makeup. She applied red rouge to her mouth more thickly than she had been told to do. The rouge was extremely expensive, being made of safflower oil and powdered mother of pearl. Baian's wife looked sharply at Okuni, but as Baian had ordered her to allow the country girls to use her makeup, she kept her peace.

They were almost finished dressing when Baian stopped by to inspect the results. Each careful appraisal was followed by a snort of satisfaction. "Such beautiful women, I'm surprised," he admitted, and his face crinkled in a smile. He looked Okuni over, front and back. "Not enough red," he snorted. He thought for a moment and then had his wife bring two silk cords dyed in brilliant Chinese vermillion. He hung the bell on the cords and tied it around Okuni's neck. After assuring himself that the red rouge, the red bell cords, and the red cloth tying the hair all shone brilliantly against the black monk's robe, he looked sternly first at Okuni and then at the other girls. He spoke each word as firmly as one would drive a nail into wood. "Good. Today you must not make one mistake. Not in singing. Not in dancing. I am entertaining extremely important guests."

In fact, Baian had taken in and trained Sanemon's troupe specifically for this occasion. Yet that was not the entire explanation. Baian had a larger plan in mind and today would be the first test of its viability. His guests were Yamashina Tokitsune, an imperial noble whom the emperor had banished to Osaka three years ago, and Shirae Zengoro, Hideyoshi's private secretary. Tokitsune cultivated Baian in the hope that Hideyoshi would intervene with the emperor on his behalf. For his part, Baian aggressively sought out first-rate intellectuals who could further his knowledge. (Baian had recently borrowed *An Illustrated Tale of Genji* from Tokitsune's library.) Baian and Zengoro both served Hideyoshi as personal attendants and so they frequently met.

"Today I have a special treat," Baian said with a teasing laugh in his voice as his two guests finished eating, "just for you." Baian had carefully calculated that if he served his distinguished guests ordinary food, the entertainment that followed would stand out. Thus the entire meal had been the plain rice gruel Densuke had cooked over the fire.

"Ah, I thought something was going on when I was here ten days ago." Tokitsune's speech was quite colloquial for a courtier, suggesting that he had contact with townsmen in the capital.

"What is it?" Zengoro was not a witty man, and he spoke without artifice.

Baian smiled but did not reply. Calling Densuke, he spoke in a formal manner, "When you are prepared, you may enter."

"Yes, Your Excellency."

The sliding door at the back of the room opened and a bell rang out clearly. At that moment Sanemon appeared in the doorway, leaning stiffly forward at the hips. He did his best to move smoothly, using the bent torso of Noh-style dance that Baian had so painstakingly taught him, but he was terrified he would make a mistake. He seemed to be on the point of death as he sang, in a strangled voice, the words of the song Baian had composed for him.

> Behind us lies our birthplace,
> The land of Izumo.
> In Kyoto spring flowers bloom,
> Spring flowers bloom.

His legs trembled and his body shook, but he managed to reach the center of the stage. Turning to face Baian's guests, he spoke in a croaking tone.

"Now then, I am a Priest serving the Grand Shrine in the land of

Izumo. Our country lies at peace. I bring my daughter, a Priestess of Izumo Shrine, to the capital so that she may dance for you."

Sanemon could not alter his muffled country accent, but at least he spoke the words Baian had written without forgetting them.

"This country style is amusing," Tokitsune said to Baian, half truthfully and half out of a courtier's habitual politeness. Baian bowed but said nothing.

Sanemon retired to the back of the stage, where he began to strike the bell hanging at his chest in a regular beat. As if in response Okuni entered, loudly striking her bell, her face hidden beneath the straw hat. She led the girls in their new kimonos to the center of the room. They chanted together in the style of a Buddhist prayer:

> Praise Amida Buddha.
> Praise Amida Buddha's name.
> Self-willed, purified body of Amida,
> The eternal Buddha.
> Neither enlightenment nor nonenlightenment,
> Nor knowing nor nonknowing
> Provide salvation.
> Praise Amida Buddha.
> Call on Amida Buddha's name.

Naturally Okuni and the other girls were dancing barefoot. Tokitsune and Zengoro found themselves gazing with fascination at the soles of the girls' feet as they lifted them and stamped.

> Speak the Buddha's name,
> Whose merit leads every man
> To aspire to Buddhahood.
> No one who desires it
> Is punished by exclusion
> From Buddha's mercy.
> Praise Amida Buddha.
> Praise Amida Buddha's name.

Sanemon and the girls struck their bells on alternating beats that grew faster and faster. The young girls' voices rose higher and brighter. Lively footsteps kicked open the hems of kimonos. The guests could not take their eyes from the girls' bare feet, now slightly flushed from striking the floor.

> Call on Buddha
> For any boon,
> His power is great.
> Call his name
> Freely, freely all our sins
> Will disappear.
> Namu Amida Butsu. Call Amida Buddha's name.

The girls danced freely around Okuni, their whirling sleeves repeatedly striking Okuni on the back and chest. They wore sophisticated clothes from the capital, but still the girls were country-bred. Their rapid dance movements soon loosened their kimonos, exposing legs and breasts. That was what Baian had expected: without altering the steps of their dance, he had coached them carefully in daring torso and sleeve movements. He had not expected, however, that Okuni would project such eroticism, hidden behind the severe monk's costume and hardly moving from the spot where she stood. Okuni struck the bell that she held by the red cords and her body emanated a joyful ecstasy. Tokitsune and Zengoro, and Baian as well, found their eyes irresistibly drawn to the figure of Okuni, rather than to the girls circling wildly around her.

When the last ringing sound of the bells died away, the girls knelt facing the figure in the monk's robe. With one deft movement, Okuni dropped the hat, revealing her face. Eyes glistening, cheeks flushed, lips red with rouge, her breath rapid, she glanced out at the guests. Then Okuni turned and slipped out of sight through the sliding door with the girls.

For a time Baian's guests did not, could not, speak. He watched them happily, saying nothing at all. Then Tokitsune sighed deeply.

"It was utterly splendid, Baian. So these girls are priestesses from the Grand Shrine of Izumo?"

"They are. Did you like the dance?"

"I've never seen such light steps. Not even in the Wind and Stream street dances of the capital."

Thirty years ago, groups of court nobles in Kyoto had taken up the popular Wind and Stream circle dances. The courtiers brought the drum and flute music of Noh and added new songs, in the end changing a townsmen's dance into a cultured court amusement. Tokitsune mentioned the term because his father had choreographed many new Wind and Stream dances in his day. The scrupulous records in his diary gave a vivid picture of their brilliance and freedom. One entry described a party of thirteen imperial nobles, organized by Prince Karasuma, dancing in the street before Shinyodo Temple. They were joined by samurai, townsmen, and even a group of local housewives as the performance grew increasingly boisterous.

Tokitsune cocked his head, musing, "And was that a Buddhist prayer dance to Amida? I'm amazed that priestesses from the Shrine of Izumo know it."

"Is the girl in the monk's robe the man's daughter? What's her name?"

" 'Kuni."

"She's a beautiful sight. Rare these days."

"The sound of the bell was splendid," Zengoro interjected. "It was unusually high and piercing."

Baian snorted. His guests were missing the point. He cleared his throat loudly, signaling the start of one of his pronouncements.

"That was the prayer dance of the Pure Land Sect of Buddhism, as performed at Izumo Shrine." Abruptly, Baian began with his conclusion. He examined his guests, first one, then the other, with a slightly disdainful gaze. Tokitsune and Zengoro looked dubious. Baian now launched into the speech he had prepared. "The origins of the Buddhist prayer dance lie in China and Korea and, in our country, with Saint Kuya in the tenth century. However, Saint Ippen personally sang and danced the *Namu Amida Butsu* prayer with great passion and he made it the basic ritual of the Pure Land Sect. He was the last of a long line of great priests, Honen, Dogen, Shinran, and Nichiren, who spread the new Buddhism among the people. Three hundred years ago Saint Ippen traveled the length and breadth of our country urging believers in Amida Buddha to abandon the world and to depend upon His mercy. They could gain Amida's Western Paradise by dancing and singing without cease Buddha's name, '*Namu Amida Butsu,* Praise Amida Buddha.' It was a time of lawlessness and people devoutly wished to leave the strife of the mortal world by calling on Amida Buddha's name. Followers swelled into the hundreds of thousands in all parts of the land. Lord Banno of Shinshu Province donated eight golden bells out of devotion. It is said that their sound aroused believers to such a pitch of ecstatic frenzy that the floors of the lord's mansion were crushed by the stamping, circling dancers. We can imagine the prayer dance of that time was almost bestial in its abandon. Illustrations in *The Priest Ippen Scroll,* painted ten years after Ippen's death, confirm this."

Baian orated his story as if reading from a book. "Now then, the shrine maiden Okuni that you just saw is dressed as Saint Ippen, the wandering bell-striking priest. Even today you can see remnants of Saint Ippen's ecstatic dancing in services at Choraku Temple in the Maruyama Hills and Kinren Temple near Shijo Street in the capital. But most of all, the prayer dance of the Pure Land Sect has been preserved at the Grand Shrine at Izumo."

"I see. As always, Baian, the breadth of your knowledge is intimidating. But tell me, why have they left their homes in Izumo to come to Kyoto?"

"Ten years ago Lord Kikkawa deposed the Amago clan as rulers of Izumo during the civil wars. Since then, the Grand Shrine of Izumo has been in decline. Lord Kikkawa confiscated most of its rice fields as spoils of war. So the priests dispatched pilgrims to all provinces to beg for contributions to the shrine. These girls serve the Shinto deities of Izumo Shrine as priestesses and they are believers in the Pure Land Sect of Buddhism. There is no contradiction." Here was an example of Baian's skill at transforming lies into truth. He cleverly wove some truths into his fabrication, so that Tokitsune and Zengoro, unable to tell what to accept and what to doubt, ended up believing it all.

Several days before, Baian had asked Sanemon if there was a connection between the girls' Buddhist Prayer Dance and Shinto dances performed at Izumo Shrine. Sanemon couldn't answer. He had gathered girls in his village to tour in the hope of earning money for themselves. The girls danced the dances they knew. They were the harvest festival dances that everyone in Nakamura village knew and danced. There wasn't anything special about them, and it was beyond his knowledge to say whether they were Shinto or Buddhist.

"You know, Baian, I would like to see it again."

All the wrinkles on Baian's face moved when he heard Tokitsune's request. He replied, very pleased, "That is an easy matter."

"Then I want to call Ochamaru, so he can watch."

"By all means. Master Ochamaru will enjoy it." Baian was thinking that Tokitsune's son, who was twelve, ought to like seeing girls his own age dance. Okuni, at seventeen, was the oldest girl in the troupe. Okaga was fifteen and the other four girls were between ten and thirteen.

Meanwhile, Okuni and the others were in the kitchen. At Baian's order they were being served the leftover gruel. Densuke watched them gobble down the food. "I saw you from the side. You were good. I know Baian is pleased, or he wouldn't serve you this food." Rice gruel was plain food to Baian, but it was a luxurious meal to villagers from Izumo. Sanemon and the others were farmers, but they had never eaten first quality rice like this before today. Every grain of the best rice they grew in Izumo went straight to Lord Kikkawa.

While they were eating, Densuke was called before Baian. When he returned and told them Baian's request, Sanemon began to tremble again. But the girls had gained confidence from the first performance. Ready to perform any number of times, they eagerly fixed their hair and costumes. "Why do I have to hide under this black kimono and hat, Densuke? Why won't Baian let me wear a bright kimono?" Okuni complained.

"You would be too beautiful, Okuni. Master Baian is protecting you from his guests." He tried to speak casually, yet this thought had been weighing on Densuke's mind from the beginning of the performance.

The reply pleased Okuni. With the bells ringing in her ears, she danced lightly and freely, her body eagerly answering the lively rhythm. Ochamaru looked like a little doll sitting beside his father, his eyes wide with delight. He clapped his hands innocently and said, "I like it. It's a child's dance."

Tokitsune narrowed his eyes, but Baian said smoothly, "Yes, that's what it is. We call it the Dance of Youth." Baian's secret plan was to show this dance to Hideyoshi. But he couldn't say it was a Buddhist Prayer Dance. The Lord of the Realm adored brilliance and would never be interested in something that reeked of gloom and ancient times. Now he knew what to call it: the "Dance of Youth." When the feet of the dancing girls lifted high, they showed pink, flushed soles. Even Ochamaru seemed to hold his breath as he watched the leaping girls. Of course, Baian did not know it, but those light steps were the natural steps of village girls in Izumo. When they drew water from the Hii River, the girls learned to leap agilely on the dry sand from one spot to the next before the water rose to dampen the soles of their feet. Unknowingly, the girls in Nakamura village practiced the dancing steps each morning and evening on the sands of the Hii River from soon after they were born.

> The light of Buddha's mercy,
> Illumines the Ten-Direction World.
> All mankind is encompassed
> By Buddha's prayer.
> Wretched nothingness,
> To strike the bell.
> Let Buddha's name strike

And fill your heart.
Praise Amida Buddha's name. Praise His Name.

At that moment the strong, reverberating beat of a Noh drum echoed in the space between the alternating sounds of Okuni's and Sanemon's bells. Sanemon blinked and swallowed in surprise. The girls, engrossed in their dancing, only sang all the louder. Among the dancers, Okuni alone reacted to the new sounds in her dance. Unlike the clear ringing of the bells that she knew and that filled her body with lightness, the drum had a heavy sound. It caught and pulled her soaring spirit down to the earth.

Tokitsune and Zengoro thought nothing of the drumming. They imagined that it was part of the performance.

The drumming caught Baian by surprise, too, but soon he relaxed. He saw that the dancing and singing he had planned were continuing, undisturbed by the beats of the Noh drum. His face creased in a broad smile and he murmured to himself, "Go to it, Sankuro, my boy."

Three

On May 4, 1588, Hideyoshi celebrated the completion of his grand Kyoto residence, Juraku Mansion, which occupied several blocks in the western part of the city. He prevailed upon the emperor to travel fourteen blocks from the Imperial Palace through the streets to Juraku Mansion. Six thousand soldiers stood guard along the route. Once there, emperor Goyozei, Retired emperor Ogimachi, the Empress, the Empress Dowager, and numerous court officials allowed themselves to be entertained at Hideyoshi's "palace of pleasures" for five days. The event was a stunning political coup for Hideyoshi and a demonstration of his all-encompassing power. Within memory, no emperor had deigned to visit the residence of a samurai. People still remembered that Hideyoshi was a farmer's son, and were impressed that he had risen so far so fast. Baian followed Hideyoshi to Kyoto in early May in order to compose *Commemoration of the Imperial Visit to Juraku Mansion*, as publicity for his master. During the many months that Baian was gone from Osaka, he left the troupe in the care of his wife and Densuke. He put Sankuro, a former Noh drum player, in charge of the troupe's training and rehearsing.

Daily rehearsals under Sankuro were less severe than they had been under Baian. Sankuro's singing voice was better than Baian's, and Okuni and the girls found it easy to follow. Sankuro was teaching them a new play that Baian had written and given to Sankuro just before he left for Kyoto. Sankuro had been instructed to teach it to Okuni and the others before Baian returned. The text was in the style of a Noh drama. Like all Noh plays it began with a Travel Song sung by a Traveler. The Traveler was the supporting, or *waki,* role. Sankuro assigned this song to Sanemon, for in their troupe he played the supporting role. Sankuro had spent many days composing and arranging elegant Noh music to fit Baian's text. Now each time Sanemon sang in his raspy, formless voice Sankuro heard his music being ruined. Nothing Sankuro could think of improved the farmer's rough singing.

When shadows of irritation passed over Sankuro's face, Okuni felt her body shrink, as if Sanemon's bad voice was her fault. In her keyed-up state, the pulse of Sankuro's drum set her whole body tingling, and she fell into a joyful reverie absorbing the new sound that she had only casually listened to before. Okuni followed along when Sanemon sang and when he made mistakes, she raised her voice to cover them. Noticing this, Sankuro led her with his drumbeats until, carried away by the music, she spontaneously began to add her own vocal elaborations.

"Okuni, you sing the Travel Song alone from now on," Sankuro finally said, exasperated. Okuni did not know how to read, but she concentrated, heart and mind, on remembering the words she heard. Each time Sankuro spoke to her, she felt her entire body tremble with excitement.

> We gaze back at our homeland of Izumo
> Through the distant haze of spring.
> Passing through Kokufu at Nagato
> Is the inn where we greet this age.
> Wide road to Hiroshima,
> Praying at Itsukushima Shrine,
> Our boat lands on the Strands of Harada.
> Sailing to Akashi, wandering through moonlight,
> One's fate is both good and bad.
> Young leaves are windblown,
> Waves of Fukushima Bay are calm,

In time we reach Osaka.
We did not intend to hurry,
But speedily we arrive in Kyoto.

Baian had followed ordinary Noh conventions when he put Okuni's journey from Izumo to Kyoto into the structure of a Travel Song.
He merely listed, one after the other, the famous shrines and historical sites that lay along the route—it was a standard poetic conceit.
But Sankuro was departing radically from Noh form when he gave
the song to Okuni. Okuni played the leading role, the *shite*, in the
troupe, and in Noh a Travel Song was not sung by a leading actor.
That did not bother Sankuro. Like Baian, he sensed that times were
changing. He was not afraid to try something new. Perhaps he would
be praised for changing the old-style Noh.

Okuni learned the song by rote. She carefully imitated Sankuro as
he sang the melody. She listened to the exact way he pronounced the
unfamiliar words. Since the song occurred before the girls came on
stage and Sanemon was no longer in the scene, Sankuro and Okuni
fell into the habit of rehearsing by themselves the long entrance
down the bridgeway onto the stage proper.

"Now, look. You aren't supposed to be dancing. Light steps won't
do. When you appear, imagine you're walking, carrying a heavy load
on your head." Sankuro taught Okuni the Noh style of movement
that he had known from childhood. He struck the drum hard to
admonish her. Okuni tried to follow Sankuro's instructions, but
when she began to sing and her body began to move, her feet stepped
lightly and quickly without her realizing it.

"If you look up the heaviness is gone. Look down at the ground
just ahead of you. Bend at the hips. Here, here, like this." He grasped
her shoulders from behind and tried to guide her into the Noh actor's
half-squatting posture. Her body grew rigid at the touch of his
hands. "I don't understand you. The force comes from here." Irritated, he stood in front of her, put both hands on her hips, and pushed
down with all his strength.

"Ahh!" As the sound escaped from Okuni's mouth, her body

melted. Sankuro put his arms around her and the heavy bell, caught between them, dug painfully into Okuni's breasts.

Her excited breath blew against his neck. In the next instant they leaped apart, as if touched by molten iron. With her eyes downcast, Okuni removed the heavy bell and slumped to the floor. Tears welled in her eyes. Fire, she thought, I have truly been touched by fire. Is this what Granny, who raised me when Father and Mother were swept away by the flood on the Hii River, meant when she said to be careful? You told me Father's blood was iron. Is the heat of Father's molten iron inside my blood? What can I do? What will become of me?

Sankuro struggled with more complicated thoughts. He had been born Saburokuro, the son of a player of the hand drum, in the Kanze Noh troupe. For generations the Kanze troupe had struggled against three other troupes of Noh performers—Komparu, Kongo, and Hosho—to gain powerful patrons. Originally, the four troupes were protected by the most important temple in the country, the Kofuku Temple in Nara. In exchange, the four troupes were obligated to perform each spring for the temple's Wakamiya Festival and present sacred torchlight Noh performances at the temple in the summer. Although some minor connection still remained, during his childhood Saburokuro had seen the Kanze troupe's income from temple performances dwindle to almost nothing. During the bloody civil wars that had raged until only a decade ago, samurai armies and rebellious tenant farmers had wrested away most of Kofuku Temple's land. The huge land rents and the rice harvest of its tenants that had so handsomely supported Kofuku Temple—and its dependent Noh troupes—were lost forever. Many Noh performers felt helpless. Other performers, among them the young drum player Saburokuro, accepted the stark reality of their position. They clearly saw that the future of their art lay in pleasing a new ruling class, rough samurai like Hideyoshi, who now wielded power.

Older actors had often regaled the child Saburokuro with the glorious history of the Kanze troupe. The Kanze troupe had prospered three-hundred years ago under the Ashikaga shoguns. Why? Because

Shogun Yoshimitsu had become attached to eleven-year-old Zeami Motokiyo of the Kanze troupe and had brought him to Kyoto to live at his side. In the sixty years Zeami spent in at the shogunal court, this master actor and playwright refined the older art of Sarugaku into the beautiful masked dance-drama that came to be called Noh. All that had come to an end fifteen years ago when Oda Nobunaga deposed the last shogun of the Ashikaga line. The leaders of the Kanze troupe did not know what to do. As the young drummer saw it, an ancient fire had been extinguished.

From as early as he could remember, he had fretted that his fate was linked to the languishing fortunes of the Kanze troupe. As the child of a Noh drummer, he was expected to carry on the drumming tradition of his father. According to the great Zeami's secret manual of instruction, *The Way of the Flower*, every child in the troupe was required to submit to a strict regime of training from the spring of his sixth year. Saburokuro easily withstood the rigors of this training for he was strong-willed and talented. He relished the intensive lessons, absolute obedience to his teacher, and doing such tasks as polishing the stage floor once a day. From an early age, however, he aspired to become more than a drummer in the declining Kanze troupe. His ambition led him to reject many inherited traditions of the Noh theater.

About three years ago, Noh had begun to flourish once more, this time under Hideyoshi's patronage. In the summer of 1585, when Hideyoshi was named Regent and Advisor to the emperor, he commanded actors of the Kongo troupe to entertain the emperor's brother and sister in the precincts of the Imperial Palace. And in the autumn, Hideyoshi invited the Master of the Kongo Noh troupe to perform for him in Osaka Castle. Hideyoshi's younger brother, the newly appointed governor of Nara, took actors of the Komparu family under his patronage and, perhaps as a result, Hideyoshi became the direct patron of the Grand Master of the Komparu troupe and his young son. Of course Hideyoshi's chief retainers also hurried to support Noh and even nobles of the Imperial Court, hearing of the regent's taste in theater, vied to show interest. Every Noh troupe was benefiting except the Kanze performers. It was agonizing for an ambitious young man to be a member of the ignored Kanze troupe.

One year later, in the autumn of 1586, Saburokuro cut his ties with the theater troupe of his birth. He had no choice. The Kanze master foolishly decided to accompany the dour samurai lord Toku-gawa Ieyasu to his provincial capital in Mikawa Province. How stu-pid, the young drummer thought. Hadn't Ieyasu been defeated by Hideyoshi? Wasn't Ieyasu merely a country vassal who served the real ruler, Hideyoshi? Mikawa was far from Kyoto, an unimporant place, and utterly without culture. Saburokuro let the Kanze troupe go to Mikawa without him. He was energetic. He was determined. He had hope. He intended to be recognized by the Lord of the Realm. With only his drum he traveled to Kyoto and then to Osaka where by chance he met Baian, personal attendant to the Lord of the Realm.

The young drummer's personality and abilities suited Baian. Densuke remained Baian's favorite among the servants who lived at Hoshi Temple, but increasingly Baian came to rely on the instinct and talent of the Noh drummer when he was composing new songs. When Baian suggested that he change his name to Sankuro, saying that Saburokuro was old-fashioned, he readily agreed. He had left the Kanze troupe behind, and he was happy to abandon his Noh name as well. With his new name, Sankuro felt reborn to a life of great possibilities. He was eager to enter a new life.

"You've been rehearsing straight through. You must be thirsty. Have some water. Drink up." Densuke entered, chattering brightly.

"Thanks. It's time for a break." Sankuro spoke brusquely. When the chilled water ran down his throat he felt his emotions cool down as well. I cannot have this woman, Sankuro thought to himself. Okuni is beautiful even compared to Kyoto women and when I held her in my arms she yielded softly, as if she had no bones in her body. But Okuni is in Baian's charge. What if he discovers us? It would be the end of everything.

Okuni's hands trembled when Densuke passed her the teacup. She drank the water in a single swallow. She took a second cup to calm herself. She closed her eyes. Not even the cold water slowed the wild beating of her heart. She did not understand what fate had brought her and Sankuro together at Baian's. But she had been waiting, with stifled breath, for Sankuro's next expression of love. And then Densuke appeared.

"I'm glad you came, Densuke. Teach Okuni one of the new Short Songs popular in Kyoto. You know them better than I do." Without waiting for a reply, Sankuro picked up his drum and left the room. Okuni felt stricken. Sankuro held me tightly and now he has pushed me away. She thought of the pain in her breasts when the bell crushed them. She knew the pain inside her heart would not go away. Densuke sensed that something was wrong, but did not know what to say.

"Yes, let's rehearse. Please teach me." Okuni took the bell from her neck and passed it to Densuke.

> Love.
> Does it make me sad or glad?
> Am I glad or am I sad?
> Do I float, do I sink,
> In this stream of tears?

Although the lyrics were modern, it was a gloomy melody, so, while singing, Densuke smoothly switched to another of the many songs tucked away in his memory. Okuni danced and Densuke sang. Since she disliked the black monk's robe, she wore a bright, short-sleeved kimono at rehearsal. She found she could fit her light dance steps to almost any song and add to that the arm and sleeve movements Baian had taught her. Yet, she was not dancing as buoyantly as usual.

> Seeing a flower,
> Who is not moved?
> Seeing the moon,
> Who is not moved
> To wet one's sleeves with tears?

"I'm sorry, Densuke." Okuni could not bear her pain any longer. She stopped dancing in the middle of the song and, weeping, she rushed out of the room. Densuke continued to sing.

> You cause the tears,
> I cry,
> I cry.

The following day, Sankuro picked up rehearsals as if nothing had happened. Yet the mere sight of Sankuro's face made Okuni happy, and she trained especially hard, her heart beating fast as she tried to follow Sankuro's strict commands. Densuke, seeing it all, said nothing.

At the end of the month Baian returned to Hoshi Temple. When he saw how much Okuni had learned, he was immensely pleased. "Yamashina Tokitsune talked to some of his friends in Sakai about you and they want you to perform there. I'm going to be busy writing for some time so I'm putting Sankuro in charge of everything." Without saying more, he dismissed them. For several weeks he went into complete seclusion to complete the manuscript of the *Commemoration of the Imperial Visit to Juraku Mansion* for Lord Hideyoshi.

Sakai was an important trading port a few miles to the south of Osaka. It was governed by a group of merchants who monopolized trade between Osaka-Kyoto and the outer provinces. Sakai was also the home port for vessels in the lucrative China trade and the base for companies trading with the Portuguese. Because it provided the crucial guns, swords, armor, and clothing that Hideyoshi's armies depended upon, even the Lord of the Realm wooed its great merchants and grudgingly accepted Sakai's status as a free city. It was one of the few places in the nation not ruled by a samurai general or warlord. Here the taste of townsmen held sway.

Their wealthy hosts treated Okuni and the others very well. They gave them presents of expensive robes and served them delicious feasts, far beyond the meager fare the small troupe had known at Hoshi Temple. "Sakai is a generous town," one of the girls sighed, as they greedily ate stewed fish, chicken, and pickles with their rich gruel, delicacies they could not have dreamed of back in Izumo. The girls tasted soy sauce for the first time, and Okuni, especially, liked its rich, salty taste. Almost every day they were asked to perform at tea ceremonies and poetry readings at different mansions around the city. Okuni's dancing gained a high reputation among the astute merchants and tea masters who made Sakai their home. After they had been in Sakai for several weeks, a message arrived inviting the "shrine maiden of Izumo" to perform in Hirano, a neighboring city with extremely close ties to Sakai. The invitation came from Suekichi Kanbei, a samurai who enjoyed a prominent position in Hirano. When Sankuro learned this, he immediately decided they would go.

When Okuni realized they would be leaving for Hirano the next day, she went outside to look for Sankuro. Or, more precisely, when night was approaching and Okuni noticed he was absent, she wanted to be with him. Ever since he had embraced her, he was constantly on her mind. When he was nearby, she watched him quietly. When he went out without telling her, she would search anxiously until she found him. Then she was content just seeing his face, and she could return home happily.

Sankuro was standing looking at the harbor, now quiet in the darkness. On the horizon a Chinese junk floated on the calm waves. Sampans were tied to the dock. No other person was in sight. She recognized him, even from a distance.

"Sankuro, what kind of place is Hirano?" She used the simple question as a pretext to come near. "Is it far from Sakai?"

Startled, he glowered at Okuni as if he had forgotten he had embraced her. "Far from Sakai?" He repeated the question looking at her with an expression of wonder. He laughed, shaking his head, "It's between here and Osaka. It's a only a few miles away, a morning's walk." Sankuro was charmed by Okuni's innocence.

Okuni fixed her eyes unblinkingly on Sankuro's moving lips. Although she heard the words he was speaking, she was not listening. It was early spring. The night wind blowing off the sea was warm. Her body was close to Sankuro and she suddenly began to sweat. As Sankuro took Okuni's wrist, she leaned her breasts against his chest. Sankuro and Okuni were standing in the shadow of large crates piled on the dock. No light reached them from buildings along the shore. Sanemon and the girls were asleep in the house.

Okuni moved as Sankuro's hand guided her. She melted, body and soul. She did not consciously think of what was happening to her, she only felt herself entering a state of bliss. At times strength would come into her arms and she would hold Sankuro tightly, but soon the strength would ebb away. She sensed her body sinking into a deep, deep place and her spirit, escaping, danced lightly upward, far away.

Sankuro moved away from Okuni, who seemed sunk in sleep. He traced his finger across her plump cheek. At last he lifted her to her feet.

"Don't talk about this. Not to anyone."

Okuni was suddenly awake. She couldn't believe what she had heard. "Not tell anyone?"

"If Baian finds out, we'll be in trouble. So don't talk about it."

"I won't." Okuni nodded agreement, but she felt unbearably sad. I feel a joy in my heart and body that I didn't feel when Kyuzo made love to me. Why do I have to hide it, she wondered. Was this being *kabuki*? Okuni did not know what made Sankuro fear Baian, but his insensitive command struck her painfully. She had to speak out. "Then were you just playing with me now, Sankuro?"

"That's a crazy thing to say. I liked you from the first time I saw you at Baian's. Can't you hear how I feel, in the sound of my drum, when you're dancing?"

"Really?

"Of course."

"Well. . .Why didn't you tell me?"

"Do you think I could do that? You're a fool."

"But. . ."

"I've endured the unendurable until this night. Don't you understand how I've suffered?"

Okuni was completely satisfied with this single explanation. Without saying more, she straightened her kimono. She was aware of the moistness of her body, and unlike the time she had been with Kyuzo, the sensation of her body's wetness made her happy, for it was a memento of Sankuro's love. One could say the act of lovemaking was the same in both cases, but to Okuni nothing about them was the same. She remembered that when her father and her mother had fallen in love, they also had to hide their feelings. A smelter's daughter could not marry an ordinary miner. Now Okuni could understand why they had run away. Hadn't my mother been caressed and hadn't she melted like this? In the past, Okuni had imagined the fire of her mother had melted the steel of her father, but now she believed their fire and steel fused together in joy. That joy gave her parents the courage to elope and the strength to find their way out of Iron Mountain and onto the plain of the Hii River. This was true. Okuni felt she now understood everything that had happened to her parents in the past.

"Sankuro," Okuni began, wanting to tell him the story of how her parents had fallen in love.

"Shhh," Sankuro stopped her and again pulled her close, pressing his lips hard against Okuni's mouth. Again Okuni grew uncontrollably passionate in Sankuro's embrace and again the strength flowed from her body as it had before. The fire her granny warned her against burned through her body until it consumed itself. She was happy. She overflowed with pleasure, in her breasts, her throat, her hips, her thighs. And she thought of Hirano. In Hirano I will dance only for Sankuro. Already she was half asleep. Even in her drowsiness her joy was such that her body wanted to dance.

Four

As Sankuro said, the walk to Hirano took hardly half a day. On either side of the dirt path sweat-covered farmers waded in groups through the paddy mud. They were pulling weeds from rows of evenly spaced, pale green rice shoots that marched in straight rows field after field, as far as they could see toward the distant, flat horizon. Water coursed through channels into the fields, returning in time through sluices to rejoin the small rivers that soon reached the sea.

"What's the name of this river?" Okuni spoke out impulsively. Anxious to hear Sankuro's voice, she seized on the first topic of conversation that came to mind. "Do you think it ever floods?"

"It might in a storm, I suppose." Sankuro was a city man, raised at Kofuku Temple in Nara. He wasn't interested in rivers, but he was in a good mood and to humor Okuni he kept the conversation going.

"The Hii River in Izumo floods every year. The water rises and washes away fields and paddies. It carries away people, too. In Izumo we call it the Eight-Legged Dragon. We say 'beware when the Dragon moves its legs'."

"That would be terrifying, a dragon on the rampage."

"My mother and father were swallowed by the Dragon. They were. . ." Like all girls in love, Okuni wanted to tell Sankuro about herself. But Sanemon's rasping voice cut in, "It's the sand in the Hii River that kills, not the water. When the Dragon moves, he brings cold sand that swallows up paddies and houses."

"Gold sand?" Sankuro was suddenly alert.

"Yes. Cold sand that runs like melted steel."

Sankuro imagined a river of shining gold. "That would be a magnificent sight."

Sanemon grumbled, "What's good about a river that buries rice fields and houses under sand?" Sankuro and Sanemon did not realize their misunderstanding. Sankuro continued in an expansive mood and Sanemon fretted that the Dragon of the Hii River would devour his small fields while he and his daughters were away from Izumo. The sand bottom of the Hii River rose higher every year. Sanemon was a lowland peasant and he hated the miners who never stopped digging for iron-bearing ore in the mountains. And he hated the steel workers at the smelters for pouring their slag of pure sand into the river day after day, year after year. It is summer now, the stream is low, and the Dragon sleeps, the shimmering scales of its eight legs glinting in the sun. But when the winter rains come, the Dragon's legs will move and the sand, carried down by the boiling water, will slice through river banks and bury rice fields so they can never be used again. Will my fields be taken this year? Sanemon worried constantly. Without a rice crop his family would starve. And he had heard a frightening rumor that land was being surveyed by order of the Lord of the Realm in order to give it to new owners. Densuke had promised he would ask Baian what was happening, but then Sanemon had to go to Hirano. He worried, and he wished he and the girls were home in Izumo.

"Let's rest here."

"Are you tired?" Sankuro frowned.

"I'm old." In fact, Sanemon's tough peasant body was much stronger than Sankuro's, which had been formed by sitting motionless on stage for hours at a time. But Sanemon was stubborn and he had his own reason for wanting to stop. "I have to rest."

The light spring breeze flushed Okuni's cheeks. Her spirit was buoyant and gay. They could see houses at the edge of Hirano ahead of them. She smiled at Sankuro, "We may have to perform right away. Why don't we run through a piece before we get to Hirano. I think it would be nice to dance under the sky."

Sankuro nodded and stretched out on the grass, not bothering to take out his drum. On a small rise shaded by a tree, the girls quickly let down their kimono sleeves, which had been tied up for walking. They waited expectantly for Okuni to begin.

> Pure white moon flower,
> Clinging to the inner fence,
> Wasted, sadly waiting.
> Can the gourd's searching tendrils
> Slip under the eaves?
> No, they cannot meet.
> The heart in love,
> Is buoyant, light.

Over the past weeks, Okuni's body had completely absorbed the severe Noh movements Sankuro had showed her. Also, in their daily rehearsals she had learned Densuke's popular singing style—her voice no longer came from her head, but from deep within her abdomen. But here in the open air and without Sankuro's strict drum beats holding her back, Okuni felt free to dance as she pleased. Although not consciously aware of this, she felt an intense happiness flowing through her body and soul. The words of the love song Densuke had taught her were sad, but she wasn't thinking of their meaning. The sleeves of her kimono whirled in a bright arc and her legs flashed in the air. Sankuro was not watching, and she sang with a brighter melody than she had been taught, and led the girls in lighter, quicker steps. The sun was shining brightly, and the song wafted over the green fields of rice, returning to the girls in faint echoes. One by one heads appeared above the waves of pale green, hands stopped working, and gradually a crowd of peasant men and women gathered around Okuni and the dancing girls. Sankuro frowned, thinking it was a worthless audience. But Okuni was pleased; they were like her friends in Nakamura village in Izumo. Some joined in singing, for these short love songs were popular everywhere in the countryside. When someone sang in a loud voice, Okuni met his eyes and danced to his rhythm. Okuni danced, intoxicated by the pleasure her body was experiencing. The farmers were tremendously pleased. They clapped and called out their thanks. At last Okuni stopped dancing. She was surprised at how elated she felt. It reminded her of the time she had plunged into the erotically swirling crowd at the Plum Blossom Festival in Osaka. When I perform at Baian's house or for the rich merchants in Sakai I'm not carried away by this wonderful intoxication, she thought.

Sankuro nodded a curt signal that the dance was over. Sanemon went quickly into the crowd. His real reason for stopping had been to find out from the farmers what was happening to them under the new rule of the Lord of the Realm. The farmers were relaxed after the dancing, and they replied openly to Sanemon's questions.

"We don't know what's going on, but life is harder than before."

"A samurai official came to the village. We had to give him our swords. He said they'll melt them down. They're going to build a big statue of Amida Buddha in Kyoto. And we'll gain merit in the next life." Many farmers spoke up.

Another man edged forward. "In our village the soldiers counted every sword, gun, and spear we had. Someone said they want our hoes and our plows, too. For the iron."

"What? How will you be able to grow your rice?" Sanemon asked, anxious and amazed. The farmers looked confused and uncertain. They did not know what was in Hideyoshi's mind. They did not know that the Lord of the Realm was considering an elaborate scheme to freeze the farmers, the merchants, and the samurai into permanent and unchanging social groups. And they did not know these local events were an initial test of the plan. Stripping farmers of their traditional right to own swords and spears would help guard Hideyoshi against rebellion. More importantly, Hideyoshi saw that if a farmer did not have weapons, he could not rise to samurai status on the strength of his own efforts, as Hideyoshi himself had done. If his plan was carried out under the pretext of giving alms to Buddhism, Hideyoshi would make mass warfare by the peasants a thing of the past. And he would forever destroy a singular, if often unnoted, feature of traditional Japanese society: the possibility that a man or woman of exceptional ability could move upward through the classes. But the people Sanemon was speaking to didn't know this. They were only farmers. They could describe but not explain the recent strange events.

Before the farmers could add anything else to what they had said, Sankuro shook his head in annoyance and said his group had to leave. He turned and started walking toward Hirano, the others following.

At Hirano the first person they met was able to direct them to Suekichi Kanbei's imposing house. Members of the household staff greeted them in the servant's compound, showing them immediately to separate quarters in a building at the rear of the main residence where they could rest. Laid out on the matting of the floor were bolts of beautiful silk material dyed with small flowers and Chinese grass designs. Okuni and the other girls were told to make new kimonos immediately. They would be performing the next day. This reflected the urgency of an old man. At the age of sixty-three, Kanbei felt the need for haste in all his actions. The girls took up the delicate silk with cries of delight and began that very minute to carefully sew new kimonos for themselves. Okuni's silk, richly embroidered with flowers in varied colors, was of foreign make, imported on one of the Portuguese ships. She caught her breath, happily imagining how attractive she would look to Sankuro, wearing this magnificent silk kimono.

"Since Master Kanbei gave me this foreign silk I must wear it when I perform." Okuni intensely disliked the dull, black priest's robe that Baian made her wear. She wanted to dress beautifully for Sankuro.

"Yes, I guess you're right, but. . ." Sanemon worried that Kanbei would be angry if she didn't wear the new kimono and he worried that Baian would be angry if they changed the play Baian had set.

"I think I know what to do. It won't be hard," Sankuro said, not pleased by the situation but feeling responsible for finding a solution. "Listen carefully. Okuni, you make a quick change of costume, like they do in Noh plays. In Noh, the actor changes offstage and the audience can't see it. But that's not interesting. I want you to change on stage, instantly, before the audience's eyes." Okuni carefully rehearsed the action that Sankuro described. She concentrated very hard, wanting to please Sankuro by not making any mistake.

The next day the troupe was politely brought into Kanbei's residence to perform. The house was very large, and Okuni was sweating by the time they reached the main room where Kanbei's guests were waiting. She was wearing a beautiful silk-brocade kimono under the black robe, so she seemed larger than usual. She felt drops of sweat trickle down between her breasts and worried that her makeup would run before they could begin. She realized she was tense, as if this were her first performance before an audience. She could not help being excited about her new dance.

Kanbei lightly greeted his four main guests, who were seated casually, cross-legged, at one end of the large reception room. "Thank you for coming all the way to Hirano. I have arranged a small diversion. Please relax. Make yourselves comfortable."

Kanbei was a small, energetic samurai who enjoyed life intensely. At an age when most men were content to do nothing, he actively directed the affairs of the Suekichi family, of which he was now the head. Generations ago the Suekichi family had lost its large land holdings when the emperor dedicated all its fields to the maintenance of the Byodo Temple in neighboring Uji. As compensation, the court had appointed the Suekichi family hereditary tax collectors for the central government. Twenty years ago, when the area came under Oda Nobunaga's control, Nobunaga himself confirmed Kanbei in the position. Kanbei had a reputation for being rigorously honest; at harvest time he scrupulously collected the required amount of rice from each farmer in the district, and he delivered every last grain of rice tax to the magistrates above him. The farmers of Hirano, who were the victims of Kanbei's probity, feared and even hated him. After Nobunaga, Hideyoshi not only continued Kanbei in his tax-collecting duties, he also granted him valuable shipping rights along the Japanese coast and, eventually, to China as well. This trade brought Kanbei great riches. The lengths of luxurious foreign silk he had given the girls to sew into kimonos were part of that wealth.

Sankuro lifted the small hand drum to his shoulder, squeezing the cords controlling the tension of the drum head in his left hand. He signaled Sanemon with a nod and struck the tightly stretched face of the drum with the fingers of his right hand, calling out sharply and rhythmically at the same time.

Sanemon entered, moving as Sankuro had instructed him. At times like this Sanemon felt utterly desolate, and, without life or energy, he struck the bell and sang in a flat voice.

> Leaving our homeland of Izumo,
> We look back.
> Kyoto is flower-filled in springtime,
> Kyoto is flower-filled.

Sanemon reached the center of the room, turned to face the spectators, and suddenly, turning as stiff as a board, broke out in a cold sweat. He could not remember what to say next. In the adjoining room, Sankuro couldn't see what was wrong, but he struck the drum strongly several times. Sanemon didn't respond. Instead, he slowly sank to his knees at the back of the dancing area, half-heartedly striking the bell, *chin-chin-chin*. Sankuro had no choice but to begin Sanemon's speech himself, playing the drum at the same time.

"To begin with, I am a Shinto Priest of the Grand Shrine of Izumo. I have a daughter named Okuni, who is a Virgin Priestess of the Shrine. Since peace now reigns throughout the land, she has traveled to the Capital to dance for you."

Sankuro had never acted in a Noh play, but he had naturally absorbed the style of Noh voice during his years of drumming. Now his voice rang out clearly and the audience, already bored by Sanemon's wooden voice and blank expression, sat up attentively. Sankuro could feel the audience without seeing them: they were listening to each word he spoke in the half-chanting style of Noh speech. Calmly, Sankuro nodded a cue for Okuni and the other girls to make their entrance.

The clear voices of the beautifully dressed young girls rose in the air from behind the black figure of Okuni. Dancing and striking their bells in unison, they entered singing of their journey from Izumo to Kyoto. During their procession into the room, Okuni's voice rose above the others, leading them, but she hardly moved her body at all. Then, suddenly, the first verse of the prayer to Amida Buddha was cut short and all the girls, with Okuni now in the center, began to dance with floating, leaping steps as they beat ever faster on their bells.

"They're absolutely delightful."

"Aren't you the sly one, Kanbei, arranging this."

"You know we adore something new and interesting."

Sankuro could see Kanbei accept his guests' praise with a pleased smile but heard him say nothing in return. He wondered if Kanbei would give some audible sign of admiration when he saw the next part of the performance.

The last section of the prayer dance was approaching. Okuni's lovely white legs began to flash out from under the hem of her black monk's robe. Each time this happened the guests were able to glimpse another color so seductive it almost made them doubt their eyes.

> Why ring the bell
> In this life of emptiness?
> Ring the bell in your heart.
> Sing praise to the Lord,
> Praise Lord Amida Buddha!

When the sound of the bells was at its loudest, Okuni glided behind the girls, who made a wall with their bodies and hid her from view. She slipped out of the black robe and Sanemon, waiting at the rear, scooped it up while the girls parted into two groups. In an instant Okuni came forward, fluttering the gorgeous sleeves of her kimono. As she took her hat off in one hand, she began unexpectedly to sing an erotic song in the popular style.

The cord of the tattered sedgehat is broken:

Neither worn,
Nor thrown away.
When I give you a sash,
You complain that it is a used sash.
If it is a used sash,
Then your body, too, is used.

No one spoke. It was a silence of men struck dumb with admiration—for the brilliant kimono suddenly revealed by an ingenious theatrical technique, for the beautiful full face that appeared in an instant from beneath the black lacquered hat, and for Okuni's effortless, leaping dance steps that melded perfectly with her soaring voice. The transformation of Okuni was so splendid, so attractive, and so unexpected, that for some time the guests did not speak.

"Magnificent. No, more than magnificent. My dear Kanbei, you have served a splendid feast. This poor priest is filled to contentment."

The formal voice startled Sankuro and Okuni, who was still carried away by her dancing. No one in the troupe had noticed that Baian was one of the dignitaries Kanbei was entertaining. Baian's wrinkled face was contorted into a suppressed grin. His jowls shook with laughter. The lie he had sent off to Sakai had taken wing and had flown here to Hirano. He had had no reason to imagine that he would be meeting Okuni's troupe at Kanbei's house, and he found the coincidence vastly amusing—and gratifying.

"Master Kanbei," Baian asked teasingly, with laughing eyes, "they sang that they served the Grand Shrine at Izumo, but is that girl really a sacred dancer from Izumo Shrine?"

"Indeed she is. One of my servants is from Izumo. He says their accent reminds him of the way his father speaks and it has made him quite homesick. In truth, she is a virgin priestess of the Grand Shrine of Izumo, just as the song says."

Listening to Kanbei's reply, Baian nodded and snorted happily.

"That girl called Okuni is splendid. Though she's young she has a bold, fearless look." The person who spoke was Mashida Nagamori, the day's chief guest and a close personal friend of Hideyoshi.

Although Nagamori was a general, Hideyoshi had assigned him to manage economic affairs. He was one of the highest-ranking officials responsible for supervising the nationwide Land Survey. Nagamori had a thin face and a cruel glitter in his small eyes. All his reactions were precise and cold. When he said that Okuni looked bold and fearless, it was only to be expected from a samurai who had killed men in the battles of the civil wars, scarcely a decade past.

A second important guest was Yakuin Zenso, a physician prominent in Hideyoshi's retinue. "I've seen many dances in Kyoto but nothing like these floating footsteps," he marveled. The eyes of the third major guest, a youth of seventeen, sparkled with pleasure, but in deference to his elders he did not speak. The young man was Hideyasu, a son of Tokugawa Ieyasu whom Hideyoshi held hostage to ensure his father's good conduct. Hideyoshi had come to like the boy so much he adopted him as his own son, giving him a name made up of one character from his father's name and one from his adoptive father's.

Baian's voice was bland. "The girls' rich kimonos amaze this poor priest. They're gifts from you perhaps, Master Kanbei?"

To Baian's seemingly innocuous question, Kanbei smoothly lied, "No, not from me. I am immensely honored to be seen in your distinguished company but I'm a poor man who could never afford to give expensive gifts to traveling artists. Before they came here, they danced in Kyoto and in Sakai, so I suppose they received the kimonos from rich patrons there. Still, since she is a Virgin Dancer from Izumo Shrine, I must give her some reward."

"Ohh? So these people have danced in the capital, have they?" Baian was intrigued to see how far his lie had flown.

"They sang of dancing in the 'flower-filled' capital in spring, and now it's the middle of summer, so. . ."

"I see. I see."

Kanbei was a perceptive host, and when it was apparent that his guests were taken by the unusual dancing of the shrine maiden from Izumo, he ordered Okuni to repeat her performance. And again a third time. A traveling Noh troupe that Kanbei had summoned, as well as comedians and jugglers, waited with mounting annoyance for their turn to perform. They were never called.

At last Baian whispered in Kanbei's ear and rose to go. "I understand," Kanbei nodded and pressed gifts on Baian. Kanbei smiled inwardly, for he sensed Baian had some special interest in Okuni's performance. Baian hurried back to Hoshi Temple, where he eagerly opened the presents. He found three gold pieces in addition to the obligatory summer gift of soy bean paste. It was exactly what he had expected. Kanbei knew Baian was close to Hideyoshi.

"Densuke," Baian chattered happily, "it was very interesting in Hirano. I ran across something at Suekichi Kanbei's villa that will surprise you."

"What was that, Excellency?"

"I saw Okuni dancing at Kanbei's house." It pleased Baian to see Densuke's small eyes light up in his large, round face. "Astonished, are you? Well, I was surprised, I must say."

"The last I heard, they were in Sakai."

"It seems Kanbei summoned the troupe to Hirano. Master Kanbei proudly proclaimed to everyone that Okuni is a virgin priestess of the Grand Shrine of Izumo. He didn't see through my lie, nor did any of his great guests." Baian laughed delightedly.

Densuke tried hard to ask in an unemotional tone, "Is Okuni. . .I mean, is Sankuro, is everyone well?"

"They're all well. Sankuro and Okuni came up with an unexpected scene in the dance. Okuni sang one of your songs, Densuke, just as you hear it in Kyoto. Master Kanbei is having them perform for other guests for a while. But they'll be coming home before long." Densuke's heart leaped. From that day on he waited impatiently for Okuni's return.

It was hard for Densuke to initiate a conversation with his master. But Baian was in an especially good frame of mind so Densuke raised the question weighing on Sanemon's mind: what did the Land Survey mean? Baian frowned, vaguely annoyed to be asked about such matters. But Densuke was his favorite servant so he gave a detailed answer.

When Okuni and the troupe came back to Hoshi Temple, Densuke rushed out to meet them. He was amazed to see how much Okuni had changed in just three months' time. Her speech and her manners were now like those of a Kyoto woman and she had taken on a refined beauty. When he saw her large, lustrous black eyes gazing lovingly at Sankuro, Densuke's heart almost stopped. So it has happened, he thought, and he felt his body collapse in on itself. Of course, she looks more beautiful than the other girls, he thought. And then, like Sankuro, he knew that Baian must never suspect the relationship. I must protect Okuni, Densuke resolved. Okuni was still a girl, hardly seventeen years old, and when Densuke glanced at the two of them, he could easily see that she was afire with love for Sankuro, while Sankuro, who was experienced, showed nothing. It is up to me to take care of Okuni. I must take care of Okuni, he repeated to himself again and again, until it roused him from his depression.

With a hangdog look, Sanemon sidled up to Densuke, "Did you talk to Master Baian while we were gone? Densuke, what's going to happen to us?" Sanemon was like a sick man begging for medicine.

"Yes, I asked him."

"What did he say?"

"It's not just that the land is being surveyed. That's been going on for four, five years. Lord Hideyoshi is going to issue a new order that all farmers have to return to their land." The girls were chattering happily, glad to be back at Hoshi Temple, but when they heard Densuke's serious voice they stopped and listened intently. "After the Great Buddha is built, peace will be restored to the land, and everyone will have a hoe or a plow in his hand. No farmer may live in a city and no farmer may make or sell things like merchants do, the Lord of the Realm will say. If a farmer leaves his land, the land will be given to someone else to grow rice and barley. Master Baian says you should go straight back to Izumo, quickly, before the edict is posted on the notice boards."

"I won't go back," Okuni broke in. "I won't leave here. I won't." The words unconsciously tumbled from her mouth in Izumo dialect. "I want to dance here. I won't go back to Izumo. I won't, I won't!"

She looked frantically to Sankuro, wanting him to say, "I won't let you go."

"Okuni, be calm." Densuke, not Sankuro, quieted Okuni. "Baian didn't say everyone had to go back. The girls can stay. Baian will look after you."

The terrible tension in Okuni slackened. As she leaned against the door of the hut, Sankuro put his arms around her from behind.

Okaga looked shyly at Okuni and spoke in a small voice, "I'm going back. I'm going with Daddy. Yokichi is waiting for me." She paused and then blurted out, "And Kyuzo is waiting for you, Okuni. Shouldn't we all go back together, Sister Okuni? We have to go back." Okaga was usually such a shy youngster, her rudeness was startling. After a moment Sankuro asked coldly, "Who is this person Kyuzo?"

"He's going to be Sister Okuni's husband. He's waiting in Izumo for Sister Okuni to come home." Okaga seemed to attack Sankuro with her words. Okaga, a terrible crybaby, had become a new and different person.

"So, Okuni has a husband, has she?" Sankuro spoke with a harsh, controlled sneer that made those listening shudder. He removed his hands from Okuni's body and walked outside.

"Wait, Sankuro. Wait." Okuni ran after him, seizing his arm. "I don't have a husband, not Kyuzo. It's a lie. I'm not going to marry Kyuzo. I never will."

"Okuni. I'm not angry. I'm not jealous. I don't say 'go home', Okuni, and I don't say 'stay'. The best thing is to talk it out among yourselves. Decide any way you want. For myself, I agree with Baian."

"Sankuro, you're saying you don't love me?"

"Don't talk nonsense. Didn't Densuke say Baian will protect you girls?"

"And you, Sankuro?"

"I will never be separated from Baian."

The two spoke in low voices, their eyes not meeting. Then Sankuro walked quickly away. Okuni returned to the room.

"Before we left Izumo, Kyuzo strictly told me to bring you home, Okuni." Now that Sankuro was gone, Okaga spoke up relentlessly. "We should go home. We should all go home to Izumo together."

"What are you talking about!" Although Okaga was a little girl, Okuni couldn't keep from shouting at her. "Go back if you want. I'll never do it. I forgot Kyuzo the day I left Izumo. Tell Kyuzo to forget me!"

"Sister Okuni, do you want to be *kabuki*?"

"What?"

"To run away from a promised husband is what a *kabuki* woman would do."

"Ohh!" Densuke saw the fire come into Okuni's eyes. She lifted her shoulders defiantly. "So I'm a *kabuki* woman? If it's *kabuki* for me to be the wife of Sankuro, the man I love, instead of Kyuzo, someone I hate, then I'm glad to be called *kabuki*." Until this moment their affair had been kept secret from members of the troupe. Okuni's words made it public. To Okuni's declaration that she was a *kabuki* woman, Sanemon and Okaga had no reply. Densuke quietly rose and went out of the room.

Five

Many things happened during the latter part of the year 1588. Sanemon, who had no reason to remain in Osaka another day, left for Izumo the following morning and took Okaga with him, while the four other girls, who did not want to go home, remained at Baian's with Okuni. The girls were still just children, not betrothed to anyone, and they had come to enjoy the free life of dancing and singing and wearing beautiful kimonos. Sankuro was greatly relieved to see Sanemon go and pleased that most of the girls in the troupe remained. Baian would have been angry with him if the small troupe had all returned to Izumo.

At the end of August, Hideyoshi issued the proclamation that came to be called "Hideyoshi's Sword Hunting Ordinance." What Densuke had told Sanemon was true enough and, as far as it went, accurate. After all, Baian was the proclamation's main author. But Baian, who was so skilled with words, hid Hideyoshi's real purpose from Densuke and from everyone who might read the lord's proclamation. In brief, it said that because a farmer could not use swords, daggers, spears, lances, or guns to plow his land, it was wasteful and extravagant for him to own arms. Weapons would be melted down in order to make rivets and clamps for the Great Buddha statue in Kyoto, thereby earning the donor merit in the future life. It was a farmer's duty to cultivate the earth diligently so his children and grandchildren would prosper in peace. Out of compassion for farmers, the Lord of the Realm so ordered.

Hideyoshi did not originate the idea of taking away the peasants' weapons. Twelve years previously, in 1576, an army of 40,000 farmers in Echizen Province had fiercely resisted Nobunaga's campaign to unify the nation. For generations, farmers of the province, who were fanatical adherents of egalitarian True Pure Land Buddhism, had ruled themselves. Indeed, the Echizen peasants' overthrowing of their samurai masters in 1470 and subsequent self-rule in Echizen for 106 years, through the entire Period of the Civil Wars, was a singular event in the nation's history. At last Nobunaga's favorite general, Shibata Katsuie, crushed the peasant army. In order to pacify the region, he slaughtered thousands of resisting peasants, women and children included, and he confiscated all the swords and spears in the province. Hideyoshi's draconian Sword Hunt was Katsuie's idea carried to its ultimate conclusion. Hereafter, farmers would be a powerless class who worked only for their samurai lords.

Densuke tried to explain to Okuni what the new order meant. "Will they take our bells?" Okuni asked.

"Not bells, of course not."

"But if they're going to make a big, big metal Buddha they'll need bronze more than iron, won't they?"

"Well, if you put it that way. . ."

Off to the side, Sankuro laughed sardonically under his breath, listening to their conversation. He knew that casting the Great Buddha was merely a ruse. More than ever he admired Hideyoshi, the cleverest man in the world. If I am always at Baian's side, the Lord of the Realm may notice me, he thought. Surely I must take that chance. If Hideyoshi sees Okuni dance he is bound to be interested, for he loves new and brilliant things.

When fall came, Baian went to Tajima for the hot baths. Ever since the Kyushu campaign he had been bothered by a lingering cold, and that was two years ago. For several months he had been at Hideyoshi's beck and call, rushing first to his castle in Osaka and then rushing back to Juraku Mansion in Kyoto more times than he could remember. Immense preparations had been necessary for the emperor's visit to Juraku Mansion. Then while Okuni and the troupe had been in Sakai, he had worked night and day at Hideyoshi's command to complete the official record of the event, *Commemoration of the Imperial Visit to Juraku Mansion*. He was exhausted and needed to rest.

While Baian was convalescing at Tajima, Sankuro and the others were at loose ends. They had wanted to stay at Kanbei's and perform, but Baian had specifically recalled them. But now that he was ill, they had nothing to do. Densuke suggested they perform in the city. Sankuro readily agreed because of his long-standing dream that one day Hideyoshi would see them. Okuni's spirits soared when she imagined performing freely outdoors as they had on the way to Hirano. Sankuro said confidently that they would perform in the center of the city, where the Yodo and Neriya rivers meet, in front of Hideyoshi's castle. Throughout the city many new stores had been opened by merchants from Hirano, Sakai, and elsewhere. But Osaka was so new that large sections of land were still not occupied, including the area directly in front of the castle.

"Shouldn't we ask Baian before we dance in front of the Lord of the Realm's castle?" Densuke asked. It annoyed Sankuro to have his idea opposed, but he knew Densuke was right. If they came to Hideyoshi's attention while Baian was gone, Baian would feel slighted, and no one could tell what he might do. No, Sankuro could not reach Hideyoshi directly.

They discussed the situation for a long time before they decided to perform in front of prostitutes' houses. The reason was that they had to perform where people congregated. In Osaka, shrine and temple festivals drew throngs of people only four or five times a year, unlike Kyoto where famous religious sites were always crowded. On the other hand, people congregated in front of the shacks of the prostitutes every day. Until city officials set aside an area in the city for licensed prostitution, women were legally free to ply their trade wherever they wished. Prostitutes gathered at crossroads and busy intersections, where they put up small shacks. In good weather, Okuni and the others often saw traveling Noh troupes or other entertainers perform in front of these cheap hovels.

When Sankuro and Densuke returned from checking over the area, Okuni was helping the girls prepare the beautiful kimonos Kanbei had given them. Coldly furious, Sankuro ordered them to put the kimonos away. They would wear the kimonos Baian had given them.

Okuni was hurt by the way he spoke to her but she had to ask, "Why can't we wear our best kimonos tomorrow, Sankuro?"

"Our audience won't be the rich important people we played for in Sakai and Hirano. They'll be townsmen, don't you understand?"

"Yes, and villagers bringing food into the city will stop to watch. I know that."

"Then you should know enough not to wear those costumes. You're a stupid girl."

She flushed as if he had struck her. Still, she would not meekly accept something she did not understand. "Ordinary people like to see beautiful clothes. Why shouldn't we look nice?"

"Even the kimonos Baian gave us are too good for commoners. We're going to be invited to perform for important audiences again, and what if you get the good kimonos dirty? Put them away." He turned on his heel and went outside. Okuni and the other girls did what Sankuro told them. Okuni had been looking forward to dancing in her beautiful kimono. Going back to the old clothes deadened her high spirits.

The next day they spread out a few straw mats in the street to mark off a dancing area in front of the shacks where the prostitutes worked. Then they fastened mats to bamboo poles to make a fence around the dancing area, leaving a gap for an entrance. Curious passersby could no longer stop in the street and watch, and perhaps drop a coin at the entertainers' feet, as was the custom. They would have to pay admission to come inside the fence. Then they could see the dance. Although members of the troupe didn't think of it this way, they were creating a new kind of urban, commercial theater system.

Sankuro and Okuni were in a bad mood because of their quarrel, and this naturally made the girls downcast, too. In the small troupe, Densuke took on the role of encouraging the others. "All right,

Okuni will sing and I'll dance. The song Okuni likes. Come on."

"The song I like?"

"Yes. Let's begin." Densuke started the song off and began to dance.

The lyrics of Densuke's song described a servant fanning charcoal to boil water. This was the first time Okuni had seen Densuke dance, and she was surprised at his skill. His melody was a currently popular Quick Tune, so of course they all knew it. Soon Okuni and the other girls were singing along with Densuke, delighted and charmed by his comic movements. Sankuro had seen Densuke dance at parties given by Baian, when guests who had drunk many cups of rice wine called on Densuke to entertain them. Remembering Densuke's comic pantomime, Sankuro's dark mood evaporated and soon he was adding lively drum beats to the gay singing. First, Densuke mimed a steaming bath tub with hot water flowing from it. He stood on his toes and leaped up and down to the rhythm of the song. Then, he half-opened his fan and waved it, as if cooling hot water in a tea cup. He repeated his gestures and his dance steps over and over, each time switching the hand that held the fan. He danced with a child's light movements, then like a doddering old man.

Okuni stopped singing to gaze at Densuke's precise hand gestures and foot movements. She had no idea he was such a talented person. She knew him only as a servant in Baian's house. He was the man who casually hummed through his nose while he fetched water or chopped wood. He was a kind man. An interesting man. A man who looked after Okuni. That was the Densuke she knew, not this wonderfully funny and talented dancer.

Densuke noticed that Okuni had stopped singing. "Come, Okuni, you sing, too. This time I'll dance to the Spinning Song."

Sankuro's drumming grew stronger. Okuni's voice rose high and clear. Densuke's dance was even funnier than before. In his usual performer's high topknot, he danced like a stuck-up woman. He whirled around and around as if he couldn't stop. His movements were so outrageous the girls burst out laughing. Even without special costume he created the impression of a woman.

"Do you know the original form of the Spinning Song?" Sankuro asked when the dance was over.

"I've heard it's even older than Noh dance."

"It is. It started as a Buddhist Dance of Longevity, centuries before Noh began. At that time it was called the Wind and Stream Longevity Dance and it was a specialty of monks at Kofuku Temple in Nara where I lived. It was a woman's dance. I remember seeing it when I was a boy. A young monk, dressed as a girl, danced like a woman and sang while my grandfather accompanied him on the drum. But it's changed a lot since it became a popular song."

"Do you remember the words?"

"Of course." Sankuro admired Densuke's performance. At the same time he would use this opportunity to show off his superior artistic knowledge to Okuni and the others.

"Please sing it. I never thought I'd learn the real form." Densuke was genuinely pleased and he waited impatiently for Sankuro to begin. Sankuro settled himself, raised the drum to his shoulder, struck it once, and began to sing in a dignified manner.

> Spin the thread, so they say;
> The thread of night is long, they say.
> Tortuously spin,
> Long through the night,
> I long for you.

"I see. So that's what the Spinning Song is about. I knew it had a woman's movements, but I never knew it was about a woman sadly spinning thread through the night waiting for her lover. I thought it was about a woman turning." The two men laughed, now in good spirits.

"Do you want to learn it?"

"Yes." And so Densuke learned the song from Sankuro.

Every day that fall when it wasn't raining they performed in the street in front of the prostitutes' shacks. But they didn't draw many spectators, for it was still an unsettled time. Hideyoshi had only been in power for three years. Merchants and their employees were busy on errands and had little time to spend watching dances. That didn't bother Sankuro, for he was only passing the time until Baian returned. The spectators who came inside the rude fence were strongly attracted by Okuni's beauty. They liked the lively dancing and Densuke's antics in the Spinning Song and gradually, by word of mouth, the troupe became known in the city.

Early in winter an event occurred that affected the troupe's destiny irrevocably. Baian came rushing back from his rest to offer congratulations to the Lord of the Realm. The rumors Okuni and the others had been hearing for several weeks turned out to be true: Hideyoshi's favorite mistress was pregnant. The excitement was palpable. At last Hideyoshi would have an heir. People loved to gossip wildly about the Lord of the Realm's libidinous ways. It was said that a hundred, three hundred, no, a thousand mistresses had felt his embrace. And none of them could give him a child. Despairing, he had made his nephew Hidetsugu his successor. The rumors grew louder when Hideyoshi commanded that a castle be built on the banks of the Yodo River, some thirty miles north of Osaka. The enormous castle in Osaka and Juraku Mansion in Kyoto had only been completed within the past year. Why did the Lord of the Realm want a third castle, and why must it be completed by spring? Many speculated it was for the birth of a child. And so it was.

The pregnant woman was Hideyoshi's closest consort, Otane. How Otane, Nobunaga's niece, came to be Hideyoshi's mistress was a tangled story. When Hideyoshi was a young man and still a vassal to Nobunaga, he fell passionately in love with Nobunaga's sister, Oichi, reputed to be the most beautiful woman in the country. Nobunaga gave Oichi in marriage to his favorite general, Shibata Katsuie. But Hideyoshi never lost his desire for her, and following Nobunaga's assassination, he took the opportunity to attack Katsuie, largely, it was said, in order to seize Oichi. She chose to die with her husband when Hideyoshi razed their castle, but her daughter, Otane, lived. Perhaps in retribution, Hideyoshi took the daughter as his mistress, for it is said she greatly resembled her mother. Such an unnatural alliance was a never-ending subject of gossip in Osaka. Otane must have hated Hideyoshi, yet she became his favorite among scores of mistresses and would remain so until his death. Now she was bearing his child and he was building a castle for her. Hideyoshi believed that if his child was born in its own castle it would be a boy. Also, people gossiped that mother and child would be in danger if they lived among Hideyoshi's other women in Osaka Castle. A woman's jealousy is a terrible thing.

Unfortunately, Baian was resting in Tajima when the news came and by the time he reached Osaka, Hideyoshi had already disowned him. Okuni and the others did not understand exactly what had happened, but from then on Baian stayed inside Hoshi Temple. He was never called to the castle and of course he wasn't summoned to Kyoto. Baian was in a desperate state of mind and no one, not even his wife, dared speak to him. Densuke had to leave the troupe and return to his servant's role. As for Sankuro, each morning he took the girls out Hoshi Temple's back gate to perform in the city. When those in power are out of sorts, Sankuro thought it was best to be invisible.

One day, as they were resting between performances, Okuni mused, "If you have the Lord of the Realm's child, do you get a castle built for you?"

"Why do you ask such a question, Okuni?" Sankuro said in a testy tone.

"I was just wondering." She said nothing more. As early winter approached and falling maple leaves danced red through the city streets, she felt something strange in her body. Day after day her legs felt leaden. Her stomach was heavy and she could not eat. Flashes of intense cold flooded her loins. When dancing, the sharp ringing of the bells and the echoing of the drum seemed to enter through her ears and penetrate her whole body. It was strange, Okuni thought. Then when she heard the talk about the new castle on the Yodo River she knew that she, too, was carrying a baby in her womb. When a man and woman join their flesh together it is natural to have a child, she thought, just as her mother and father, fleeing from the steel furnaces in Iron Mountain, had conceived her. Just as the Lord of the Realm is having a child after embracing his mistress. Now he is building a castle for his child. What about me?

"Don't tell anyone." Okuni recalled the words Sankuro had whispered fiercely in her ear the first night he embraced her, on the pier in Sakai. Okuni lived openly with Sankuro, now that Sanemon and Okaga were gone, and while Baian was at Tajima she proudly acted like Sankuro's wife before Densuke and the girls. How sad, she thought, that I have to love Sankuro secretly again, now that Baian is back. The Lord of the Realm is happy to have a child. Why can't Sankuro be happy that I'm going to have his child? Don't tell anyone, he said. If Baian finds out I'm pregnant, it will be terrible. He'll send us away. I can't tell anyone, she said to herself again and again. Tell no one, tell no one, she cautioned herself.

Okuni took the lead, as usual, singing, dancing, and striking the bell that hung from her neck. The sound of Sankuro's drumbeats pained her, like a nail being pounded into her heart.

"It's snowing." Sankuro looked up. The audience had disappeared. "It's going to be a heavy snow. We'll have to stop performing for a while." The girls immediately began taking down the fence and rolling up the mats.

Powdery snow fell softly over the streets and alleys of Osaka, seeming to quiet the busyness of the year's end in that merchants' town. Tiled roofs throughout the city were transformed into angles of white.

Walking along the riverbank on the way back to Hoshi Temple, they saw boats enter the channel of the Yodo River one after the other, seemingly without end, carrying rocks of gigantic size.

"They must be stones for Yodo Castle. The Lord of the Realm is anxious to have the castle finished. They can't even rest on a snowy day." Sankuro stared at the rock-laden boats sliding by, impressed by the power of the Lord of the Realm. Beside him, Okuni silently watched the current of the Yodo River devour the falling snow. What kind of castle is being built just so a woman can have a baby, she wondered deep in her heart. Suddenly, she wanted to go there and see it.

Six

Early the next morning, Okuni said she was going out to see Yodo Castle. Sankuro looked at her, unbelieving: "In this snow?" None of the girls would go with her. In a single night the city of Osaka had been buried under a thick blanket of snow and dense flakes swirled through the air with no sign of stopping. A snowstorm this bad was rare in Osaka. The others thought it was crazy to go out and they tried to persuade Okuni to wait.

But her mind was made up. "No matter what, I'm going," she cut them off, and began to get ready.

"Go then, it's your funeral. You won't find a coolie moving in a storm like this," Sankuro rebuffed her.

Densuke was uneasy about the situation. "Well then, why don't I go with you? It isn't safe for a woman to walk alone in such snow." It was unclear whether she heard his kind offer or not. Gritting her teeth, she put on layers of everyday kimonos as well as several more kimonos that the worried girls put in her hands. Densuke, too, put on layer after layer of clothes until both of them were as round as balloons. He tied a piece of linen cloth over his head and another over Okuni's for extra warmth.

"You're strange-looking creatures, I must say," Sankuro laughed at them from a corner of the room.

"If the snow gets worse, we'll turn back." Densuke spoke as much for Okuni's ears as for Sankuro's. He led the way outside.

The snow had piled high during the night. Yesterday, opened

doors had sported welcoming curtains; today they were shuttered tight. It was mid-morning, but snow falling through the air muted the light so it seemed like afternoon. The city was utterly without sound.

"You're not cold?"

"No."

They were passing through the merchants' quarter. Osaka was a castle town and its districts were laid out in the standard fashion: castle at the center, mansions of the samurai immediately surrounding it, further out, in a larger concentric circle, stores and homes of merchants, and finally, at the city's edge, clusters of artisans' shops and workers' hovels. Houses were getting farther apart. They reached the Yodo River and walked silently along its wide dike. Except for the black river, the whole world was white. Ships loaded with stones and tree trunks moved slowly against the current. On the dike, groups of men, chanting *"eiya eiya,"* leaned their shoulders against thick ropes that inched the heavy boats upstream. Flesh showed through tattered clothing, and though they walked barefoot in the snow, sweat poured from their bodies because of the extreme exertion. The feet of many were raw and bleeding. When a man collapsed in the snow, too weak to move, he was dumped into an empty boat that carried him swiftly downstream and out of sight.

"If you're tired, let's go back. You can see the castle any day. They won't finish it before spring." Densuke tried to speak cheerfully.

Okuni did not reply. She would not admit that the bitter wind, hurling snow across the river into their faces, had already sapped the warmth from her body. She determinedly placed one foot before the other on the steep, snowy slope. The snow was getting deeper, and even carrying no load, it was hard to move forward. Every few minutes Densuke turned to look back at Okuni. Her face was pale, he thought. Her eyebrows were beautiful, powdered white by blown, unmelting snow that clung to them, but beneath them her large eyes were watery and unnaturally bright. Densuke did not want to show his worry. He turned into the wind and they plodded on. At an unknown village, Densuke took out some food he had brought.

They had to eat while walking, for the cold became unbearable if they stopped moving even for a moment. It was dusk when they reached the fork made by the two joining rivers.

"There. I can see it." Densuke pointed across the river. Huge rock walls of a central fortress were already in place. The great size of Yodo Castle was apparent in the framework made of giant trees that masses of workers, even in the midst of this terrible snowstorm, were raising as high as the fifth story. At that distance, the swarm of moving laborers and the samurai who commanded them looked like a nest of ants: the worker ants carrying loads much larger than themselves, the warrior ants urging the workers on. If sword-bearing samurai had not been present who can tell how many workers might have frozen to death. Men worked desperately without stopping to escape their supervisors' curses and cracking whips, until the blood beat so wildly in their breasts there was no possibility of becoming cold.

Okuni looked silently across the river. This is the castle? The Lord of the Realm is building this castle for the woman who will bear his child? Okuni's thoughts came randomly. Snow is covering the stone foundations like a white kimono and the black tree trunks carried by dozens of men are turning white in the snow. The snow will continue falling, she thought, but work on the castle will not stop for anything.

"You've seen it, Okuni. It's enough. Let's go back."

Without even a nod, Okuni turned and started to retrace her steps. But she wasn't content. She didn't know why she had wanted to see the castle in the snow. She wasn't even sure that seeing the castle had been her object in trudging up the Yodo River.

"Wait, Okuni. If we walk back it will take until morning." Densuke flagged an empty boat coming down from the castle, and they climbed on board and asked to be taken to Osaka. Sitting still in the open boat was far colder than walking. Densuke wrapped Okuni in his arms. It was cold. Bitter cold. The wind from the river pierced their clothes. The snow lashed their faces. At first Okuni rubbed her hands together to warm them, but after awhile she lay still. Densuke looked at her and was frightened. Her slack face was blue and she seemed only half-conscious.

"Okuni. What is it?"

She looked at Densuke and smiled bleakly. Then she groaned and collapsed into the bottom of the boat. She felt a wrenching pain in her abdomen, a pain that seemed to be crushing the bones of her pelvis. In spite of the intense cold, sweat poured from her body.

"Okuni!" Densuke lifted her in his arms.

The boatmen noticed something was wrong. "Moriguchi village is just ahead. There's a house on the river road where you can get her warm. It's the cold. It's too much for her." Saying this, the head boatman steered for the bank and soon the boat landed on the shore. Okuni regained consciousness in time to crawl onto the riverbank when the boat stopped.

"Are you all right, Okuni?"

"Yes. I'm going to walk." She ignored Densuke's hand and, standing up alone, she staggered forward through the snow, one halting step after another toward a house whose lighted windows could be seen through the swirling storm. Three unbearable spasms of pain ripped through her body in quick succession and she fell forward in the snow. When Densuke knelt and tried to raise Okuni to her feet, he realized at once what was happening. The white snow was bathed red with her blood. Clots of blood smeared her clothes. Each time she coughed rivulets of blood streamed from the bottom of her kimono.

"It's all right, Okuni. I'll carry you. Hold on, please." Densuke put his own kimono over the unconscious body of Okuni and lifted her strongly in his arms. He was a young man and well built, but in his haste and anxiety he lurched and staggered toward the lighted house. When he reached it, he pounded on the door, "Is anyone home? Is anyone home? This woman is very sick. Help us, please!"

At last an old woman came to the door. Looking annoyed, she poked her leathery, wrinkled face out. "If you're a samurai, go away. There's no one left but the old man and me."

"She's awfully sick. Can you help her?"

Looking at Okuni the old woman saw that she was dangerously ill. "Bring her inside. Is it a miscarriage?"

"I think so. Please help her."

"Lay her down and do as I say." The old woman was strong-willed and sure of herself. She ordered the old man to light a fire, and she carefully removed Okuni's bloody clothes. Densuke stared hypnotically as Okuni's large breasts and voluptuous body were revealed. She seemed to shine with a terrible whiteness. The old woman washed between Okuni's thighs and, tearing off a kimono sleeve, placed it between Okuni's legs. Densuke had thought that only the two old people were in the house, but two girls now edged shyly into the room. The old woman gave them a rough cloth and had them vigorously rub Okuni's neck, shoulders, arms, and breasts. "Lie beside her and warm her. Rub her body, but do not touch her stomach. Do you understand?" The two girls lay on either side of Okuni, alternately rubbing and embracing her. The old woman put two layers of heavy men's kimonos over Okuni and took her bloody clothes into the kitchen, where she began to wash them.

"Will she live, Granny?" Densuke asked.

"I don't know."

"Please save her."

"Is she your wife?"

"No. She's under the protection of Reverend Baian, who is a retainer of the Lord of the Realm."

"Is she his woman?"

"Oh, no. She's not the Lord of the Realm's woman." Densuke evaded her scornful look.

"Of course not. His woman wouldn't be in rags, she'd wear a silk kimono, and she wouldn't be walking in the snow. If you're the lord's servant, tell him that every farmer hates him." The water was red with Okuni's blood.

"You're talking about the Lord of the Realm." Densuke was frightened.

The old woman went on rancorously, "When the samurai went to war, they made our men carry their tents and armor. They stole our food. If a farmer resisted he was killed, just like that. So when we hammered out hoes and plows we always made some swords and spears, too. We weren't going to wait meekly to be killed. But then the monkey-faced farmer, who calls himself the Lord of the Realm stole our swords and spears!"

"I know. The wars are over."

"They say that. And he's the only one who's gotten rich. Farmers are starving and Monkey Face has money to waste building another castle. He took our food, even the rice seed, last spring. Now he's taken our men to carry rocks and wood to build that woman's castle. In the winter!" Her eyes flashed with deep hatred.

"Granny, it's dangerous to say such things to other people."

"I've seen nothing but war, killing, burning houses. Not one good thing has happened. I won't regret it if I'm killed."

Before long Okuni regained consciousness, and the old woman said that Okuni would live. In the night Densuke ran back to Hoshi Temple to tell Sankuro. Okuni was Sankuro's woman and Densuke would never pass the night with another man's woman, no matter what the situation. Sankuro was awake, waiting for them to return. Densuke could tell at a glance that Sankuro knew.

"Why did you let her go out in the snow?" Densuke burst out in sudden rage.

"Okuni does what she wants to do. You know that."

"Your child died! Don't you care?"

Sankuro closed his eyes for a long time and then sighed. "I don't know, Densuke. I don't know what I feel. About Okuni or the child."

Densuke's mind was in turmoil. I'd run away with her if it was me. Deep into the mountains, leading Okuni to safety. I'd care for her and I'd bring her child into the world with my own hands. Why didn't I notice she was sick? Why didn't I bring her back before her child died in the snow? He was sick with regret. Forgive me, Okuni. Forgive me. It was my fault. Please, forgive me. He could not get the words out of his mind. He blamed himself, not Sankuro.

The next morning a bright sun began to melt the snow. Sankuro walked the muddy, slippery path to Moriguchi village. When he appeared at the door the old woman eyed him suspiciously, fearing he was a samurai. Sankuro spoke politely, "May I come in?" and with a feeling of relief, she knew he was not. She took Sankuro into the room where Okuni was lying motionless. Nodding to the old man and the two girls to follow her, the old woman went outside into the sun to look for firewood.

Okuni and Sankuro looked at each other for a long time without speaking. Okuni's face was as white as snow and her lips had lost their redness. But as she continued to gaze at Sankuro, light gradually returned to her eyes and soon her eyes began to sparkle. How beautiful, Sankuro thought. This beautiful woman is my woman. When I think that she almost died in the snow, I feel the happiness of a man who has recovered a treasure. His heart overflowed with tenderness for Okuni as he took and held her hand.

"I lost your child." Okuni's throat was dry. Her shoulders shook uncontrollably.

Sankuro bowed his head. "Forgive me, Okuni."

This apology from her man was so unexpected Okuni wept. She closed her eyes, but the tears did not stop. I haven't cried for such a long time, Okuni thought. I was thirteen when I cried the night Granny died in Izumo. Now she wept with all her might. She cried as if every last drop of moisture in her flesh would pour out in tears.

Almost every day Sankuro walked to Moriguchi village to visit Okuni. Often Densuke wrapped up dried fish or bean paste and rice from Baian's kitchen and gave it to Sankuro. They were gifts to the old woman for taking care of Okuni. Since they weren't performing, they didn't have money to pay the old couple in Moriguchi. Okuni grew stronger, day by day. She felt close to Sankuro and he was always kind. She was pleased that he was attentive to the old woman's grandchildren, whose names were Otsuru and Omatsu. He brought them candy and toys. These two country children were entranced by the girls from the troupe, whom Sankuro made a point of bringing with him several times a week. Had Okuni thought about it, she might have realized it was strange that he let the girls wear their most colorful kimonos on these visits. But she was simply happy to see Sankuro. It wasn't in Okuni's nature to suspect that his thoughtfulness might have another purpose behind it.

Hideyoshi pardoned Baian on New Year's Day, 1589. Once again Baian was in an excellent mood. He regularly went from Hoshi Temple to the castle to attend Hideyoshi, and several times he accompanied the Lord of the Realm to Juraku Mansion in Kyoto. He was extremely busy through late winter. One day in early spring, he noticed he hadn't seen Okuni around Hoshi Temple. He questioned Densuke. Densuke replied, with some foreboding, that she was sick with "the way of blood." Baian snorted loudly and then chuckled. All women's ailments were known as "the way of blood." He recalled distastefully the fits of hysteria that overcame his daughter when she was menstruating and he imagined that that was Okuni's problem, too. He dropped the subject and didn't mention it again.

Spring that year was wet and the grass grew quickly in Moriguchi village. "A heavy snow means a good harvest. This should be a good year. I want to have the fields planted before our son comes back from working on Yodo Castle," the old woman remarked. At last Okuni was able to get out of bed, thanks to the old woman's careful attention through the winter. Also, through the winter Densuke had held aside for Okuni some of the pills Baian was receiving from Tokitsune at court. Although Densuke didn't know what they were intended to cure, they helped Okuni recover. Now that Okuni was up, she talked to the old woman about herself, how she lived at Hoshi Temple in Osaka and how they had traveled to Sakai and Hirano. She said she liked dancing with Densuke and the girls who visited.

"Dance?" The old woman looked sharply at Okuni. From that moment the old woman turned cold. She stopped treating Okuni like her daughter. A barrier came between the old farming woman, who loved the land, and Okuni, who ached to dance on the stage. Okuni was still very weak, she could scarcely walk, but she knew she had to leave. She couldn't trouble the old woman any more.

Spring had come. Okuni walked outside in the warm weather to regain her strength. Seeing the spring flowers, vivid memories of her childhood in Izumo came back to her. As she relived the times she had run along the Hii River as a child, her steps unconsciously turned toward the Yodo River. The girls caught sight of her slow-moving figure.

"Where are you going, Sister Okuni?"

"Up the riverbank."

"I'm going, too."

"Me too."

Omatsu was eight and Otsuru was ten. They were happy to run alongside Okuni, who climbed heavily to the top of the bank. After three months together, the two girls were comfortable with Okuni and treated her like an older sister.

"What's that?"

"A line of soldiers."

A brilliantly colored palanquin was being carried along the river road from the direction of Osaka in the midst of a long column of warriors. Okuni had met many processions of warriors during her journey with Sanemon and the girls from Izumo to Kyoto. She had learned that it was dangerous for a commoner to approach too close-ly. You could never tell what incident might arise. She led the two girls behind a large tree that hid them from view.

The leading foot soldiers wore battle dress and carried spears and guns. The mounted warrior who commanded the company appeared to be a ranking general. Eight men carried an unusually large palanquin on their shoulders, four in front and four behind. Gaily colored silk curtains covered the sides of the palanquin, mak-ing it impossible to tell who was inside. A dozen young women walked behind the palanquin, their thickly powdered white faces visible under wide straw hats. The women walked in silence, appar-ently tired by their long journey. Behind a second company of armed soldiers, porters carried all manner of boxes and luggage. A third group of soldiers brought up the rear. The procession was so long it seemed to have no end.

"It's the lord's woman, isn't it?" Omatsu asked.

"Uh-huh. She's moving to her castle up the river," Otsuru said.

Okuni didn't speak but she looked piercingly toward the palanquin. The woman with the bulging stomach who was riding inside was intensely happy. Just thinking of it, she had the impulse to rush up the bank and kick the palanquin to the ground. Was this the jealousy approaching madness that a woman who has lost a child might feel? Or perhaps the terrible anger of a woman whose pregnancy goes uncelebrated? In truth, it was the natural rage of a deeply unhappy woman, seeing another woman living in the extremity of luxury. Malice and enmity boiled up in her breast and became unbearable. Before the children's frightened eyes, Okuni paled and crumpled to the ground.

Seven

The day Hideyoshi's heir was born, people in their houses and in the streets of Osaka gathered to gossip avidly. It's a boy. The Lord of the Realm is so happy, he gave the baby a "fortunate" and an "unfortunate" name. That's right, two names. His fortunate name is Tsuru-matsu. I heard that, too. So he'll live a long life like the stork, *tsuru,* and the pine, *matsu*. And his unfortunate name is Sutegimi. The lord named him Thrown-Away Boy to ward off bad luck. Of course. An evil spirit won't bother a castoff child. These and other comments were excitedly bandied about in each of Osaka's many districts.

It was summer. Okuni was resting in the hut at the rear of Hoshi Temple. Her body was slowly healing half a year after that snowy day. When she heard that the woman in Yodo Castle had safely given birth, she felt calm and happy. She hadn't forgotten the cruel sight of the palanquin being borne to the castle nor her jealousy, but Okuni was a woman and the birth of any child made her glad.

Sankuro was in a buoyant mood. After Tsurumatsu's birth, Baian quickly wrote and presented to Hideyoshi a commemorative scroll, *Birth of a Young Prince*. Hideyoshi was so pleased, he ordered Baian to remain at his side constantly. Sankuro often accompanied Baian to the castle and to Kyoto. Okuni found that Sankuro was often away in Kyoto for periods of a week or more. He talked excitedly when he returned. "Baian says it, too: Kyoto is going to be Hideyoshi's capital. Osaka is just a port town. Kyoto was the capital of Japan under the rule of the Ashikaga shoguns for hundreds of years and the emperor lives there, too. That's enough reason for the Lord of the Realm to move to Juraku Mansion. Get well, Okuni. The next time you dance, it'll be in Kyoto. In Kyoto." Sankuro described the Golden Throne in Juraku Mansion and the 26,000 gold and silver coins that Hideyoshi had thrown into the crowd from his castle gate in celebration of his son's birth. Sankuro was not exaggerating when he spoke in awe of golden pillars and ceilings, gold dishes, and even stables and toilets of gold at Juraku Mansion. Hideyoshi's latest edict, the Land Survey, was providing him with immense wealth, which he spent as lavishly as he pleased.

"How does the Lord of the Realm get so much gold?" Okuni was thinking of the old woman living in Moriguchi village who was so poor.

"Soon after the lord took away the farmers' swords, he ordered a new land survey. As a result, he knows where every grain of rice in the whole country comes from. Everything belongs to the lord. If he wants it he only has to take it. He rules the world, China and India, too." Sankuro thought Okuni's question childish and he burst out laughing.

At that moment Otsuru and Omatsu arrived at Hoshi Temple from Moriguchi village. "Did Granny say you could come?" Okuni immediately asked in surprise.

As if he'd been expecting them, Sankuro interjected, "The names Otsuru and Omatsu together make Tsurumatsu. How lucky. Baian will be delighted. He'll like the idea of adding two more dancers to the group."

"You must tell me what Granny said," Okuni demanded several times.

"We came without asking," Otsuru finally answered.

"How could you do that? Granny will be worried. Go home. Go straight home to Granny." The girls were taken aback by Okuni's strict tone, but Omatsu, the younger sister, pouted and said, "I won't go back. I want to dance."

"You can dance if Granny says so."

"She won't let us. That's why we didn't ask."

"Then you have to go home to Moriguchi."

"Master Sankuro said we could come any time. Master Sankuro said we could dance with the other girls."

Okuni sucked in her breath. She owed her life to the old woman. Yet Sankuro had planned this. She sent the girls outside so she could be alone with Sankuro. "Granny saved my life, Sankuro. It's wrong to tempt the girls to dance unless she says they can. Why did you do it?"

"Look Okuni, for a while you won't be well enough to dance. So you see, we need more girls. This is a good way to add to the dancing chorus."

"It's kidnapping."

"Don't say that. I gave the old folks plenty for nursing you. In fact, I should get something back in return."

"You gave money for the girls?"

"I did."

"Then you're a slave trader, Sankuro."

"Is that so?" Sankuro, who had been bantering good-naturedly, was angered by Okuni's accusation. "When did I kidnap anyone? When did I buy anyone? I'm pleasing Baian. There's nothing wrong with that."

"Granny will go crazy with worry. Don't you know she and Granddad will cry if they don't know where their two grandchildren are?"

"That strong-willed old woman won't cry."

"Even so, she'll be angry with me and I won't know what to do."

"You don't have to worry about it, Okuni. She hasn't any reason to be angry. Otsuru and Omatsu want to be here. They'll eat better here than in Moriguchi, won't they? They'll be happy wearing beautiful kimonos, nicer than anything they have in the village. The old woman won't be upset. She ought to give a prayer of thanks."

Okuni's body shook. She was quarreling with the man she loved. Since her illness, Sankuro had not made love to her. It frightened her to oppose Sankuro, yet she couldn't accept what he'd done.

The girls did not go home. Every day they tried on the bright kimonos, and they practiced singing and dancing out of Okuni's sight. Okuni was very aggravated with Sankuro, but she didn't have the strength to argue with him. All she could do was tell the girls again and again to go home. Perhaps Sankuro found Okuni's sullen looks irritating, or perhaps he was tired of seeing the bedridden woman. In any case, one day he left the hut and went with Baian to Juraku Mansion, taking his drum with him.

Not many days had passed before the old woman, whom Sankuro had correctly called strong-willed, appeared at the back gate of Hoshi Temple. "Heh! Okuni! Sankuro! Densuke!" She spit out the detested names. "Come out, you kidnappers. Child stealers. You stole my granddaughters. Otsuru! Omatsu! Don't try to hide. Do you think Granny doesn't know you're here? Stupid girls, come out!" The old woman's eyes smoldered with anger. She knew Hoshi Temple was under the protection of Tenmangu Shrine and that its head was a personal retainer of the Lord of the Realm, but she screamed for everyone to hear, as if prepared to lose her life for the sake of her granddaughters.

"Granny, I'm here. Please come in," Okuni called out, half sitting up in bed. What she had feared had happened. Or was about to happen. I'll accept her anger without resistance, she thought. I'll let her hit and kick me if it relieves her resentment. Then she can take the girls home. Sankuro's gone to Kyoto. It's a good time.

The old woman stood in front of Okuni, cursing her. "If you're still in bed you should remember that I saved your life."

"Granny, I couldn't forget that."

"Don't lie to me. Aren't Otsuru and Omatsu here?"

"Yes."

"Then you're a kidnapper, a child stealer. You returned evil for the good I did you."

"Granny, I didn't steal them. I've been in bed. When they came I told them to go home."

"That's easy to say. Bring them out. You can't hide them from me."

Okuni called, "Otsuru, Omatsu," but they didn't come. She knew the girls were listening outside the room. She called them again, raising her voice. Then, "Densuke, bring Otsuru and Omatsu here." There was the sound of a scuffle outside and in a moment Densuke brought the two girls in by the scruff of their necks. Densuke hung his head sheepishly, but the old woman did not even look at him. She saw her granddaughters wearing the bright dancing kimonos.

"Otsuru! Omatsu! You're disgusting! You're dressed up like harlots!" She ordered them firmly, "Come along. You're coming home with me to Moriguchi. The rice is planted. There's weeding to do. Come home and work."

"I don't want to," Otsuru exclaimed, rejecting her grandmother's words. "I won't go home."

"I won't go back either," Omatsu continued. "Dancing and singing are better than weeding rice."

The face of the old woman flushed. "What are you talking about, you cursed children? Listen to me! Does something grow from dancing? Is something harvested? Can you fill someone's stomach with singing? But look at the fields and paddies. The earth is our blessing. If you put a seed in the ground and you water it, it grows. It blossoms and the grain ripens. Rice, wheat, barley, millet are what make people live and get strong. What do you children think you grew up on? Your mother bore you, but when you left her teats you lived by eating rice gruel. Everything you eat is born in the soil except the fish from the river. It's damned nonsense to grumble that singing and dancing are better than farming the land. The devil take you! Lewd women, *kabuki* women, take money for singing and dancing. *Kabuki* women are plants that haven't got roots in the ground. They're vegetables yanked out of the earth and carried around the city for sale. They wither in front of your eyes. Otsuru, Omatsu, is that what you want to be?"

Omatsu hardly listened but Otsuru, the oldest, waited for the old woman to pause for breath and then said, "I won't go home. In town there's money, Granny, and you can buy rice and vegetables with it, even if you don't work in the rice fields."

"And what do you think would happen if all the farmers stopped growing rice and tried to use money to buy it? There wouldn't be any rice. You could sing until your voice was gone and dance until your legs fell off and you still couldn't eat. Stupid girl."

"I don't understand." Omatsu, who was only eight years old, found the arguments beyond her. "I don't want to understand. I'm not going back to Moriguchi."

"I'll drag you home if I have to." The old woman looked hard at Densuke. "They made a law that farmers can't leave their land, Densuke. The Lord of the Realm made it, and you and Okuni serve one of his retainers, so you'd better obey it."

That was true. It was the third sweeping measure in Hideyoshi's ambitious plan to regulate every aspect of national life. Disguised as a Population Census, the latest edict's purpose was to bind farmers to the land they were cultivating. After the Sword Hunt and the Land Survey had been completed, Hideyoshi's officials ordered a meticulous count of each man, woman, and child with their place of residence clearly shown. Under the new law, the registry in Moriguchi would show the birth and death of each person in the village. If a person's name was in the book, that person could not leave the village or take another occupation. The old woman's son, who had been impressed into a construction gang working on Yodo Castle, was now home. The old woman had worried constantly that the samurai would take him away again and that she and the old man would be left to care for their rice fields alone. She saw that the new law would keep her son at home. And it would not allow Otsuru and Omatsu to leave their village. The old woman forgot that she hated Hideyoshi and welcomed his new law.

"Granny's right," Okuni told the girls, "even Sankuro has to do what the law says. Go home to Moriguchi with Granny." Okuni was relieved to have it settled.

"Take those clothes off. You can't wear such things at home. You'll never find a good husband. Throw them away and come home." The girls wailed and clutched their beautiful kimono sleeves tightly to their breasts, but in the end the old woman's implacable words defeated them. Their fate was settled by the fact that no one could defy Hideyoshi's command. Disobey the order of the Lord of the Realm, the lord most powerful, the lord most intelligent, the lord most fearsome, and retribution beyond imagining would follow.

The old woman dragged the girls, crying as if their hearts would burst, back to Moriguchi village. Okuni lay quietly in her bed. The old woman's words rang in her ears. They filled her mind. What grows from singing and dancing? Can it fill your stomach? Lewd women, *kabuki* women, take money for singing and dancing. *Kabuki* women don't have roots in the soil. Carried through the city for sale, they wither before your eyes. You can sing until your voice is gone and you still won't have food to eat.

Every word the old woman spoke seemed true to Okuni. People need food, a place to sleep. These needs aren't satisfied watching people dance or hearing them sing. She knew this was so. Yet tired as she was, Okuni felt the desire to dance racing like a fire through her body to her toes and fingertips. As a child in Izumo, the sound of the water flowing in the Hii River had urged her to dance. Her arms and her legs naturally moved in rhythm to the sounds around her, the sigh of the wind, the ringing of bells, the beat of a drum, the singing of a bird. Why is this, she wondered.

"Densuke."

Densuke has been sitting quietly near Okuni. "What's the matter, Okuni?"

"Why do you think people pay to see us dance and sing?"

Densuke had been thinking about the old woman's words, too, and he had an answer ready. "Because it gives pleasure. It's beautiful, interesting, funny. It's a good thing."

"Is something beautiful good?"

"Yes, it is."

"Is something interesting good?"

"Yes."

"Is something funny good?"

"Oh, yes."

"Then that's why people pay money? And afterward, what's left?"

"What do you mean?"

"After we sing and after we dance. After our singing is heard and our dancing is seen. I mean, does something remain?"

"The heart that enjoyed pleasure remains."

"The heart remains?"

"It remains. Certainly it remains. Joy in the heart is something greater than money can buy."

"Greater than money can buy." After a time Okuni sighed deeply. "Oh, I want to dance."

"I know you do."

Otsuru and Omatsu returned to Hoshi Temple two days later. The next day, the old woman came and took the girls back to Moriguchi. After three days the girls returned again. This time Sankuro was at Hoshi Temple, having arrived from Kyoto the previous night. He took the girls to a place in the city he wouldn't reveal. When the old woman appeared for the third time and she saw Sankuro, her face reddened with rage. "So you're the ringleader, Sankuro! May you burn in hell for what you've done! Tell me where they are."

The old woman screamed at Sankuro. She begged. She cajoled him. Through it all he stood coldly with arms crossed over his chest. He would only say, "They're not here. Search the place, you won't find them."

She searched under the floorboards and in servants' rooms filled with cobwebs, first frantically and then with growing despair as she realized they were not there. The strength seemed to leave her old body and tears appeared in her eyes. "All right. I'll let them dance. Only tell me where they are."

"I can't tell you what I don't know."

"Their names are in the village record book. What will we say?" she finally asked in desperation.

"Say they're dead. The samurai will take their names out of the book."

"You're a terrible man, Sankuro. I'll tell Reverend Baian. I'll go to the castle and scream to the Lord of the Realm that you're breaking the law. They'll cut off your head for what you've done!" Cursing him, she left Hoshi Temple. Of course she couldn't carry out her threats. She was just an old peasant woman wearing rags. If she tried to get into Hideyoshi's great castle, Baian's servants would throw her into the street and she was likely to lose her own head. Sankuro was unfazed by the scene. He knew he had won. He kept the girls hidden for a few more days, in case the old woman returned. When she did not, he brought them back to Hoshi Temple.

"I'm going to Kyoto," Sankuro told Okuni. "I want Densuke to teach Otsuru and Omatsu while I'm gone. By the time you dance before the Lord of the Realm, Okuni, I want the mud of the farm washed off these two."

Okuni was too weak to argue with Sankuro. She felt sorry for the two thin girls who crouched breathlessly behind this proud man with the cold, pale face. She despised the way he had lured the innocent girls here and she pitied the old woman who had raged and cursed to protect her grandchildren. But she also understood the youngsters' desire to escape from their village. It was natural to want to sing and dance.

Densuke did as Sankuro said. He taught Otsuru and Omatsu to sing, while the older girls showed them their dances. Lying in her bed, Okuni watched Otsuru and Omatsu practice.

> Desire to see you
> Brings me running, secretly.
> Release me, let me speak:
> I love you, what shall I do?

Densuke was an excellent singer and a kinder teacher couldn't be imagined. The four girls from Izumo, remembering that it had been hard for them at first, tried to make the two younger girls feel at home. They enthusiastically demonstrated the troupe's special dance steps time and time again. It was now midsummer. With all their might and with the sweat streaming from their bodies like a waterfall, Otsuru and Omatsu danced the dances and sang the songs, step by step and note by note, exactly as instructed. The rehearsals continued day after day. Whenever he was free, several times each morning and afternoon, Densuke came to the room to teach. The Izumo girls did everything they could to help Otsuru and Omatsu absorb the arm and leg movements correctly. In the end, they stood behind the two girls and moved their young hands and feet as one would manipulate a puppet.

Sankuro, Okuni called out in her heart, what have you done?

For the two girls, singing and dancing before Okuni as if their lives depended upon it, had no talent at all. Otsuru's singing was lifeless in spite of Densuke's careful, patient instruction. Omatsu's movements were awkward, if energetic, and her steps didn't match the words of the song. The harder they tried, the clearer it became that neither of them would bring joy to a listener through her song, nor lift a man's heart with the rhythm of her body. The desperation with which these two plain-featured country girls rehearsed was more than boring, it was ugly.

It shocked Okuni to admit that such ineptitude was possible. Until now she had imagined that anybody could sing, anybody could dance. She hadn't doubted it for an instant. But Otsuru and Omatsu couldn't dance, they couldn't sing. No matter how many years they practiced, they would never be any good. Their bodies simply weren't suited to singing and dancing. When she considered that the girls had run away from their granny to take up a life for which they had no ability, Okuni's heart sank. It pained Okuni to watch and she closed her eyes. But she could not close her ears.

"Stop it!" She hadn't meant to speak sharply. She smiled weakly at the girls. "You must be tired. Rest a bit. I'm tired, too."

Eight

The Kamo River that runs through the center of Kyoto is a limpid, gentle stream. It isn't like the rampaging Hii River Dragon in Izumo or the broad, heavy-flowing Yodo River that empties into Osaka harbor. Like the capital itself, the stream is bright and gay.

After two years' convalescence at Hoshi Temple, Okuni's health was much improved. Even though she was not fully recovered, Sankuro was anxious to bring the troupe to Kyoto, where they could be close to Baian. Earlier in the year Hideyoshi, with Baian by his side, had methodically directed his armies against the last warlords who opposed him, in the end destroying the fortress at Odawara, his final opposition. Baian was now staying with Hideyoshi at Juraku Mansion. Baian was in a euphoric mood, and he readily agreed that Sankuro should bring Okuni and the girls to the capital.

The small troupe traveled north along the Yodo River in leisurely fashion, deliberately avoiding the village of Moriguchi. When they reached the juncture of the Yodo and Kizu rivers they were amazed to see that Yodo Castle was gone. Only gaunt frames of buildings remained. Rocks that had formed the towering walls were being loaded on boats and sent up the river to Kyoto. Painful memories of her lost child filled Okuni's mind and she walked alone in silence. Sankuro and the girls chattered heedlessly.

"Where does the Lady of Yodo Castle and her child live now?"

"They went to Osaka Castle long ago."

"If the lord doesn't need a castle any more, he tears it down."

"It shows he's powerful."

They slept in farmhouses along the way during the two nights of the journey. At midmorning of the third day the small troupe of Sankuro, Okuni, and the six girls entered Kyoto through the great south gate near Kujo Street. It was April, 1591. Kyoto was beautiful. The scene along the bank of the Kamo River was incomparably elegant. Young willow leaves, the color of amber, waved in the spring breeze. They passed the foot of Mount Inari, rising close at hand in the east. The girls were carrying heavy bundles of costumes and stage properties, but even so they ran excitedly ahead to see the interesting sights. Merchants and workers moved briskly across the bridges over the stream, intent on business. As they began to encounter dense crowds of people, Sankuro had to warn the girls not to get separated from each other. At Shijo Bridge they looked west along the busy street.

"That is Shijo Muromachi, the center of Kyoto. In the summer the floats gather there for the Gion Festival, so it's called the Corner of Floats," Sankuro explained to the girls.

"Who are the women wearing the bright-patterned kimonos and head coverings?" Okuni was exhausted from the journey, but the fashionably dressed young women she saw strolling near the bridge sparked her interest.

"Nobles' daughters. They must be on their way to see a procession. There's one in Kyoto almost every day."

The girls were exhausted and wanted to rest, so they agreed that they would wait by the bridge while Sankuro showed Okuni more of the city. "Don't move from this spot. We'll be back by noon," Sankuro warned them. The two turned west from Shijo Bridge and threaded their way through many narrow streets tightly packed with stores and businesses. Hurrying tradesmen and laborers pulling carts of food and lumber made it difficult to walk at a steady pace until they came into the spacious area called Kinri Rokucho, marking the outer reaches of the Forbidden Palace of Sixth Ward. Turning north, Okuni saw all around her workmen tearing down the old houses of imperial aristocrats and, in their place, hurriedly building new mansions for Hideyoshi's generals and officials. The imposing tower of Juraku Mansion could be seen just to the north and perhaps a mile further was the emperor's Palace. It was the Lord of the Realm's deliberate plan to pack the area between the two palaces with the residences of men loyal to him. The air was filled with the pungent odor of freshly cut cedar as carpenters worked at a frantic pace day and night to meet Hideyoshi's impatient orders. "Well, what do you think?" Sankuro asked proudly.

"I never imagined that the capital would be so much more magnificent than Osaka," Okuni said. When Sanemon's group had stopped in Kyoto three years before, he kept the girls inside, so Okuni was seeing the city for the first time.

"Twice as many people live here."

"The feeling is different; it's happy and gay," Okuni said with a smile. "At Shijo Street I saw poor people, dressed almost as badly as the farmers in Moriguchi or in Izumo. But their faces were lively." Okuni was exhilarated by the atmosphere of the city.

They began walking in the direction of Juraku Mansion, where Baian lived. As they neared it, people coming from all directions began gathering in the streets. Soon they were surrounded and people pressed tightly against them, as they had pressed against Okuni during the Plum Blossom Festival in Osaka.

"What's happening, Sankuro?"

"It's a procession. As I said before, people are coming out to see it."

Okuni gasped with astonishment. A long procession of men on horseback came into view. As the lead horseman approached Hideyoshi's mansion, the masses of spectators parted to let the colorfully dressed group pass through.

"It's a parade of foreigners, the Southern Barbarians," Sankuro said.

There were some twenty horses. Strange men were riding them, dressed in the most outlandish clothes that Okuni had ever seen. Two grooms walked ahead, faces as black as iron kettles, heads wrapped in white cloths. They wore jackets without trailing sleeves, quite unlike kimonos, and striped trousers in the shape of a paper lantern, puffed out in the middle and tight at the ankles. In striking contrast to the black-skinned grooms, the first four men on horseback had sickly white complexions, and their blue eyes seemed half asleep beneath light, tan hair. The four men who followed were clearly Japanese in their features, but their dress was the most bizarre of all. Over brilliant kimonos they wore sleeveless cloaks—a style that Okuni had never seen before—and pants of magnificent silk gathered at the knee. Circles of lace, like white flowers, decorated their necks. Each carried a large, decorated cross and had a long sword fastened at the waist. Instead of the usual thonged slippers or straw sandals that a Japanese would wear, their feet were encased in leather boxes that reached as high as the ankle.

"Who are they?"

"Japanese coming home from the Southern Barbarian lands. They call themselves Kirishitan, the name of the barbarian god."

"Who are the big men behind them?" Okuni indicated the dozen white men who came next in the procession.

"They're Southern Barbarian merchants. They came to Japan from the seas in the south to trade silk and spices for copper and gold."

"My, what huge noses."

"Look at their bluish eyes. It's frightening. I wonder if they can see with eyes like that."

"Look, that helmet's shaking. There's a bird's feather on it."

"That's called a *chapeau*. It's not a helmet. Southern Barbarians wear such things on their heads."

Southern Barbarian. Kirishitan. *Chapeau*. The words overwhelmed Okuni's ears. I see, in the capital you can come across interesting things like this. Sankuro was right. If you're going to dance, dance in the capital. And I can see that the capital is the place to live, too. Oh, what a beautiful and strange procession. Okuni's heart beat with excitement.

The leader of the procession was Alessandro Valignano, the Italian Visitador General of the Jesuit Mission to Japan. During the past twenty years, a dozen Italian and Portuguese Jesuit priests had successfully converted many tens of thousands of souls to the Kirishitan faith. For ten years and more, the city of Nagasaki had been ruled directly by the Company of Jesus. The city and surrounding villages had been ceded to Jesuit control "for all time" by the region's baptized samurai lord, Dom Bartholomew Omura, in 1580. Now eighty-six churches in Nagasaki served a local populace that had been converted en masse to the religion of Iesus. Following the model of this Kirishitan fief, the eventual Christianization of Japan seemed possible. Then four years ago Hideyoshi, without warning or explanation, had ordered the foreign priests to cease preaching and immediately leave the country. Although the priests pretended to leave, nearly a hundred quietly remained, waiting for the chance to resume their preaching.

Now that Hideyoshi was the undisputed ruler of the nation, he was in a position to enforce that earlier, somewhat casual, edict. The fate of the Kirishitan cause depended on Valignano's meeting with Hideyoshi. Could the priest persuade Hideyoshi to lift the decree? Valignano calculated that a grand and colorful procession might please Hideyoshi and put him in a favorable frame of mind to accept the Jesuit petition. It was wellknown that Hideyoshi loved ostentatious display and that he especially liked to dress himself in European finery. Valignano therefore included in his retinue three distinguished-looking European Jesuit priests whose rosaries and crucifixes sparkled brightly in the sunlight, and four elegant young Japanese who were the sons of Kirishitan lords in Kyushu recently returned from Rome, where they had undertaken study of the catechism. And indeed, the four Jesuit priests, the four Japanese, the thirteen Portuguese merchants from Macao, and the twenty-six Indian servants carrying gifts made a splendid sight in their colorful doublets, hose, cloaks, feathered hats, and lace collars.

Valignano also hoped to flatter Hideyoshi. The Lord of the Realm loved to think that his fame extended to foreign countries. Therefore, Valignano planned to present himself to Hideyoshi in a theatrical manner as the "Plenipotentiary of the Viceroy of Portuguese India," not as the mere Jesuit *Visitador*.

In front of the gold gate of Juraku Mansion, Valignano waved his feathered hat and smiled broadly at the crowd. *"Ola! Boã tarde!"* he called out in a loud voice. Others in the procession took off their hats and greeted the crowd extravagantly, *"Boã tarde para todos."* Of course, people in the streets had no idea what the pale-skinned creatures were shouting. And while some shrank back, frightened, a few braver spectators edged forward to peer curiously at the foreign costumes. The procession continued through the gate into the grounds of Juraku Mansion.

Okuni thought excitedly that it would be wonderful to dance in those brilliant and strange barbarian clothes. The bold patterns were so unlike the birds, the flowers, and the moon that decorated her kimonos. She imagined herself on stage wearing the shining foreign beads around her neck and a silver cross over her breast. Her feet danced and the pulse in her neck raced. The image of the foreign barbarians remained in her mind as she turned away. She and Sankuro were silent walking back to join the girls at Shijo Bridge. The girls were relieved to see them. They all shouldered their bundles and started east across the bridge. Still in a reverie, Okuni was slow to react to the woman's voice that suddenly called out, "Sankuro. I didn't expect you so soon."

"Oh. Oan." Sankuro spoke flatly.

"I'm glad you're here," she said in a laughing voice, pressing herself against him. "Let's go home. I've food and wine." She tried to take his arm but he shook her off.

"I've got to find a place for the girls."

"Ah. Are these the girls from Izumo Shrine you're always talking about? Bring them home with us."

Sankuro stood a moment thinking and then made up his mind. "All right. We'll go."

"Of course we'll go. Of course the master goes to his house." Oan laughed happily.

Oan and Sankuro led the troupe to a small house. Oan chattered gaily to Sankuro along the way but all he said was, "We're hungry. Fix some food."

Oan took the girls to the kitchen, where they eagerly lit a fire and began to prepare their food.

"Change your clothes and relax, Sankuro." Bringing out a kimono from the inside room, Oan started to help Sankuro undress.

"I can change myself. Go to the kitchen and cook."

"The girls can do that. I want to take care of you."

"No. Keep away."

"Why are you in such a bad mood? Well, I'm in a bad mood, too. I expected you to come home alone." Oan went back to the kitchen.

Okuni just stared at Sankuro. She wanted him to say something, but he turned away without speaking. Soon a gruel of rice and vegetables was put on a low table in the middle of the room. Oan lit an oil lamp and the room brightened. The girls ate ravenously, laughing freely when Oan spoke to them as if she were their older sister. Sankuro ate in silence. Although Okuni held a bowl in her hand, she felt as if her heart and stomach were frozen. She could not swallow a bite of the soft rice. This is Sankuro's house. This is where he stays when he comes to Kyoto. I've been a fool, she thought. For two years I've been sick and we haven't made love, and I never even considered that Sankuro might have found another woman. Her complacency disgusted her. She should be furious with Sankuro, but Oan was the one she looked at with animosity shining in her large eyes.

There was nothing special about Oan. She was ordinary looking, seven or eight years older than Okuni. Compared with Okuni she was shorter and thinner, and her breasts were not as large. Okuni did not understand how Sankuro could be attracted to such a woman.

Otsuru and Omatsu put down their chopsticks. They could now feel the tension among the adults in the room, and they were afraid to move. Naturally, Oan noticed that Okuni neither spoke nor ate, but as if to demonstrate that she was mistress of the house, she continued to laugh and to talk to Sankuro in a familiar way, although he said nothing in return.

Okuni faced Sankuro. "Who is this woman, Sankuro?" The words burst from Okuni. She had meant to be fierce but her voice broke.

"What do you mean, who am I?" Oan turned to Okuni, but Okuni was looking hard at Sankuro.

"This woman. Who is she, Sankuro?"

Since Sankuro remained silent, Oan replied haughtily, "I am Sankuro's wife. We've lived together six years. This is Sankuro's house."

Okuni gazed unblinkingly at Sankuro, but she heard each word that Oan said. For six years this woman has known Sankuro. Six years ago Okuni was a child running in the Hii River in Izumo. A violent jealousy raged through her body. Okuni waited doggedly for Sankuro's answer. Until he spoke, she would not say one word. The girls sat breathless, like stones.

"What's his name? Kyuzo?"

"What?"

"You've a husband in Izumo."

It was as if Sankuro had struck her heart with a stone. Okuni couldn't breathe. She felt horrified and sickened that Sankuro would remember the name Kyuzo. Kyuzo was before I met you. For three years we've been together, and all that time you've had a wife in Kyoto. I ask about Oan and you reply by asking about Kyuzo. Kyuzo and Oan are different. Different, she wanted to shout, but she swallowed her anger.

Okuni's silence unnerved Oan. Oan fidgeted, trying to restrain herself. "Who is this woman, Sankuro?" Oan finally demanded. When Sankuro didn't stir, she turned to Okuni. "Who are you?"

Okuni did not answer. The truth is, she did not know what to say.

"Don't act superior. You stole my man."

"Stole?" The word leaped out, but Okuni did not shift her gaze from Sankuro's face. "You'd better ask Sankuro if I stole him or not."

"Sankuro's mine."

"That's for Sankuro to say."

"This is my house. Get out. Get out!" Oan was losing control of herself in the face of Okuni's icy composure. Sankuro, who had been watching the two women, at last rose and spoke. "All right, we'll go."

"I didn't mean you. This house is ours. I told that woman to get out." Oan clung to Sankuro's legs.

"This woman is Okuni. We can't perform without her. Since you want her to go, I have to leave, too."

Oan clung to him frantically. "No, you won't go. You can't leave me for that woman. I won't let her take you, I won't, I won't!"

Okuni watched as Oan became hysterical. Okuni did not know if she would ever be able to forgive Sankuro for sleeping with this plain woman, but she felt a deep strength growing in her body, a strength she had lacked for a long time. Oan would not give in easily and she would battle Okuni fiercely, but Okuni knew that her own will to win, born of fire and steel, would defeat Oan. Okuni looked as cool as the river's stream, but inside she wanted to shout, I've won, Sankuro is mine, he will never leave me.

The next day they moved into an abandoned farmhouse that Sankuro had come across in Toribei Field on the southern outskirts of Kyoto. Its crumbling roof and the untilled fields surrounding it were paradoxical evidence of the power of Hideyoshi's land policies. As Hideyoshi had intended, the rigorous Land Survey, starting in 1585, six years past, was producing a windfall in government revenues from land and rice taxes. However, many farmers couldn't pay the new taxes, and rather than risk frightful punishment, they fled the land and sought work in the cities as anonymous craftsmen or servants. That was the case here.

Oan brought Sankuro's clothes along with her own household things, and she moved into the farmhouse as well. "Though I may die, I won't leave him!" she shouted wildly. From that time on, Sankuro refused to speak to Oan. He couldn't stand to look at her twisted face and he wondered what he'd ever seen in her. When she came into the farmhouse, he would leave. When the troupe set up on a street corner to perform, two guards hired by Sankuro kept Oan from entering the theater. As summer wore on, Oan began to lose her senses. In the farmhouse she would shout at Okuni for hours at a time, and Okuni's icy calm only fed her hysteria. She must give up soon or she will go insane, Okuni thought. One day, Okuni spoke quietly to Oan. "Please understand. Sankuro plays the drum and I dance. Sankuro doesn't want to change this. He and I will never be apart. You must understand this."

Oan stared, stricken, at Okuni. Her face went lax. Her eyes stared vacantly. Like a ghost she rose to her feet and drifted out the door. When morning came and she hadn't returned, Okuni went out to look for her. Okuni had won, but she couldn't help pitying Oan. She ran through the abandoned fields around the house, calling, "Oan, Oan," and through the neighboring rice fields. She searched all day, along the streets leading into the city and at the crossroads where the troupe sometimes performed. At dusk Okuni returned home alone. Sankuro was waiting for her. He barked crossly, "Where have you been?" When she told him Oan was gone, he paid no attention, but continued as if she'd said nothing, "The lord's heir died."

"Oh."

"He died at Osaka Castle. No matter how many prayers Hideyoshi ordered, it didn't help."

The child of Hideyoshi's favorite mistress, Otane, did not live to celebrate his third birthday. Over the past several weeks, rumors had spread through Kyoto that Tsurumatsu was gravely ill. But Sankuro was so irked by Oan's tantrums, he didn't have time to think about the sick infant. Now that the child was dead, he realized what the consequences would be for them and he sighed bitterly, "During his mourning they won't let us sing or dance. It'll be a long time."

Okuni began to cry.

"Stop it. Don't be a fool," Sankuro snapped, irritated.

Okuni's heart overflowed with sadness. She had lost her child in the snow three years ago. The woman who had a castle built for her has lost her child. It was sad that she had attacked Oan with her silence and hatred and that she had driven her away from the man she loved. She pitied Oan. One sadness lay on top of the other. Sankuro was a cruel man. What he had done to the old woman from Moriguchi disgusted Okuni. But he was a part of her and she could not exist without him. She could not stop the tears.

"Will you quit bawling?" he barked at her two or three times.

When she didn't stop, he ignored her crying and returned to his own concerns. He was deeply dejected. He had abandoned a career as a Noh drummer in order to fulfill his great ambition to meet Hideyoshi. Then he had met Baian, who created the lie about Okuni's origin and schemed to have the Lord of the Realm see them perform. Sankuro dreamed that in time Hideyoshi would proclaim his troupe Best in the World. One of Hideyoshi's many ideas was to recognize one master in each craft or art and to bestow on him the title Best in the World—one potter, one basket-maker, one tea master, one silversmith, one sword-maker was so recognized. Sankuro would be Best in the World in the theater. Sankuro had brought the troupe to the capital to be near the Lord of the Realm. But Baian seemed to lose interest in them as the months passed. He didn't call for Sankuro and he didn't ask the troupe to perform. And now Tsurumatsu's death would stop them from performing before Hideyoshi, or any other audience, for months to come. The beautiful picture Sankuro had painted of his future was ruined. They wouldn't even be allowed to perform on the street corners to earn spending money. The cries of summer cicadas drummed on Sankuro's ears without cease. The cicadas melded with the sound of Okuni crying. He rose and strode outdoors.

Since they could not perform that summer, they pooled their money to buy wheat seed that they planted in the abandoned field next to the farmhouse. The young shoots grew rapidly, warmed by the sun and watered by the streams that flowed down from the hills surrounding the capital. As the months of the hot summer passed, Okuni and the girls from Izumo happily tended the growing grain. Otsuru and Omatsu may not have been good on stage, but they were peasant girls who thrived in the fields. The two guards Sankuro had hired for the theater helped them. Kanji, who was from Kyoto, had never farmed before, but he had a good singing voice, which he used to encourage the girls as they worked amid the wheat. Mame was from Omi Province, just east of Kyoto. He was a farmer who had run away to escape the crushing new taxes, a fact he carefully concealed from Sankuro and everyone else. Mame was content to work silently in the wheat field alongside the women. All together, there were now ten members in the troupe.

In late summer Hideyoshi issued a fourth decree. It was posted at Sanjo Bridge, where the Tokaido post road led out of Kyoto toward the eastern provinces. All of them ran to see it except Sankuro. Kanji, who could read, explained the message in simple words.

"The 'Edict of Class Divisions' is what it's called," Kanji said. "Article One: After the battle of Odawara, some samurai and their servants have moved and taken jobs in the city. Some merchants have left their shops. This is forbidden. Return to your homes. Article Two: Some farmers have left their land and are working for wages. This is forbidden. Return to your land. Article Three: Do not help a runaway. Do not take a stranger into your house, no matter who it is. If you disobey this law you will be killed. If relatives or friends help a runaway, three will be killed." Hideyoshi's intention was to fix each man and woman permanently in the social class to which he or she was born. To achieve this end he would threaten the death penalty, and use it without reservation.

Kanji felt uneasy. He had left his job as an apprentice of the Paper Guild in Kyoto to taste the freer life of the troupe. He had no intention of going back to the dull, hard work of picking up and sorting waste paper. Fortunately, he thought, the masters of the guild would not remember him, and his name was unrecorded. Mame was terribly frightened. He was an escaped farmer in danger of execution. Not only that, members of the troupe could be executed for helping him. He tried not to show his fright. The new edict's severity surpassed any previous command issued by the Lord of the Realm. Everyone in the troupe talked about what it meant.

"What are we? We're not warriors, or farmers, or merchants. And we aren't servants to a lord." Okuni questioned Sankuro about the edict when the group arrived back at the farmhouse. "When we were girls in Izumo we worked in the fields. Does that mean we have to go back to Izumo and farm again?"

"Of course not. That was a long time ago. Still, we have to belong to some place or be someone's servant. That's what the order means."

Sankuro thought about it for some time. Then he decided. "There's no other way. We'll become Baian's servants."

Okuni spoke vehemently, "Never. I won't be Baian's servant!"

"Why not? He's been good to you."

"I want to live like this. I could have another child, Sankuro. I won't have a miscarriage next time."

Sankuro was surprised by Okuni's confident tone. They could have a child only if they were independent of Baian. But he worried that they weren't safe under the strict new edict.

"We're dancers," Okuni said, "and the law doesn't mention dancers. We don't belong to any place or any person. I just want to live here."

Sankuro didn't press the matter and so they stayed in the farmhouse and waited for the wheat to ripen. Okuni looked at their field of growing wheat day and night. The seeds they had planted had grown from frail, pink shoots into tall green stalks that were blossoming. White wheat flowers danced in the warm wind. Okuni loved the earth, and the rice and wheat that came from the earth. She knew it was true that, as Granny from Moriguchi had said, not even the Lord of the Realm could live if farmers did not grow the five grains. But the love of dancing bubbled within her, and it seemed strange to her that the lord's order did not mention people who danced.

Through the late summer and into early autumn, each morning Kanji and Mame went fishing for trout in the Kamo River. They sold their catch in town and bought rice and vegetables with the money, so the troupe ate quite well even though they weren't performing. Kanji and Mame tried to forget the latest edict of the Lord of the Realm.

But the world around them could not forget. One day their pleasant life was crushed without warning. Elders and farmers of the neighborhood gathered outside their house. They shouted harshly, "Who are you? Come out. Who said you could live here?"

Farmers guarded the backdoor so no one could escape. Okuni came outside, followed by Kanji, Mame, and the girls. They fell to their knees in the wheat.

"We're dancers from Izumo," Okuni said.

"Why do you live here?"

"The house was empty. We need a place to sleep."

"Sleep? Why did you plant wheat?"

"We can't sing and dance in the city now and we need to eat."

"It's forbidden," an old man screamed. "Don't you know the law? We can't let other farmers use our land. We'll be punished."

"We aren't farmers. We're dancers."

"If you aren't farmers why are you planting wheat?"

"Is that wrong?"

"Of course it's wrong. If you're from Izumo, cultivate the land in Izumo. This is our land and outsiders can't use it. That's the lord's order."

"If we can't dance and we can't grow food, what will we do?"

"How should we know? Just get out. Get out now, or we'll report you to the officials!"

Hideyoshi's plan to force farmers back to their land in order to increase food production was having the opposite effect. Okuni would not give up, so the village elders ordered the farmers to tie them up. At that point Sankuro came out of the house, arms folded nonchalantly. "Stop it."

"Who are you?"

"I am a servant of Omura Yuko Hogen Baian, retainer of the Lord of the Realm. If you put ropes around our necks you'll regret it. I'll have your heads cut off."

"Huh?" The farmers' sun-blackened faces creased with anxiety. They weren't clever at talking. They didn't know who Baian was, but the coolly arrogant young man standing there frightened them. "If you're a servant of the Lord of the Realm, can you prove it?"

"Our master Baian lives in Juraku Mansion with the Lord of the Realm. Go and see him if you want proof."

Of course, they couldn't do that. "We'll report what you say to the officials."

"Fine. Tell them."

Grumbling and looking back suspiciously, the farmers had no

choice but to go away without molesting the performers further.

"Sankuro, was it safe to say that?" Okuni asked.

"Yes. I'm going to see Baian now. I'll ask him to make us his servants."

"Can you do that?" Mame tried to keep the terror, and eagerness, from his voice.

"Leave it to me. I'll manage."

Okuni couldn't think of any reason for Baian to hire them. He had lost interest in them and performances were forbidden by Hideyoshi. But when Sankuro returned in the evening, he brought good news.

"From this day on we're Baian's servants."

"All of us?" Mame asked, his mouth still dry with fear.

"If any official asks about any of us, Baian will say we serve him." Looking pleased with himself, Sankuro confided to Okuni that he had paid Baian to agree to do this.

"You paid him money? Must we pay our master to serve him?"

"It was a cheap price for our freedom. The law can't touch us now." Sankuro didn't let Okuni's disapproving look disturb him. He laughed loudly, announcing, "All right, we're servants, not farmers. Servants aren't allowed to grow food, so let's harvest the wheat tonight. Then we're going to perform."

"The wheat won't be ready for another twenty days," Mame said without thinking. No one noticed the slip.

"Perform?"

"When can we perform?"

"Soon. I've heard a new rumor. The Lord of the Realm is going to conquer China. Baian told me. The lord is going to go to Kyushu with a huge army, build a castle at a small port called Nagoya, and launch an invasion from there. Of course, Baian will be by his side."

"Then we'll go with Baian to China?"

Sankuro shook his head and laughed. "Oh, no. We'll perform in Kyoto."

"How can we? It's forbidden."

"Only because Hideyoshi is in the capital. When he goes to

Kyushu in the spring, things will be bright and lively again in Kyoto. You'll see." Sankuro's spirits were restored. Money will flow into the capital if there is a war, and our audiences will be large. When Hideyoshi returns from China he will want to celebrate his victories. If we build up a good reputation, surely he will want to see us. And because we're now Baian's servants, Baian will want to show us off to the Lord of the Realm. The small amount of money I paid Baian was a good investment. And the wheat will carry us through the winter when it's too cold to perform. Sankuro smiled happily to himself—it was a clever plan.

"It's sad," Mame grumbled as they all went into the wheat field that night. "Wheat shouldn't be cut when it's flowering. Soon we'd have a perfect harvest." The others were pulling the wheat up by the roots. Only Mame used a sickle, a rusty one abandoned by the farmer who had fled his land. Mame honed it with a stone and water from the Kamo River until it shone. He loved farming and it showed in the way he fondly held the sickle in a light grip. The white flowers bowed before his keen blade. Okuni ran behind him, picking up the fallen stalks. The flowers of wheat that had floated like a white mist over the ground gradually disappeared from sight as the evening deepened.

"Oan." Okuni did not know why the name suddenly came to her lips. The white flowers Okuni was holding in her arms trembled and fell to the dark earth.

Nine

It was no secret that for many years Hideyoshi had thought about conquering China and becoming its emperor. As early as 1586, he had hinted at the plan when he met with Gaspar Coelho, Vice-Provincial of the Jesuit Mission in Japan. But why now, six years later? People said Hideyoshi chose that particular moment to launch an invasion of China in order to escape from the deep grief caused by the death of his son, Tsurumatsu. Also, Hideyoshi had no more domestic opponents to defeat now that Odawara Castle had been leveled. People also gossiped that a foreign war offered the great advantage of keeping his dangerously ambitious generals occupied and far away. Hideyoshi resigned as Regent and Advisor to the emperor, passing the title to his nephew, Hidetsugu. The new regent would rule the nation from Juraku Mansion, while Hideyoshi devoted himself to the conquest of Korea, China, and if it suited him, India as well. In the winter of 1591, he commanded each vassal lord to assemble soldiers, horses, weapons, and stores for an invasion. Since most of the burden fell on farmers, their lives became desperate. Kyoto, on the other hand, prospered. Military preparations continued through the following spring until the capital burst with a dozen provincial armies jostling for space and privilege. Street performances gradually resumed in the capital, although the official year of mourning for Tsurumatsu had not passed.

"Let's perform on the riding field next to Kitano Shrine," Okuni said.

"Kitano Shrine?" Sankuro thought for a moment, then shook his head. "We can't dance at Kitano."

"But why? That's the busiest place in Kyoto." Living in the city for a year, Okuni had become familiar with its important sites. "The crowds are even bigger than the ones we saw at Tenmangu's Plum Blossom Festival."

"That's why we can't play at Kitano." It was simple to Sankuro. Kitano Shrine was Baian's rival and they were Baian's servants. So, they could not perform at Kitano.

"I see. We can't dance at Kitano Shrine." Okuni did not understand the logic of giving money to Baian or of worrying about Baian not wanting them to dance at Kitano Shrine, but she would not oppose Sankuro. The terrible memory of Oan was often in her mind. I won't be able to bear it, Okuni thought. If I anger Sankuro and he turns against me, the way he turned against Oan, I'll go mad just as she did.

Okuni thought the huge grassy area outside Kitano Shrine was an ideal place to perform. But she also knew they could attract a sizable audience in almost any busy part of the city. So they sang and danced on street corners, as did many other troupes in that hectic time. Densuke and the girls liked to see what other groups were doing during breaks in their own performance. They found that the Fast Song had been taken up by a number of artists, drawing large audiences wherever it was sung. Okuni rarely went out. She did not need to see other performers. She was confident that nothing matched the lively footwork of their Izumo dances.

As winter ended and spring leaves began to open, one by one the armies that had assembled in Kyoto began to depart for Korea. Thirty-two lords had mobilized 187,000 soldiers for the invasion, most of whom were camped in or around the capital. They would march some four hundred miles to the invasion port of Nagoya in Kyushu. Even professional dancers could not compete with the magnificent processions that left the capital between April 27 and May 7 of 1592. When their audiences melted away, Okuni and the others decided to join the swelling crowds who had come to watch this brilliant, real-life spectacle. On the morning of April 27, the army of Lord Maeda Toshiie of Kaga marched out of Kyoto, followed by an even larger army led by Lord Gamo Ujisato of Aizu. The latter procession was an arresting sight. The kimonos of the warriors were made of exotic foreign silk filigreed with gold, and the ends were tucked into ballooned European-style trousers. Broad white collars and rosaries with crucifixes made of polished wood encircled their necks. Portuguese-style capes of brown velvet fringed with gold tassels fluttered around their shoulders as they rode forward. Outlandish combinations of European and Japanese dress had become fashionable among Hideyoshi's lords in the year that had passed since Alessandro Valignano had introduced the Southern Barbarian style of clothing to Kyoto. Naturally, Kirishitan lords were the first to embrace the European style of dress. And Lord Ujisato, with all of his men, had been converted by the Jesuit fathers: they were Kirishitan samurai.

A breathtakingly handsome youth rode by Lord Ujisato's side. The charming adolescent forelock that framed his dark, stern face suggested he was his Lord's lover. His trousers, fastened at the knees, were in a European fashion called *karusan* (originally *calecon*). The trailing ends of a purple velvet sash flew in the air behind him. He was truly beautiful in Okuni's eyes. A flute was tied to his back and he carried a gleaming spear in his right hand. Much later Okuni would learn this handsome young warrior's name was Nagoya Sanza.

On the following morning, April 28, a brilliantly dressed Lord Date Masamune swaggered through the streets at the head of a glittering procession. From that day the term "Date dandy" entered the language. In the afternoon, Hideyoshi's two favorite generals, Uesugi Kagekatsu and Satake Yoshinobu, departed with their armies. But by far the most impressive procession that left Kyoto that day was led by Lord Tokugawa Ieyasu from the Kanto region in the east. Not one soldier in his huge army was elaborately dressed. Horses and men carried what was needed for battle and nothing more. Ieyasu himself wore a plain kimono, quite unlike the ostentatious finery the other lords favored. His sober attitude marked him as a man apart.

A week later, on May 5, a parade of glittering palanquins departed from the women's quarters of Juraku Mansion carrying Hideyoshi's wife and her retinue. Two days later, on May 7, the Lord of the Realm himself departed from Kyoto. The procession route was jammed with spectators, for everyone knew this would be the most splendid parade of all. Hideyoshi made it known that he expected every resident of the city to see him off. It was a festive event. Even inveterate homebodies, grumbling they'd been forced out-of-doors for nothing, were soon caught up in the indescribable excitement of this remarkable occasion.

The first part of the procession was not exceptional. At the head marched an elite band of samurai with European muskets on their shoulders, and they were followed by a battalion of archers. Two generals on horseback, surrounded by aides, commanded the troops. The first colorfully dressed men in the parade were eighteen mounted warriors bearing large red, yellow, black, and white armor on their backs as protection against arrows. Fifty-three tall banners, dyed with the paulownia leaf crest that Hideyoshi had chosen to identify the Toyotomi family, waved in the wind as they were carried by. Then came troops of spearmen.

A dignified old man rode slowly by on a gray horse. He was Ashikaga Yoshiaki, the deposed shogun of the old regime, whom Oda Nobunaga had defeated and put out to pasture twenty years earlier. Hideyoshi forced Yoshiaki to ride helplessly through the streets without armor, a public symbol of the Lord of the Realm's absolute power. In compensation for his peasant upbringing, Hideyoshi indulged in a mania for collecting things and people of high quality. Riding behind the former shogun were a large number of mild-mannered courtiers of the former aristocracy whom Hideyoshi kept at his beck and call.

"Master Baian!" The girls from Izumo gave a cry.

"Is that Master Baian?" For the first time Kanji, Mame, Otsuru, and Omatsu were seeing the man they served.

Baian was riding a chestnut mare. A brilliant red sleeveless cloak was draped over his black monk's robe, and a flat crimson hat covered his head. The combination was so strange and Baian was so large that people could not help gaping at him. Densuke was leading his horse by the bridle. When he saw Okuni's face, he unconsciously started, pulling on the reins, so that Baian's horse shied and whinnied and shook its mane. Baian looked down at Okuni, snorted with pleasure, and passed on.

Baian was one of twenty advisors and counselors who accompanied Hideyoshi. They were followed by the lord's corps of personal physicians, led by Zenso, who, Okuni remembered, had been at Kanbei's house. After them came twenty-three tea masters and then ten men of letters, Hideyoshi's poets and chroniclers, among them the imperial aristocrats Tokitsune and Zengoro, who had seen Okuni dance at Hoshi Temple. When Okuni recognized their faces she asked Sankuro to explain who they were. Kanji and Mame, standing alongside, misunderstood his proud description of their titles. They thought Sankuro was intimate with these important people and they gazed at him in awe.

Next came Hideyoshi's three changes of horse and his twenty-two falconers. A long line of attendants carried Hideyoshi's gold-handled sword, burnished spear, helmet, leggings, and umbrella of state plumed with white swan feathers. They held his gold fan, wine gourd, and folding campstool high in the air for everyone to see. Scores of bearers passed by shouldering brilliantly lacquered chests secured with tasseled vermilion cords. These contained Hideyoshi's personal effects. Then three hundred men marched past flourishing feathered javelins.

Finally, "It's the Lord of the Realm!"

"The Lord of the Realm is coming!"

"Lord of the Realm! Lord of the Realm!"

It was amazing how the people of Kyoto unconsciously shouted out Hideyoshi's title when he appeared. In former times, common people were forced to press their faces to the ground when a lord passed in a show of abject deference. But Hideyoshi wanted everyone to see him in all his magnificence. Somehow people began to stand and shout out his title, and this became the new custom. Today people all around were excitedly calling out, "The Lord of the Realm! It's the Lord of the Realm!" when Hideyoshi appeared.

Colorful Chinese brocaded silk, beautifully ornamented with gold and silver, draped his snow-white horse. Hideyoshi sat like a bantam rooster astride a gold-inlaid saddle, over which was spread a tiger and a leopard skin. He had wrapped his small frame in scarlet silk and a beard made of bear's hair covered his face. The plume of a white hat trailed in the air down to his hips. The six-foot sword he carried at his waist was so much longer than his puny body that people had to wonder if the lord was able to pull it from its scabbard. In truth, he was an overdressed peasant and he looked ridiculous. Had the sophisticated residents of the capital not been so dumbfounded, and frightened of the consequences, they surely would have laughed out loud. Sankuro, though he was impressed by Hideyoshi's power, could not find words to express what he felt seeing Hideyoshi for the first time. Okuni saw a tiny man hiding his face behind a fur mask, and noting his small, sunken eyes, she knew he was old. Why does Sankuro want us to perform for this shrunken old man, Okuni wondered. I wouldn't feel the least excitement dancing for him.

After the Lord of the Realm passed, people weren't interested in watching the battalions of marching soldiers who followed him. They turned away and began drifting home. As they were working their way through the dense crowd going east toward Shijo Street, a palanquin came up behind them. "Okuni. Is it you?"

The door of the palanquin slid open. When Sankuro saw who was inside, he dropped to his knees. "Ah, Master Kanbei. We haven't seen you for a long time."

Suekichi Kanbei was there to see off Hideyoshi. "Okuni, why don't you come and dance for me? In summer I'll send a messenger. Where do you live?"

"In Toribei Field, just south of here."

"I know it. Hm. In three years you've grown truly beautiful. Splendid." He smiled quietly at Okuni and nodded in parting. As an attendant began to close the door, Sankuro hurriedly asked, "Master Kanbei, when will the war in China end?"

Kanbei hesitated to tell a low-ranking servant what he knew. But because Sankuro was Baian's servant, he cautiously spoke his true thoughts: "It won't last long. You see, the farmers are tired."

Sankuro stood watching the palanquin go out of sight, trying to absorb what Kanbei had said. Because farmers are tired the war won't last long? Sankuro couldn't fathom Kanbei's meaning, but he felt elated. The sooner the war is over, he thought, the sooner we can perform before Hideyoshi.

Through the summer they waited for Kanbei's message. But a summons to Hirano never came. Kanbei was wrong: the war did not end quickly. Hideyoshi's strategy had been wonderfully simple: he would march the Japanese army, 200,000 strong, peacefully through Korea and make a lightning attack across the Yalu River into China. In Hideyoshi's warped view, the meaning of the recent visit of the Korean embassy and of Valignano's mission to Kyoto was that Korea and India had already submitted to his rule. A true megalomaniac, he believed the whole world wanted him to be its king and that he and his army would march virtually unopposed into the Chinese capital. This is not, of course, what happened. Within weeks of leaving Kyoto, Japanese armies had taken Pusan, and by June they occupied Seoul. However, Korean soldiers harassed the Japanese army every step of the way. By late summer a few of the invading units had managed to reach the Yalu River, where they were met by unexpectedly large Chinese forces. The Japanese were forced to retreat. From his temporary castle at Nagoya in Kyushu, the Lord of the Realm issued repeated commands to his generals to win victories, but in truth the Japanese samurai army was being defeated. Hideyoshi's grandiose "Campaign to Enter China" was in grave danger. Hideyoshi was eager to lead his armies in the field personally, and to die there if necessary, but he was dissuaded from leaving Japan by urgent admonitions from the imperial court.

In one important respect Hideyoshi's personality was deeply flawed: he was unable to separate his private and public lives. Within months after setting in motion the largest war in Japan's history, he allowed his attention to be completely absorbed by personal matters.

In the autumn of 1592, Hideyoshi's mother died. In his grief he forgot everything about the war and hurriedly returned to Osaka. He organized and led the funeral ceremonies for his mother. When that was done he moved to Kyoto, then east to the Kanto region, and back to the capital again. He had scarcely settled in when he suddenly ordered officials to start building a new castle at Fushimi in Kyoto's southeastern hills. Hideyoshi had raised great castles in Osaka, Kyoto, Yodo, and Nagoya, and now, to people's astonishment, he stayed on in Fushimi busying himself with details of building yet a fifth castle. When he at last returned to Kyushu it was midwinter. Turning a deaf ear to the dire news his generals were sending from Korea, he spent his time giving banquets. He entered into dilatory truce negotiations with an embassy from the Chinese court, but that led nowhere. In late winter Japanese forces fell back from Pyongyang and took up defensive positions in Seoul. By the beginning of 1593, the Korean navy was sinking every Japanese ship that ventured from port. His troops were beginning to starve from lack of supplies and to die in the bitter cold of the Korean winter. Yet in spite of the ominous war news, Hideyoshi did nothing. Because the soldiers received no leadership from home through that spring, it can be said that the Korean war was being lost because it was not being won. In the summer of 1593, Otane gave birth to Hideyoshi's second son, who was named Hideyori by the proud father. Hideyoshi lost all interest in the war after his son's birth.

"We're going back to Osaka, Okuni."

"Why?"

"Why? Why are you so dull? Because the Lord of the Realm is in Osaka. And Baian will be with him. So we have to go back to Hoshi Temple."

"Because we're Baian's servants?" Okuni had not forgotten her unhappiness at being a servant, bound to a master.

Sankuro was exasperated. "If you don't understand, there's no point explaining it."

Immediately after the child's birth, Hideyoshi broke off negotiations with the Chinese embassy, heedless of his generals' anger. He returned to Osaka Castle in a jubilant mood, accompanied by a great train of courtiers, warriors, and attendants. Of course, Baian returned to Osaka with Hideyoshi, and Densuke accompanied him. Densuke had not seen Okuni and the others for more than a year, so it was a pleasant reunion. The troupe settled into Hoshi Temple. Sankuro diligently rehearsed the girls in the jesting songs currently popular in Kyoto, hoping these would interest Baian. Baian had not seen them perform for a long time and Sankuro wanted to show him something new.

> My hair, carefully groomed just now,
> Is disheveled.
> By someone, my heart, too,
> Is disheveled.

The girls tied up their long hair in front with strips of gaily colored paper and silk, following the new Kyoto fashion. In contrast, Okuni left her hair loose, so that when she danced it whirled in an exciting way.

> My heart, how annoying,
> Day and night does not leave you.
> Never extinguished,
> Since arriving,
> Wily, sly, oh, cunning love.
> Tossing, turning, tossing, turning,
> My body sleepless in its love.
> How sad it is, to sleep alone,
> Having slept together,
> How sad to sleep alone.

Kanji was a good singer. He had a splendid voice. Okane, the oldest of the four girls from Izumo and not especially attractive, was his regular companion. When he sang and she danced you could feel a bond tying his voice to her movements. Otsuru and Omatsu had not improved at all, although they imagined they danced and sang as skillfully as Okuni. It saddened Okuni when she saw how pleased they were with their bad performance. It would be kind to tell them, she thought, but she did not have the heart. In any case, since Sankuro had brought them into the troupe it was his responsibility and, of course, he did not care if they were good or not. He didn't expect them to do more than add to the spectacle. Sankuro taught Mame to play the Noh stick drum, the *taiko*, to add color to their music. Mame played only passably, but sometimes Sankuro sat to the side and watched while Mame accompanied the girls.

As they continued to rehearse, Okuni became more aware of the difference between the heavy Noh style of singing that Sankuro had learned as a Noh performer and Densuke's light, buoyant style of singing that was so popular among street entertainers in Kyoto. She realized more and more that when Sankuro played the deliberate rhythms of Noh on his hand drum, her lively dance steps slowed and became heavy. At the same time, she loved using Noh's beautiful hand gestures. As she practiced, she found she was trying to join the two styles of dance together: the leaping steps, *odori,* she had learned in the sands of the Hii River, that fit naturally to the popular music Densuke liked to sing, and the graceful gestures of Noh dance, *mai,* that Sankuro's singing and drumbeats drew from her hands. Sankuro did not know what was going on in Okuni's mind and so he resisted, using the drumbeats to bring her body under his control. She was in a contest with Sankuro that she was determined to win, but in the meantime she felt proud that her body could answer Sankuro's drum so well. I will never leave him, she thought. She was happy struggling against Sankuro's drum, searching for a way to meld Noh *mai* and popular *odori* into a new kind of dance. She felt close to Sankuro when she danced. There was no room then, as there was at night when Sankuro embraced her, for the terrible fear that he might reject her. As he had rejected Oan.

Baian was often away from Hoshi Temple on errands for Hideyoshi during the day, so Densuke was usually free to come by and look in on rehearsal. Okuni felt happy when Densuke sat watching, smiling quietly at her.

"In Kyoto, we saw interesting dances, Densuke," Okuni said returning his smile. "We saw traveling Noh troupes and five hundred people circling down the middle of road in a giant street dance. But Densuke's Spinning Song is the most entertaining of them all."

"That can't be true," Densuke said somewhat embarrassed.

"Densuke, sometime I wish you could dance with me when we set up our theater in the street."

"Would you really like that, Okuni? That's all I thought about in Kyushu." Densuke caught himself before he said more. But that was the way he felt. He could not forget the image of Okuni's face, when he had looked up and unexpectedly seen her in the crowd the day Hideyoshi left Kyoto. Even now, a year later, his heart raced when he remembered that moment. On the trip to Kyushu there had been nights he couldn't sleep, thinking of her. Some nights in Kyushu when the soldiers were given cheap whores, his longing for Okuni was so great he would get drunk and take one of the prostitutes to bed. He was so miserable afterward his heart would ache. Although he told himself again and again that she was Sankuro's woman, he was helpless to love anyone else.

Gradually, Sankuro withdrew from the daily rehearsals at Hoshi Temple. He had planned the move to Osaka to regain his previous close relationship with Baian. But he found no opportunity to ask Baian when he would show their performance to the Lord of the Realm. Baian stuck to Hideyoshi like a burr to a saddle. He did not visit their rehearsals at Hoshi Temple once. Hideyoshi was ecstatic over the birth of his son. He dashed from one pursuit to the next as if he were dancing on air: to Fushimi Castle to urge the construction along, to Osaka Castle to play with his heir, to Atami Spa near Edo to take the baths, to Osaka Castle again to play himself in a series of Noh plays about his life that Baian had dashed off, back to Kyoto to oversee a gigantic tea ceremony to which he invited half the city of Kyoto, and on and on. Baian was at his side at every moment. Sankuro slowly began to accept the fact that Baian had forgotten them. And with that he lost interest in training the troupe. He sat by himself in a corner of the room, letting Mame play the drum for rehearsals.

In the autumn, Sankuro decided to leave Osaka when the occasion arose. One day, when Okuni was practicing the Spinning Song with Densuke, she remarked casually that she longed to dance for Kyoto audiences again. Sankuro immediately agreed and said they would do what Okuni wanted. Although the troupe members were surprised at Sankuro's sudden enthusiasm, they happily left Hoshi Temple for the capital the following day. Densuke walked partway with them. He turned back reluctantly when they reached the Yodo River. The picture of Okuni's white body and her red blood on the snow was painfully etched in his memory.

Though Kyoto winters are cold, the days were mostly sunny and not much snow or rain fell that year. The troupe set up their mat fence and danced in the street whenever the weather was fair. In time Okuni began to gain a reputation for her dancing. The troupe performed together in the streets during the day and at night they slept in the old farmhouse in Toribei Field. Sankuro's good mood did not last long, and often he did not go with the group into the city. Okuni understood his disappointment but she could do nothing about it. What a pity that in the midst of this bustling, cheerful city, Sankuro is unhappy, she thought.

Hideyoshi moved into Fushimi Castle in May 1593, even before the workers had finished it. True to his impatient nature, that same month he began ceremonies to mark the event. In Korea his armies were sunk in a quagmire, victory no longer possible, but the Lord of the Realm celebrated. He celebrated the birth of his son at the most elaborate cherry-blossom viewing party ever witnessed in the capital. He entertained guests at banquets in his magnificent new castle and he acted in Noh plays for their enjoyment. The festive atmosphere engendered by Hideyoshi spread among all classes of people in the city. Wherever Okuni and her troupe put up their theater, they attracted enthusiastic audiences.

For several days it rained and they could not perform. The willow leaves were beautiful along the riverbanks but the troupe members were depressed because they were cooped up inside. Sankuro sat bleakly, arms folded, thinking over his situation again and again. He had not left the Kanze Noh troupe in order to be a street performer. He regretted the years he had wasted waiting for Baian's assistance. Should he kill himself? He left the house and began walking in the direction of Fushimi Castle. If that is where the Lord of the Realm lives, I want to see it, he thought. He stood in the rain, gazing at the impassive stone walls that separated him from the Lord of the Realm.

When he returned the rain had stopped. "Let's set up a theater in the riverbed at Gojo Bridge," he said with a determined set of his mouth. Okuni and the others were surprised at his change in attitude, but they readily agreed because Gojo Street was in the busy heart of the city. Sankuro did not tell them that he had a special reason for choosing that location: Gojo Street connected Fushimi Castle and Juraku Mansion. Hidetsugu, Hideyoshi's nephew, was living in Juraku Mansion now, so Hideyoshi was bound to travel that road, Sankuro reasoned. One day, when Hideyoshi crosses the bridge, he will look down and see us perform.

The next day, under Mame's competent supervision, they built an unusual theater on the grass-edged bank at Gojo Street, on the east side of the Kamo River. Instead of laying out straw mats to dance on, they put up a square dance stage made of wooden planks. Around this they raised a pole fence over which they draped a light brown cloth to keep casual passersby from peering in free of charge. Although the stage wasn't roofed, its shape was very close to that of a Noh theater. But Sankuro was not just copying from Noh. He had his reason for wanting a permanent, wooden stage. Sometimes Hideyoshi rode out of Fushimi Castle on horseback and sometimes he was carried in a palanquin. Sankuro calculated that in either case, if the stage was raised above the ground, Hideyoshi would have an unobstructed view of their performance when he looked down from the bridge. And he thought that an extravagant theater was likely to capture Hideyoshi's attention.

"Now, when you dance at Gojo Street I want you to put on your brightest and finest kimonos. Decorate your hair. Look your very best." When Sankuro said this, Okuni and the other girls shouted joyfully. It was the end of spring, and falling petals of late-blooming cherry blossoms drifted in the gentle wind. They didn't need to wear extra kimonos to keep warm anymore, but Okuni thought it looked luxurious to display several layers of colorful silk, so she showed the girls how to hike up their outer hems to show the inner kimono clearly. This arrangement of the costume left their feet free to move in quick steps when they danced and beautifully accented the line of their twisting hips and torsos.

"That's not a bad idea," Sankuro said, nodding his approval. Okuni had the girls tie their hair high in front, which made their heads look large and striking and made the proportion of their bodies especially attractive.

The willows growing along the Kamo River stretched out their pale green leaves. Sankuro vigorously beat the hand drum with the flat of his hand. Mame struck hard on the large drum with two stout sticks. Okuni rang the bell. Kanji and the girls sang out in unison with all their hearts. Even people across the river at the far end of Gojo Bridge crossed over to find out what the interesting sounds coming from the new theater were all about. Many spectators came down into the riverbed to watch. That day Sankuro was inspired and all the members of the troupe did their utmost.

Just past noon on the third day of their performance on the new stage, Hideyoshi burst onto Gojo Bridge surrounded by a small personal retinue. Usually guards ran ahead announcing the approach of the Lord's procession, "The lord comes! The Lord of the Realm comes!" But today he appeared without warning. Hideyoshi was extremely impatient by nature, and it gave him perverse delight to confront people unannounced. It served his purpose to surprise them. Today Hideyoshi was in a foul mood. Although he had built Fushimi Castle for his newborn son, Otane would not bring the child from the Second Tower of Osaka Castle, for she remembered that Tsurumatsu had died after being moved from his place of birth. Hideyoshi was forced to agree, for evil forces might be lurking in the move, but it irritated him to live alone in the new castle apart from them. From Korea he heard only bad news—casualty figures, food shortages, the immensity of China—yet it was difficult to blame others when the war was so clearly his own doing.

He had tried to calm himself that morning by conducting the tea ceremony, but a terrible omen had occurred. He was stirring tea in his finest bowl, a lustrous piece made by the ceramist he himself had titled Best in the World, when he dropped the bowl from his left hand. It broke into three pieces and tea spilled on his guests. Again, he couldn't blame anyone but himself. He flew into a rage and hurled the pieces into the garden, where they smashed into fragments on the rocks. Later in the morning, at a meeting of the Grand Council, veiled criticisms had been made of his nephew Hidetsugu. It was Hidetsugu's duty as regent to advise emperor Goyozei on domestic matters. When his first son died three years ago, Hideyoshi had passed on to Hidetsugu his own title of Regent to the emperor and had given him Juraku Mansion as his seat of rule. But Hideyoshi now had a second son, and Hidetsugu's shortcomings irked him. It was not clear what Hidetsugu had done to annoy the Grand Council, but Hideyoshi turned his anger on his nephew.

"I'm going to Juraku Mansion," Hideyoshi spat out, and immediately set out with a small group of attendants. He did not want to summon Hidetsugu and then wait hours for him to arrive at Fushimi. He wanted to settle the matter now. The reason for his anger was hazy. Perhaps that is why he allowed a palanquin to carry him, rather than go on horseback. The tiny Lord of the Realm, shriveled arms crossed over his thin chest, impatiently fumed inside the magnificent gold-encrusted box that bearers rushed down Gojo Street.

As the palanquin crossed Gojo Bridge, Hideyoshi looked out the window and saw the theater. He heard the sound of music and singing.

"What's that?" the Lord of the Realm called out in his usual high-pitched voice.

The attending warrior running alongside the lord answered that it was only a group of riverbed entertainers doing a type of Buddhist prayer dance.

"Eh? I'm not interested."

With Hideyoshi's muttered reply, the procession passed on without incident. Indeed, glimpsing the theater was an inconsequential matter for Hideyoshi. As he turned away from the window, it was already past and forgotten. But those who served the Lord of the Realm lived at the whim of his dangerously volatile temper. They could not ignore a single word he uttered. Reports of the incident filtered down the line of retainers in murmurs and whispers. What did he say? He looked out the window, I think. Did he see entertainers under the bridge? They're despicable, he said.

Baian was riding toward the end of the small procession. His face blanched and then turned red when he heard these comments. He snatched the reins from his groom and spurred his horse to the railing of the bridge. Standing high in the stirrups, he could see everything inside the theater. "Sankuro! Okuni! Come out! Or I'll smash that stage to bits!"

When they heard his booming voice they fell to their knees, astounded. "Master Baian. What is it, Your Excellency?" Sankuro edged forward on his knees, bowing obsequiously.

The agitated clattering of his horse's hoofs punctuated Baian's furious shouts, "Don't come near me! Filthy beggars!"

"What are you saying, Master Baian?"

"I'll say it once. I'm not your master, you're not my servants. If anyone asks, I don't know you. Don't approach me again!"

"What is it, Master Baian? Have we displeased you?"

"Don't speak to me, you beggars of the riverbed! This road belongs to the Lord of the Realm. Trash like you have no right to put up a stage in the lord's sight. Take it down!"

"But, Master Baian..."

"Silence!" Spitting out the word, he turned his horse toward the disappearing procession and galloped across the bridge.

Stunned into silence, they watched him ride out of sight. Then Sankuro felt anger rising in his stomach. Beggars of the riverbed, trash, Baian had said. I'm not good enough to be seen by the Lord of the Realm. "Baian, you bastard!" The words leaped from his enraged throat. He stared off after the procession.

Okuni thought Sankuro had never looked more beautiful or brave. Gazing at his proud profile, she felt a tide of happiness flow through her body. For some time Okuni had worried that they were growing apart, but that night when Sankuro roughly held her in his arms, she felt the joy of their bodies becoming one. It was because their hearts had become one, she believed.

"Sankuro." Okuni abandoned herself to receiving Sankuro, body and soul. No love is as strong as ours, she thought. Before she sank into a deep, moist sleep, she thought, I will have another child.

This hope filled her dreams.

Ten

A fragrant breeze heralded the coming of summer. It was 1596, two years after Baian had disowned the troupe. Sankuro was drinking heavily, keeping to himself, and little interested in the troupe. Okuni, however, kept dancing. Nothing could keep her from dancing.

The softly flowing stream of the Kamo River reflected the figure of an unmoving, exhausted man on the river bank. His ragged workman's jacket was caked with mud. Even the patches on its ripped fabric hung in tatters. His feet were bare, unprotected even by straw sandals. Matted hair covered his face and his naked chest was like a bear's. The top of his head, which should have been clean-shaven, was black with stubble. He wore no sword and looked as if he never had, so he couldn't be a masterless warrior, a *ronin*. It was hard to believe he was young, yet he didn't have the white hair and bent back of an old man.

The man hesitated, then approached some women washing their laundry at the river's edge, "Shijo Street. Where's that?"

His rough voice and dark, shaggy appearance startled the women, for beggars and wandering *ronin* were not an uncommon sight in this capital of flowers. When it seemed he meant no harm, they answered airily.

"That's Gojo Bridge over there."

"Shijo's the next street up."

"Everything west of the bridge is Shijo. What part do you want?"

"They say women from Izumo are dancing by the river. Yah?" The women flinched at the man's harsh country speech and scowling face. They turned back to their washing without answering. The man said no more. He turned and walked along the river toward Shijo Bridge.

The man was Kyuzo from Izumo. His appearance in Kyoto at this particular moment was the result of a series of unplanned events. In the aftermath of a disastrous flood on the Yodo River that winter, Hideyoshi had commanded certain provincial lords to construct levees along the river's lower reaches where the flooding was the worst. Farmers in the area were already destitute from building Yodo Castle, so Hideyoshi singled out three distant fiefs, including Izumo, to provide forced labor. Hideyoshi's deliberate policy was to demand that vassals contribute huge sums and provide labor for massive public works in order to impoverish potential rivals. The rice fields of Nakamura village, where Kyuzo and Sanemon had been born and Okuni had been raised, were dedicated to the upkeep of the Grand Shrine. Hence, traditionally, its farmers were exempt from conscripted labor. But Izumo's new lord, Yoshikawa Hiroie, resorted to a drastic move to curry Hideyoshi's favor: he rounded up almost every farmer in his fief, including those who lived in Nakamura village. In the bitter cold of February, less than a month after Lord Yoshikawa received Hideyoshi's order, Kyuzo and Okaga's husband, Yokichi, found themselves carrying earth and rocks up the banks of the Yodo River.

Construction supervisors worked the conscripts mercilessly. Men who collapsed from exhaustion were kicked out of the way until they could struggle up to work again. The seriously ill were forced to go on without medicine or rest. When a man died, a new conscript immediately took his place. Kyuzo carefully considered his situation. He had experience working on the high levees where the Hii River flowed past Nakamura village. He knew that no matter how hard they worked they could not build dikes high enough to control a river as broad and long as the Yodo in three or even six months. He would be dead before the levees were finished. He would die working like an animal. Why must he die, he thought, raising his face to the sky. But where could he go? He couldn't return to Izumo. He'd be arrested. He couldn't go to friends because of the new law against harboring criminals. One night he heard conscripts from the Kyoto area talking among themselves about a group of women from Izumo who were dancing near Shijo Bridge in the capital. Could Okuni be in Kyoto, he wondered? If she was, he was determined to see her again.

He didn't reveal his plan to Yokichi, for his friend's strength was visibly failing. In late spring, Yokichi became feverish. Even so he was forced to carry heavy loads every day. One afternoon he slipped carrying a large rock and his spine was crushed in the fall. Yokichi died, coughing blood while Kyuzo watched helplessly. Kyuzo gritted his teeth in silent rage; he would not die. The next time a large group of replacements arrived at the river, he slipped away and hid until darkness came. By day he moved north, avoiding people and houses, and at night he rested. It was easy to find his way. He merely walked upstream following the Yodo and the Katsura rivers to the Kamo River, which brought him into Kyoto. He was ravenously hungry, but the desire to escape drove him on. When he passed through the south gate into the capital, his only thought was to meet Okuni.

Approaching Shijo Bridge, he asked several passersby, "Are dancers from Izumo at Shijo?" No one bothered to answer the man who looked like a beggar. It didn't matter. Soon he heard the clear sound of bells and the familiar words of the Buddhist prayer song.

> The light of Buddha's mercy
> Illumines the Ten-Direction World.
> All mankind is encompassed
> In our prayer to Buddha.
> Praise Amida Buddha.
> Praise Amida Buddha's name.

Kyuzo ran down the bank toward the theater. Mame blocked the door with his long wooden staff. "You can't come in here. Buy a ticket."

"She's Okuni, isn't she?"

"Of course."

"Then tell her Kyuzo's here. From Izumo. Tell her to come out and see me."

"I can't interrupt when she's dancing. You have to wait."

"No, I won't wait any more. Okuni! It's me, Kyuzo! You can't have forgotten me!"

Startled, Mame jumped forward. Onstage, Okuni's dancing body sensed the rough challenge of Kyuzo's voice. Kyuzo. . .The name, the voice, nearly forgotten through the passage of nine years. Could he be here?

"Hold on. You can see her after the performance." Although Mame was a small man, he pushed Kyuzo out of the theater entrance with all his strength. Kyuzo staggered, weak from hunger, and fell on the grass.

"Damn it! Get Okuni. I'm Kyuzo. I'm from Izumo. Call her out here!"

Okuni's whole soul was absorbed in her dancing. As if in a trance, she wondered if Sankuro had heard the hoarse shouts. When she was able to glance in his direction, she saw that his face was expressionless as he struck the drum. It was common enough for drunks and vagrants wandering in the riverbed to quarrel outside the theater. Okuni felt a little relief. She must have imagined the voice and the words. How could Kyuzo suddenly appear in the capital? How could he possibly find her? There was no way Kyuzo could know Okuni was at Shijo Street.

> At times, the infatuated heart
> Reveals itself.
> Unfeeling man, can you pretend
> Not to notice?

Okuni sang the final verse loudly and fervently as though to erase the moment. The dance ended but the hoarse shouts in Izumo dialect were still ringing. She couldn't possibly ignore what was happening outside.

Okuni saw Mame struggling to hold a filthy, hairy man to the ground some distance away from the entrance. He had one hand over the mouth of the man, who was trying to shout. Many people came to the riverbed to see sideshows. A group began to gather to watch this free show. At first glance, Okuni thought that the man Mame was holding couldn't possibly be Kyuzo, so she approached. Her gorgeous silk kimono, elaborate hairdo, and velvet accessories set her apart from the working women who had stopped to gawk. Kyuzo recognized her immediately.

"Okuni. It's me, Kyuzo." He crawled forward on his knees and in his excitement clutched her hips, trying to embrace her. She recoiled instinctively.

"Kyuzo!" There was no question that beneath the animal-like appearance this was the man she had known in Izumo. "What are you doing in Kyoto?"

"Yokichi and I were sent to the Yodo River in February to build levees."

"You're with Yokichi?"

"He got hurt."

"He's injured?"

"He's dead." He described Yokichi's painful death. "I can't go back and tell Okaga. She'll die if she hears Yokichi's dead. But that's better than thinking he doesn't want to go back."

"What?"

"I'm bitter, Okuni. Why didn't you come home with Okaga? It still galls me. I couldn't hunt for you, after the Land Survey we were locked in the village. I'm not letting you go again, Okuni. I'll join your troupe."

"Kyuzo, you're not a performer."

"I can sing. At festivals I played the bell, and I can drum. I can do anything Sanemon did. Okuni, I can't go back to Izumo. I'm going with you."

Okuni was caught unprepared. She searched for any excuse to refuse his sudden demand. "Kyuzo, it's impossible. This isn't my troupe. You can't join just because you play the drum."

"This guy here. He's a guard, isn't he? I can do that," Kyuzo insisted. He paused, "You got pretty, Okuni. People thought you were good-looking in Nakamura village, but you're beautiful now."

Kyuzo gazed at her lustfully, for the moment forgetting his deep grudge that had grown stronger over the years. He had roughly made love to her when she was sixteen, an immature, budding flower. Now she was as beautiful as a peony in full bloom. Okuni watched his eyes trace the line from her plump cheeks to her neck and to her shoulders. It disgusted her to see him stare at her full breasts as if he wanted to lick her body. She shuddered. I can't let Sankuro meet him, she thought. She didn't know what to do. She desperately wanted to escape Kyuzo's devouring eyes.

"Is that you, Okuni?" A voice called out from behind her.

Turning, she saw Densuke with an enormous bundle strapped to his back, coming down the bank. She quickly ran over to him and spoke in an undertone, "What's happened, Densuke? Why are you here?"

"Baian died. I can be a regular member of the company from now on. How is Sankuro?"

Seeing Densuke's smiling face, an idea struck her. "Densuke, please, say you're my husband."

Seizing his hand, she turned to face Kyuzo. "I'm sorry, Kyuzo, but I have a husband. You can't join this troupe." Singing and the music of drums and bells rose from inside the theater, calling her. She ran inside, leaving Densuke and Kyuzo on the riverbank.

"You're Okuni's man?" Kyuzo stood up, bristling with envy.

Densuke nodded. "Who're you?"

Kyuzo answered with country honesty in spite of his anger. "I'm Kyuzo. Okuni was supposed to come back to Izumo and marry me." He told how he had escaped from the Yodo River and how he had found Okuni's theater.

"I'm sorry, but you can't come with us. You can see it wouldn't be any good."

Kyuzo looked strangely at Densuke. "Okaga and Sanemon wouldn't say if Okuni had a man. So, she's turned into a *kabuki* woman, has she? And with you? That's a laugh." And he laughed, a bitter, mocking laugh.

"If you love her, please don't stay here. Please leave."

"Is the cuckolder asking the cuckold for a favor?"

"I didn't know Okuni was promised to you. She left Izumo years ago."

"It's been nine years."

"The years and months have separated you from Okuni and they've brought me close to her. Don't hate anyone. It's better if you just go. Here, take this." Densuke reached into the sleeve of his kimono. He felt the packet of fifteen silver coins Baian's wife had given him when he left Hoshi Temple.

Smiling thinly, Kyuzo accepted the offered packet. "You're paying me to go?"

"You had a hard time on the Yodo River. The money will help you escape. You have to live."

"Yes, I'm not going to die like Yokichi." He looked coldly at Densuke. "I'll borrow the money. The years have taken Okuni away, this money will separate us even more. I'll pay you back, I promise. Everything." The ominous undertone escaped Densuke's notice.

Kyuzo turned abruptly, climbed the stone steps of the riverbank, and, without altering his determined pace, crossed over Shijo Bridge. Densuke watched him disappear. It was cruel to send him away like that. He and I are alike: Okuni turns her back on both of us. It would be better if Okuni sent me away, too, he thought. He smiled ruefully and went into the theater, carrying his heavy bundle.

Everyone in the troupe liked Densuke, so he was warmly welcomed as a member. He told them that Baian had died after going into a coma a few days earlier. When Sankuro related the incident at Gojo Bridge three years before, Densuke replied, "So that's what happened. Baian came home from Fushimi Castle in a terrible mood, saying that if Okuni or you ever appeared I had to send you away. I was really worried. Then I heard you had a theater in the riverbed here."

Okuni spoke up. "Last year our stage was washed away by the rain."

"The Kamo River flooded?"

"I always thought it was gentle, not like the Hii River in Izumo. But overnight it rose and took away our big new theater, the pillars, the roof, everything. It was a wonderful stage, Densuke. The floor was polished wood and it was raised off the ground. It made an echo when I stamped my feet." Okuni's nervousness showed in her rush of words.

"The Yodo River flooded at the same time."

"Yes, Granny in Moriguchi village drowned."

"The old lady? That's sad." Densuke looked at Omatsu and asked, "Where's Otsuru?"

"After the flood, she went home. But I'm going to dance with Okuni, always."

It saddened Okuni to see Granny's spirit and energy in her grand-daughter. After years of dedicated practice, Omatsu still moved like a crab on the stage. Her thick voice reminded Okuni of Granny, as well.

Mame, excited by Densuke's appearance, plunged into a fevered account of horrors they had witnessed, events Densuke knew of but had not seen. "Last summer, Densuke, we saw the most awful thing. The Lord of the Realm killed all of Hidetsugu's women and children. It was on the riverbank below Sanjo Bridge. We saw the soldiers do it."

Hidetsugu, twenty-four years old, had been the Lord of the Realm's designated heir. But from the moment Hideyoshi's second son was born, Hidetsugu knew he would never succeed to the title. Soon after the boy's birth he became cruel and arbitrary. The first incident came one day when he was practicing archery; he used a farmer tied to a tree as a living target. The people of Kyoto were shocked. No one could remember a ruler who had acted so capriciously. A town wit coined the sardonic phrase that the regent was "an arrow-straight" ruler. Then Hidetsugu took up hunting with Portuguese guns, shooting at farmers rather than animals. Tiring of archery and shooting, he offered a handsome reward to anyone who would allow his head to be cut off. Of course, no one was willing to sell his life for money. The rumor spread that the regent took prisoners out of jail and used them for sword practice. People began locking their doors in broad daylight. Many were afraid to go out at all. Early that summer, Hideyoshi banished Hidetsugu to the Buddhist monastery at Mount Koya and a few days later ordered him to commit ritual suicide by cutting open his belly.

Mame went on. A month and a half later, they saw a square of soldiers guarding a large pit dug in the riverbank near Sanjo Bridge. A purplish lump of meat was jammed on a pole, baking in the sun. It was the regent's head. It faced west, in the direction of Amida Buddha's Western Paradise. Except for the regent's widow, who prayed quietly while gazing at her husband's head, the mistresses, female servants, and children of Hidetsugu pleaded piteously for their lives. Dressed in silken robes, they had been hauled from Juraku Mansion without warning and brought to the execution site crammed into carts. Three magistrates sat on folding stools, orchestrating the scene. Mashida Nagamori, the official whose cold eyes had watched Okuni dance at Kanbei's villa in Hirano, impassively nodded a signal to begin. First the soldiers seized the children, pierced their bodies two times with their swords, and threw them into the pit. A few of the women tried to flee, screaming wildly. Soldiers caught their long hair and cut them down with one or two sword strokes. In a few minutes' time, thirty-nine ladies from Juraku Mansion and the three young sons of Hidetsugu were slaughtered in the bright sun like beasts. After their bodies were kicked into the pit and Hidetsugu's head thrown after them, laborers filled the hole with dirt. What Mame and the others had seen was almost too cruel to be believed. Among those killed were an old woman of sixty and a bud of a maiden, scarcely twelve years old. The same day, Hideyoshi ordered workmen to raze Juraku Mansion, distributing its most valuable gates and towers to favored temples. Priests of the Nishi Honganji Temple received the mansion's beautiful Noh stage, which they installed in the temple's northern courtyard. In the end, not one stone was left to mark the site. In the blink of an eye the regent and his family were transformed into red streams of blood on the black earth, demonstrating the fearsome power of the Lord of the Realm.

Okuni wanted to shake off these dark thoughts. The lie Baian had created was now true. Dancing ecstatically, Okuni now felt that she really was the shrine priestess he had described. She felt that Baian lived on in her dancing and felt a rush of affection for him.

Now, after a long interval, Okuni's body floated lightly, dancing to Densuke's wistful song.

> Secret lover,
> Speak with your eyes.
> Don't talk,
> Or rumors flow.
> Let's be unseen like the grass,
> That hides beneath the eaves.

"Densuke, your singing's better."

"And your dancing's improved, Okuni." Neither of them seemed to tire, no matter how much they sang and danced.

> If our secret love
> Is widely known,
> I don't care,
> Except for you.
> If rumors fly
> About our love,
> Hidden gossip
> Cannot hurt.
> Let's do it, let's love,
> While we can,
> All we can.
> I am here, depend on me.

Densuke was calling out to Okuni through the words of his song. Spurred on by his voice, Okuni danced lightly and freely, no longer saddened that their beautiful theater had been swept away by the waters of the Kamo River.

"I danced wonderfully on the wooden stage. It boomed like a drum when I stamped on it."

"Yes, but it was washed away." Densuke felt a twinge of regret that he had given his money to Kyuzo. It would have been enough to buy a new stage, he thought. Yet, words alone would never have persuaded Kyuzo to leave.

Seeing that Sankuro had gone and she and Densuke were alone, Okuni abruptly stopped dancing. "Densuke, please forgive me. I didn't know what to do. When I saw you, I thought Buddha had come to save me from hell. I can't ever repay you."

"It looks like emergencies are my specialty."

"All I could think was, what if Sankuro came out and saw him?"

"I knew that."

"Did he go back to Izumo?"

"Well. . .he said he'd repay the loan."

"Loan?"

"It wasn't much. I gave him some money."

She placed her palms together and bowed. Her gratitude was deep and she knew no other way to thank him.

Sankuro returned, boasting to Densuke, "The Lady of the Western Tower invited us to perform last spring, Densuke."

"Really? You performed before the Lord of the Realm's lady?"

"Master Zenso arranged it. He heard we were playing at Shijo Street and remembered the time he'd seen us at Master Kanbei's. We performed for the Lady at a cherry blossom viewing party on the slopes of Higashiyama."

"That sounds wonderful."

"The party was arranged so that cherry blossoms made a canopy overhead, with carpets spread out on the grass under the trees. White curtains, with Hideyoshi's paulownia leaf crest on them, were hung all around us. It was so elegant. Surprised, aren't you? We did it without Baian's help."

"How did it go?"

Sankuro frowned, but answered, "A great success. The Lady was entranced."

"What did you dance, Okuni?"

Okuni did not like the conversation and she answered reluctantly,

"Do you remember the Water Wheel Song? I danced to that."

"Of course I remember." Recalling the song, he sang lightly.

> Water wheel on the Yodo River,
> Do you wait for someone,
> Turning, turning, turning?

"The ladies liked it, Densuke. They laughed," Sankuro added.

But the truth was that the Lady of the Western Tower had not even given them a gratuity when they were done. Okuni looked down, waiting for the topic to pass. Sankuro saw Okuni's guarded expression and his mood changed. He reviewed the events of that day in his mind once again, trying to understand what had gone wrong. Okuni and the girls had finished the performance at dusk. They were praised by all the nobles in the Lady's party. Sankuro had felt so confident of their success that he had begged Zenso to introduce their dance to Hideyoshi and the young heir. Zenso had been startled by Sankuro's forwardness but he agreed to ask the Lady's permission to speak to the Lord of the Realm. The next thing Sankuro knew, Okuni had begun to dance again. Then the Lady abruptly left, with Zenso and the others following. Sankuro could not make out what had happened because of the gathering darkness, but their best chance to reach Hideyoshi had come to nothing. Remembering his humiliation, Sankuro's confident mood disappeared. He looked at Okuni sullenly and walked away.

Through the summer of 1596, the troupe continued to perform on the east side of the dry bed of the Kamo River, just downstream of Shijo Bridge. But a series of natural disasters struck Kyoto one after the other, driving their audience away. An earthquake and its aftershocks half destroyed Fushimi Castle and toppled the statue of the Great Buddha which the Sword Hunt had built ten years before. The thick earthen wall that surrounded the city was shattered in many places. Later, gale winds caused extensive damage to temples, the mansions of Hideyoshi's lords, and businesses. Finally, a blazing comet was seen streaking through the summer heavens. Rumors said it was Hideyoshi's punishment for murdering the regent and his women.

In the midst of these calamities, a messenger from Suekichi Kanbei found Okuni in the riverbed. "The Heavens are displeased. Let the Priestess Okuni from Izumo Shrine come to exorcise this evil." And so the troupe was led to a small house at the foot of Fushimi Castle where Kanbei now conducted his affairs. Kanbei welcomed them and immediately asked Okuni to perform, as a kind of ceremony, the Buddhist prayer dance the troupe had done when they first came from Izumo. Kanbei paid no attention to Sankuro and Densuke. It was clear to everyone that he was only interested in Okuni's performance. After the prayer dance was over, he looked at Okuni with a warm smile and said, "You haven't changed at all, Okuni. How wonderful. I'm going to invite many guests. Won't you stay here and perform for them?" Okuni was pleased by the invitation and it was quickly agreed that they would move into Kanbei's household that same day.

The following day, heavy rains and violent winds began. The terrible weather continued intermittently for an entire month, causing frightful devastation throughout the capital. The Kamo and the Katsura rivers flooded again. But Kanbei's house was never in danger, for it stood just below Fushimi Castle, high on the hillside of Momoyama. Since they could not perform, the girls happily spent their time making new kimonos from the luxurious silk cloth Kanbei gave them. The cloth was wider and more extravagantly patterned than the silk he had given them when they had performed for him eight years before in Hirano.

Okuni stood before Densuke wearing a man's kimono of light green material figured with large white cranes. Laughing, she asked, "Do you like it on me, Densuke? I sewed this for Sankuro, using Kanbei's best silk, but he won't wear it."

Densuke swallowed hard. "You look wonderful." Densuke felt his heart beat faster, for the man's kimono emphasized the voluptuousness of Okuni's body.

"Then I'll wear it. It might be fun to impersonate a man."

"Play a man?"

"Why not? People like it when you impersonate a woman, don't they? It might be interesting if I come out as a man when you're doing your woman's dance." Okuni smiled to herself and shifted her weight onto one hip like a man.

After many weeks, the sky cleared and Kanbei sent for them. "I am inviting Lord Hideyasu. Do you know who he is?" Kanbei asked quietly.

Sankuro bowed low. "Of course, Master Kanbei. He is the son of Lord Ieyasu and the Lord of the Realm's adopted son."

"I don't want any mistakes. Make your dance interesting. Okuni, I want you to dress in *kabuki* style." He handed Okuni a Kirishitan rosary made of crystal beads. "Wear this around your neck and hang the bell from it."

Young men were called *kabuki* if they dressed extravagantly in Southern Barbarian clothes. The craze for exotic dress began after Alessandro Valignano's visit to Kyoto. Lords and vassals serving Hideyoshi had been the first to flaunt in public the sleeveless vests, bloused pantaloons, round hats, velvet belts, Kirishitan crosses, and rosaries of the Southern Barbarians. Then the fad was taken up by foppish young samurai, sons of officials, and well-to-do commoners. A foreign accessory, like a Portuguese white silk scarf worn over one's collar, was very *kabuki*. Originally the word came from the verb *kabuku*, meaning "to be slanted." While in the past *kabuki* had meant someone who was eccentric, and in Izumo the word had been used to shame a person who deviated from the norm, it now indicated a trend setter in the foreign fashion. In Kyoto, if one wasn't *kabuki*, one was behind the times.

Okuni looked extremely beautiful with the Southern Barbarian rosary lying on the breast of her brilliant kimono. Its crystal spheres sparkled in the light when she stamped her feet and waved her silken sleeves. She had dreamed of dancing with such a rosary on her breast from the moment she had seen the tall priest Valignano that first day in Kyoto so many years ago. Now she could find no words to tell Kanbei of the unexpected joy it brought her.

"It suits you perfectly. Yes, I think Lord Hideyasu will like it."

Throughout the day the troupe waited, anxious and excited.

Hideyasu, who took the seat of honor in the banquet room in Kanbei's house, was twenty-three years old. He was in the unique position of being favored equally by Ieyasu and Hideyoshi. As a child he had been a hostage for Ieyasu's good conduct and had lived close to Hideyoshi for many years. As the boy grew to manhood the Lord of the Realm came to admire his honesty and manly bearing. Hideyoshi was so fond of him and trusted him so much he even allowed him to return to his father's fief in the east from time to time. The young man now lived in Fushimi Castle as Ieyasu's emissary to Hideyoshi. Today, Hideyoshi had gone to Osaka Castle to meet with ambassadors from China. Hideyasu was not involved in the negotiations, so he accepted Kanbei's invitation as a pleasant diversion. After Hideyoshi had conducted the Sword Hunt and had promulgated the strict division among social classes, Kanbei had renounced his samurai status: if he had to choose, he deemed it more profitable to be a merchant in the new society. With skillful diplomacy, he had obtained trading privileges simultaneously from Hideyoshi and from Ieyasu. Whichever way the political world might go, the two men in this room, one a samurai and one a merchant, were safe. The young Hideyasu was in his usual good spirits.

"Does Your Excellency recall the young lady perhaps?" Kanbei spoke politely but good-naturedly.

Hideyasu looked at Okuni and smiled. "How could I forget? The dancing priestess from Izumo. What is her name?"

"It's 'Kuni."

"Of course. 'Kuni did a special dance. The Child's Dance, I think it was called."

"The late Baian said it was the Dance of Youth." Kanbei corrected him deferentially.

"Ah, yes."

Okuni and the others were surprised to learn that Hideyasu had seen them perform at Hirano. Six years ago they hadn't noticed the teenage boy among Kanbei's important guests, but he had remembered them. They were encouraged to do their best. Hideyasu watched the opening prayer dance with great pleasure, for it was almost unchanged from the way he recalled it from six years before. Then, when Okuni removed the black hat and robe and emerged wearing the light green man's kimono with the crystal rosary on her breast, he slapped his knee, greatly amused. "Okuni has become *kabuki*!" he exclaimed. In all likelihood this was the first time Southern Barbarian costumes had been incorporated into Japanese popular dance. Kanbei's gaze moved between Okuni and Hideyasu, as he smiled and nodded to himself. His idea was even more successful than he had expected.

Before Okuni finished dancing, an urgent message from Osaka reached Fushimi Castle, where it was relayed to warriors and officials inside and outside the castle walls. Hideyasu, who was the commander of Fushimi Castle in Hideyoshi's absence, turned pale when he received the message. He immediately rose and hurried from the room.

No one in the troupe knew what had happened. Sankuro went out to ask Kanbei's servants and returned after some time. "The war is starting up again."

"Why?"

Sankuro spoke deliberately, as if convincing himself of the truth of the news he had heard. "The Lord of the Realm agreed to see ambassadors from China at Osaka Castle in order to accept the surrender of China and Korea. But the lord didn't like the Chinese emperor's message and he turned red in the face and smashed the emperor's gifts on the floor."

It was true. The state proclamation read out by the Chinese ambassadors described Hideyoshi as "the King of Japan, who serves the Emperor of China." Further, it said Japan could trade with China on the condition that Hideyoshi served the emperor well. It was an intolerable insult to the man who dreamed of ruling the entire world. Within the day, Toyotomi Hideyoshi issued orders to mount a second Korean campaign.

"More war?" Okuni wondered.

In his room, Kanbei was also murmuring, "War again. Hm."

Kanbei knew Hideyoshi's generals in Korea had finally convinced him to withhold further attacks. In the interval, the generals hoped peace discussions with the Chinese government delegation would bring an end to the useless bloodshedding. Hideyoshi, in a moment of personal pique, had shattered those careful preparations and lost their best opportunity to extricate themselves from a hopeless war. Kanbei felt Hideyoshi had tempted fate with his first Korean venture. Now, he thought, Hideyoshi's very survival, and the survival of his heirs, was at stake. Kanbei guessed, from reports of his secret agents, that only Hideyoshi's closest allies would send armies to Korea for a second campaign. Ieyasu and others would keep their warriors home. Kanbei thought carefully about the future balance of power between Hideyoshi and Ieyasu. As a merchant, he had no favorites. He favored only caution.

Eleven

Okuni and all the members of the troupe were fortunate that they had Kanbei's patronage during this difficult period. Later that year, Emperor Goyozei changed the era name to Eternal Happiness, hoping to avert further disasters. Subsequently floods and earthquakes subsided but there was great turbulence in society as fresh armies were dispatched to Korea from Fushimi and Osaka castles. Kanbei rarely went out, for he was now over seventy. He was content to sit at home and receive a constant stream of guests who came to conduct business, primarily merchants but also warriors and nobles. Kanbei did not smoke and he did not drink. Nor did he serve his guests wine, either hot Japanese rice wine or the red Southern Barbarian kind. He did not flatter his guests with the tea ceremony, a pastime many merchants cultivated in the hope of pleasing Hideyoshi. Perhaps Kanbei had learned a lesson from the death of the renowned tea master Sen Rikyu some ten years past. Rikyu had been honored as the greatest master of this polite art. Even so he was ordered to kill himself when he displeased Hideyoshi. Kanbei believed people were linked in this world by profit, not by friendship. When he had visitors, he showed them Okuni's prayer dance and the newer dances and popular songs that Densuke had taught the troupe. Kanbei did not entertain guests in order to curry their favor; he simply liked a relaxed atmosphere in which to carry out his business. When he did not have guests, he had the troupe perform for his own pleasure.

Although uninterested in dressing in Southern Barbarian fashion himself, Kanbei enjoyed giving Okuni's troupe the most recent exotic foreign clothing he received in trade. At first, Okuni wore European ornaments and a lace collar at his insistence, and Sankuro and Densuke dressed in Portuguese pantaloons to amuse him. As the months passed, they found themselves falling into the habit of wearing striking clothes every day. Densuke favored a red sleeveless vest worn over his Southern Barbarian pantaloons, and he was fond of buckling a foreign sword at his waist.

"Densuke, we really are *kabuki* people, aren't we," laughed Okuni.

"Oh, we're gorgeous *kabuki* people. I like it when you wear ornaments on your collar, Okuni. It suits you."

Time moved slowly on the days Kanbei did not entertain guests. "Ahh," Okuni said, stretching, trying to stave off boredom, "I wouldn't be wearing beautiful clothes like these, but I think dancing on the riverbank is more fun. Sankuro, I want to dance by the river when Kanbei doesn't ask us."

"What? Throw away this luxurious life? Once we leave, we can't come back here. Kanbei gives us good food, wonderful clothes. He treats us well. What else do you want?"

"Nothing. But Kanbei's guests don't clap to the music when I dance or sing along with Densuke. I feel like I'm dancing to a wall. It discourages me."

"You can't compare audiences on the riverbank to the people who come to this house. It's crazy to say you enjoy dancing for them. They're scum."

"They encourage me."

"Shut up!" Sankuro snapped in irritation. "It's your fault we weren't invited back by the Lady of the Western Tower. It was our chance to be seen by the lord. It's because you're content playing for commoners that your dancing and singing don't improve. Don't you understand that, Okuni?"

"No, I don't."

"What?"

"I dance best when I'm happy. When the people I'm dancing for are happy watching me, Sankuro."

"You're a fool. That's nonsense. This isn't Izumo, this isn't the backwoods. This is the capital, where refined people appreciate artistry. I don't want to play for an audience of stupid, dirty peasants and shopkeepers and servants. What do you think I'm working for?"

"Do you think if you stay here the lord will notice you one day, Sankuro? Do you think all your effort will accomplish that?"

Okuni no longer tried to please Sankuro as she had done when she was a young girl. She spoke her mind. Sankuro flushed with anger, then glared at her and stalked out of the room. At that, Okuni burst into tears, wailing loudly. She could not stop crying. The relationship between Sankuro and Okuni was becoming strained as Okuni matured and asserted herself and as Sankuro's dream of success failed to materialize. Still, no one in the troupe dared mediate when the two quarreled in front of them.

Densuke finally spoke, placatingly, "Okuni, it's hard for Sankuro when you speak to him like that."

"Sankuro talks about the lord every time he opens his mouth. I don't want to dance for the Lord of the Realm. It was enough to have danced before his lady. When I think of the Lady of the Western Tower it makes me sick. She accused me of dancing while I was drunk, Densuke." Then she related to Densuke details of the flower viewing party, things she had kept from Sankuro.

"We started dancing in the late afternoon and when dusk came torches were lighted so we could continue. When we were finished, the Lady of the Western Tower said she wanted to meet me. She was sitting a little distance away on a flowered carpet spread on the grass and was drinking rice wine from a big cup. I left the dancing area and knelt in front of her. Then she asked me to share her drink, Densuke, but I said no."

"Not directly?"

"Yes, I looked at her and said that when I danced I became intoxicated, so I didn't have to drink wine. Dancing on the grass in the open air reminded me of my childhood, when I skipped on the sands of the Hii River. I had danced that afternoon before the Lady like I was in a trance. I didn't want her wine."

Densuke looked at this woman with deepening admiration. Commoners were forbidden to speak directly to their rulers. And to refuse a ruler's request was unthinkable, even for a noble or a general. The Lady of the Western Tower was, of course, Otane, Hideyoshi's favorite mistress and the mother of the heir, Hideyori. She was commonly known by the name of the castle in which she lived. When she had given birth to Tsurumatsu in the castle on the Yodo River, she was called the Lady of Yodo. Later, when she had shared Osaka Castle with Hideyoshi's wife, the Mistress of the Second Tower. Now, living in the westernmost ramparts of Fushimi Castle, she was the Lady of the Western Tower. Needless to say, people around Hideyoshi indulged her whims without stint, for her slightest displeasure could mean banishment or execution for an offender. What Okuni had done was incredibly daring. "Was the Lady angry?"

"Not really. Zenso turned pale, because he was handling the conversation up to then, repeating to me what she said, and then repeating what I said to her. Like I was a foreigner who couldn't understand. When I said, directly to her, I don't need wine, she smiled and then laughed." Okuni remembered her warm feeling for the Lady that day. Dancing on the fresh grass under clouds of pink cherry blossoms that beautiful spring afternoon, she had felt close to the woman who had lost her child beside the Yodo River. She was like Okuni. Okuni did not think it was special to look at her and speak to her.

"Did something else happen? Sankuro said. . ."

"He doesn't know. After the Lady laughed, she looked at me and said, 'You've been drinking and that's why you refuse wine now. Noh actors are praised because they don't eat or drink before they dance. Perhaps you should stay in the riverbed if you cannot dance before me without drinking'." Okuni's face tightened into a frown. "I couldn't let her say that. Sankuro didn't hear, so I told Zenso I wanted to dance again, to show the Lady I wasn't drunk."

Okuni's generous feeling had been transformed into a daring challenge. Zenso and the attendants watched in stark terror while

Okuni fiercely, rapturously whirled on the green grass before the Lady of the Western Tower, as if she and not the Lady were in command. Kanji sang, Mame played the stick drum, and Sankuro joined his drumbeats to Okuni's dance. A chill wind blew down from the mountains but the Lady seemed oblivious. The tension between the two women was broken only when a worried lady-in-waiting whispered that the young prince was waiting. The Lady rose, walked between the prostrated warriors, and disappeared inside her palanquin with a shrill, condescending laugh. Zenso hurried after his mistress, loudly remarking, "That woman went mad when our Lady rebuked her." Okuni continued to dance, oblivious to everything. Naturally, Zenso never mentioned Okuni to the Lady again. For reasons that Sankuro could not fathom, his request had come to nothing.

"So that's what happened. Hm." Densuke folded his arms across his chest and considered the situation. Okuni was not aware of the gulf separating her from Sankuro, he thought. She loves him too deeply. They are bound together by their bodies, but their goals and ideas are worlds apart. How strange is the relationship between man and woman, he thought miserably. Densuke couldn't find the words to say it, but he worried about the future of their small company.

"Sankuro? Haven't you come home, Sankuro?" Okuni rose in the middle of the night and wandered outside. Sankuro had been gone two nights. Is he seeing another woman, like Oan, she wondered? She wept silently.

By the time Sankuro reached Yanagi Ward, off Nijo Street, he had put Okuni out of mind. She was just a woman. If he spent two or three nights away from home, she would weep and love him all the more. Every man in the street thought that way. The prostitutes' quarter at Yanagi Ward had been organized seven years before, in 1589, by two of Hideyoshi's former grooms. It was the major area of prostitution in the capital, catering to merchants and the lower classes for the most part. When a noble or a samurai wanted to visit Yanagi Ward discreetly, the new *kabuki* fashions provided a convenient disguise. Though Hideyoshi had banned the Kirishitan religion, he continued to relish Southern Barbarian fashions; he ate meat and eggs and drank European wine. It has always been that the lower orders mimic their masters' ways. Sankuro entered Yanagi Ward this early evening wearing a Portuguese cape over bloused foreign pantaloons. Women who peered through the grilled windows facing the street thought he might be a noble or a samurai and called out to him, "Come in, sir," "Do visit me, Excellency." It flattered Sankuro to be treated well, especially after his annoying argument with Okuni.

Sankuro stopped before an entryway covered by a crimson curtain. The building was plain, like a shop or a store, and it made him wonder if this house sold women like over-the-counter merchandise. The name painted on the lantern beside the entrance read "Court Maidens." He went in.

"Welcome, sir." Speaking politely, a man knelt to greet him, quickly took off his guest's clogs, and washed his feet with a damp towel. Several women pulled on Sankuro's sleeves, wheedling him to come to their rooms. After he had chosen one, the man led the way to a matted room on the second floor. Again the man knelt and spoke deferentially. "Would you like wine to drink, sir?"

"Yes, I'll have some."

The man hurried out, returning in a few moments carrying two porcelain bottles of hot rice wine. He bowed politely and left. Sankuro did not pay attention to the man. He was excited by the looks and smell of the woman he had chosen. Sankuro hadn't seen the man before. He couldn't know the man was Kyuzo.

In fact, Sankuro would not have recognized Kyuzo's face at the Court Maidens even if they had met the year before. Kyuzo was a changed person. He had wandered into Yanagi Ward by accident and stumbled into the Court Maidens. In spite of his appearance, the master gave him a job drawing water and cleaning the rooms. He did these menial tasks without rest, day and night, with a peasant's single-minded diligence. The first person awake in the morning, he was also the last to go to bed. The master of the Court Maidens soon noticed that Kyuzo was not only hardworking but also extremely clever. He promoted Kyuzo to a position of greeting and handling customers. Kyuzo now wore merchant's clothes made of linen, and he shaved the top of his head like a townsman. Seeing him, no one would imagine he was a peasant from the Izumo countryside.

"Why don't you enjoy yourself, Kyuzo?" The girls of the house tried to seduce him now that he looked respectable and had money.

"I haven't time."

"Kyuzo, have a drink with me."

"I don't drink."

"What's the matter with you? Are you made of wood? Is your heart stone?" It didn't bother him when customers or prostitutes made fun of his strict behavior. He had not imagined that such luxury existed as he had found in Yanagi Ward. Men came here partly to satisfy their lust, but they also came to celebrate, eating and drinking gaily through the night. When they returned home in the early hours of dawn, they were still floating in a world of dreams. They spent money like water, never bothering to add up their bill when it was presented to them. How foolish he had been to plow the rice fields like a beast and be a samurai's slave on a river dike, Kyuzo thought. Nor did he intend to become the quarter's victim. It did not take him long to see how easily even innocent country girls became slatterns when they accepted the loose life of the brothel. Kyuzo knew that women were machines to suck money from men and that wine was no more than expensive water.

When Kyuzo received a tip from a customer, he saved it. If a kimono was thrown away by one of the girls, he cleaned and mended it and sold it for a small amount. His one pleasure in life was raising a puppy he named Black on the leftovers he scrounged from the kitchen. He had a single-minded aim: to save enough money to buy a prostitute who could earn him money. Just now a girl could be purchased easily and cheaply. Hideyoshi had forbidden selling girls into brothels, but for the past two or three years, times had been hard and girls were openly sold on street corners. Most were daughters of peasants impoverished by floods or by conscription in the Korean war. The girls were too young to imagine the sorrow they would in time experience. At first, life in Yanagi Ward seemed a veritable paradise compared to the hard farm work they were used to.

In all his work, an unquenchable desire to avenge himself against Okuni drove Kyuzo. "Damn that woman," he bit his lips in hatred, thinking of how she had made a fool of him. Often he walked with Black along Shijo Street looking for Okuni's theater. As Black grew, the dog became vicious and utterly devoted to his master. Kyuzo talked to Black, as he did not talk to any person. "How can I get back at Okuni and her man, Black? I want to hurt her. Where is she? Where has she gone?" Black would wag his tail, as if he understood what his master was saying.

Kyuzo did not find Okuni, who was staying at Kanbei's residence in Fushimi, but he saw many other shows in the riverbed during his search. Most were common freak shows: a fake porcupine-raccoon hybrid, a dwarf horse, an armless archer, an amazon, trained monkeys. Hoarding his money, he chose the cheapest place, where a barker was shouting to passersby, "Come see the woman's head! A freshly chopped-off, bleeding head! Step right up and see it!"

Before Kyuzo's eyes could become adjusted to the dark of the shed, Black started to snarl. Women's terrified voices shattered the air. "Quiet, Black. Quiet." Kyuzo looked down and saw the heads of three women on the ground, hair matted and cheeks smeared gray and red, as if dead. But their eyes were open and their lips twitched. It was obvious the women were buried up to their necks in a hole. "Come on, Black. Let's go." Kyuzo was angry that he had wasted money on a stupid trick, but on the way back to the Court Maidens an idea suddenly occurred to him. If men will pay good money to see dead women displayed in the riverbed, what would they pay to look at live, beautiful women from the brothel lined up in front of them? Yes, it was a good idea, he thought. He began laying a plan.

Twelve

The Lord of the Realm energetically commanded vassals and lords of all fiefs to contribute new armies for a Second China Campaign. But he left it to his generals to carry on the war. He himself did not go near invasion headquarters at Nagoya in Kyushu. Instead he gratified his taste for spectacle by traveling in glorious processions back and forth between Osaka Castle and Fushimi Castle. And he continued to hold lavish tea ceremonies, direct Noh performances, and organize extravagant entertainments, of which the most notable was the ostentatious cherry blossom viewing party he arranged at the Sanbo Temple at Daigo, a day's journey from the capital, on April 20, 1598.

Three days before the party was to be held, people serving Hideyoshi felt their world turn upside down. Daigo is renowned for the profusion of its cherry blossoms in early spring, but on the afternoon of the 17th the Lord of the Realm pointedly noted to his retainers that he was not satisfied with the number of trees in the temple compound. He would only be happy if he could see every inch of the northern and southern courtyards covered with a canopy of pink blossoms. It may have been a capricious remark, but for the next two days dignitaries in nearby provinces frantically dug prize cherry trees from their gardens, in full blossom, and transported them to Sanbo Temple. Suekichi Kanbei owned three magnificent cherry trees in the garden of his Fushimi home and he entrusted Kanji and Mame with the urgent task of moving them to Daigo.

"Flower viewing?" Okuni asked, frowning. "But what is happening with the war in Korea and China?"

Okuni's question was asked by many people, for the lord's behavior was erratic indeed. Kanbei had long admired Hideyoshi's willpower and intelligence, but as he watched his trees being uprooted, he was amazed by the Lord of the Realm's frivolity. Kanbei received almost daily reports from informants telling him that the new campaign in Korea was failing. The Japanese had been defeated in many battles and it seemed likely that only the powerful army led by Kato Kiyomasa, dubbed the Devil General of the campaign, would be able to escape. Kanbei also knew that only Hideyoshi's closest vassals from western Japan were fighting in this second campaign. Just as Kanbei had suspected he would, Tokugawa Ieyasu found a pretext to keep his armies safely home, and he continued to strengthen his position in the eastern provinces. From the beginning, Kanbei had thought Hideyoshi acted rashly in going to war. With an eye to the future, Kanbei had been quietly cultivating Ieyasu's favor. He felt a deep sense of satisfaction that his earlier, difficult decision was proving to be correct. Bidding farewell to his beautiful cherry trees, Kanbei was moved to the wry reflection that no flower blooms forever.

The Lord of the Realm, who loved display in all things, ordered people to line the route of his procession to Sanbo Temple. Of course, Sankuro went out to see his lord, and most of the members of the troupe did as well, even though Daigo was a tiring walk from the city. Okuni and Onei stayed behind to care for Yata, the baby that had been born to Onei and Mame that winter. The boy, growing day by day, loved to have Okuni hold him in her arms. Sometimes a band tightened around her heart when he laughed or smiled, and grief welled up because she remembered her own dead child. But usually she felt a great sense of peace when she played with Yata. He was not her child, but he was dear to her. People are being killed in a war and the lord is looking at cherry trees, but there is also this kind of happiness, Okuni thought. She watched Onei quietly nursing Yata. And she wept.

Sankuro and the others were noisy and excited when they returned. They had seen the lord's golden palanquin arriving from Fushimi Castle and six palanquins arriving from Osaka Castle meet at exactly the same moment in front of the gates of Sanbo Temple. Each palanquin seemed more beautiful than the next. Each was accompanied by bearers, guards, and mounted warriors wearing colorful costumes. They saw the lord's palanquin enter the massive gate and the palanquins from Osaka follow him in. And they wanted to tell Okuni and Onei all they had seen.

"You should have come, Okuni. The Lady of the Western Tower's palanquin was second. It was splendid."

"She was second?"

"Well, after the lord. The lord's wife was first, she was second, and the third, fourth, fifth, and sixth palanquins carried the lord's other favorite mistresses. It was a spectacular sight."

The Lord of the Realm brought all his women together to enjoy themselves for the first time at the sumptuous day-long party among the cherry blossoms of Sanbo Temple. Naturally, this exceptional event became the subject of gossip among people for a very long time.

"Sankuro."

"Hmm?"

"I think the lord's women must be miserable. I'm surprised they don't die of jealousy. I think I'm much more fortunate than the Lady of the Western Tower, because I don't share my husband's arms with other women." Sankuro did not reply to Okuni's happy boast. He didn't think it necessary to tell her about the woman in Yanagi Ward. In Sankuro's opinion, the large number of aristocratic women Hideyoshi kept as mistresses was proof that the Lord of the Realm wielded great power. Sankuro changed the subject.

"The invitation from the Lady of the Western Tower could have changed everything. What a waste."

"What do you mean?"

"If you'd pleased her with your dance then, we could have performed under the cherry trees at Sanbo Temple for the lord himself today."

It was Okuni's turn to keep her silence. The happiness filling Okuni's heart a moment ago was gone, but she loved Sankuro too much to tell him what she really felt. She knew Sankuro would be angry if she said the Lady of the Western Tower was her enemy. She knew he would be angry if she told him she was happy just to dance in the riverbed. Okuni remained silent. Each withdrew further from the other.

When summer came many people called on Kanbei at his home. However, Kanbei did not ask the troupe to perform for his guests. The visitors spoke to Kanbei in hushed voices, they stayed a short time, and they hurried away. They seemed to have no spare time in which to watch dancing or listen to singing.

"The Lord of the Realm is sick. They're offering prayers at Hoko Temple for his recovery." Sankuro spoke with a worried expression on his face. He was the first to hear the rumor.

"The lord is sick?"

"Very sick. The emperor held a performance of sacred dances at the palace to ask the gods to heal him."

"If the Lord of the Realm dies, will the emperor be the new Lord of the Realm?"

"Of course not." Okuni's naivete irritated Sankuro. "The emperor is the emperor. The lord's son will be the new Lord of the Realm."

"The child the Lady of the Western Tower gave birth to?"

"Yes. Master Hideyori."

"How old is he now?"

"Well, he was born in 1593, so he's five now."

"Five years old? How can a five-year-old Lord of the Realm rule the world?"

"The lord isn't dead yet, so don't talk like a fool." Stung by her simple question, Sankuro turned his back on Okuni.

Since Sankuro wouldn't answer her, Okuni went to find Densuke.

"I don't know what will happen, Okuni, but I know Kanbei won't ask us to perform while the lord is sick. And this year the Gion Festival will be used to drive away the vengeful spirits that are making the lord ill. All the people are supposed to come and offer prayers."

So when the evening of July 16 arrived, everyone in the troupe put on their best kimonos and walked to the Gion area of Kyoto to join the tens upon tens of thousands of people gathering to celebrate the Gion Festival, the largest mass religious celebration in the nation. They saw the floats that would be pulled or carried through the city's streets in the festival's climax the following day. The Gion Festival had begun in the summer of 876, when priests carried a figure of the Ox-Head God through the city to suppress malevolent spirits that were causing a fearful plague. Each summer thereafter, various deities were paraded in the four directions as protection against pestilence. Now in Hideyoshi's time, the festival was as much a show of the wealth of Kyoto's merchants as it was a religious ritual.

There were two kinds of floats, Mountains and Towers. A Mountain was a beautifully carved and painted float often topped by life-sized figures from mythology or history. Twenty or more men carried the Mountain on their shoulders. A Tower was a mammoth wagon weighing five or six tons. Each of its four wheels stood as tall as a man and it took one hundred or even two hundred men to inch the wagon on its great wheels through the streets. Singers and dancers continuously performed in a room raised several stories above the street. Finally, a slender tower of bamboo and pine branches set on the elaborate, peaked roof soared eighty or more feet into the air.

Each of the one hundred or so Mountains and Towers was the property, and responsibility, of a merchant guild or residents of a particular ward or district. Men gladly spent the entire summer painting and refurbishing the float that belonged to their group. Silks from China and rare imported Flemish tapestries decorated the sides of the largest Towers. Although Hideyoshi had prohibited the practice of the Kirishitan religion in 1587, celebrants wore their Southern Barbarian costumes with elan. Dolls with Western features, like protuberant noses, graced the tops of some Mountains. The night of the sixteenth was dedicated to the floats and was known as the Evening of the Mountains. Men and women who had worked hard on the floats celebrated by drinking and singing until dawn.

"It's too hot and crowded. If we get separated, I'll see you at Shijo Bridge in the morning." Sankuro spoke irritably. He wasn't interested in seeing the floats.

"Where are you going?"

"I can't stand this heat. I want a drink."

"I'll come with you, Sankuro."

"No." Sankuro looked directly at Okuni. "I want to drink by myself."

Okuni watched Sankuro turn north and walk into the crowd. Suddenly her mouth went dry and the thought flashed into her consciousness: he has another woman. All these nights he has been away from my bed. Elbowing and pushing people aside, she ran after him. Where is Sankuro going? Oan has to be dead. She can't be alive. To whom is he going? She followed Sankuro as he entered upper Kyoto, where the crowds were less dense. At the corner where Nijo Street enters Yanagi Ward, Sankuro stopped and straightened his clothes. Okuni stepped into a small alley to keep from being seen and in that instant Sankuro vanished into the licensed quarter. When Okuni peered out he was gone.

"Sankuro..."

The name came to her lips unconsciously as she stood looking down the street where he had disappeared. Then she noticed young women behind latticed windows lustily calling to men in the street. Sankuro is going to a prostitute, he's going to drink and sleep with her, Okuni thought in confusion. She could not understand what made Sankuro go to a prostitute. Still, it was Okuni's nature to feel relieved that it was not a woman like Oan.

Okuni was staring at the houses of prostitution, wondering which one Sankuro had gone into. In front of the Court Maidens a man lighting a lantern turned and looked in her direction. Their eyes met. Okuni blanched. Kyuzo, in such a place? It's unbelievable but he's here, dressed in a merchant's kimono.

"Okuni!"

When she heard his voice, she gasped and fled. The sight of Kyuzo revolted Okuni. Forgetting everything, she turned and ran wherever the streets led her. She raced headlong without glancing back. At last, wildly out of breath, she reached Shijo Street, where the crowd was so tightly packed she had to stop.

"Okuni, there you are, I've been looking for you." It was Densuke. The familiar voice calmed her. "Look. There's Moon Tower. It's beautiful, isn't it?" Okuni and Densuke may have met by chance, or Densuke may have been looking for Okuni here at the center of the festival crowd. In any case, he was shy now that they were together. The Tower was something to talk about. Moon Tower was the largest and most famous float in the Gion Festival. Its half-moon ornament rose above all the others and was instantly recognizable. Glowing lanterns hanging from eaves spoke of approaching evening. Densuke and Okuni watched the tops of Towers and Mountains fade into the soft black of the deepening summer night.

"It's too late to go back to Fushimi, Densuke. Where are the girls?"

"They went back with Kanji."

"What will I do?"

"I can hear flutes and bells from Oracle Mountain. They'll play all night. Why don't we go there?"

Okuni walked behind Densuke. Her mind was blank. She could not think. She moved as if in a daze and she stumbled when the surging crowd pushed against her.

"Okuni, you're going to get lost again." Mechanically, Okuni reached out and took Densuke's extended hand and they began to edge forward, clinging to each other for support. The crowd was so dense it took them many minutes to move one block to the small alley where Oracle Mountain was kept. Several children, gathered around the float, were singing to the accompaniment of bells and flutes. Densuke was deeply touched by their young voices, and he was aroused by the physical energy emanating from the excited, sweating people pressing in around them. Densuke trembled as he became conscious of Okuni next to him. He drew Okuni close against his body and the two of them stood, as if embracing, before Oracle Mountain.

On the evening before the procession, offerings of lighted candles and other kinds of fire offerings were brought to honor the Empress Shinko, the deity who was enshrined at the top of Oracle Mountain. All night people streamed in, carrying new flaming offerings, so the area around the float was continuously bright. The worshipers then stayed on to drink and sing. Some were singing boisterously as the bells and flutes played uninterruptedly. Inebriated men rose and did impromptu dances.

"Do you want to drink, Okuni?"

"Oh, yes."

That night Okuni learned to drink. In one breath she swallowed the cup of cold rice wine Densuke poured for her. She didn't bother tasting the second or the third cups either but drank them down like water. A warm glow spread through her body. The bell rang, *chan chiki chi, chan chiki chi*, its sound drawing her into a warm state of abandon. She heard the singing. They weren't ancient festival songs, but popular ditties every city person knew. A man or woman began a song and then it was taken up by the crowd. Okuni sang along with the others. She sang and she drank. Densuke, too, felt exhilarated. He held Okuni close in his arms. She was soft and unresisting. He lived in the same room with Okuni and he had not touched her once because she was Sankuro's woman. He was miserable with desire for her, and his drinking helped him forget Sankuro. Densuke embraced her tightly and at last cried out, "Okuni. I love you, Okuni. I've loved you since the day we met. I've yearned for you all this time." But the woman in his arms lay limp and unmoving. "Okuni?"

Densuke looked down at her face. Long black eyelashes formed bows under her two closed eyes. Tears wet her lashes and coursed down her full cheeks.

"Why are you crying, Okuni? I love you." He shook her gently but she did not move. She was asleep.

Okuni had put on weight living at Kanbei's house, and the thin cotton summer kimono she wore could not conceal the fullness of her youthful breasts and hips. She was drunk and weeping and didn't even know she was being embraced. When Densuke realized this, his own drunkenness vanished like the receding tide.

He looked around at the men and women sprawled on the ground in advanced stages of inebriation. There is nothing wrong with this, since singing and drinking please the Ox-Head God of the festival. Densuke's desire for Okuni was transformed into a feeling of tenderness toward her. He didn't care if he couldn't love her like a man. He cradled her head on his knees and he straightened her clothes. Although her large breasts showed plainly, her sleeping face was childlike. When the sky was beginning to lighten, Densuke fell into a shallow sleep. If I had a child with Okuni, he dreamed, it would be beautiful like her.

The scattered members of the troupe met at noon the following day at Shijo Street near the bridge. Kanji, Mame, and the girls walked in from Fushimi. Sankuro looked bathed and spotless, all evidence of his lovemaking to another woman washed away. When he saw Okuni he smiled weakly and said, "Ah, there you are, Okuni." He seemed embarrassed.

Surprisingly, Okuni suffered no ill effects from her drinking of the night before. She felt as she always did after a good night's sleep. When she woke, she confessed to Densuke that she didn't remember anything she had done at Oracle Mountain. Densuke said she had slept through the night, and she thought no more about it. She did not return Sankuro's greeting but, looking straight at him, she smiled slightly. It isn't pleasant to think of Sankuro making love to a prostitute, but my love is large enough to hold this small pain. We are leaders of the troupe and our lives are irrevocably bound together, Okuni thought as they stood in the dense crowds watching the procession of Mountains and Towers move slowly past them. The parade continued through the stifling heat of the afternoon. Only when the sun began to set did the floats return home.

The rhythm of the festival would not leave their bodies. They all sang and danced as they walked back to Fushimi that evening.

Oh, don't we know,
Oh, don't we know,
Why the sleepless man,
Says it's too bright
To sleep on a summer night?

And Densuke sang out at the top of his lungs.

My love is a firefly,
Flickering on the water.
I cannot speak,
Foolish firefly love.

"Quiet. The lord is sick." Sankuro frowned and spoke sharply as they entered the streets lying at the foot of Fushimi Castle. Coming directly from the noisy festival in Kyoto, they thought the silence in the castle town was eerie.

Okuni answered back, "We sang prayers to the Ox-Head God to help the lord get well."

"Well, the festival is over."

Indeed, the Gion Festival was over and many had prayed to Buddha and to the myriad of Shinto gods. But those appeals had no effect. Two months later, on September 18, Hideyoshi died at Fushimi Castle at the age of sixty-two. The afternoon following the lord's death, Kanbei called the troupe before him. He greeted them warmly and then gave them generous gifts of money and expensive silk cloth.

"You have served me diligently for a long time. I've decided to live in Hirano for a while. I may summon you later. I don't want you to forget me."

Okuni and the others were dismissed from Kanbei's service as if they had been temporary servants. The members of the troupe bowed their heads politely and gathered up their gifts.

Sankuro asked anxiously, "Is it true the Lord of the Realm has passed away?" Rumors of Hideyoshi's death were rife, but there had been no announcement.

"I wish you good fortune," Kanbei said to Okuni, smiling at her as she left the room. He ignored Sankuro's question.

Sankuro was reluctant to leave and asked another question. "Master Kanbei, who will be the next Lord of the Realm?"

Kanbei glanced briefly at Sankuro through his small eyes and replied without emotion, "The Crown Prince is the heir."

"The lord's son?"

"Naturally. Crown Prince Hideyori. Each lord in the country has sworn an oath."

"What oath is that?"

"An oath to serve Prince Hideyori should Lord Hideyoshi die."

Kanbei had spoken frankly to Sankuro once, giving his opinion that the war in Korea would not last long. He had been foolish to confide valuable, indeed dangerous, information to someone who was hardly higher than a servant. Sankuro could ask as often as he wished, but this time Kanbei did not reveal his true feelings or his insider's knowledge. He looked blandly at Sankuro without giving a hint whether the Lord of the Realm was alive or dead. And he kept to himself his absolute conviction that the nation's next ruler would be Lord Tokugawa Ieyasu.

Thirteen

When Kanbei dismissed them, Okuni and most of the other troupe members immediately thought of going back to the riverbed at Shijo Street. This did not sit well with Sankuro, whose disdain of a common audience had only deepened. The troupe faced an unsettled and dangerous time. Bands of excited samurai galloped in and out of Fushimi Castle every day, terrorizing people along the southern road that connected Fushimi and Osaka Castle. It was clear to everyone in Kyoto that the Lord of the Realm was dead. At least, Sankuro reasoned, Shijo was several miles north of Fushimi and well out of the way of the nervous warriors and their swords. Okuni, of course, was elated at the thought of performing beside Shijo Street again. Kanji and Mame were enthusiastic about using the money Kanbei had given them to build a new wooden theater. In fact, with Kanbei's gifts they could build an even finer theater than the one that had been washed away in the flood. If Sankuro would allow it.

"You can raise the stage floor as high as you want. You can turn the entrance into a damned temple gate, for all I care." Sankuro showed no interest in the kind of theater they would have. Sulking, he let Kanji and Mame take on the responsibility.

Four days passed after Hideyoshi died on September 18, 1598, before the death notice was posted in the city. The announcement said a brief funeral service would be held that day, September 22, in the Hall of the Great Buddha of Hoko Temple to honor his spirit. It struck many people as strange that the passing of such a powerful ruler was so little mourned. In the four days that had transpired, the armies fighting in Korea were told to withdraw and return to their home provinces. It is not clear who issued the order, but thus ended Hideyoshi's grandiose dream of ruling China, Korea, the world.

In those same four days, passersby saw a large, new theater rise in the bed of the Kamo River. It was the most elaborate theater in Kyoto. The back wall of the stage was made of fragrant, freshly cut pine wood. The stage floor of broad, smoothly polished cypress planks was protected by a peaked roof resting on four square pillars. Patrons entered the theater enclosure through a low "mouse door," the high sill of which discouraged gate-crashing by drunken passersby. One guard easily handled the flow of spectators in and out of the small entrance. The troupe's crest was emblazoned on a cloth that was draped around a drum platform rising over the entrance, called the "tower" by theater people. Kanji laid five spears horizontally over the tower as a decoration, following a tradition of traveling Noh troupes who once used the spears to control unruly crowds. Copying the bridgeway of a Noh stage, they built a splendid bridgeway leading onto the stage from the right, to allow them to make long and impressive entrances and exits. In fact, their theater looked very much like a Noh stage, except that the workmanship was inferior and the bridgeway was shorter. Kanji erected a large sign in front of the theater that read "Okuni, the Shrine Maiden from Izumo."

Many people remembered Okuni, so when Mame beat the large drum in the tower in the morning to signal the start of the performance and the bells rang out and the girls' happy voices were heard singing the familiar songs, spectators soon filled the space in front of the stage. Okuni danced vividly, as if all her pent-up feelings were at last being released. Kanji sang better than ever and even Omatsu danced with such energy that her face flushed brightly. When the girls entered the stage dressed in the beautiful Southern Barbarian clothes Kanbei had given them, spectators applauded and cried out in admiration. Nothing in the riverbed compared to the brilliance of Okuni's dancing or to the faddish spectacle the girls presented. Many people enjoyed the show so much they returned three and four times.

They sang along with the girls. They urged Okuni on, clapping out the rhythm as she danced. Okuni looked out at the laughing, happy people in the audience and thought, they don't care if the lord is dead. They enjoyed themselves at the Gion Festival, like I did, singing and drinking and sightseeing. And they didn't bother praying for that shriveled-up, dying little man.

Although audiences crowded the small theater, Sankuro remained aloof from their success. It irritated him to see the kind of people who entered their theater every day. He was already over thirty and this was not what he had expected. His voice was coldly sarcastic as he said, "We're wasted on this riverbed rabble. Our costumes, our performance, everything. We're too good for them."

"Well, Sankuro, isn't that exactly why so many women sit in the audience? They want to see our new *kabuki* fashions so they can copy them. When I'm dancing I see lots of men, too, studying our Southern Barbarian kimonos. We need to be beautiful so people will want to copy the way we look. It's not wasteful, Sankuro."

"You don't have ambition, Okuni. The Lord of the Realm is the only audience that matters to me."

"The Lord of the Realm is dead."

"The young prince is Lord of the Realm. We had a great opportunity when the Lady of the Western Tower saw us perform. But you threw that chance away. I want to know why, Okuni!"

"That again? It's past."

"It's not past. She's the mother of the new Lord of the Realm. If she'd liked you then, we wouldn't be dancing in a riverbed now."

"I'd rather dance in the riverbed than for a woman like that."

"Well, maybe that's what you're worth, Okuni."

Nowadays, when Okuni contradicted Sankuro, as she often did, he would cut her off with a contemptuous remark and stalk out of the theater.

Sankuro was gone, so Okuni directed her hurt and anger at the others. "What does he mean, 'maybe that's what you're worth'? If he thinks he's so wonderful, why did he leave the great Kanze family and the Noh theater? Why is it good to play for important people?

Yes, the riverbed suits me. It's better to dance here by Shijo Street than at Baian's or Kanbei's. Isn't it wonderful when the people here laugh, clap, and sing with us? Well, Densuke, isn't that so?"

Okuni did not follow Sankuro when he left the theater. She knew he was going to his woman in Yanagi Ward and for that reason perhaps she was unconsciously stubborn and argumentative. Unable to agree with Sankuro's ideas, Okuni was beginning to openly quarrel with their troupe leader. This worried Densuke. He wondered what would come of their rift, but he couldn't think of anything he could do. He was caught in the middle. Even though he usually agreed with Okuni, he was afraid to say so.

Every minute Sankuro was gone, Okuni tried to fill the aching void in her heart by rehearsing. Singing, she raised her voice in combat. Her body danced as if to challenge him. I will turn everything I feel into a dance, she vowed.

"Some day, Densuke, I'm even going to dance to your Spinning Song." It was a kind of dare. Could a woman do the dance of a female impersonator?

"It'll be hard," was Densuke's only reply.

Early in 1599 the Lady of the Western Tower moved out of Fushimi Castle and took her child Hideyori, the new Lord of the Realm, to Osaka Castle. Then, in late spring, after the immense Toyokuni Shrine had been erected on the top of Amida Mountain in Kyoto's eastern hills to honor Hideyoshi as a human god, a Bodhisattva, and a guardian of the Japanese nation, Tokugawa Ieyasu occupied Fushimi Castle as his residence. People began to call Ieyasu the Lord of the Realm.

These events confused Okuni. "How can that be?" she asked, amazed. Sankuro glared at Okuni.

No one answered, for they were intimidated by Sankuro's fierce scowl. He could almost taste the bile of his envy. Sankuro had calculated that the Kanze family of Noh performers had buried itself in oblivion when it followed Ieyasu to his provincial fief of Mikawa eleven years ago, and even more so when, four years later, in 1590,

Ieyasu had moved his place of residence to the tiny fishing village of Edo in the distant Kanto district. It was bitter for Sankuro to realize that if Ieyasu became the country's ruler, the Kanze troupe would achieve the fame he had sought all these years. Sankuro could not control his anger: he put down his drum and rushed out of the theater. Once again, he did not come back that night.

Yata, Onei's and Mame's child, was now two years old. Living in the theater, Yata had been surrounded by singing and dancing from the day he was born, and he unconsciously imitated what he saw. Tottering on tiny legs, he would dance a few steps and then fall down. He was adorable and he laughed constantly, even when he fell. Okuni, Onei, and the others clapped and sang to encourage him.

> Little flower,
> Pick the young flower.
> Splash the water,
> Climb the hillside.
> Hide like the deer,
> Little one.

Okuni held her bell out to him. He struck it once before falling down. Again and again he tried to hit the bell and dance. I wish I had a child to teach my dances to, Okuni thought.

Absorbed in Yata's amusing performance, at first they did not notice the stranger entering the theater. Rough clothes scarcely better than a beggar's hid the outlines of a small figure that might have belonged to either a girl or a woman. Straggly hair fell over her face and her feet and legs were coated with dirt. She stood watching. They all sensed her presence at the same time and turned. She pushed back her hair to show a lovely, white face.

"Sister Okuni. Sister Okuni," she called out in a beautiful voice.

Okuni stood up. "Okiku? Is it you?" She could hardly believe that the person in front of her was Okiku. But she could not mistake the voice of the child she had clasped to her breast when she said good-bye more than ten years ago in Nakamura village. Okiku had been six then; now she was a grown woman.

"Yes, it's 'Kiku." They rushed into each other's arms and in an instant they were locked in an anguished embrace. They wept and called each other's name. Gradually Okuni became aware of the mature curves of Okiku's heaving, tired body. And the memory returned to her of the strange excitement she had once felt in Izumo, her throat tightening and her heart pounding wildly, when young Okiku's body had pressed against her. Okiku is not a child, she is a woman, Okuni thought, remembering the long years that had passed.

"But how did you get to Kyoto, Okiku? Did you come alone? How incredible." Okuni looked at Okiku with staring, amazed eyes.

Exhausted and excited, Okiku did not know where to begin. Okuni made her drink hot water and eat some food. Gradually she settled down and began to talk about everything that had happened in Izumo since Okuni went away.

"You know how the Grand Shrine at Izumo used to own twelve villages and seven ports? Well, after you left, we got a new Lord of Izumo and he took most of them away. Not Nakamura village. That's still the same. But the shrine got poorer and poorer. Then the samurai did the Land Survey and after that the lord took more and more of the rice crop. And Okuni, every year the river washes more rice paddies away." The words tumbled out in a torrent.

"The Hii River still floods?"

"Worse then before. Now the Dragon is split in two."

"We used to say, 'the Eight-Legged Dragon is thrashing its legs'." Okuni had always liked the image of the eight channels of the river moving like dragon legs.

"Now it's two separate rivers, Okuni. The sand piled up higher and higher, until half the river started flowing west and half east."

Okuni tried to imagine it and then sighed. She had changed since leaving her home in Nakamura village. Why shouldn't even the course of the Hii River change as well with the passing years?

"How is Okaga? Is she well?"

"Sister Okaga became a nun." It was the custom in the country for a girl to call a playmate "sister," as Okiku called Okuni "sister." But Okiku and Okaga were real sisters, the daughters of Sanemon.

"An official letter came from Osaka saying Yokichi had died work-ing on the riverbank. Sister Okaga cried every day and she couldn't stop. After a while she entered Renga Temple. Father was angry, but she wouldn't listen to him or anyone. She went to the temple and became a nun."

"Didn't she have a child?"

"No."

Okaga had loved Yokichi so much she gave up dancing to marry him. Then her husband was taken away before they had a child. He died and she became a nun. A woman's happiness is so fragile, Okuni thought.

"Sister Okuni. Didn't Kyuzo come?"

Okiku's question pierced Okuni like a knife. "Why?"

"Kyuzo said he was going to look for you when he was sent to the Yodo River. He didn't come?"

Okuni didn't answer. "Well, he must have died, too, then," Okiku said lightly, putting the matter out of her mind. Okaga and Okiku were blood sisters, but Okiku had an independent, resilient, and cheerful nature, quite unlike Okaga.

"So why are you here, Okiku?"

"I've come to dance with you, Sister Okuni. I always wanted to."

It was true, Okiku had wailed and begged to be taken along when Okuni, whom she loved as much as her own sister, had gone off with Sanemon and Okaga. And when Okaga brought back a gorgeous dancing kimono of flower-patterned silk to wear at her wedding with Yokichi, Okiku decided she would go to the capital to dance in a beautiful kimono just like it. But she couldn't leave. Resi-dents of Nakamura village were registered in the Land Survey book and no one, not even a little girl, was allowed to travel outside the vil-lage without special permission. Okiku waited eight years before she finally found a way to come to the capital. She proudly explained what she had done. When the Lord of Izumo took away the land that had supported the Grand Shrine, priests organized bands of pil-grims to sell shrine blessings and thereby add to the shrine's income. The shrine was allowed to sell throughout the country. Okiku decided this was her chance. She gathered her courage and joined a group of pilgrims going in the direction of Kyoto, without telling Sanemon. They had left that spring. It was not an easy journey but the amulets sold readily because Izumo's Grand Shrine was an ancient sacred place. Long before they reached Kyoto, all the talismans were sold and the group started back. At that point Okiku escaped, and after nearly a week of arduous searching she found Okuni's theater.

"It must have been hard." Listening to Okiku's story, Okuni's eyes filled with tears.

"Sister Okuni," Okiku said, as she eagerly put her hands on Okuni's knee and shook her, "let me dance with you. Teach me your songs, please."

"Sanemon must be terribly worried, Okiku."

"Father gave up, I told him so many times I'd find you. He always said I was like you, Okuni."

Okuni held Okiku's hands tightly in hers and looked into Okiku's large, shining eyes. "If you want it, no one can stop you. Dance if you want. And we'll see how you sing."

The next day Okuni was waiting when Sankuro returned to the theater. "I want to teach Okiku," Okuni said ardently.

"She's from Izumo? Hm." He glanced at Okiku without interest. "Go ahead."

Okiku was sleeping blissfully in a corner backstage. Later in the day the boisterous laughing of the audience and the sharp sound of bells and singing woke her. She edged forward eagerly to watch. She was surprised to see that, except for the leaping steps, the dances were not at all like the ones they did in Izumo. She adored the rosary that bounced on Okuni's large breasts as she danced. Looking into the audience, she was amazed by the clothes people were wearing. People in Kyoto were used to Southern Barbarian dress, but Okuni was seeing it for the first time. Wide-eyed, she noticed that the fanciest kimonos were worn by men. Ladies covered their heads with delicate veils, tempting men to peer at their faces. Servants passed dishes of fish and rice to their masters and mistresses, who ate as the show went on. Some men, already drunk, clapped and shouted encouragement to the girls onstage. I'm going to make them applaud for me one day, Okiku thought, her heart racing excitedly. Her attention went back to the stage when Densuke danced to the Spinning Song. When she saw this funny man moving his hips like a woman she laughed until tears came to her eyes. His imitation of a baby learning to walk and talk was even funnier. The idea for the baby routine had come to Densuke the previous day when he was playing with Yata. His fans cheered Densuke and the new sketch. It was a huge success.

Okiku looked at Sankuro playing the drum at the rear of the stage, wondering who he was. His face was somber but she thought she had never seen a more handsome man. In the days that followed Okiku realized he was Okuni's husband. No one told her. She knew by the familiar way they spoke to each other.

For several days Okiku rested. She walked to the river's edge and washed her face in the clear water of the Kamo River. Onei and Okane, whom she had known in Izumo, combed and put up her hair. Okuni gave her a silk kimono. She was small and looked no more than fourteen or fifteen, but Okuni saw with pleasure that she was a beautiful young woman. Okuni set aside most of each morning to personally teach Okiku their songs and dances. Okiku learned quickly. Her singing voice was sweet and clear, so different from Okaga's. And she moved naturally in the dances, displaying her slender body to good advantage. Her talent was immediately apparent. Because she did well, Okuni hugged Okiku and praised her after almost every rehearsal.

"Okiku will be able to dance in the center with me, Sankuro." Okuni sounded like a proud parent when she spoke to Sankuro.

"Oh?" Sankuro had been in a bad mood since the day Ieyasu occupied Fushimi Castle. Nothing pleased him these days, and he made no response to Okuni's excited plans for Okiku.

In the shadow of a fan,
Your eyes allure me.
Oh, my lover,

What shall I do?
Have mercy,
For I am like the dew
On the morning glory.

"Densuke, isn't Okiku's voice beautiful?" Okuni was bursting to tell someone and since Sankuro would not listen, she turned to Densuke.

"Uh-huh."

"And she dances so well. Don't you think she does?"

"Umm."

Okuni floated through each day. She truly loved this girl whose ardent dream of dancing with Okuni had brought them together, as if by fate, after they had been separated for a dozen years. Okuni gave her most valuable kimonos to Okiku without a second thought. She gave Okiku ornaments for her hair and silk cords to tie around her waist. She forgot about herself as she taught Okiku to sing and dance. If she seldom played with Yata any more, it was surely because she was creating her own child.

Densuke was not prepared for this change in Okuni. Certainly, he thought, Okiku has talent, but Okuni's possessiveness toward the girl struck him as somehow unnatural. Then he sighed. When Okuni had wept in his arms on the night of the Gion Festival, wasn't she grieving because she had lost Sankuro's love? Wasn't Okuni merely giving Okiku the passion she no longer could give to Sankuro? Omatsu, too, noticed Okuni's obsession with Okiku. She stared at Okuni, biting her lips to remain silent.

In late summer Okuni declared that Okiku was ready to make her stage debut. Naturally, Okuni made a big thing of it. She would not put Okiku in the chorus with the other girls. In her first performance, Okiku was allowed to perform solo, in the center of the stage. Okuni carefully dressed Okiku in Okuni's most valuable kimono of pink and orange Southern Barbarian silk. Because Okuni was considerably larger than Okiku the long sleeves covered all but the tips of Okiku's fingers. When Okiku started to dance her hands moved in and out of the kimono sleeves in unexpectedly alluring ways.

> I've asked you on rainy nights,
> Let me ask in the full moon:
> Will you change your mind?

Okiku's lips were bright red with the lip rouge Okuni had applied. Her face was flushed with exhilaration. The troupe's steady patrons, caught unawares when she first appeared, were soon captivated by the troupe's new performer. They clapped along with the music and shouted out, "Wonderful," "What a beauty," "Keep dancing." Okuni observed that Okiku's first performance was better than anything Omatsu would ever accomplish. Okiku's mere presence on stage thrilled the audience.

> Plovers of Suma and Akashi,
> Crying in bitterness,
> To ourselves.
> We cry in the capital,
> In the countryside.

"She's wonderful," Okuni sighed, as she watched Okiku dance. Indeed, the audience was captivated by Okiku's presence. Previously Okuni alone had aroused and excited the men and women who came to the riverbed. Okuni was Okiku's most avid spectator. Her attention didn't waver as Okiku spontaneously danced encore after encore. Her eyes clung to Okiku as if she were seeing herself.

That night when Okuni asked, "How did you like Okiku, Sankuro?" he replied with uncharacteristic pleasantness, "We've picked up a good one. If she's trained well, she can be your successor, Okuni."

Okuni felt ecstatic at Sankuro's words, for he seldom spoke well of anything nowadays.

"Do you think so, Sankuro? I think so, too. And the audience liked her."

"Of course. She's young."

Okuni's breath caught in her throat. Okiku was seventeen. Okuni was twenty-eight. Why didn't I noticed the difference in our ages before, she cried out silently.

Fourteen

The war was over in Korea, but in Japan the political situation threatened to explode. Hideyoshi had named Tokugawa Ieyasu as one of the Council of Five Ministers charged with guaranteeing Hideyori's safety and succession. Yet Ieyasu had not only occupied Fushimi Castle, he subsequently moved into Osaka Castle, supported by a large body of troops. Hideyoshi's most loyal generals, now returned from Korea, denounced Ieyasu as a usurper. But most of the ministers spoke of peace, or perhaps they judged Ieyasu to be more powerful than Hideyoshi's heir. Sitting in Osaka Castle, Ieyasu declared himself young Hideyori's protector, a strategy that silenced Ieyasu's opponents for the time being, at least.

Fall passed into winter. Okuni experienced immense pleasure dancing each day with Okiku at Shijo Street. Week by week Okiku became more beautiful and self-assured. Okiku's youthful spirit responded to Okuni's skill. This in turn spurred Okuni to try new ideas in performance. It was a reflection of the times that although reports of impending civil war floated through the capital, people did not seem disturbed. Places of entertainment thrived in the capital. The area around Shijo Street boasted more theaters than when Okuni had first performed there six years before. Several traveling Noh troupes put up theaters in the riverbed next to theirs. The number of pleasure-seekers coming to the riverbed greatly increased as well. Okuni danced before large and loyal audiences in spite of the intense competition. Several young aristocrats were regular customers who passed entire days lounging on rugs and mats spread on the grass, somewhat apart from the townsmen and workers who crowded up to the stage. They hid their faces beneath wide-brimmed straw hats and playfully dressed in Southern Barbarian clothes. They came in elegant disguise, for the riverbed was not a reputable place for a noble to be seen.

> We love, and in love we doubt.
> For whom is my heart
> A tattered hat?
> Cold-hearted,
> Do not wear me,
> I seek another
> To cover with my love.

Summer came. Okuni and Okiku danced joyously each day to a full theater. On one particular afternoon, Sankuro sat alone on the river's edge, withdrawn from the performance, oblivious to the calls and cheers coming from the theater. He dangled his toes in the clear water, letting its coolness flow into his body. He placed his drum on his knee and slowly loosened its red silk cords. It was the small Noh drum, six inches across and about twelve inches long. He had inherited it from his father, who had died while Sankuro was still a boy. When his grandfather had placed the drum in his hands, he had said, strike it hard, you must strike a drum hard to make a good sound.

Sankuro's drum was a symmetrical cylinder, with a taut leather head stretched over a steel ring at the two ends of the cylinder. Each head consisted of doubled leather, a thin skin taken from the belly of a seven-day-old colt on the inside and a thicker skin from the animal's flank on the outside. The body of the drum was a hollowed-out block of cherry wood in the shape of an hourglass. The heads were attached by cords laced between the two steel rings and stretched tight. When the top head was struck, sound reverberated through the drum's narrowing and then expanding waist, producing a slight answering sound, a delicate echo, when it reached the bottom head.

The silk cords controlled the tension of the heads and therefore the pitch of the drum. Using pressure from his left hand, the drummer could tighten the cords to offset the effect of a rainy day or hold them more loosely when it was dry and the head skins were already tight. The drummer held the cords and the narrow body in his left hand, rested the drum against his right shoulder, squeezed the cords to the proper tension, and struck the head with the flat fingers of his right hand. Soft, sharp, or heavy, the tone changed depending on the tension of the cords, the force of the right hand, or the place on the head where the fingers struck. It was said that a fifty-year-old drumhead sounded the best. It must be fifty years since my grandfather played this drum, Sankuro mused. Its sound is brilliant. When will someone of importance hear it?

He struck the drum. The drum sounded. Struck in anger, its sound was magnificent. It echoed over the cold water. Lonely and angry. Brilliant, hard, and beautiful. Sankuro struck and struck, the edges of his mouth stretched as hard in anger and bitterness as the leather of the drumheads. Okuni was a woman without aspirations. It was useless to play for her. If I could return to the Kanze troupe, I would. He laughed mirthlessly. He knew the Kanze troupe would not take him back, especially now. When Ieyasu had moved to Fushimi Castle, the Kanze troupe had followed him. Then when Ieyasu had decided to celebrate the New Year in Osaka Castle, he had summoned the Kanze troupe to Osaka and commissioned the headmaster to stage five days of felicitous Noh dramas in the castle grounds. The news he had just heard was the worst: a week ago Ieyasu had left for Aizu in the north but the Kanze performers, who had already spent six months in Osaka Castle, were settling in for a long stay.

> Man's heart is unknown,
> The true heart is unknown.
> In sad disordered exile,
> We probe each other's thoughts,
> And do not understand.

Sankuro's strong voice and the masterful beats of his drum carried over the flowing water. The sound was so beautiful people crossing Shijo Bridge stopped to listen.

"Hello. You there. Hello." A young man leaning on the bridge railing called down several times before Sankuro heard him. When Sankuro turned to look, he saw a pair of soft eyebrows painted high on a smooth forehead, the unmistakable mark of an imperial courtier. "Aren't you the drummer with the troupe from Izumo?"

"I am, sir."

"You play for the priestess called Okuni. But not today."

"Yes, sir."

"Well, well. I first saw you at Baian's house."

"Ehh?" Sankuro looked carefully at the slender, fair young man gazing down at him. The young man had the confident grace of someone born of aristocratic blood.

"I'm Yamashina Tokio."

"Sankuro at your service, sir."

"So, you don't remember me, Sankuro?"

Sankuro naturally felt apprehensive addressing such a person. His body broke out in a cold sweat as he tried to recall the face, but he couldn't place the elegant young man or his two attendants.

"My father is Yamashina Tokitsune."

"Ah, were you the young master they called Ochamaru?" Sankuro was relieved to be able to dredge up the memory of a small boy clapping happily as he watched Okuni dance.

Tokio smiled at him brightly. "Yes, I was Ochamaru. Now my name is Tokio." When a boy came of age it was customary for him to change his name. "Don't forget it."

"Please forgive me. It was rude that I didn't recognize you, sir." Tokio had been about ten years old then, so he would be, Sankuro quickly calculated, twenty-two or twenty-three now. Sankuro hastily straightened his clothes and bowed.

"It's natural, I was a child then. But I didn't forget you. I've just come from your theater. I'm often there. Didn't you know?"

"I'm grateful, sir. I humbly apologize, sir." He did not know how

to respond. Sankuro seldom noticed the audience when he was playing. He was also careful about looking out into the audience because
samurai and nobles did not like to be stared at. Sankuro thought it
was remarkable that he should meet the child Ochamaru twelve
years later as a grown man. Tokio's next words were even more sur-
prising.

"Come to the imperial palace the day after tomorrow."

At first the words did not register. Sankuro's mouth sagged open
as he stared at Tokio.

"I'm arranging a command performance for the emperor." Looking down at Sankuro, he smiled again. "Do you understand?"

"Yes, yes. What should we prepare, Your Excellency?" Sankuro
was on his knees among the stones of the river edge. His voice broke
and tension constricted his chest in a vise.

Tokio's reply was casual. "What you usually do is fine. The day
after tomorrow, in the afternoon. Come to my house. A servant will
guide you." Saying this, he crossed over Shijo Bridge and disappeared from sight.

On the morning of August 10, 1600, Sankuro, Okuni, and the
other members of the troupe followed their guide to Tokio's mansion
on Imadegawa Street. From there they walked to the Imperial Palace
a few streets away. A servant showed them to the open, grassy area of
a garden separating the Hall of Benevolent Virtue and the Hall of
Silk Brocade. Straw mats were spread on the grass for dancing.
Directly facing the dance area was the building the Emperor favored
for parties, the Hall of Refreshing Purity. While the troupe set up for
performance, Okuni looked around her. Compared even with the
outside of Hideyoshi's extravagant mansions and palaces, the emper-
or's palace was plain. The sliding doors of the Hall of Refreshing
Purity had been removed and Okuni could see the simple room,
undecorated except for a gold-lacquered blind hanging in the center.
How disappointing, she thought, the emperor will be hidden behind
a blind. How can I dance well for someone I can't see?

Okuni's cool reaction was not shared by the others. Okiku,
Okane, Onei, Mame, Kanji, and even Omatsu were nearly frantic

with excitement and awe: in a few minutes they would perform directly before the Son of Heaven, the emperor. For Sankuro, this moment marked the rebirth of his great dream. Tokio and a dozen other nobles entered and moved solemnly over creaking wooden floors to take their assigned places in the hall. After bowing low toward the lowered blind, Tokio turned toward the troupe gathered in the garden and nodded. Sankuro began to sing in a beautiful voice. Mame's drum beat sharply. The girls struck the bells and their voices rose clearly in the warm summer air. Okuni and Okiku danced flawlessly. The small audience gravely watched.

When Okuni stopped dancing, the nobles in the hall bowed toward the golden blind and withdrew. Apparently the emperor had already left. Servants gave them money, kimonos, and a roll of cotton cloth from India. Although this did not compare with Kanbei's usual largess, it was as much as they earned in one month at Shijo Street. No one in the imperial party had laughed or clapped and no one spoke to them now, but Sankuro took the gifts as a sign that the emperor was pleased. Sankuro was elated.

When they returned to Shijo it was still barely noon, but they were too keyed up to perform for the riverbed audience that day. Okiku's eyes sparkled and her cheeks were flushed. She could not stop talking. "Sankuro said a refined audience is best and he's right. Imagine dancing for the emperor himself! I felt so light. I can't dance like that in the riverbed. It's much better to dance for cultivated people."

Okuni was the youngest member of the troupe and the least experienced, and Okuni was offended by her supercilious prattle. "The people in the riverbed are our true audience. They clap and sing and are part of our performance. I won't have you say you don't like them."

Okiku felt ashamed to have been rebuked by Okuni and stopped talking. But Sankuro snickered, baiting Okuni. "There's so much you don't like, Okuni." Yata began to cry and wouldn't stop. Sankuro went outside, saying crossly, "Noisy kid." After he cooled off, he returned, and they all silently went to bed. But in the deep of the night, few of the company could sleep.

The next day Tokio came to the riverside carrying unexpectedly good news. His appointment at court was undemanding, and he was left with a good deal of free time to devote to private pursuits. That day he was coming to the riverbed on just such a private errand.

"You did well at the palace yesterday. Both the emperor and his consort liked you, and she wants to see you again. Come to my house tomorrow afternoon."

The emperor's consort, Sakiko, was from the Konoe family, one of the five imperial lines. She was the daughter of former Regent Konoe Sakihisa. Although most people no longer remembered it, when Hideyoshi was campaigning to be appointed shogun, he adopted her and presented her to Emperor Goyozei as a consort. It had been Baian's plan to connect Hideyoshi to the aristocracy and so bolster his claim to the title but of course nothing came of it. Sakiko, who had become the emperor's mistress at the age of eighteen, was now twenty-six. She was the emperor's favorite and the mother of seven imperial princes and princesses. Her family was not only politically important but highly versed in poetry and the arts, and since Emperor Goyozei did not have a wife, she was the dominant female presence in the palace. She was vivacious and headstrong in personality, and very fond of taking up new fashions.

Okuni took the invitation pleasantly. "Sankuro, why doesn't Densuke do his funny Spinning Song dance?"

Sankuro dismissed the idea out of hand. "That outdated slapstick! How could we dare show that to Lady Konoe?" By saying "outdated," Sankuro was deriding the folk origin of Densuke's act, the crude longevity skits and dances priests had put on in the old days. Remembering the Lady of the Western Tower's reaction, Okuni thought that perhaps Sankuro was right and she did not argue with him.

The next day the troupe went to Tokio's house and from there they were led into a large open courtyard on the grounds of the Konoe family mansion. When the Konoes sponsored official court dances, this was where they erected a meticulously built and carpeted dancing stage enclosed by a thick red railing. Today, a beautiful stage was not in evidence, but rather a dozen rough wooden planks had been laid flat on the ground to form a square. The August sun poured down unrelentingly, and the troupe members were nearly dizzy from the heat. Even in the riverbed, Okuni thought, their theater had a roof overhead that kept them cool when they danced. Nor was there a bridgeway for entrances and exits as there was in a Noh theater. Okuni frowned, but they had to get ready to perform immediately, so she couldn't consider what it meant for them to be dancing in such poor circumstances before an imperial audience.

The Lady Sakiko and a large group of court ladies, attendants, and friends of Tokio's were already gaily eating and drinking when they began the performance. In the middle of the Buddhist Prayer Dance, just before Okuni took off the straw hat to reveal her face, Lady Sakiko's small voice was heard from behind the blind.

"It is hot. Will someone not bring me snow from Korea?" The Lady's maids quickly rolled up the gold-lacquered blind separating their mistress from Okuni, for everyone present knew the classic Chinese poem she was referring to. And they knew the famous episode in *The Pillow Book,* Sei Shonagon's personal diary of life in the ancient court, in which she had raised the blind when Empress Teishi quoted this line. Ostensibly, Lady Sakiko had asked for the blind to be lifted because of the heat, but in fact she wanted to see Okuni better.

When Okuni saw Lady Sakiko, she was struck by her innocent and unaffected attitude. Okuni thought she had the fair skin, open eyes, and plump cheeks of a child. On the spur of the moment Okuni decided to dance the Water Wheel Song for Lady Sakiko, for it had once been a children's song.

> Water wheel on the Yodo River,
> Do you wait for someone,
> Turning, turning, turning?

Lady Sakiko laughted delightedly, for she recognized the song as an improvisation on a verse from *The Tale of the Heike.*

Water wheel on the Uji River,
For whom in this floating world
Do you turn?

She turned to her entourage and said, "She's called 'Kuni. Isn't she the Best in the World?" She used the popular expression deliberately, to show her familiarity with fashions outside the court. Several ladies chorused, "As you say, my Lady, Best in the World." And they laughed decorously.

That afternoon, Lady Sakiko enjoyed the troupe's presentation so much she had Okuni repeat many of the dances. She laughed often and clapped her hands when Okuni sang a clever line or when Okiku danced especially well. When darkness came, servants lit a bonfire in the garden. They danced until late at night. Lady Sakiko's attendants murmured to themselves that they could not remember when their mistress had enjoyed herself more. After this success, other nobles invited them to their mansions as well. And so, throughout the late summer, the troupe embarked on a round of private performances at homes of important members of the imperial family. Each time, Tokio sent a messenger with an order to appear at his house at a certain hour and day. Invitations were sent to him and he made whatever arrangements were necessary. It was as if he had become their manager and they were at his disposal. The atmosphere was usually gay and pleasant at these informal parties so Okuni did not object to performing there, although she still preferred the audience at the riverside. Okiku, on the other hand, relished being seen by a cultivated audience and Sankuro was exhilarated at this unexpected turn in their fortunes. After the shogun, an imperial noble was the next best patron, he thought.

"Is the Lord of the Realm the master of the emperor?" Okuni naively asked one day.

"Of course not. The emperor is greater. Even the lord must bow to him. And the lord is given his title by the emperor."

"Then why did you want to perform for the lord all those years instead of for the emperor?"

Sankuro flared, his usual asperity suddenly returning. "The emperor is highest, but the lord has more power, Okuni."

"Even if the lord is only six years old?"

As if she hadn't spoken, Sankuro went on, "I've told you before, the lord owns everything in the country. He takes any amount of rice or gold he wants. He gives the emperor gold so the emperor can live."

"If the emperor is the highest why doesn't he take the gold himself?"

"Because the lord commands the soldiers. Let's drop it. You'll never understand." And returning to his old patterns, Sankuro abruptly ended the conversation and strode outside.

One stifling morning at the very end of summer they were resting in the theater when Mame ran in saying that Fushimi Castle was being attacked. "They say war has started again."

At last, the jockeying for advantage between Tokugawa Ieyasu and supporters of Hideyori was at an end. Upon hearing that the Lord of Aizu had declared himself for Hideyori, Ieyasu led a large army of foot soldiers and mounted warriors from Osaka Castle and began marching north toward Aizu. Allies of Ieyasu raised another 70,000 men and waited in Edo. Ieyasu's armies were now three weeks' march to the north of Kyoto. It was the opportunity Hideyori's supporters had been waiting for. Minister Ishida Mitsunari, Hideyori's most forceful advocate among the Council of Five Ministers, ordered his troops to attack Fushimi Castle. It was now only lightly defended and certain to fall.

"Who's inside the castle?"

"Retainers of Lord Ieyasu."

"And who's attacking the castle?"

"Lots of soldiers from western Japan. More are on the way."

"They're against Lord Ieyasu?"

"They support the Lord of the Realm, Prince Hideyori."

"Will they capture the castle?"

"Nobody knows. They might, they have Southern Barbarian guns. They aren't doing anything yet, just sitting outside shooting into the castle."

For ten days the western army gradually consolidated its position for the final assault. There were feints and skirmishes along the outer walls to test the castle defenses. The defenders were called on to surrender, with no result. Had members of the troupe looked up they would have noticed that traffic across the bridge was heavier than usual. Hardly anyone was coming into the riverbed to see them perform.

Finally, Okuni announced that she was going to Fushimi. The girls looked frightened, but Sankuro and Densuke immediately agreed.

"Yes, let's watch the battle."

Early in the afternoon of September 7, 1600, Okuni, Sankuro, and Densuke changed into inconspicuous clothes, packed some food, and started walking south toward Fushimi. The castle was only a few miles from where their theater stood on the east side of the Kamo River next to Shijo Street. Okiku and Omatsu followed at a safe distance. Their plan was not as dangerous as it might seem; for they knew the area well, having lived at Kanbei's house. Fushimi Castle was separated from the town by forests and a hill. Taking back streets and seldom-used paths so they wouldn't be seen, they arrived in the late afternoon and climbed to the top of the hill. Several hundred townspeople were sitting on the grass, as if picnicking. Looking down, they could see the castle and the soldiers surrounding it. Muskets were going off constantly. They followed the path of fire arrows arcing high and then falling inside the castle grounds. Smoke and fire rose from the Western Tower. Soon masses of soldiers, looking like columns of ants, swarmed up and over the castle walls. A part of the Inner Citadel crumbled and slid into a moat like an avalanche of snow. Defenders on the ramparts were cut and pierced by attacking soldiers. They toppled off the walls, making slow cartwheels in the air. Distant sounds of guns, battle drums, and moaning conch shells drifted up the hillside. People must have been shouting and others screaming in agony, but these sounds did not reach the spectators on the hilltop. It was like watching a play staged for children, with toy soldiers fighting for a toy castle.

Okuni watched Fushimi Castle burn through the night. At dawn a muffled cheer of victory signaled the end. In truth, the Inner Citadel of Fushimi Castle had been a golden, shining jewel, its luxurious decorations even more beautiful than those of Juraku Mansion. Hideyoshi had built Fushimi Castle to be unconquerable, but Hideyoshi's soldiers destroyed it. The subjects of the lord have burned the lord's castle, Okuni thought. How strange. Okuni was exhausted, and she clung to Sankuro's sleeve as they walked home in the morning. She could not get the thought from her mind: first the lord builds a castle and then it is torn down. Yodo Castle, Juraku Mansion, and now Fushimi Castle. Something that takes such effort to create is so easily destroyed. Why is that, she wondered.

Minister Mitsunari ordered workers to obliterate all traces of Fushimi's walls and moats and with his army marched south to occupy Osaka Castle. There he gathered two armies totaling some 90,000 men and dispatched them north in two columns. He would attack Ieyasu from the south while the soldiers from Aizu attacked Ieyasu from the north. They would crush the usurper of Hideyori's rights between the jaws of two powerful armies. In all, nearly 300,000 soldiers were being marshaled for the coming battle that would, it was said, decide the fate of the nation.

A few days after the battle of Fushimi Castle, the troupe received an order from Tokio to perform at one of his friend's garden parties. Even Sankuro was surprised. The invitation was not to be refused, however, and they went out to perform the next day. This small event in the lives of ordinary performers showed that only the samurai were involved in the military conflict. The common people of Kyoto carried on their daily lives undisturbed. Even the imperial nobility did not care.

When the heat of late summer gradually passed and as the cooler days of autumn returned, the trees along the Kamo River began to change their coloring from deep green to yellow, to orange and then red. Throughout the fall, when the troupe was not entertaining at a noble's party, they danced in the riverbed. People brought tea and hot rice wine to warm their stomachs in the autumn wind. They spread mats and rugs on the ground and bundled up against the increasing chill. Okuni and the others were absorbed in dancing and singing, as were the spectators, and they forgot about the war.

> I wait for a lover,
> Who is fickle as the floating grass.
> I sadly yearn
> And drift into sleep,
> As the moon sets.

It was Sankuro's idea to get rid of the mouse door that traveling Noh troupes had invented many years ago to discourage gate crashing. He had Mame and Kanji build a large double door, like a Buddhist temple gate. Now people had a clear view of the girls dancing on the raised stage when they passed by. They stopped to watch. This in turn attracted more people. It was a cold spectator who was not lured into the theater when the door was being closed, with a ponderous creaking sound, in his face. It was a clever come-on.

"Wait. Wait, I tell you." A man carrying a black dog hurried up as Mame was swinging the heavy door closed.

Mame went into his usual patter as he turned back from the door. "If you don't hurry, you'll miss the dancing. Step lively. Pay your money and see the show."

"Money, eh." Kyuzo growled. He reached under his sash and pulled out a pouch tightly closed with drawstrings.

"Hey, that dog can't come in."

"No? Why not?"

"He'll annoy people."

"He won't, but here's money for two." He slapped the coins into Mame's hand and pushed into the theater. Okuni was standing on stage, singing emotionally with her arms stretched out to the audience. Kyuzo, gazing fiercely at Okuni, held the dog so tightly they were like one person, hard and unmovable as a rock. This wasn't the childish Okuni he had parted from in Izumo. This was a mature, voluptuous woman. Her colorful sleeves were butterflies fluttering in circles around pure white arms. Her legs opened like flowers in bloom when she raised her feet to dance. Her face was flushed, eyelids pink and half-closed, and her red lips were slightly parted. She had a smile that suggested some private ecstasy. This woman is Okuni? Although it was cool, sweat poured from Kyuzo's body. Kyuzo was becoming sexually aroused and he hated her for it.

When Kyuzo looked around the theater he saw that most of the spectators were young men, dandies out for a good time, the same kind of customers that frequented the Court Maidens. They were ogling Okuni. Many were inflamed by drink and by the rhythm of her dancing body. When he realized this, his heart hammered with a furious, jealous rage. He felt a snake writhing in his bowels.

> I cannot meet my love,
> In dream,
> Or on the mountain of reality.
> Today is the past of tomorrow,
> Yesterday the past of today.
> Love passes in a dream, a dream.
> Have mercy,
> Cruel dream.

Kyuzo thought he would suffocate watching Okuni. Then she disappeared from the stage and in her place three women entered along the bridgeway dancing. Kyuzo did not know Omatsu, on his right, but he recognized Onei, on the left. When he saw that the girl dancing in the center was Okiku, he almost shouted out. She shouldn't be in Kyoto, she should be back in Izumo. Now that Okuni was out of sight, the stifled feeling in his chest gradually dissipated and he regained his usual composure. When Densuke entered, the audience began to clap and shout. People roared with laughter at his simpering impersonation of a woman singing the Spinning Song. Kyuzo watched the scene with a sneer on his face and cruel contempt glittering in his eyes. How could this creature be Okuni's lover? It was unbelievable. But she had said he was and so had he, so it couldn't be doubted. Kyuzo's flesh crawled.

His eyes moved to the back of the stage where Kanji was striking the bell. Next to him Sankuro sat expressionless, playing the drum.

"Him? Why, that's the fellow that comes to the whorehouse," Kyuzo growled. Kyuzo pressed on his chest to calm his breathing. He took his purse, opened it, and deliberately counted out twice the number of coins that Densuke had given him. He slowly rose to his feet.

Abruptly the black dog barked.

Surprised by the unexpected sound, people turned. Kyuzo threw the coins as hard as he could at Densuke dancing on the stage. Then, without saying a word, he turned on his heel and went out, Black running behind him, barking loudly. The barking continued in the direction of Shijo Street until it was no longer heard.

"Densuke, that's a nice bit of money. Do you know who it was?" Sankuro asked when they closed the theater that evening.

"No. I only saw his back."

"I wonder if I've seen him around. Hm." Sankuro thought it over but he did not recognize the hurrying figure as Kyuzo.

Sankuro and Densuke didn't attach any significance to the incident. Pleased spectators often threw coins onto the stage. It was the accepted way to tip entertainers in the street. Of course, Mame collected an admission fee from each person who entered the theater. Still, it was common enough for fans to shower coins on a favorite like Densuke. When Densuke came offstage and told Okuni excitedly that the man had thrown more than thirty silver coins onstage, she felt uneasy. Puppet theaters had started coming into the riverbed to take advantage of the many customers drawn there by the troupe's dancing and other entertainments. The women in the puppet companies were known to be prostitutes, and Okuni wondered if their appearance in the riverbed had anything to do with Densuke's large gift of money. Did prostitutes in the puppet troupes collect money during performances that way?

One afternoon that autumn, when their audience was small, Tokio came to the theater with an attendant. In the midst of the performance the nobleman got up and strolled out, leaving his attendant behind. At the end of the performance, the attendant came backstage with a message. "Come to Tokio's house," he said, looking at Okiku, and he walked out of the theater.

"What is this about?" Okuni asked suspiciously.

"Well, he wants Okiku alone," Sankuro replied, showing no emotion.

"Why does he want Okiku alone?" As soon as she spoke, Okuni realized it was a foolish question. She tried to gloss over the situation. "It must be a court noble's idea of a practical joke. Or the attendant is trying to trick us. What a thing to say. It's funny." Okuni tried to laugh. It was a hollow laugh that no one joined.

"No, it's not a joke and it's not a trick. He wants Okiku alone," Sankuro said forcefully, folding his arms.

Okuni responded with fury, "Well, refuse. Okiku isn't a loose girl. You tell him clearly she's not a prostitute and that she won't go."

When Sankuro remained silent and no one else spoke up, Okuni felt apprehensive. "You're going to refuse, aren't you, Sankuro? Do you want us to sell ourselves like women in puppet troupes do? Should we be whores like them? If he needs a woman, he shouldn't come here. Let him go to Yanagi Ward. And if Lord Tokio doesn't know where it is, you can show him, Sankuro!"

Her grievance, pent up inside for so long and even now not risen to the level of consciousness, triggered Okuni's outburst on behalf of Okiku and of course herself. She said what she had never intended to say. Sankuro stood with his arms folded, staring at Okuni's face, silent as a mute. Okuni's words poured out in a torrent. "Lord Tokio is only a court noble, isn't he? He isn't a warrior. He doesn't wear swords, he can't kill you. You're thinking Lord Tokio introduced us to the emperor and to his lady, aren't you, Sankuro? You think if you refuse, Lord Tokio won't invite us again. We don't care. If there's no emperor and no Lord of the Realm, we can dance in the riverbed and not be afraid of anyone, Sankuro. We don't need the emperor or a child Lord of the Realm. We don't need them! You should get rid of those ideas, Sankuro!"

Sankuro did not disguise the pain he felt listening to Okuni's uncharacteristic tirade.

Okiku was intently watching Sankuro's face in profile. She turned quietly to Okuni and said, as if to soothe her, "It's all right. I'll go."

That was the last thing Okuni expected to hear. "What are you saying, Okiku? Don't you know why he's invited you?"

"Of course I know. I'm not a child."

Even Sankuro looked at Okiku in surprise. Okuni went on, "Okiku, you're not a prostitute. You're the daughter of Sanemon, from Nakamura village in Izumo."

"I'm a *kabuki* woman in a dance company."

"Being a *kabuki* dancer isn't a disgrace. You can't go to Lord Tokio's house. I won't let you."

Okiku's tone was openly mocking. "Sister Okuni, if you were invited, wouldn't you go?"

"Me?" Okuni was flustered by the turn in the conversation. "Why would I go? Sankuro is my husband."

"Are you positive that's the reason?"

"What do you mean?"

"I think you're jealous Lord Tokio invited me and not elder sister Okuni."

"How can you say such a thing, Okiku!" Okuni turned hot with anger and her lips trembled.

Okiku continued, coolly, "I haven't got a husband and Lord Tokio doesn't displease me. He wants me. I'm happy to go."

"Don't sell yourself like a street whore, Okiku!"

"Ah, then it's all right if I'm not paid?"

"He only wants to play with you."

"Well, that's up to the woman's skill, isn't it? Whether a man plays or stays?"

Okuni caught her breath. What kind of girl could utter such terrible words? Is this Okiku? Is this the girl Okuni had held in her arms in Izumo? Okiku turned away and began to dress, indifferent to the accusing eyes around her. She deftly put on her best kimono and added heavy rouge to her cheeks and lips. Okiku was aware of her attractive body and while she adjusted her hair, she proudly thrust out her breasts. At the same time, Sankuro changed his clothes.

"Sankuro, where are you going?"

"I'll take her. A woman shouldn't go out alone." He led the way out of the theater. Okiku followed close behind. After hesitating for a moment, Okuni picked up Sankuro's drum and ran after them.

"Sankuro!" She caught up to them as they were crossing Shijo Bridge. Sankuro took the drum from her without a word and continued on his way. Okiku didn't look at Okuni.

"Don't come home late." Okuni knew how foolish she sounded. Her voice trailed off as she watched them go.

The attendant at Tokio's house would not admit Sankuro. Sankuro, however, insisted on meeting Tokio, if only for a moment. Tokio bristled at Sankuro's impertinent request. He had not sent for Sankuro. He was eagerly waiting for the girl. Brusquely he told the attendant, "In the garden. Just him."

Sankuro was forced to prostrate himself face down in the dirt of the garden, while Tokio looked out coldly from inside the house, not even bothering to approach along the verandah.

"Speak." It was a haughty command, addressed to an inferior.

Until now, Sankuro had supposed that the smiling young nobleman was genuinely friendly. In previous meetings, the fact that Tokio was an aristocrat and Sankuro a drum player had not been an issue. It was galling to grovel in the dirt like a servant. But Sankuro did not let pride distract him from his purpose in coming.

He pressed his face to the ground. "Your Lordship is a noble in the house of the emperor to whom all events in the world are known. I beg to ask Your Lordship what will happen in the coming war." Sankuro spoke as flatteringly as he dared.

"Do you mean you want to know who will become the next Lord of the Realm?"

"Yes, Your Lordship."

Tokio held the most junior rank in court and he had never been asked an important question before. He was pleased.

"Do dancers and musicians in the riverbed worry about such things?"

"I do, Your Lordship."

"Well, if you, a trifling person, want to know the war's outcome, imagine how desperately the samurai who are fighting would like to know." Amused by his clever sally, Tokio tittered in a shrill, womanish voice. "Well, things are in an uproar, don't you think, Sankuro?"

"As Your Lordship says." Baian and Kanbei were gone. But Okuni's taunt required an answer. Sankuro patiently waited for Tokio to continue.

"Still, the question of who rules the world should not perturb the imperturbable. In Kyoto we are not perturbed. Chance decides who wins a war and who loses it. The winner will be received at court, the loser will not. That is all. Do you see, Sankuro?"

"Yes, Your Lordship."

Tokio had been drinking while waiting for Okiku. Slightly flushed, he continued to lecture Sankuro, enjoying the feeling of superiority it gave him. "The victors come to the capital, they build rich buildings, they present the emperor with gold, they lavish money on the Five Imperial Families trying to buy their favor. They are social upstarts coming to us to decorate their rule, coming to us to refine their vulgar warriors' manners. Nobunaga and Hideyoshi did it. And two hundred years ago the Ashikaga shoguns did the same. Since my family is custodian of court etiquette regarding official dress, generals beg us to instruct them in the proper way to appear at court."

Tokio began telling with great relish anecdotes of ancestors who had taught newly risen warriors, for a price, how to cover the worst defects of their country upbringing. Sankuro knew nothing about the subject, and he was soon bored with Tokio's stories. He repeated his original question, "Then who do you think will win this war?"

Tokio was irritated that he had been interrupted. He stared icily down at Sankuro, his delicate face showing his utter disdain; Sankuro had not understood one word he had said. "It does not matter who the winner is. He will be the one who comes to the palace. When he does, I will be waiting."

The smooth white face disappeared into the mansion's depths, as if swallowed by the darkness where Okiku waited. Sankuro was dismissed and told to return in the morning for Okiku. He turned toward Yanagi Ward, determined to erase this distasteful experience from his memory.

Lighting with oil had recently come within the reach of commoners living in the capital. The prostitutes' quarter was especially radiant, glowing in the light of hundreds of small flames. Lamps burned in windows and in lanterns on the street. When Sankuro passed into the brightly lit entry of the Court Maidens, Kyuzo abruptly pushed him back. Caught off-balance, Sankuro fell heavily in the dirt. He looked up at Kyuzo, astonished rather than angry. "Didn't you see it was me? I was just walking in."

"Don't come here again! Never!" Kyuzo shouted violently.

"What are you talking about? Why not?"

"You know the regulations of the licensed quarter. Riverside beggars aren't allowed to enter a house of prostitution."

"What?" Sankuro turned red.

"You have nerve, crawling up here from your shack by the river to buy a woman. What's that under your arm? A drum? Get out of here."

Sankuro stood up, yelling furiously, "I'm a regular customer. You just work here. Treat me with respect."

Kyuzo folded his arms on his chest and laughed deeply. "Respect? You? If you don't shut up I'll call the police. Not a girl in the Court Maidens would dirty herself sleeping with a beggar entertainer from the riverbed. They are all above you. Or if you don't want to go, why don't you walk through the center of Yanagi Ward and announce it: 'I'm a filthy entertainer from the riverbed, what house will take me in?' Or should I do it for you?"

Sankuro was enraged at Kyuzo's calling him a "riverbed beggar." This insulting slang, for performers who made their living along the Kamo River, was just entering the popular argot of Kyoto. Each time he heard it, Sankuro bridled at the unfair insult. He was descended from a family of Noh performers. He was not a beggar.

People gathered around to see the sideshow. It was fun to watch a whorehouse pimp get the best of a customer. Sankuro was furious and shamed. And he knew it was the law. Regulations that were two hundred years old prohibited entertainers from mixing with prostitutes. That was why Sankuro had worn the Southern Barbarian clothes as a disguise when he first came to Yanagi Ward. He had been foolish to bring the drum with him tonight. He had no choice but to accept his humiliation and leave. He cursed between clenched teeth, "Damn Okuni!" He blamed her for everything. He hated her.

Kyuzo's taunts followed him. "I know your face. Don't show up in Yanagi Ward again."

The owner of the Court Maidens wondered what the shouting was about. It was unlike Kyuzo, he thought.

Kyuzo entered the owner's room and spoke quietly. "It was just a riverbed entertainer from Shijo Street. He tried to come in. I sent him away."

"You're always careful, Kyuzo. Thank you for taking care of it."

The two men did not speak for several minutes, the master comfortable in the silence of old age, Kyuzo physically gripped by powerful emotions. Kyuzo ended the silence.

"Master?"

"Yes?"

"Some of the theater women along Shijo Street sell themselves to men."

"I've heard that."

"We can't ignore their competition. Many of our customers go to the riverbed."

"Hm. I wonder what we should do."

"Yes, Master, I wonder."

A dark light flickered in the depths of Kyuzo's eyes. Kyuzo was still inwardly trembling with excitement. The palpable animal pleasure of publicly debasing the man from Okuni's troupe had not subsided. It would be more gratifying to degrade the effeminate comedian Okuni calls her husband, he mused, but even this thought didn't satisfy him. The fact that he still wanted to cry out, that he felt an implacable desire for revenge against Okuni, was assurance that he was alive. Kyuzo found solace in his profound rancor.

Fifteen

On October 21, 1600, Tokugawa Ieyasu's 80,000 warriors, drawn from the eastern and northern fiefs, triumphed over the western armies of Hideyori on the reedy plain of Sekigahara. This was indeed the battle that decided the fate of the nation. It lasted half a day. Ieyasu's first public act as the victor was to execute the generals he had defeated. In the warm morning sun Minister Ishida Mitsunari was paraded in a wooden cage through the streets of the capital to the riverbank at Rokujo Street. He stood under a canopy of maple leaves flaming orange-red, his neck bound in an iron collar, as he calmly waited to die. He was flanked by two of Hideyori's faithful supporters, the Buddhist warrior-monk Ankokuji Ekei, and Konishi Yukinaga, the Kirishitan general who had led his troops brilliantly in the Korean campaigns. People from all around Kyoto gathered behind picket fences to gape as they might at a festival. In midafternoon, under a clear sky, soldiers with spears pierced Mitsunari, Ankokuji, and Yukinaga, front and back, and sword-bearing soldiers lopped off their heads with a single slash.

Because the execution was a free show and only two blocks down river from Shijo Street, no spectators paid to enter the theater that day. Okiku and Kanji hurried off to the execution site. When they returned and tried to describe the event, Kanji was distraught. "It was terrible. Lord Mitsunari was as thin as a corpse, but his blood spurted in the air after they cut his neck."

"His face was writhing in a grimace when his head fell on the ground!" Okiku was giddy with excitement. She laughed and imitated the yelling crowd. She described details of the execution in a high-pitched voice, as if she were in a delirium.

"Okiku, we saw the execution of the regent's ladies, but it wasn't like this," Mame said, trying to calm her.

"His women were killed? I wish I'd seen that. I hope they kill some women again." Her eyes shone unnaturally. Okuni felt so sick she turned her back. Okiku's behavior shocked the others, too, and they found excuses to move away. Sankuro was restless and not listening. He was thinking of the Kanze troupe and Ieyasu's patronage. He walked out of the theater and stood pondering, arms folded, by the clear flowing stream.

"Sankuro." Okiku stood next to him, her skin hot and flushed and her eyes glowing like an animal's. "I know why you're angry. Okuni doesn't have ambition. I'm different. I want to do better than dance in *this* place." She tossed her head contemptuously toward the theater. She looked full into his face and smiled. "I'm younger than Okuni. Teach me. I can dance to your drum better than she does."

She touched his arm coquettishly and leaned her breasts close to his body. She is twelve years younger than Okuni, Sankuro thought. He stood quietly, considering Okiku for the first time as a woman. Okiku licked her lips and smirked wantonly.

Sankuro's smile was cynical. "What a fickle woman you are, Okiku. Is that what you picked up at Tokio's?"

When he turned his back, her scream was like silk tearing, "Because you didn't speak! Who took me to his house? You did!"

"What?"

"All the way there, I waited for you. If you'd touched my shoulder, I was ready to fall on your chest."

"Really?"

"What kind of wife is Okuni? She sleeps beside me every night. You don't make love to her and you don't get along. Still Okuni says, 'Sankuro is my husband.' I have to keep from laughing. It's like a line from a song."

"Okiku!"

This time, Okiku turned her back on him. Laughing, she ran into the theater. She knew how to lead a man by the nose.

Often at night Sankuro thought bitterly of the Kanze Noh troupe and its patron, Tokugawa Ieyasu. Ieyasu was a cautious and deliberate person, unlike Hideyoshi, who had acted on impulse so many times. Gradually and without incident, Ieyasu consolidated his position. Since no other warlord felt strong enough to challenge him after his victory at Sekigahara, Ieyasu tacitly began to occupy the position of Japan's supreme ruler. In Kyoto people were adjusting to the new regime. An influx of country warriors from Mikawa, Ieyasu's home province in the east, replaced Hideyori's supporters. Among performers, the striking beneficiaries of Ieyasu's rule were the Noh actors of the Kanze family, who had followed him for more than a dozen years.

That winter was cold and wet. As the long nights continued, Sankuro increasingly found himself thinking of Okiku, lying nearby. She replaced the Kanze troupe in his thoughts.

In the spring of 1601, rich veins of gold were discovered on Sado Island, which faces the Japan Sea on the back side of Japan. Ieyasu put Kanbei in charge of a new goldsmithing district in Fushimi, where the gold ore mined in Sado was brought to be minted into coins. Kanbei was appointed to this lucrative position because he had gained the cautious ruler's complete trust. Pleading old age, Kanbei seldom went out, and people who had business with him came to his house in Fushimi, always bearing some gift of jewels, gold, silver, or precious articles from Europe or India. Ieyasu was a conservative country warrior who did not approve of lavish display or new fashions. Even though Ieyasu was currently far away in the north and east, strengthening his political alliances, Kanbei was careful to do nothing flamboyant that might be adversely reported. And so, in spite of his immense wealth and his influence within the new government, Kanbei led what amounted to a hermit's life. Okuni's former patron had no occasion to invite her to entertain the plain, dour men who served Ieyasu. The fact was that Kanbei was too busy working to be able to enjoy himself.

"It's still pouring."

"Um. Everything's clammy."

"Will the Kamo River flood again?"

"If it doesn't stop raining it might."

Although the rainy season of June had passed, rain continued without letup through the summer. People were listless, as if their minds as well as their bodies were sodden with water.

"Densuke."

"Yes, Okuni?"

"The sound of the rain."

"Um?"

"The tone changes. Strong, weak, it strikes, it pounds. Sometimes it sounds like weeping."

Okuni sighed. She was making casual conversation and Densuke was the only person around. He sat pensively, listening to Okuni without speaking. Inasmuch as spectators had to sit in the open without protection from the rain, performances in the riverbed had long since ceased. Troupe members did as they pleased to pass the time. Usually Sankuro and Okiku went out together during the day. Okuni never asked Sankuro where he was going. She assumed Tokio was whiling away the rainy days with Okiku and that Sankuro was accompanying her. Perhaps he went to Yanagi Ward, too. It didn't matter any more.

"Can you dance in the rain, Densuke?"

"I don't know. But I wish we could do a rain dance. One to stop the rain instead of start it." Densuke smiled and slowly got to his feet. He danced while he improvised a comic song about the rain. Okuni burst out laughing, then said, "Tomorrow the weather will clear for certain." Densuke coughed and cleared his throat. He had felt tired for several months. He lay down, pulled a padded kimono around his chest, and tried to sleep.

The weather did not clear. Earthquakes and bad weather continued through the year, but perhaps because of Densuke's prayer dance, the Kamo River did not flood. Some grumbled that Hideyoshi's angry spirit was punishing Japan.

The seasons returned to normal in the spring of 1602. The people of Kyoto were glad the wars were over. They enjoyed the lush cherry blossoms and the warm days the blossoms ushered in. During the clear summer days Ieyasu had Fushimi Castle restored, and he built a new residence for himself in upper Kyoto at Nijo Street.

"Who is going to live in Fushimi Castle now?" Okuni asked.

Sankuro replied sardonically, "What does it matter? You don't want to perform there." Okiku laughed and looked slyly at Okuni. Okuni was aware of a change in their relationship, but thought it was because they disagreed about Okiku seeing Tokio.

Splendid weather continued throughout that year. On a bright, cool afternoon the following February, a small body of warriors from Mikawa entered Kyoto. It was Ieyasu and his personal bodyguard. Ieyasu established himself in Fushimi Castle and waited. On March 24, 1603, Emperor Goyozei conferred on Ieyasu the titles of Imperial Minister of the Right, Leader of the Genji Clan, Protector of the Junna and Shogaku Academies, and, most coveted of all, Great Barbarian-Subduing Commander, or Sei Tai Shogun. Two of the highest imperial nobles lead a magnificent procession from the emperor's palace through the streets of the capital to Fushimi Castle to make known the Imperial Proclamation. People openly spoke of a "new era of shoguns."

"Why does the emperor call Lord Ieyasu 'Shogun' ?" Okuni put her simple question to Densuke. Sankuro was in the theater, but she did not care to endure another condescending reply.

"Well, it's the same thing as Lord of the Realm. Maybe it's an older word. There were shoguns before but I don't know much about it."

Sankuro knew a great deal about it. Elders of the Kanze troupe never ceased to tell the story of their past greatness. In ancient times, four great Noh troupes had been attached to the Kofuku Temple in Nara—the Kanze, the Hosho, the Komparu, and the Kongo. Then, boasted the elders, Yoshimitsu, the second Ashikaga shogun, chose the Kanze troupe as his favorite. Shogun Yoshimitsu was sixteen in 1373 when he attended a sacred performance at which he saw Zeami, the eleven-year-old son of the Kanze troupe leader, perform with "youthful flower." Zeami became Yoshimitsu's constant companion at court and his boy lover. The elders stressed that Yoshimitsu's lavish patronage enabled Zeami's artistic genius to flower. Because fourteen generations of Ashikaga shoguns had supported Kanze actors, the Kanze name had been preeminent in the world of Noh for two hundred years. In Sankuro's lifetime the Kanze family had fallen to a pitiable state, yet in less than twenty years they were again back in favor. Sankuro thought bitterly that he should be playing drum before the Tokugawa shogun in Fushimi Castle now.

"Omatsu. Buy some wine."

It was midday. They were preparing for a performance. Sankuro liked to drink, but always after a performance. To him the drum was sacred. Omatsu asked, not believing what she had heard, "Buy what?"

"Wine. Get it, quick." Sankuro tossed some coins at her. He was pacing furiously from the stage into the house and back again when Omatsu returned with a large jar of rice wine.

"Hey, Okiku. Come here and pour." Sankuro and Okiku sat out in the audience area and began to drink. It was time for Mame to open the gate. Spectators began to enter in twos and threes.

"Sankuro, aren't you going to come backstage?" Okuni finally had to speak.

"You're on your own. I'm a spectator today. I want to see what the Lord of the Realm and the shogun won't ever see, the dance of the riverbed beggars." Sankuro was already quite drunk. His eyes did not focus and his face was pale.

When the house was full Okuni signaled Kanji to strike the bell. Okiku hurried backstage as the girls began to sing. Many customers liked to watch a performance while they were eating or drinking, so Sankuro's conduct didn't draw attention, at least at first.

Okuni entered and sang the old, well-known melody of the prayer to Amida Buddha.

Descending the rapids
Of the River of Tears,
Ever-changing views
Dampen my pillow.
Hurrying clouds
Transport the moon.
Absently my heart
Wanders in love.

They changed the lyrics for the Buddhist Prayer Dance every year, fitting the words of a current hit song to the familiar melody. When Okuni took off her hat and black robe and started to dance, kicking up the hem of her beautiful kimono, the audience felt a sudden release. Some people applauded, others called out. Many sang along with Okuni. Sankuro, sitting in the midst of the spectators, drank his wine and gazed at Okuni, nursing his smoldering rancor. I was stupid to waste years with her. She understands nothing. He drank and closed his eyes to shut out the scene.

The audience began laughing as soon as Densuke appeared onstage. Sankuro squared his shoulders. He looked at Densuke waggling his hips like a woman in the Spinning Song, and he shook his head. "What a stupid fool," he snorted. Sankuro knew. He knew Densuke loved Okuni but hadn't the courage to touch her with even one finger. At least Sankuro felt proud that no other man could have her. Although he hated Okuni, she belonged to him.

His tension eased when Okiku took center stage. What a delectable creature, he thought. She throbbed against my breast like a little bird. I waited for you to love me. I want to dance for a refined audience. Teach me, she had said. If I could do it over, Sankuro thought, I'd bet on her.

Sankuro got to his feet in a surge of drunken anger. "Come here, Okiku," he called. Okiku, who had just gone off, returned to the stage. After their initial surprise, the audience began to applaud. Eager hands reached out to lift Okiku down from the stage. The men were excited by her closeness. Yelling, they moved forward and surrounded her. They tried to touch her body. Okiku couldn't reach Sankuro because of the many groping hands.

"I'll see you outside. In back," Okiku shouted, running back onto the stage. The audience was delighted by this unexpected scene. They applauded Okiku's exit wildly. People cheered, they wouldn't stop clapping.

Standing offstage, Okuni heard the clapping, as loud or even louder than the applause she received when she took off the monk's robe. Her heart raced. She thought she was going to faint. Biting her lip so hard she could taste the warm blood, she fought to keep calm. It was not just Okiku's success. She thought of that hot summer when Oan had been driven to madness. Okuni had been younger than Oan and Sankuro had needed her. She had driven Oan away. A black cloud of despair stifled Okuni's breath. She was suffocating. This time, am I Oan? Okiku is younger than I am. Okiku is a good dancer. And Sankuro has chosen her. How fooolish, why didn't I recognize it before? They've been lovers for a long time. She felt she was sweating dark blood. She clenched her fingers and tried to control her breathing. I am not Oan. I won't go mad. I won't be driven away by Okiku. Her body shook and her lips trembled violently. Densuke looked at her, frightened, but did not speak. I'm not Oan. I can dance. I won't be defeated by someone like Okiku, she vowed.

Okiku had been secretly giving herself to Sankuro for more than a year but he would not openly choose her over Okuni. Now Okiku saw her opportunity to change that relationship. Sankuro, extremely drunk, found her at the river's edge behind the theater. She stood close to him and said, "Sankuro, play your drum for me. Forget the Kanze troupe and Lord Ieyasu. I will dance for the emperor, who is greater than the shogun. If you please the emperor, you are far superior to the Kanze troupe."

Sankuro breathed deeply, trying to steady himself. He looked down into Okiku's small face, rapt with passion and determination, and he admired her. She aroused a fire in his body and in his heart that had died out during the years he had lived with Okuni. I love her. With her I can begin again. She'll bear me a son, a second Zeami.

I will found a theater family that will last for a hundred years.

"Ah, yes," he sighed and fumbled to touch her breasts. I have won, Okiku exulted. He pulled her down onto the grassy bank. He has chosen me. She wrapped her arms and legs tightly around Sankuro.

They appeared in the theater the next morning, walking together shoulder to shoulder. Okiku no longer feared Okuni. She boldly showed she was Sankuro's woman, not caring what the others thought. That same day Sankuro stopped drinking and took back control of the performances. The normally cheerful Okuni became morose from that day on. Except for the words she sang onstage she didn't speak. She took almost no food and what she put in her mouth she could scarcely swallow. As the days passed she seemed to shrivel like a fish drying in the sun. Kanji, Mame, and the girls tried to act as if they noticed nothing. Densuke was miserable about what was happening. What kind of a man was he, he thought, not to tell Okuni he loved her? She can't survive like this. Densuke, however, could not say what he felt, even now. He wept at night when Sankuro and Okiku left the theater to make love but he didn't approach Okuni, even in her deepest misery.

Okuni felt adrift, abandoned. She did not know what to do. So she closed her eyes and tried to withdraw from the pain of seeing Sankuro and Okiku together. Sankuro's drum beat at her. In rehearsal, his voice was cold, deliberately sarcastic. "Can't you learn anything, Okuni? How many times do I have to tell you to keep your hips low? Do you think you're the only one that can attract an audience, you idiot? Your pride stretches out your body. That's wrong. Drop your hips." Okiku, whose body was young, eagerly responded to Sankuro's instructions. She did exactly as Sankuro and his drum demanded. She bent her knees, settled her hips, and tilted her body forward in a frozen position. Sankuro taught her the dance posture used by Noh actors.

Okuni only half heard Sankuro's caustic words. As she repeated the familiar movements, again and again, Okuni realized she stretched her body upward when she danced in order to be free. Her buoyant dance came from a child's carefree steps in the river's sand. She leaped in the air because she was happy. The audience in the riverbed felt that happiness flowing up through her chest and bursting out in movements of her hands and feet. They sang and clapped along with her because they shared her feeling of joy. Okuni's body refused to stoop or bend the way Sankuro ordered, not because she thought the dance movement was old-fashioned, but because she rejected the subservient spirit the basic Noh posture expressed—a person of the lower classes crouching obsequiously before a samurai lord. Sankuro didn't mind bowing to nobility because of his ingrained belief that a patron would assure his success, as it had Zeami's. But Okuni instinctively rebelled. Sometimes, Okuni thought, I wish my body could fly or I could leap as high as the stage roof. I won't listen to Sankuro's drum pulling me back to earth. I want to dance my own way, not the way Noh was hundreds of years ago.

After Okiku had been training with Sankuro for several weeks, Okuni noticed that Okiku's dance movements were becoming more and more inhibited. Onstage Okiku's slight figure seemed to shrink inside her kimono. Her knees and wrists were frozen. Her waist was a solid block. You could feel Okiku's small movements being controlled by the spare, rigid beats of Sankuro's drum, not by the lively rhythm of Kanji's bell.

Okiku, it's wrong, Okuni wanted to cry out. Remember how we danced as children in Nakamura village. Okiku happily obliterated her naturally beautiful style of dance while Okuni watched, deeply depressed. Okiku was proud of herself. Sankuro, too, was pleased that she was learning so quickly. The two worked together as diligently as had Okuni and Sankuro in the first years of the troupe. They were so intent they didn't notice that the cheers of the audience were fading. The spirit of the company's performance is changing, Okuni thought in despair. But she kept her thoughts to herself and didn't speak out against Sankuro.

In the midst of a rainy cherry blossom season, the shogun conducted elaborate ceremonies to honor the late Lord of the Realm. The year was 1603. Ieyasu commissioned three days of Noh performances at his residence in Nijo Castle, inviting many lords and nobles. By good fortune the usual spring drizzle abated, and audiences saw plays by the Hosho, Kongo, Komparu, and Kanze Noh troupes. Most of the nine plays chosen for the important occasion were reserved for the Kanze headmaster, Ieyasu's favorite Noh actor. Ieyasu donated a new kimono to each performer, down to the lowest Kyogen comedian. Throughout Kyoto people told the story of how Ieyasu had stacked four-hundred silver coins in piles on the left and right sides of the stage and how he had personally presented 250 silk kimonos to the Kanze headmaster as a gift of appreciation on the final day. Considering the new shogun's reputation for being niggardly, people said the event showed that Ieyasu intended to confer official favor on Noh actors and in particular on the Kanze troupe. When Sankuro heard these stories he flew into a terrible rage. Even Okiku couldn't calm him.

"The widow of the Lord of the Realm has been on Amida Mountain all morning praying for her husband's spirit," Kanji said brightly. "We're going to watch her procession start back."

"Why don't you come, Okuni?" Densuke asked. "It's not the Lady of the Western Tower, it's the dead lord's real wife. She came up from Osaka Castle and now she's going back."

Okuni wanted to see the shrine on the top of the hill. It was also a way to escape Sankuro's anger. The group went to the foot of Amida Mountain, where they saw the departing procession setting off for Osaka. When the crowd thinned, a light spring rain resumed. The others followed Okuni up the hundreds of stone steps leading to the Toyokuni Shrine, where the spirit of the late Lord of the Realm was enshrined. The dripping stone steps were covered with clumps of pink petals torn by the rain from the cherry trees. Okuni was disappointed at what she saw when they reached the top. The Gate of Heaven, that had led into the shrine compound and was said to be the most beautiful structure in Kyoto, was gone. It had been dismantled at Ieyasu's order and set up on a remote island in Lake Biwa. The gray wooden building, dedicated to the lord's spirit, seemed lonely, even desolate, to Okuni. Why was it deserted so soon, she wondered? They were the only people there. Men's minds change, she thought, as easily as you can turn your palm up or down.

Okuni had come to the shrine hoping to lighten the pain of being excluded from Sankuro's and Okiku's love. "I'm going back." She turned and bolted down the steep steps. Densuke and Kanji could not follow her flight. Leaping two and three steps at a time, her large breasts bounced loose from her kimono. Her long hair, uncut since birth, streamed out behind her. She rushed through the rain past people who thought her possessed or mad. At the foot of Amida Mountain, she ran past Kenni Temple in the eastern part of the capital. She rushed down lanes and back roads to Shijo Street and stopped only when she reached the riverside. She scooped up water with her hands, gulping it down. She was drenched by the rain. Her hair was tangled. She ran up the bank toward the theater to change her clothes. She automatically walked past the front entrance, without even thinking about it. This was the theater where she had danced and lived with her theater family for ten years. When it rained the front gate was locked because there was no performance. Lightly, she pushed open the small backdoor to the stage. It was the middle of the day, and even though it was raining the stage was bright. Okuni saw a couple entwined in each other's embrace, like two fish caught in a net, beneath the roof that covered the stage.

Okiku noticed Okuni first, then Sankuro. The lovers jumped apart as if touched by molten lava.

Okuni stood frozen. She didn't consider turning away. "You don't have to stop. That's a stage. I'll watch the show." Her voice shook, but the words were sure and came from her lips with unforced ease. Okiku, who was slowly straightening her clothes, looked up. Sankuro stood facing Okuni for a long while, his face twisted into a grim smile. The silence weighed on the three like a heavy stone.

"Don't talk like a fool," he harshly barked at Okuni. Then, as he usually did, Sankuro turned abruptly and walked out of the theater, and away from his problems.

Okiku did not move, but sat gazing at Okuni like a wary animal. Okiku hasn't flinched, Okuni thought, she can bear anything. Okuni stood in the center of the audience area, oblivious to the rain. She was exhausted from running, empty, her emotions washed away. She knew now that all things in this world change. What Sankuro and Okiku did was not for her to deny or approve. Her anger toward Sankuro was gone; her grudge against Okiku had been washed away.

Singing cheerfully, Kanji, Mame, and the girls returned from Amida Mountain.

"Getting wet, getting wet."

"Lovers in spring."

"Don't mind getting wet."

They trooped into the theater, followed in a few minutes by Densuke, who was completely worn out. The girls wiped mud from their feet and put on dry kimonos. The men sat on the stage drying their heads, chests, and legs. Okuni noticed that Okiku was gone.

The weather the following day was clear and warm. By noon the sand in the riverbed was dry. Everyone set to work cleaning the theater and getting costumes dried out after the several months' break from performing.

"We'll have a good audience today."

Okuni shivered with apprehension. How can I dance in front of people after what happened yesterday? Still she never doubted that she would. If she stopped dancing and singing she would die. I've got to do something before they come, she thought desperately. But what?

Spectators arrived at the theater early that day, happy to be out in the good weather and anxious to be entertained. Kanji and Mame began to play. Okuni looked at Sankuro, calmly playing the drum, his handsome profile placid. He hadn't felt a bit of pity for Oan when he rejected her and she went insane. He coolly struck his drum, as if Okuni's unhappiness meant nothing to him. Okiku was dressing in her most brilliant kimono, the one she had worn for her numerous meetings with Tokio. She seemed determined to compete with Okuni. But she did not look well. Her eyes were red; she was pale and nervous. She completely lacked Sankuro's unruffled assurance.

Suddenly Okuni realized the truth of their situation: because she and Oan and Okiku were women they suffered, and because Sankuro was a man, he did not. I want to be a man, she thought, and then shuddered, as if she had touched some deeply hidden, unconscious yearning. Not hesitating for an instant, she combed back her long, straight hair and cut it to shoulder-length with a knife. Okane and Onei cried out in surprise: a woman only cut her hair when she became a Buddhist nun.

"Okuni, what's happened?" Densuke asked.

"Nothing's happened." Okuni spoke as if trying to persuade herself it was true. She ignored the woman's kimono Omatsu had laid out for her. Instead she put on the large man's kimono Kanbei had given Sankuro, but which he had never worn. It was made of luxurious light green Southern Barbarian silk embroidered with white flying birds. She wound a broad silk sash low around her hips in male fashion, rather than tightening it at the waist like a woman. Around her neck she hung the Kirishitan rosary of crystal beads that had also been Kanbei's gift. She was dressed as a young man-about-town. Standing in the middle of the staring troupe, she covered her costume with the usual black hat and priest's robe. She picked up the bell. She took a deep breath and sang the Buddhist Prayer Song they had brought with them from Izumo fifteen years before.

> Lord Buddha,
> Man desires goodness
> Which cannot be preserved.
> Man fears hell's tortures,
> Which are easily received.
> Praise Amida Buddha! Praise Merciful Buddha!

Over the years they had constantly changed the lyrics to the Buddhist Prayer Song. Now Okuni was staking her life that in a single step she could return to the original way of performing.

Okuni sang in beautiful, limpid tones while she danced down the bridgeway and onto the stage. At center stage she faced the audience and her voice rang out clearly. "Now then, know that I am a Priestess serving the Grand Shrine in the land of Izumo. My name is Okuni."

When they heard Okuni declaim the old Name-Saying speech, Kanji and Mame joyously struck up a rhythm on the bell and stick drum and the girls' hearts leaped with excitement. The girls rushed onstage to surround Okuni, beginning the prayer dance with the high-spirited steps they knew from childhood. When they blocked Okuni from view, she dropped the hat and black robe. When they parted, Okuni stepped forward dressed like a man. At the unexpected sight the audience spontaneously burst into cheers. Okuni reverted to the old practice of singing one verse or two of a popular song. As she danced, she noticed that her body was automatically moving like a man in its man's clothes. She performed the second half of the dance in an ecstasy of self-discovery.

As Okuni was exiting down the bridgeway to fervent applause, Okiku danced past her toward the stage, fluttering the sleeves of her brilliantly colored kimono. She, too, was cheered by the audience. Okuni whirled around and glared furiously at Okiku. Instantly she followed Okiku, dancing back to center stage.

Densuke was intently watching this new bit of stage action from backstage. Suddenly he threw off his hat, draped a woman's scarf over his head, and daubed red rouge on his cheeks. He slipped on the bright woman's kimono that Okuni usually wore. Holding one end of the scarf in his teeth in an elegant feminine mannerism, he danced onto the stage after Okuni.

Before the rapt spectators the following scene took place: Okuni plucked the sleeve of Okiku's kimono. Irritated, Okiku jerked away. This happened a second, a third, a fourth time. Okuni was trying to stop Okiku's beautiful dance. Okiku wanted to draw the audience's attention away from Okuni. The audience, however, could not see into the hearts of Okuni and Okiku. They saw two characters in a play—a handsome young man flirting with a coquettish woman. Male spectators immediately imagined a scene in the prostitutes' quarter. They thought it was marvelously amusing and they whooped with delight.

Next Densuke, in woman's kimono and cheeks garishly rouged, danced between Okuni and Okiku. He gestured comically while he sang the Spinning Song. Pushing them apart, he whispered in Okuni's ear, "Don't do that, Okuni. Stop it." But Okuni was gripped by a jealous rage. Oblivious to what he was saying, she whirled on Densuke and pushed him so hard he did a thudding pratfall.

The audience burst out laughing. They held their ribs; they held their stomachs; they had to wipe away the tears. Laughter rocked the theater. It flowed over the stage. When Okuni paused to look at Densuke on the floor, Okiku fled, dancing, offstage.

"Dance, Okuni. Follow me in the Spinning Song." Densuke shouted loudly, hoping Okuni could hear him over the thunderous noise of the audience. Okuni noticed for the first time that Densuke was doing his female impersonation in her kimono. The audience clapped in rhythm to encourage Densuke. She could not help responding to the insistent beat of so many hands and to the avid chorus of voices rising from the audience.

> Ah, beloved lacquered hat,
> Souvenir of life's battlefield:
> Life is gay.
> Let it turn, let it turn.
> Let money run like water
> From the spout:
> Life is gay.
> Let it turn, let it turn.

Okuni tried to transform Densuke's female impersonation into a male dance, using all of her experience and ingenuity. She found she was able to take far larger steps dancing as a man. Arm gestures and leaps as well were unimaginably freer. Okuni lost herself in her dancing, her body intoxicated by rhythm and song. People strolling along the riverside and even spectators in other theaters hurried over to see why explosions of laughter continued to rock Okuni's theater. Okuni danced before her large, passionate audience as if its emotions possessed her.

The audience would not leave the theater until, in the darkness, they could no longer see. They demanded that the new scene be played again and again. Still choking with jealousy, Okuni seized Okiku's sleeve and danced like a jaunty, carefree man. Okiku, despairing that she could not hold her audience against Okuni, tried to dance out of Okuni's grasp. Together with Densuke, they repeated the scene they had accidentally created. In the hearts of the performers, a tragic event was being enacted. Onstage, the first Kabuki play was born. A comic scene of dalliance in the licensed quarters became the heart of Kabuki. For three centuries the scene of a town dandy flirting with a beautiful courtesan would be dramatized with ever more complexity and finesse, while never departing from the core of Okuni's invention on that spring afternoon in 1603.

That evening, when the spectators scattered to their homes, they carried the news to the upper and lower parts of the capital that the priestess-dancer Okuni was doing a new play in the riverbed. The next afternoon many returned to see it again. Within days it seemed that everyone in the city knew Okuni's name. People crowded into the little theater at Shijo Street day after day. Okuni hadn't foreseen such success but she didn't waste time wondering why or how it had occurred. She was completely and happily absorbed by the challenge of performing the new scene.

Not everyone took this startling turn of affairs as matter-of-factly as Okuni. One morning Kanji and Mame ripped a bolt of white cotton cloth into two long, wide strips. They fastened each strip to the top and along one side of a tall bamboo pole, so that the strip hung straight down like a banner. Kanji mixed black ink powder with clear water drawn from the river. With an old brush he stroked firm, bold characters onto the white cloth: "Best in the World" on one cloth, and "Okuni's Kabuki" on the other. He stood back, looking with satisfaction at his handiwork. He and Mame raised the banners, one on either side of the entrance to the theater.

Okuni's Kabuki. Best in the World. The banners fluttered and snapped in the gusting spring breezes. Placed against the wall of the theater, they were not unlike a general's war banners set up to identify his battle camp.

"What in the world is that?"

"Okuni's Kabuki?"

"Kabuki, did you say?"

"Are they calling it Kabuki now?"

"Best in the World, it says."

"Let's go and see."

Talking noisily, people came down from Shijo Bridge into the riverbed and entered the theater. Kanji and Mame stood with arms folded, nodding happily.

"We don't have enough hands."

"I think we need more dancers and musicians."

"That's what I think, too."

Kanji and Mame went on with their animated discussion for some time. They did not go to Sankuro to ask for his approval. Kanji, Mame, and the others did not consider Sankuro their leader anymore.

In a single gulp, the last of the throng of spectators who had come to see the best dancer in the world was swallowed by the large closing door. The bell and the drums sounded out brightly. Singing voices floated on the air. The banners reading "Best in the World" and "Okuni's Kabuki" called out in the wind, as proudly as a conch shell announcing victory in war.

Sixteen

Okuni was as surprised as anyone at the birth of Kabuki. Kabuki had been created through an accident. Okuni couldn't have known that her rancor toward Okiku would explode into a public scene onstage. And Okuni certainly didn't plan to repeat that spontaneous action onstage a second time. But from that day on, spectators streamed into the theater at Shijo Street and wouldn't leave until they saw Okuni flirt with Okiku and Densuke impersonate a woman. They came to see Okuni dressed like a *kabuki* dandy. People were tired of girls dancing to popular songs, pieces that had been the troupe's mainstay for a decade. If the girls danced too long, the audience clapped impatiently and shouted for Okuni to start the new scene. And so Okuni danced as a man.

The shouting spectators who packed the small theater did not bring pleasure to Sankuro and Okiku. Every time Okuni interrupted Okiku's solo dance, Okiku was infuriated. Worse than that, Okuni acted the male role magnificently. Okiku could see that both men and women in the audience were attracted to Okuni more than to her, although she was younger. Okiku was even more irritated because she was forced to admire Okuni's ability. Control of the troupe passed from Sankuro's hands. The audience itself was deciding what would be performed. Spectators were utterly enthralled by Okuni's male impersonation, which was in fact a sexual inversion of Densuke's female impersonation. Okuni was performing a double sexual transformation of fascinating ambiguity. They loved Densuke's slapstick. Sankuro despised what Densuke and Okuni were doing but the audience was not interested in his opinion. In the face of the audience's noisy acclamation, he played the drum at the back of the stage while bitter scorn boiled inside him.

Okuni danced and continued to dance as a man. When she breathed, it was as if every spectator in the crowded theater breathed with her. People's hearts were stolen by the mysterious, bewitching image of Okuni as a man. Flirting with Okiku, Okuni danced in a delirium, buoyed by a dimly understood happiness. Even though she thought Okiku was a detestable person, when they danced side-by-side Okuni forgot that and responded to Okiku's talent as a dancer. She was happy dancing. Yet she worried that this happiness would not last long. When the performance was over and the spectators were gone, the atmosphere backstage was rancorous. Sankuro and Okiku would not speak to Okuni, and as this continued it became intolerable for Okuni. Her life was bearable only when she could dance, stamping in anger and seductively pulling Okiku's sleeve. It would be paradise if the audience was in the theater twenty-four hours a day, she thought. Also, Okuni found that she experienced an intolerable emptiness when Okiku left the stage. It was painful to dance alone with Densuke. The audience held their sides laughing at Densuke's clowning. They did not see what was in Okuni's eyes.

One day, in the stillness following a huge laugh at Densuke's scene, the delicate notes of a flute arose from the middle of the house, and slipped across the stage like a shaft of light in the dark.

"It must be Sanza."

"It's Nagoya Sanza," spectators whispered among themselves.

Okuni stood onstage as if she were suspended in time. How long it has been since I've heard such a beautiful sound, she thought. The flute's tender melody flowed into her body, reminding her of the sound of water in the Hii River when she was a child in Izumo. Okuni opened her fan and began to dance lightly, like a butterfly. Her body seemed to float on the flute's playful stream. How different from Sankuro's drumbeats that pull me down, she thought. Densuke was backstage. He looked out at the audience and saw the man boldly playing the flute. He swallowed hard. It was Nagoya Sanza.

Sanzaburo. Sanzaemon. People did not know very clearly what his name was, so they called him Sanza. He had a strong jaw, thick, dark eyebrows, and eyes as large as a woman from the south, framed by long and black lashes. He was a somewhat mysterious person. Few people in Kyoto knew he was Oda Nobunaga's grandnephew (through his mother, the daughter of Nobunaga's brother), that his true name was Oda Kyuemon, and that at sixteen he had been the first soldier in Lord Gamo Ujisato's army to spear an enemy for Hideyoshi during the Kyushu campaign. From the time he was a boy, it was Sanza's burning ambition to rule a fief that would be his reward for fighting bravely for his lord. But his lord was Gamo Leo Ujisato, a Kirishitan convert who fell from favor when the foreign religion was forbidden. Ujisato had died in 1595, reportedly of a high fever. He had been a man of great ability, and Ujisato's death was so sudden that rumor said Hideyoshi had had him poisoned out of fear. Sanza did not have the heart to shift his loyalty to another lord. He abandoned a warrior's career to enjoy himself in Kyoto, living well on money provided by his sister. He made a reputation as one of the most dashing playboys in the city, for he was a man of easy assurance—a product of his samurai background—and dark good looks. He frequented theaters at Shijo Street in the daytime and at night he visited famous courtesans in the licensed quarter. Recently the houses of prostitution had been moved from Yanagi Ward, which was uptown, to the area around Rokujo Street not far from Okuni's theater. Spectators in Okuni's audience were familiar with the sight of Sanza walking in the area, dressed in costly Southern Barbarian clothes, a taste he had acquired under Lord Ujisato's tutelage. Sanza also liked to play the flute. He played whenever the mood struck him. Consequently, a cherished flute of burnished bamboo was always tucked in his sash. The man in the audience could only be Nagoya Sanza.

Sanza had heard about Okuni's new play a few days after its first performance. He wondered why a woman becoming a man and a man becoming a woman had attracted praise. Half in curiosity and half because he had nothing better to do, Sanza wandered into Okuni's theater that afternoon. He lived on Teramachi Street, just around the corner from Shijo Street, and this was not the first time he was seeing Okuni dance. But when the new image of Okuni appeared before him, his heart nearly stopped; he had the eerie feeling he was seeing himself. After all, he had helped set the *kabuki* fashion in Kyoto. And here was Okuni dressed as a man in Southern Barbarian clothes, dancing with a dreamy expression on her face. Okuni's sensuous beauty agitated him inexplicably. To calm himself, he took the flute from his sash and began to play. After he had settled into a melody he glanced up and saw Okuni open her fan. She began to dance as lightly as a flower, matching her steps to his floating melody. When the flute's notes soared, her steps lifted higher. When its tone shifted, her steps changed. Sanza played with all his heart, his eye returning to the alluring image of Okuni on the stage. It disgusted him to think of the time he had spent in Kyoto carousing in the licensed quarter. He couldn't count the number of women who had fallen in love with him in the past three years. Yet the most beautiful, the most voluptuous woman of all was dancing in front of his eyes. He lost himself in the melody of his flute.

"Nagoya Sanza was there."

"He played his flute."

"They say Okuni danced to Sanza's flute."

Next day talk spread through the city that Sanza was playing at the theater, and more people than ever wanted to see Okuni's Kabuki play. From the time Okuni woke in the morning, she waited tremulously for the moment when the notes of Sanza's flute would rise from the audience, floating, shimmering in the air. Sanza, too, could not get Okuni out of his mind, and for the next three days he appeared at the theater with his flute at the same time each day. Sanza and Okuni were not interested in what people were saying: they were absorbed in melding his music and her dance.

When night came, the fresh warm odors of spring urged Okuni to leave the theater. She walked along the riverbank, breathing deeply, unable to sleep. She had danced, but her body was not satisfied. She longed for the man called Nagoya Sanza. Her woman's body, tightly closed and untouched by Sankuro for several years, trembled violently with a passion that threatened to devour her bones and flesh. Sanza. She said his name and, without realizing it, she found herself running across the bridge and down Teramachi Street as if her limbs possessed a life of their own.

"Okuni? I've been waiting for you."

When Sanza took her hand, she lowered her face on his chest as if it were the first time she had been loved by a man. Okuni felt ecstasy. She had thought such a thing would not happen again in her lifetime. Every part of her body radiated her pleasure. She laid her head in his lap and sobbed. Okuni's body burned. Her full breasts swelled, her thighs and shoulders, firm from dancing, softened, answering Sanza's love. Sanza, too, felt pure love. He drew Okuni softly into his arms, greatly aroused by the richness of her body. He lowered his face. Okuni's body was magnificent. It responded naturally to every movement of Sanza's love. Thoughts of where Okuni was from, her age, or what kind of person she was, were far from Sanza's mind at this moment.

"Dear Sanza."

"Okuni."

When they spoke their names together, each thought, ah, this is the person I've been waiting for, and they gazed long into each other's eyes. Okuni is beautiful, Sanza thought. This is a woman I can make a new life with. Okuni thought Sanza a man she could trust completely. How fortunate I am to meet and be loved by someone like Sanza. They did not need to put their thoughts into words for the other to hear.

When dawn came and it was time to part, Sanza casually picked up the short sword he wore in his sash. "Use this. A *kabuki* dandy doesn't look right without a sword at his side." He gave the sword to her.

It was two feet long and the scabbard was richly ornamented in gold. She lifted it reverently to her forehead. The sword was heavy. It was the most magnificent gift Okuni had ever received. The thought that it came from Sanza made her intensely happy.

"Will you be in the theater today, Sanza?"

"I'll be there. To play the flute."

Okuni's life as a dancer existed in that flute. Returning to the theater with Sanza's sword enfolded in her arms, her entire body was overflowing with a woman's happiness. There was no room in her joyous heart, even in its smallest corner, for Sankuro and Okiku.

> The thing that delights,
> After a night of making love,
> Is your letter of love
> In the morning.

> If our secret love,
> Is widely known,
> I don't care,
> Except for you.

That day Okuni's voice was as sweet as an early summer breeze wafting through budding leaves. Her swaggering, masculine figure fascinated the audience crowded into the small theater. Sanza's flute called out. Holding the sword against her hip with one hand and an open fan in the other, Okuni danced as freely as the air. Moving with the heavy samurai sword took extra energy. But Okuni's body was tireless. She danced lightly, even with the heavy sword at her side.

Her self-assured manner took Densuke by surprise. The radiant smile that blossomed on her lips when she heard the first notes of Sanza's flute left no doubt about what had occurred the night before. The strongest evidence of all was Sanza's sword in her sash. Okuni was transformed. On previous nights she had simply dressed up to look like a townsman. From this night on she became a true samurai dandy, swaggering with a warrior's confidence. It suited her perfectly, Densuke noted. As if to drown his pain, Densuke sang out at the top of his lungs.

> Step in, step in, step in!
> Your name will gain fame,

If you'll just step in!
So, don't be shy, step in!

Densuke had perfected the role of the foolish woman over many performances. He decorated his pulled-up hair with flowers. From his eyebrows to the lower part of his cheeks he rouged his face bright red. Like a coquettish woman, he pulled the back of his kimono collar low, to reveal his heavy male neck and upper back. His woman's kimono trailed on the stage and it shook when he waggled his hips. Approaching Okuni, he sang seductively into the samurai's ear. The audience roared. The louder he sang, the louder the audience laughed at Densuke.

Okuni half hid her face behind an open fan, and when the laughter died the samurai sang his rejoinder to the woman's proposition.

I don't care,
If my name gains fame,
As long as my body
Is willing.

The scene didn't belong to Densuke anymore. He made his exit to noisy applause. From backstage he watched Okuni. She danced alone, totally absorbed in Sanza's flute music. Without warning, tears welled in his eyes. It was happening while he watched; once again Okuni had passed him by.

At the beginning of summer an unseasonable hot spell settled over Kyoto. One sleepless night Densuke embraced Omatsu, pulling her against him with all his strength. Omatsu didn't resist. We're companions in misery, Densuke screamed silently in his heart. He knew it was an act of despair, but he had few regrets. As for Omatsu, her dull face showed not the slightest change of expression. And her dancing showed no improvement. But she slept better.

The fame of Okuni's Kabuki grew with each passing day. Court nobles and samurai, as well as rich merchants and outcasts from the river bank, heard about her performance. Okuni's theater at Shijo

Street became the place where high and low, rich and poor, gathered together.

Shortly after the new moon, they received a message from the Emperor's mistress, Lady Sakiko. When Sankuro read the message he saw a chance to regain his authority in the troupe. It is always worth waiting, he thought. It had galled him to watch impotently as Okuni changed their performance and did exactly as she pleased, without once asking his opinion.

"An invitation has come from Lady Sakiko. We're to be at the women's quarters of the Imperial Palace the day after tomorrow at ten o'clock." He spoke to the members of the troupe with a leader's authority, something he had not done in a long time.

"We've got a big audience in the riverbed. Are we just supposed to leave them?"

Sankuro was prepared for Okuni's objection and he replied smoothly, "You can entertain the audience in the riverbed, Okuni. I'll go to the palace with the rest of the troupe."

Okuni felt a jolt of fear. She could read what was in Sankuro's mind. "No. I'm going. Lady Sakiko has invited Okuni's Kabuki. And this time we'll show her Densuke's scene. I want her to see everything we do, so she'll know what makes Okuni's Kabuki the Best in the World."

Three years ago, Sankuro had forbidden Densuke to dance for Lady Sakiko, saying his act was too vulgar for aristocratic tastes. This time Okuni rudely cut Sankuro off. She looked around at the others for support. They nodded their heads in agreement.

"Then Yata should dance, too." Mame's serious words caught even Okuni by surprise. Yet wasn't Yata as much a part of their performance as her warrior or Densuke's woman, Okuni asked herself.

"All right, he can dance. Yata, dance your very best." Yata was six, small and compact like his father. His eyes were sparkling when he nodded that he understood. He was proud that Okuni was treating him like an adult.

"And what about Lord Sanza?" Okiku asked sarcastically through tight lips, as if to attack Okuni.

"Sanza's a customer. He wasn't invited," Okuni answered simply. Even Sankuro felt that Okiku's remark was offensive, and he turned away.

The day of the performance, July 14, was warm and clear. That morning a lady-in-waiting brought the troupe into the women's quarters of the Imperial Palace. A splendid Noh-style stage had been set up in an adjoining garden. It was the same height as a Noh stage and there were small Noh-style pine trees set next to the bridgeway along which they would make their long entrances from the dressing room to the stage itself. The Noh bridgeway was gradually being taken over for popular performances. Although it was only a temporary stage, it was made of smoothly polished and fragrant cedar wood, infinitely superior to their theater in the riverbed. Okuni exulted; it was worth coming to dance on this stage.

The performance began with Yata's dance. It would seem Lady Sakiko and the Empress Dowager, who were hidden behind a gold-colored hanging blind, were greatly amused by Yata's childish manner. Murmuring voices seeped through the thin bamboo slats of the blind as each succeeding scene was played—the prayer dance, Okiku's solo, Okuni as a man, and Densuke as a woman. Court ladies sitting outside the blind covered their mouths in an attempt to hide their laughter. Sanza had sent his servant Sarujiro in his place to play the flute, and he did acceptably well. All in all the performance was a success, and they were given many wrapped gifts. But when they opened them back at the theater, they were disappointed to find rice and wheat instead of silk or cotton cloth. Still, it was as much food as ten or eleven days performing at the riverside would bring in. Almost everyone in the troupe was gratified, including Okuni.

Sankuro and Okiku returned home dejected. The imperial audience had not reacted as expected. There were no men present to appreciate Okiku's beauty, and she didn't stand out among the many elegantly dressed noblewomen. On the other hand, the strange sight of Okuni dressed as a samurai titillated the secluded women, even the elderly Empress Dowager. Not only that, they laughed openly at Densuke's foolishness. How could aristocrats have the same taste as commoners? How absurd it was. Why, damn it? Sankuro spit the words furiously. Yes, he thought, we need a male audience. The Lord of the Realm and the shogun wouldn't be amused by Okuni's and Densuke's stupid sketches. But the lord was dead and the shogun liked the Kanze Noh troupe. Where was there room for Sankuro?

"I can't stand it any more," Okiku shouted spitefully at Sankuro. "Do you think I like it?"

"Then do something. Every day Okuni stops me in the middle of my scene. No one looks at me any more. They come to see Okuni, the 'Best in the World'." There was cruel, implacable hostility in her voice.

"Wait," Sankuro said. He would have to create a new performance for Okiku that was more interesting than Okuni's. But it couldn't be done now, when Okuni was so popular. They would have to wait. Okiku bit her lips in anger. Although she had taken Sankuro from Okuni it wasn't a source of pride. The gossip in the capital wasn't about Sankuro and Okiku. Nobody cared. But the love affair between Okuni, Best in the World, and Sanza, the *kabuki* dandy, was talked about from upper to lower Kyoto. It irked Okiku, and it was impossible for her simply to put such thoughts out of her mind.

"What, Okuni danced for Lady Sakiko at the palace?" Kanbei wanted to see Okuni dance again the minute he heard the news. He dashed off a simple letter, sending it by a servant to Shijo Street. He was seventy-eight years old, an old man. All his life he had calculated which way the winds of power would blow. He lived with the caution of a merchant ruled by capricious warriors. But today he thought that this might be his last chance to see Okuni and he acted on impulse. "I'm inviting Lord Hideyasu to see Okuni's Kabuki. Don't bother yourself about it." Kanbei spoke brusquely to his son Magozaemon, whom he thought, correctly, would disapprove.

"Are you really going to watch Okuni's Kabuki here? Isn't Hideyasu out of favor?" Magozaemon, who was already middle-aged, was more conservative than Kanbei. When he was younger he had been constantly on the road doing business for his father, so he was unaware of the side of Kanbei that savored extravagant pleasures, and he had no idea that his father was a close personal friend of Hideyasu's.

"Never mind," Kanbei grimaced unhappily, "I won't ask them to perform here." Kanbei made special arrangements to preserve his son's image of him as a sober and responsible person. He would have Okuni perform out of Magozaemon's sight, in Fushimi Castle. Hideyasu was staying at Fushimi Castle en route to Echizen Province, the fief Ieyasu had recently awarded him, as a consolation it was said. Echizen was a raw district without any of the pleasures of the capital. Kanbei felt deep compassion for Hideyasu. When Hideyasu had been young, it seemed he would be Ieyasu's heir. Ieyasu adored him, and everyone paid court to the brilliant and charming second son of the Tokugawa lord. But when Ieyasu became shogun, he promoted Hidetada, his third son, to Junior Minister of the Second Rank and made Hideyasu Junior Minister of the Third Rank, signifying that he had changed his mind. Hideyasu's bright star was in eclipse; he was now merely another provincial lord. Hence, Kanbei was not acting in self-interest but out of fondness for Hideyasu. He hoped that Okuni's dance, which Hideyasu had seen before, would entertain the unhappy young lord.

On the morning of the performance, three days later, Kanbei was in his palanquin waiting in front of Fushimi Castle when Okuni and the rest of the troupe arrived. Kanbei had not bothered to see them at his house in the days before this. He smiled gaily. "I hope you're all well? Good. We should try to make Lord Hideyasu happy." His eyes twinkled as he said, "I'm just going along to enjoy myself. I'm relying on you." Okuni was moved by Kanbei's confidence. When they had received his message, they immediately went to his house in Fushimi. As in the past, his servants brought them many rolls of expensive imported fabrics to make into costumes. Okuni divided the beautiful material carefully, so that each girl would receive a color and design most suitable to her. She gave the most splendid silk to Okiku, who was surprised but pleased. For herself, she made a costume that imitated from head to foot the Southern Barbarian clothes Lord Ujisato had given Sanza and that marked him as a *kabuki* dandy: hand-dyed underkimono of pale blue silk, a short kimono over that with a shiny, flowery design, foreign-style balloon trousers, and a sleeveless cape tied with cords of gold-colored silk. Kanbei did not inspect their costumes. Nor did he ask what they were going to perform for the shogun's second son. He trusted them. No one is a better man than Kanbei, Okuni thought. She resolved to do her best.

Fushimi Castle stood almost exactly as it had in Hideyoshi's time, rebuilt by Ieyasu to match its previous splendor. At the main gate, Kanbei was taken to the audience hall of the Western Tower. Okuni's troupe was led through a garden adjoining the Western Tower into a small waiting room, where they began to put on makeup and costumes. It was midsummer and very hot. Okuni stripped down until all that covered her upper body was a thin, almost transparent underkimono. The others were busily occupied. But Densuke could not help staring at Okuni's voluptuous form across the room.

Hideyasu, now thirty years old, loved Fushimi Castle more than any other place. As a young man, he had learned to like Southern Barbarian fashions when he had lived there with Hideyoshi, his adoptive father. Just that morning he had bathed using imported soap. He no longer enjoyed scrubbing with the traditional pouch of rice bran. The fragrance of the soap lingered pleasantly on his skin. As much as anything, Ieyasu disliked Hideyasu's preference for foreign ways. Ieyasu was cautiously building the foundations of a ruling dynasty. He had decided that, whatever Hideyasu's brilliance, younger brother, Hidetada, was a safer choice to become the second Tokugawa Shogun.

Hideyasu was wearing a cool cotton kimono. "Ah, it's been a long time, my old friend."

Kanbei chose his words carefully. "I am happy to see you looking healthier than ever, my Lord." He bowed low.

"You seem in good spirits, Kanbei. Well now, tell me what you've planned. I know it's something special. Quickly, tell me this instant."

Hideyasu had been in a mood of pleasant anticipation ever since Kanbei's message had arrived three days ago.

"Perhaps your Lordship remembers seeing a Priestess of Izumo Shrine dance at my house some years back?"

"Ah, you mean the day the Lord of the Realm dismissed the Chinese embassy and the second invasion of Korea began? I haven't forgotten, Kanbei."

"Your Lordship is too generous. The woman who performed the Buddhist Prayer Dance on that occasion is now titled Best in the World. She has a theater in the riverbed at Shijo Street and her performance, called Okuni's Kabuki, is highly praised."

"Best in the World. Hmm. Okuni's Kabuki, you say?"

"I thought it might be a tasty side dish while you drink to assuage the summer heat."

"I am grateful, Kanbei. If this Kabuki is the best in the world, it should be something to see." Hideyasu remembered watching the Buddhist Prayer Dance while he drank a strong foreign liquor from a Southern Barbarian goblet. Kanbei had kept the sparkling crystal glass filled to the brim. The sounds of the girls' stamping feet and ringing bells, and the firm beat of the drum remained pleasant memories. Acting like the lord of Fushimi Castle, Hideyasu called all the servants and attendants to watch.

The performance reached the point where the girls' lively steps stopped. The Buddhist prayer dance was finished. In the center of the stage the familiar monk's black robe and hat were whisked off, and a girl in a beautiful kimono began dancing. Hideyasu shook his head slightly. She was comely, young, and she danced well enough. But this was not the woman he remembered seeing as a child and again at Kanbei's house seven years before.

"Kanbei."

"Yes?"

"Isn't the woman, what's her name, here?"

"You mean 'Kuni?"

"Um."

"Yes, she's with the troupe."

"That's not her."

"No, my Lord."

Kanbei was impressed by the keenness of Hideyasu's memory. He, too, wondered where Okuni was. What had happened was this: when Okuni heard that Hideyasu was to be the main guest, she decided not to do the Buddhist Prayer Dance. It will bore him to see me dance the same thing three times, she said firmly after Mame had read out loud Kanbei's second message ordering them to perform in Fushimi Castle. Okiku immediately said she would do the role. Both Okiku and Sankuro saw a chance to supplant Okuni, and they seized on it. Now Okiku was singing out confidently and smiling boldly at Hideyasu as she danced, even daring to catch his eye with a flirtatious glance. The sound of the bell and drums evoked warm memories of past performances, but Hideyasu had been expecting to see Okuni, and he felt disappointed.

In the middle of Okiku's dance, Okuni stepped before the audience. She tugged Okiku's sleeve. Okiku pulled away. One hand pulled, one hand pushed away. Two hands met with a clapping sound. Is that a woman or a man?

"Ah, that's Okuni."

"Yes, it's her."

Now that he had identified Okuni, Hideyasu relaxed. Then Densuke sashayed between them, hips waggling. All the people gathered in the Western Tower of Fushimi Castle burst out laughing.

So that's what Kabuki is, Hideysu thought. He mused that Hideyoshi would have enjoyed this comic dance called Kabuki. The bright red of Okuni's kimono, from neck to breast, thrilled Hideyasu.

> Sleeve waving farewell,
> Leave love behind,
> With your love.
> Journeying together,
> Red petals fall in the wind,
> They bloom on the water.
> Leave the shadow

Of the moon's dewy tears
On your sleeve.

At the sound of Sarujiro's flute, Densuke danced off the stage, leaving Okuni alone.

What is the name of the grass
That I mingle with,
Beneath the eaves?

When Okuni had finished her dance, Hideyasu spoke to her directly. "So, you're Okuni. Come closer."

Frightened, Kanbei tried to interrupt diplomatically. "Forgive me, Lord Minister, but entertainers from the riverbed do not deserve to be addressed by your Excellency. Let me speak on your behalf."

"Never mind, it doesn't matter." Hideyasu stood and walked over to a suit of his armor that decorated an alcove of the room. He lifted from the breastplate a Kirishitan rosary made of coral. Abandoning etiquette, he spoke directly to Okuni as he placed the coral rosary in her hands. "Your crystal rosary is unsightly. Use this instead." He returned to his seat among his startled vassals, and explained to Kanbei, "Among millions of women in the nation, only one is called Best in the World. I didn't succeed in becoming best in the world of men. Don't you think that makes me her inferior? Don't you think it is cause for regret? Ha, ha, ha." Hideyasu's laugh was bright and good-natured but Kanbei broke into a clammy sweat; I've made a mistake, he thought, regretting his rashness. When Hideyasu saw the sparkling rosary on Okuni's breast, wasn't he reminded of an earlier time, when his future as Ieyasu's heir had been shining just as brightly? It had to be a painful memory. Wasn't that why he called the crystal rosary unsightly?

"Okuni, won't you dance once more, with this rosary?" Okuni replaced the crystal rosary around her neck with the rosary of pink coral. She half opened her fan and began to dance.

Water wheel on the Yodo River,

Do you wait for any man?
Turning, turning, turning.

The song that Lady Sakiko and her attendants had found so amusing caused Third Minister Hideyasu to weep. Kanbei was stricken to see this, and he hurried from the castle while Okuni was still dancing. His plan to cheer the unfortunate warrior through sprightly song and dance had evoked shadows of the past, producing the very opposite result. Kanbei returned home in a foul temper, vowing never to be so foolish again. Okuni and the troupe went back to the riverbed without seeing Kanbei. Yet, they were pleased by the splendid new costumes they had received and were happy to have performed at the castle.

As soon as Okuni reached Shijo Street she ran to Sanza's house. They embraced without saying a word, like lovers separated for a dozen nights instead of only three. Okuni sank into Sanza's arms, drowning in his love. She forgot herself completely when she made love to this quiet man. She had never been so fulfilled. When she had fallen in love with Sankuro, she had still been a girl, too timid to tell him what she felt. Sanza had waited for Okuni anxiously, for he did not know when the troupe would return. He loved to hold her soft, yielding body and to touch her smooth skin. When they finished making love and Okuni's breathing slowed, he thought coolly that she was, after all, only a woman. Then he frowned. Why was he thinking such a thing, he wondered. For he loved her totally.

When Okuni woke, she smiled with dreamy eyes. "Where do you think we went? To the castle."

"The castle?"

"Fushimi Castle. Kanbei took us there and we danced in the Western Tower. For Lord Hideyasu. He's now called Junior Minister of the Third Rank." She ran on gaily, hungry to tell him every detail before he heard the story from his servant, Sarujiro.

"You know so much, don't you?" Sanza bantered with Okuni, but he also felt a stirring of jealousy. Sanza had been in the Western Tower himself several times when he was serving Gamo Ujisato. But his time as a samurai had passed, and for three years Sanza's only knowledge of the world of power had come from street gossip. He usually was amused when Okuni prattled on about this and that, as she liked to do when they were together, but listening to her now he felt a dull ache in his chest.

"Seven years ago when I danced for Lord Hideyasu, he slapped his leg and said, 'Okuni has become *kabuki*.' Yesterday I dressed exactly like you, Sanza. And he gave me a necklace of pink coral."

How ironic, Sanza thought. Dressed to look like me, Okuni can meet Hideyasu, while I cannot.

She lowered her voice, "Lord Hideyasu wept, Sanza."

"What?"

"I don't understand too well. He said, 'Okuni is the best woman in the world, but I am not the best man in the world,' and then he laughed. And then he cried."

Sanza could well imagine that Hideyasu wept. He could understand Hideyasu's pain at not becoming the Best in the World. Wasn't he, Sanza, in the same situation? His dream of ruling a castle was gone. Okuni was only a woman, but she was the Best in the World. Could he compare to her? Sanza thought back to the night Okuni had told him with innocent delight how the Lady from the Western Tower had commanded her to drink and she had blithely refused. Sanza had been incredulous when he heard how she had disobeyed the mother of Hideyori while Hideyoshi was living. Hideyoshi acted arbitrarily and cruelly in his old age; no warrior would have had the courage to defy the Lady as Okuni had. Sanza had recognized that Okuni was not boasting but only explaining why she did not like to perform for the Lady of the Western Tower.

"So, what did Lord, that is Third Minister, Hideyasu say after that?" Sanza spoke quietly, looking down at Okuni's face, but her eyes were already closed and she was breathing softly. Perhaps I am merely the man who makes love to the best woman in the world, Sanza thought sourly. He took up his flute and went outside, walking along the bank of the Kamo River through the heavy, settling dew until he reached the arching bridge at Shijo Street. At times the flute sounded a harsh note. At the sound, Sanza's lips turned down sardonically.

Seventeen

Kanji and Mame had been talking about expanding the theater ever since Okuni's new scene had started bringing overflowing houses. However, a larger stage would make their performance seem skimpy. Kanji and Mame decided the answer to the problem was simple: add more dancers to the troupe. Just as they were considering ways to do this, a group from Nakamura village in Izumo appeared at the theater. Like Okiku, they had escaped from Izumo by joining a selling brigade traveling on behalf of the Grand Shrine. There were four women and three men. They knew Okiku and they guessed where she had gone when she did not return with her selling group. They were too young to have known Okuni personally, but everyone in Nakamura village had heard that Okuni was dancing in Kyoto.

"Why did you come?" Okuni asked.

"People are starving in Nakamura village," one of the girls said, "so we left."

Another continued, "The new lord is cruel. He takes all the rice we grow. Izumo is hell."

"How can you say Izumo is hell?" Okuni objected. She had a fond childhood memory of Izumo. "Don't talk like that about the land where you were born and grew up. You'll be punished. Izumo is a beautiful place."

The girls couldn't answer back. They were afraid of Okuni. One of the young men spoke up, "Izumo isn't beautiful any more, Sister Okuni. The Hii River floods every year and eats up our rice fields.

The Dragon brings sand down from the mountains in the flood, and it covers the fields. And wind in the summer blows the sand into huge dunes that move right over the crops. It's terrible in Izumo. We had to escape."

"In Izumo we sang and danced. We want to dance in Kyoto with you, Sister Okuni."

Okuni thought sadly about the changes in the land she loved so much. She sighed. When will I see Izumo again, she wondered. She smiled at the young people from Nakamura village and welcomed them into the troupe. "Of course you can dance with us."

They rebuilt and enlarged the theater under Kanji's and Mame's skillful direction. They added a small building behind the stage to serve as combination dressing room and living space. They expanded the size of the stage itself, and they hung brightly colored cotton bunting under the eaves as decoration. The young men from Izumo were enthusiastic singers. The girls, who shared with Okuni the childhood joy of leaping in the Hii River sand, rapidly learned the troupe's dance steps. The Buddhist Prayer Dance became breathtakingly beautiful with the addition of seven new singers and dancers. The sound of the bells was richer. The singing was stronger. Eight girls in gorgeous kimonos now danced in unison alongside Okuni and Okiku on the new stage. Tipsy spectators who witnessed this ravishing spectacle imagined they had been transported into an enchanted garden of nodding flowers.

Soon after the fame of Okuni's Kabuki was established, the riverside at Shijo Street grew more crowded and more lively than ever. Commoners, merchants, servants, samurai, and nobles mixed here as they did nowhere else in the city. To cater to these pleasure-seekers, most of the capital's street-corner entertainers moved to the riverbed. Wandering *ronin* demonstrated the art of swordsmanship to earn pennies from passersby. Blind bards appeared, chanting *The Tale of the Heike* while they accompanied themselves on the thick-throated *biwa,* the large, old-fashioned lute. Other entertainers plucked a smaller lute, new to Kyoto, called the *jabisen.* Its sounding box was covered with snakeskin. Black bears snarled in cages. Freaks of many kinds displayed themselves to the curious. Trained monkeys from Tamba, west of the capital, jumped through hoops and did humorous tricks. Dance troupes from different regions of the country came and went. Professional puppet troupes and groups of women performing Noh often set up theaters. Entertainers of every stripe gathered beneath the bridge at Shijo Street for one major reason: the dry land between the riverbanks had not been recorded in the Land Survey register. Officially, the land didn't exist. Consequently an enterprising producer could build a theater in the riverbed without getting government permission, as was necessary elsewhere. Even more important, there was no land tax to pay. The riverbed at Shijo Street was a no-man's-land in the heart of the capital. Naturally it attracted thieves and rascals as well as performers, but that did not keep people away. Curious and venturesome folk from around the nation were drawn to this makeshift entertainment district.

A dark-browed, heavyset man carrying a black dog in his arms went unnoticed in the moving crowds of the riverbed. Certainly no one in Okuni's troupe saw Kyuzo carefully observing all that was going on around him. The previous year Kyuzo had helped his master hurriedly move the Court Maidens from the old gay quarter at Yanagi Ward to a new location along the Kamo River at Rokujo Street. Ieyasu wanted to have a palatial residence built in the center of the city. And he wanted it finished before spring. The city magistrate chose the Nijo district, in the upper city near the Imperial Palace, as the site. Yanagi Ward was only a few blocks away, so the houses of prostitution were ordered to relocate to the lower city, at Rokujo Street. In the new licensed quarter, houses were built along three broad cross streets, marking upper, middle, and lower districts. Those in turn were divided in two, making six areas. Their regular layout facilitated control by the owners, and, if necessary, the police. Many of the house owners grumbled about the move to Rokujo Street. Kyuzo, however, showed great acumen. He advised his master to accommodate the city magistrate willingly. He urged him to capitalize on the move by building a larger house. Kyuzo also worked behind the scenes to create an organization that would deal directly with the magistrate on behalf of the owners. When Kyuzo urged that the owner of the Court Maidens serve as the first head of the Brothel Owners Guild, not surprisingly his suggestion was accepted. Kyuzo's foresight and ability so impressed his employer that he was promoted to general overseer of the house, a position of considerable responsibility. Kyuzo was now a respectable merchant.

Gossip quickly traveled the short distance from Shijo to Rokujo. Kyuzo had heard about the banners announcing Okuni's Kabuki and Best in the World the same day they went up. He heard, too, that Sanza, a man famous among the ladies of the quarter, was Okuni's lover. He could laugh at Densuke, a foolish, moonfaced fellow, but not at Sanza. According to one story, Sanza had had an affair with the highest-ranking courtesan in Yanagi Ward, a beauty named Katsuragi. Her love for Sanza was so true that she refused to see other customers, which made her all the more popular. When Sanza left her for Okuni, she killed herself in grief. Probably the story was just advertising for the house that owned her, Kyuzo thought. In Yanagi Ward, the Court Maidens had been too small to own an important courtesan like Katsuragi, but Kyuzo had gathered many beautiful prostitutes in their new house. Perhaps he could start a similar rumor about Kashiwagi, their top woman. The jealousy he felt toward Sanza knotted his stomach until the pain was almost unbearable.

Was Okuni really Best in the World?

Kyuzo stopped in front of Okuni's theater and looked at the tall banners flying in the wind. He could not read, so the characters spelling out Okuni's Kabuki didn't mean anything to him. However, the phrase Best in the World was written over many shop fronts, so he recognized those characters. He heard the crowd's excited laughter. The fence around the theater could not contain the singing and ringing bells. Then sweet notes of a flute floated in the air. Brief stillness. Wild cheers. Kyuzo imagined Okuni dancing to Sanza's flute music during the day and sleeping with him at night. His face tightened into a bitter grimace. Black ran about at Kyuzo's feet, barking excitedly. Kyuzo squatted beside the dog and spoke to him earnestly. "Black. I tell you, I'm going to do it!"

A few days later, workmen began to tear down small theaters and sideshow shacks kitty-corner from Okuni's theater, just downstream from the bridge. An open fence of crossed bamboo poles went up, enclosing an area three or four times the size of Okuni's theater. Lumber was stacked inside. A large crowd gathered to watch a gang of carpenters set about their work. Kanji and Mame walked across the street to join the crowd.

"I hope people aren't going to have their heads cut off again," Mame said when they saw the fence. They both shuddered, remembering the bloody execution of Lord Mitsunari and the other defeated generals. The executioners held the crowds back by an open lattice fence just like this, Mame remembered, but the area inside the fence hadn't been as large. As they watched, the shape of a building emerged.

"It looks like they're building a theater," Kanji reported excitedly to the others. "A big one."

Sankuro went to see and soon he was back with his own report. Laughing, he said, "Well, it may be a stage but they aren't going to make money with it. You can see everything through the fence. What fool would pay to go inside?" Every day people hunted for knotholes in the solid board fence around Okuni's theater to avoid buying a ticket. It was ridiculous to build a theater and then let everyone watch free.

Later, though, Densuke and Kanji asked each other the same worrisome question. Why, if it's such a crazy idea, is someone doing it? "Who's building it," Densuke asked, "that's what I want to know." The carpenters at the building site didn't know who was paying to have the stage put up, but they knew what the stage was for.

Densuke and Kanji hurried back. Densuke's usually placid face was creased in a frown. "A prostitutes' house from Rokujo Street is going to use it."

"A prostitutes' house!" Okuni exclaimed indignantly. "They can't have a stage. It's not allowed."

They thought this was so: that performers were strictly forbidden to work as prostitutes on the side. Recently the Kyoto city magistrate had ordered several theaters in the riverbed demolished because their actresses had propositioned spectators after performances. Everyone in the troupe welcomed this. A woman in a house of prostitution enticed a man, got him drunk, then let him sleep with her. A performer showed the public an artistic skill. It was not that they believed in monogamy or the virtue of virginity. But Okuni and the others made a distinction between a woman who gave her body out of love and a woman who sold her body in a whorehouse. For that reason, troupe members accepted Okiku's relationship with Sankuro, but they disliked it when she went to sleep with Tokio. Everyone knew that Okuni loved Sanza, so it was natural and good for her to sleep nightly with him. Society allowed a man to buy a woman in a house of prostitution, but the theaters at Shijo Street were places to show artistic skill. In the minds of Okuni and the others, the situations were very different, and it was wrong to mix them together.

At the time that the prostitutes' theater was being built, the Kyoto city magistrate, Itakura Katsushige, promulgated new regulations for the licensed quarters. Three articles were posted on boards throughout the city:

> **One:** No house of prostitution may be erected outside a
> licensed quarter and no woman may engage in prostitu-
> tion outside a quarter.
> **Two:** No licensed quarter may be established outside
> designated areas.
> **Addition:** The Kyoto city magistrate is responsible for
> maintaining strict order. In the event of violations, all
> residents of the area will be held accountable.

This extremely severe edict prescribed the death penalty for most violations. The edict contained all the provisions that the Brothel Owners Guild had urged the magistrate to issue. The first and the second articles would eliminate competition from streetwalkers and informal red-light districts, under the guise of regularizing social intercourse. The additional article had been suggested by Kyuzo. He argued that it was in the owners' interest to involve the magistrate in Rokujo's affairs. Quarrels over women occurred almost every night in the quarter and many involved drunken and abusive samurai whose higher status put the merchant owners in a weak position. The added article put the magistrate's authority squarely on the side of the owners in any dispute. The brothel owners did not discuss the final sentence. Kyuzo was not asked why he had proposed it and he kept his reasons to himself.

Over the next several days, troupe members went across the street in twos and threes to look for themselves. Yes, it did seem to be a theater. But why did prostitutes need a theater? And how could a house of prostitution move to the riverside when that was against the law?

"Are prostitutes going to take their customers in there?"

"With only a few crossed bamboo poles for a fence, you could see every move."

It was ludicrous to think of people standing in the street watching a prostitute make love to a customer. They laughed and they hooted, imagining such a scene. Even the young people from Izumo knew what prostitutes did and they joined the laughter.

"So what are they going to do?" Densuke could not even guess.

Okuni showed no interest. In all her time at Shijo Street she had not once gone inside another theater. It was Okuni's nature to concentrate on her own life and affairs and not worry about what other people did. And what concerned her these days was the sound of Sanza's flute. She first noticed the change when autumn began. The pure sound of his summer melody was gone. Sometimes his floating notes strayed away from the rhythm of her dancing feet. Sanza's heart was somewhere else, Okuni thought. And not just when he was playing the flute. Sometimes when Sanza's arms enclosed her, Okuni shivered as if the chill autumn wind was blowing between them.

"Sanza."

"Hm?"

"Tell me what you're thinking."

Sanza did not answer. Was he tired of Okuni? He had first

appeared in the audience playing his flute nearly half a year ago. Would he come to the theater and play for her every afternoon if he had found someone else? No, she knew he loved her. "It's cold of you not to tell me." Irritated, she slapped his thigh. In their relationship, she was the one who talked, while he listened. In the beginning, he would nod pleasantly as she prattled on about everything that had happened during the day. But now he rarely responded to what she said, and his gaze seemed far away. Pouting, she said, "If there's something about me you don't like, tell me." She knew that wasn't the problem but she wanted to provoke a response. It was terrible not to know why Sanza was unhappy.

He sighed and looked at Okuni. He spoke quietly. "It's not you, Okuni."

"Then what is it?"

"I dream. Of a castle."

"A castle?" Castles were built with the blood and effort of farmers. She hadn't expected Sanza to say this.

"If you're a man, you should rule a castle."

Every warrior dreamed of someday ruling his own castle. Hadn't Hideyoshi been a sandal-bearer for Nobunaga, and hadn't he risen to become Lord of the Realm and the builder of as many castles as you could count on your hand? When the Battle of Sekigahara was imminent, Sanza saw this as his last chance to win recognition. He honed his spear and was about to leave for the battlefield when he learned that Ieyasu had already won his victory in a single day. The time of wars had ended under Ieyasu, and the time for Sanza to earn a fief and to build a castle of his own had irrevocably passed.

Sanza rolled over. He reached for his rosary of square wooden beads, an ordinary Buddhist rosary, like the rosaries thousands of people owned. He gazed at the polished beads gleaming darkly in the candlelight. And he looked at the brilliant Kirishitan rosary made of coral that lay beside Okuni's pillow. Okuni wore either the coral or the crystal rosary around her neck day and night, taking it off only when she lay down to be embraced by Sanza. He could not help comparing the two. He was like his rosary, he thought to himself. He was nothing compared to the woman who was Best in the World. He smiled sardonically.

"Dearest Sanza," Okuni wrapped her arms around Sanza's chest. Sanza saw fear in Okuni's face, an expression he had not observed before.

"What is it?"

"I'm afraid."

"What are you afraid of?"

"If I knew, I wouldn't be so frightened. I'm afraid of what makes you draw away. Please tell me what you're thinking."

"I'm. . .I'm dissatisfied with myself."

"You're dissatisfied with yourself, Sanza?"

"I dream too much."

"No," Okuni instantly rejected the idea, "you don't need a castle."

"What?"

"Even if you build a castle, when times change it'll be torn down."

Sanza gazed at Okuni's determined face, which now had no shadow of her earlier fear, and listened to her confident voice. Yes, a woman who's best in the world would say she doesn't need a castle. I'm no match for such a woman. Sanza's sigh came from deep within him.

People strolling nearby whooped with excitement. The Sadojima House from Rokujo Street was parading its attractive prostitutes across the stage opposite Okuni's theater. The voices of more than a dozen men and women joined a din of old-style flutes and drums, *biwa*, bells, and gongs rising up into the air. People from all around the riverside converged on the new theater. Tickets were so cheap it didn't seem possible the troupe could turn a profit. The audience area was tightly-packed and outside, around its perimeter, a mass of people's heads poked under the flimsy linen curtain draped over the open fence of crossed poles and peered inside.

Hardly any spectators came to Okuni's theater that day, but Okuni would not accept the humiliation of calling off their performance. Like a woman possessed, she danced angrily. She wouldn't stop, but

Kanji and most of the girls slipped across the street as soon as they were off stage. They stood on tiptoe and crawled on their hands and knees to see past the men and women surrounding the theater four and five deep.

"More than twenty prostitutes are packed on the stage and they're dancing," Kanji whispered to Sankuro when they came back. "The costumes are pretty good. It's a big show."

"You call that dancing? They're showing off the girls, that's all." Even the young girls from Izumo weren't impressed.

"It's like a sideshow."

"That's right."

As might be expected, Sankuro preferred not to be bothered, but Okiku's curiosity would not be satisfied unless she saw for herself. She returned with a puzzled expression on her face, "How can they have a house of prostitution outside Rokujo Street? The magistrate's order says you can't do that."

Sankuro replied thoughtfully, "They haven't really opened a house of prostitution. And the law doesn't say prostitutes can't dance outside the licensed quarter. That must be it."

"Well, if it's all right for prostitutes to come outside Rokujo and dance, Sankuro, no one can complain if we try to take some of their customers, can they?"

Okiku was worried that no matter how well they danced they couldn't match the scale of the performance next door. She did not want to stand idly by while her patrons slipped away like an ebbing tide.

It was typical of Okuni that she shut the problem of the new performers across the street out of her mind in the days that followed. Truly, she did not care what they did. As long as she could dance for herself or for even one spectator, she was happy. So she was totally absorbed in dancing alone onstage after Densuke's exit, when the realization struck her that the notes of the flute were not Sanza's. She glanced anxiously to the back of the audience area where he always sat. She saw Sarujiro, Sanza's servant, playing the flute. Okuni broke from her dancing and ran through the audience to confront Sarujiro.

"Sanza. Where is he?"

"I can't tell you."

"What?"

"I'm not supposed to say."

"Why not? I only asked where he is. Is he across the street?"

"No."

"Then where is he?"

"He's left Kyoto, and he isn't coming back. You shouldn't try to follow him. He won't let me say any more."

Sanza gone from Kyoto? Okuni stood stricken.

The few spectators left and Sarujiro took Okuni to Sanza's house. "Master Sanza left you these." Lying on the floor of his room were a gold-filigreed long sword with sharkskin hilt, a lacquered stamp case, six pouches of gold powder, an elegant silk kimono brocaded with gold thread, and all of his Southern Barbarian clothes. Sanza had left behind all of the objects associated with his life as Kyoto's greatest *kabuki* dandy.

Okuni felt weak and she had to sit on the floor. At last she spoke: "Sanza's gone back to his family."

"Yes."

"He's thrown me away, and I'm the best woman in the world." Huge tears welled in her eyes. She was conscious both of the sound of her words and of the sound of tears spattering like blood from her breast to her stomach. She tried to stand, but crumpled to the floor.

"Okuni, Okuni." Densuke, who had followed her, put his hand gently on her shoulder. As if her heart were shattered, Okuni let out a terrifying cry. She roared and cried like a wounded animal. Densuke's blood turned cold hearing her. He knew Sanza had left, and he understood Okuni's grief. He wanted to embrace Okuni himself, but instead he returned to the theater. He went to Omatsu, who was now his wife, and said, "I don't want you to leave Okuni's side for a while. Do you understand?"

Okuni wept through the night, dropping off into a fitful, exhausted sleep just before dawn. Omatsu sat by her side, her crablike face expressionless, not moving and not speaking a word through her clenched teeth. Okuni woke with a dull pain throbbing in her head. The joints of her arms and legs were stiff, and when she moved, her bones ached terribly.

Each day when the sun came up, Mame was the first person to rise in Okuni's troupe. He would go out in the street and put up the banners that read Okuni's Kabuki and Best in the World. When the wind blew, the banners snapped loudly, catching the attention of people who were walking by. That morning they hung motionless in the windless autumn air. Okuni came into the theater when the sun was high. Densuke caught his breath. Overnight Okuni had become a different person. Her face was bloodless and deeply wrinkled. She seemed ten years older. Both of us are getting older, Densuke thought, his chest feeling painfully heavy. Okuni shuffled into the middle of the theater like a walking ghost.

"Okuni, let's rest today." Densuke's voice was broken and hoarse.

A glint appeared in Okuni's deep, staring eyes. "Are you saying I can't dance?"

Densuke was relieved to see a spark of life. "I don't mean you can't dance. Just that you don't have to today. Not many people will come. Why not rest?"

"The audience will come if I dance," Okuni said stubbornly. Sanza is gone, and if I don't dance, I will die, Okuni thought. No matter how tired I am, I must. Sankuro and Okiku watched coldly from the side of the stage as Okuni sang.

> You cannot know another's heart,
> You cannot know the truth
> That lies in another's heart.

Densuke danced along with Okuni, struggling to hold back the tears that her choking voice drew from his heart. Singing loudly, he answered.

> Leave a corner in your heart
> For my secret love.

I who know you
Can only weep and weep.

Okuni would not stop dancing. She danced on and on, until even
her warmest fans became bored and walked out. When Okuni finally stopped, her body was filled with an overpowering weariness. She
fell into a deep sleep in a corner of the stage. Okuni was fortunate to
be able to sing. It was her salvation that she could dance. Sanza did
not appear in her dreams.

Sarujiro stayed at the theater for the next several weeks, following
Sanza's detailed instructions. He patiently taught several of the
young men from Izumo how to play Sanza's flute music. And bit by
bit Sarujiro told Okuni about Sanza's departure. He spoke quietly
and simply. His master had not left a letter because Okuni could not
read. His master's life as a warrior had ended when Lord Ujisato
died. Now his life as a *kabuki* playboy in Kyoto had ended, too. He
was going to work as an official in Mimasaka Province under his
brother-in-law, the Lord of Mimasaka. His sister had written him
many long letters, inviting him to live with them. He had decided to
go. Okuni was best in the world, but Nagoya Sanza was nobody. He
wasn't Nagoya Sanza any more. Using his samurai name, Nagoya
Kyuemon, he would become a minor provincial bureaucrat. He had
left Kyoto wearing a sober gray kimono and a pair of straw sandals.

"He didn't look back?"

"No, not once. He was in a hurry. To build a castle."

"A castle?" Okuni looked dully at Sarujiro.

"The Lord of Mimasaka wants Master Sanza to help him build a
castle. The letter came from Master Sanza's sister. She told him to
come quickly."

Building a castle was always an urgent matter. Then the castle
was destroyed. What was the point of it? She was disappointed that
Sanza was the kind of man who needed a castle to be happy. And it
will not even be his, she thought despairingly.

Okuni danced every day, trying to attract an audience. But Okuni's body had lost its vitality, her movements were listless, her voice

dull. Densuke's comedy, too, was not the same. There was a desperate quality to it. He was trying to be amusing. The girls danced brightly enough but they could not dispel the gloomy atmosphere Okuni brought to the stage.

Eighteen

Through the increasing chill of autumn, Okuni's dancing failed to entice back the audiences the troupe had once enjoyed. Several of the small stages and sideshow shacks in the riverbed disappeared. Their places were taken by large new theaters. Each was managed by one of the wealthy houses of prostitution in Rokujo Street. Admission was absurdly cheap, but it didn't matter. When the girls lured the spectators back to their houses of prostitution in the evening, they made up any money the owners had lost in staging the performances.

One day workmen came to tear down the small dancing stage that stood next to Okuni's theater. The men enclosed a particularly large area with a green bamboo fence.

"It's going to be a prostitutes' Kabuki theater."

"Another one?" Okuni grew angry when she heard that still another group of prostitutes had stolen her name and were calling themselves "Courtesans' Kabuki."

"I wonder how they got the troupe next door to move out?"

"Money."

"Eh?"

"They paid for the land."

"Whores must be rich to pay for land in the riverbed no one owns."

"Well, the house owners are."

Densuke and Mame went outside to watch the new theater going up. They were depressed and talked in subdued voices. Sankuro and

Okiku stood by themselves, examining the expensive construction of the new stage floor.

Okiku faced Sankuro, eyes smoldering with resentment. "Since prostitutes are allowed to come here to steal our customers, I say let's move into their business. We can call ourselves prostitutes from Izumo. We'll make a big hit."

Okiku's boldness and strength still astonished Sankuro. He chuckled and said in a bantering tone, "And will you advertise Okuni as a whore, too?"

Okiku was serious in her reply: "Okuni couldn't be a prostitute if she wanted to."

"Oh, and why is that?"

"No one would buy her." Okiku's large eyes glittered maliciously. "She struts around and she boasts that she's best in the world. But if you think about it, she's an old woman, Sankuro. If she was a prostitute, she'd never catch a customer!"

"Hmm." Sankuro could feel the deep hatred toward Okuni that lay behind Okiku's words. He noted with satisfaction that he felt no emotion at all. "Maybe it's time we abandoned Okuni."

"Do you mean that, Sankuro?"

He did mean it. When talk of Okuni's love affair with Sanza was on everyone's tongue, Sankuro was terribly humiliated. But his masculine pride hadn't allowed him to be driven away from the troupe by gossip. That was now past, and no feeling of any kind remained to tie him to Okuni or the troupe. "It's more than Okuni," he explained. "Prostitutes' Kabuki is going to take over Shijo Street, and we should leave before it does."

"Where can we go?"

"Edo. That's the only place."

That night, winter blew in on a bitter wind. The coldest place in the city was along the riverbank, but when morning dawned snowless and bright, men came from all parts of the city to see their favorite whores at Shijo Street. Through that long winter customers filled the prostitutes' theaters. In spite of her resolve, there were days when Okuni was forced to stop dancing because not one patron entered their gate.

"That interesting music is the *jabisen*. Should we go over and see?" Densuke turned and spoke to Okuni. It worried him to see her sinking deeper into apathy with each winter day. She didn't go outside and spent her days in the theater doing nothing at all. Densuke wanted to suggest some diversion but it wasn't easy to think of one in the wintertime.

"I don't want to see prostitutes." Okuni frowned. She was in such a bad mood that Densuke was the only person in the troupe who could speak to her.

"It's just next door. We can peek through the fence." He tried to be gently persuasive.

"I don't want to peek in."

"Then I'll buy two tickets for us."

"It's all right if you go by yourself, Densuke."

"If I wanted to go alone, I'd step out the door and look. I want you to see it, Okuni."

"Why?"

"Aren't you the *kabuki* dancer who sets the latest styles, Okuni?"

"I won't see prostitutes."

"Not prostitutes. Prostitutes' Kabuki. Don't you wonder what it's like?"

"They're just copying Okuni's Kabuki. They're using the name I made."

"If they're imitating us, don't you want to find out what they're imitating? Besides, merchants and soldiers from all over the country go in and out of the gay quarter. The prostitutes must have picked up something from them that's new. Come on, Okuni. Stand up, let's go." Okuni resisted, but Densuke took her by the hand, led her across the street, paid their admission fee, and took her inside the theater of prostitutes.

They entered as the performance was starting. Although the stage of Okuni's theater had been enlarged after she earned her reputation as Best in the World, the stage before her was easily twice its size.

The music began and twenty girls dressed in gorgeous kimonos danced in a sinuous line onto the stage. Although only a few of the girls were beautiful, their faces, armored in thick layers of makeup, radiated self-confidence. In spite of the fact that their gestures were ragged and often did not match the music, they danced audaciously, oblivious of their faults. Because they were all dressed alike they made a spectacular impression.

Ten to twelve singers and musicians, all men, sat along the back and sides of the stage. They almost certainly were professional street musicians, recently recruited for this kind of performance, because they were fairly skillful and knew all the current popular songs.

> When you do not come at night
> I strike my guiltless pillow,
> Upright, on its side,
> Every which way.
> Pillow, pillow, guiltless pillow.
>
> Females, small fry,
> Moving up and down
> Beneath the bridge,
> Never sleeping alone.
>
> Be compassionate, for to man
> The world is dew
> On the petal
> Of the rose.
>
> The passing world is a dream,
> An illusion,
> No more than madness.

Densuke didn't particularly watch the stage but he listened carefully as the singers moved from one song to the next. They're not bad, he thought. This music was far richer and more harmonic than the drum and bell music of Okuni's group. Melody-carrying instruments made up the core of the ensemble: several types of flutes and a dozen lutes, both the old *biwa* and the new *jabisen*. The strings were able to carry the vocal melody when the singers rested, which was an interesting development. Because the promoters were brothel owners, most of the short songs were about sexual passion. The tone of the *jabisen*, too, was lasciviously suggestive.

When the group dance was over and the stage was clear, a large square pillow covered with silk brocade was placed in the center of the empty stage. A magnificently dressed courtesan, with a vain expression on her face, entered like a ship in full sail. She settled herself grandly on the pillow, making it clear she was the star of the troupe. She wore several layers of kimonos, the hems of which trailed on the floor. Over them she wore a robe of heavy silk, embroidered with designs of flowers and birds in a rare Southern Barbarian style. Two young girls offered her a *jabisen* with a great show of reverence. The courtesan held the slender instrument diagonally across her knees and plucked the strings with her fingers while she sang:

> And now it is told that in the reign of Emperor Toba, the Courtesan's Dance was born. Wearing white trousers and lacquered hat, and clasping a short dagger at her side, the most beautiful woman in the land, the courtesan Gio, danced before his majesty.

It was a well-known section from the epic *The Tale of the Heike*. Gio was a professional female dancer who had brought the White Dance, so called because of its costume, into the imperial court. Usually *The Tale of the Heike* was chanted by a blind beggar-monk, like the man Baian had encountered at the Plum Blossom Festival in Tenmangu Shrine the day he first saw Okuni dance. The three-stringed *jabisen* could not reproduce the music of the old-style *biwa*, which had six strings, but its sound was brilliant and strong. The courtesan sang rather than chanted the words, and the ancient melody of the *biwa* had been extensively revised for the *jabisen*. The sensuous timbre of a woman's voice was mysteriously appealing, especially in this episode from the tale about a seductive female singer-dancer. After each sung phrase, piquant reverberations from the taut *jabisen* strings hung in the air.

With the brazen attitude of a woman who knows she has captivated her male audience, the courtesan rewarded her fans with a come-hither smile over her shoulder as she swept offstage. On cue, percussionists played a quick rhythm on the drums and bells.

The chorus line of prostitutes, costumed in fresh kimonos, re-entered, singing and dancing. The performance was called Kabuki, but the prostitutes appeared as themselves and no prostitute played a man. About the only thing the troupe had borrowed from Okuni was her innovation of opening the kimono at the hem to accommodate active footwork. The prostitutes moved languorously, and certainly never considered leaping, but the opened kimonos showed a good deal of white female leg. The twenty primping women were ludicrous dancers. They walked in a circle, they flipped their sleeves from one side to the other, they waggled their hips, and that was all.

No. That is not Kabuki.

A painful cry arose in Okuni's heart. How dare they call this Kabuki? This isn't art. This isn't dance. This is a show to seduce men, a way to sell whores. Were the prostitutes shocked to see Okuni staring at them with fierce malevolence in her eyes? In any case, they quickly lifted their skirts and ran offstage. The show was over. The women formed a long line in the street in front of the theater, paraded across Shijo Bridge, and turned south, parallel to the riverbank. Men from the audience, aroused by the brief performance onstage, followed after them. The men and women together made a long, long procession. After them came stagehands and musicians and other workers at the theater. Finally, the brothel owner who sponsored the show strolled along at the rear, a sly smile on his face. The true purpose of Courtesans' Kabuki was not the performance onstage, but this processional "performance" of whores and their customers from Shijo to Rokujo each day. What better way to advertise a whorehouse than by displaying its wares in public, both on a stage and in the street? And, of course, it was completely legal, thanks to Kyuzo's foresight.

Okuni was physically revolted as she left the theater. Densuke's normally pale face, however, was flushed with excitement.

"Well, it has something, don't you think?" Densuke spoke to Kanji standing in the entrance to their theater.

"You can say it's gaudy, I suppose. It's over soon. Then that parade."

"What's interesting is the *jabisen*. It makes a lot of different tones and colors depending on how you pluck it." He turned to Okuni, "The prostitute dances are ridiculous, I know, but the *jabisen* is different. Its sound is interesting. Why don't we buy one and learn to play it, Okuni?"

Okuni stopped and glared at Densuke, "*Jabisen, jabisen*? What are you talking about, Densuke? That's whores' music. Why should Okuni's Kabuki copy a whore's performance?"

Just as Okuni would not let her eyes see the expressions, half fear and half despair, on the faces of Densuke and the others, she would not allow her ears to hear the sounds of the new *jabisen*. It's not clear when Okuni, in her stubbornness, first began to close off her heart. But surely this was the moment she resolved to stand fast for the art she had created and to defend her reputation as Best in the World. How could she possibly imitate prostitutes? The challenge further strengthened her obstinate spirit. I will not use the *jabisen*. I can dance without it. I am Best in the World.

Jabisen players in the riverbed did not wait for spring breezes to lift their melodies and intermingle them in the air. Before the plum blossoms were out, bright streams of notes spread out past the green lattice fences into Shijo Street. When the *jabisen* was played alone, its melody was impressive and splendid. When its reverberations were joined by the notes of a flute, the sound was ravishing.

Kanji waited until Okuni and Densuke were not near before he approached Sankuro. "If Okuni doesn't like the *jabisen*, why can't we use it just when the other girls dance?"

"I've already thought about that. The problem is, who will play it?"

"I will," Okiku broke in, "I'll play it."

The *jabisen* was still a relatively new instrument in Kyoto, so merchants were able to ask exorbitant prices for it. Sankuro had been reluctant to invest in a *jabisen*, but now that Okiku wanted to play it, buying one became another matter. Using the troupe's money, Sankuro bought Okiku a *jabisen* that had been imported from the Ryukyu Islands. The dealer explained that this style of lute had been invented in China, where it was called *sangen* or *san hsien*, "three strings," and then it had been taken up in the Ryukyu Islands. Its three strings stretched down a long, thin neck to a square sounding box covered with a tightly-stretched snakeskin. In the past ten years, Kyoto merchants had begun to import instruments made in the Ryukyus. Some people called the lute a *jamisen*, which later was to become *shamisen*, but mostly it was called *jabisen*, meaning snakeskin, *jabi*, and strings, *sen*. Okiku was proud to own such a rare object, and she would not allow any other troupe member to touch it.

Okiku found a blind monk-minstrel named Ganjo to teach her. He had been a wandering *biwa* player, a chanter of *The Tale of the Heike*, but now he was too old to travel the country playing and singing for a living. He had easily learned to play the new instrument, and he was happy to take Okiku as a pupil. She went to his house every day to study. Ganjo's singing style was old-fashioned, but he knew every trick of lute playing. He listened intently to Okiku's playing and made exacting corrections.

"No. That's wrong. Move your middle finger higher on the string."

"Like this?"

"Higher. Slide your finger up."

"You mean this way?"

"Hm. Good."

Okiku learned quickly. Ganjo's corrections did not upset her, indeed she welcomed them, for she was determined to learn to play as well as any professional. In fact, as the lessons went on, Okiku's naturally aggressive nature asserted itself and before long their positions were reversed. Okiku acted like the teacher, commanding Ganjo to do whatever she wanted. She was impatient to learn as much and as quickly as possible; she also looked down on him as her social inferior. She expected him to serve her. For his part, Ganjo was used to being ordered about. All his life he'd been a wandering beggar; he didn't resent her demands. Ganjo was teaching her *Chikubu Island*, a slow, plaintive piece from the old repertory, that he especially liked.

"That's dull. It's too slow," Okiku snapped, irritated. "Don't waste my time. Sing something lively that men in the audience will like."

"Next lesson I will."

"No. Do it now, Ganjo. Hurry up." And so Ganjo taught her a current popular song, set to *jabisen* music. "Yes, that's what I want. Now, teach me another song."

Each afternoon when she returned from her lesson, Okiku took her place proudly in the center of the stage to practice finger exercises and complicated runs for hours at a time. The detailed fingering on the neck with the left hand was particularly difficult to master. It also required unwavering attention to keep the nails of her right hand from tearing the delicate snakeskin when she plucked the strings. At first, others in the troupe admired Okiku, for she was diligent, but after a few months, the *jabisen*'s harsh, insistent sound began to get under people's skin. Precisely because Okiku was so engrossed in practicing, she was utterly oblivious to how much ill will she was creating with her self-centered attitude. Kanji had a special reason to feel resentful: he had suggested buying the *jabisen* in the first place, and now Okiku wouldn't let him play it. He spoke in a deliberately loud voice, "It's absurd. Does she think she can draw an audience by herself?"

And, of course, Okuni was the most furious of them all.

The *jabisen* is for whores' Kabuki. Do you want us to imitate prostitutes? Surely both Sankuro and Okiku remembered Okuni's biting comments. Sankuro bought the *jabisen* knowing I hate it and Okiku constantly plays it to spite me, she fumed to herself. It wasn't a question of whether Okiku played the *jabisen* skillfully or, like Omatsu, was talentless. Each time Okiku returned to the theater cradling the *jabisen*, and began to strike its strings, Okuni felt as if those sharp nails were scratching her face. No matter how well she plays, I will never dance to the *jabisen*. Never. Never.

Looking across the river from their dressing room toward the cloud-shrouded hills east of Kyoto, the city was cloaked in a gentle rain.

"The flower rain is here." Okuni spoke loudly, peering up at the sky.

Early summer in the Japanese islands is marked by a steady drizzle, poetically known as "flower rain" or "plum rain." From June and into July traveling was a wet, muddy, miserable chore to be avoided, if possible. During the rainy season the theaters next to Shijo Street were closed. Not even the most avid patrons of the prostitutes were seen along the riverside.

Densuke felt grumpy that morning. He put a cloth on his head and went outside to relieve himself. A figure approached in the rain. It was Sarujiro, who had left the troupe several months before to join his master in Mimasaka.

"Sarujiro? What are you doing back in Kyoto? Come in, come in," Densuke cried out, ushering him through the door. Sarujiro didn't reply, but went inside, his face drawn and expressionless. "Look who's here," Densuke called out.

Okuni caught her breath. Without thinking she blurted out, "Sanza. Where is Sanza?"

Sarujiro slowly lifted his gaze from the ground, "Master Sanza is dead."

"It's a lie. You're making fun of me," Okuni cried. Surely he's making a joke, she thought. No one spoke.

"No. It's not a lie," Sarujiro said finally.

After Densuke and Kanji helped Sarujiro change into dry clothes, he described to Okuni what had happened. When Master Sanza arrived in Mimasaka, Lord Tadamasa, his sister's husband, treated him kindly. But his lord didn't give Sanza any specific responsibility. Tadamasa was young and inexperienced in governing, and he was in a torment trying to decide if he should build his castle on the plain or on a hilltop. Sanza immediately argued in favor of putting the castle on the plain, where it would serve as an administrative center for the surrounding fief. There wouldn't be any more wars, Sanza reasoned, so a defensible site, like a hilltop, wasn't needed. Tadamasa's chief retainer was a fearless samurai named Ido Uemon. He mocked Sanza to his face, calling him a coward and an effete Kyoto dandy. Uemon insisted the castle be built on Tsuru Hill to satisfy clan honor. A castle perched on Tsuru Hill would be guarded by two swiftly flowing rivers and a moat, making it nearly impregnable to assault. Eventually Lord Tadamasa selected the mountain site for his castle. After that, Sanza was very discontented.

Uemon insulted Sanza every chance he got. One night Sanza casually mentioned the beauty of the shining moon. Uemon laughed sarcastically, saying any fool knew that the sun shone, but the moon did not. In early spring, Sanza galloped close to Uemon while out riding, deliberately splashing him with mud. Uemon turned red with rage, but he couldn't retaliate just then because he was escorting several clan elders.

Sarujiro narrated the final incident. "One day at the beginning of spring, I was walking beside Master Sanza while he was out riding. Before we knew it, we were surrounded by Uemon and a group of his soldiers on horseback. Uemon tied back his sleeves, getting ready to fight. He shouted at Master Sanza, 'You're a little man, Sanza. You'll die before you interfere with my plans to build the castle.' Master Sanza calmly rode up next to Uemon, smiling quietly as if he didn't care about Uemon's threat. Master Sanza didn't even have his hand on his sword. That criminal, Uemon. He screamed and suddenly cut Master Sanza across the head and chest."

Okuni said thickly, "And what did Sanza do?"

"He spurred his horse away. When I found him he was weak and couldn't drink the water I gave him. He died in my arms." Sarujiro began to weep.

Okuni turned white. Okiku's cheeks flushed crimson, and she tensed with suppressed excitement. "And Ido Uemon, what happened to him?"

"Lord Tadamasa was very angry because Uemon didn't have the right to kill. Lord Tadamasa was the only one in Mimasaka who could do that. So the lord sent soldiers to catch Uemon, a strong man who wouldn't surrender. Uemon cut and slashed and hacked until a dozen soldiers were wounded. They finished him off with spears."

"What an interesting story!" Okiku laughed and clapped her hands, as if she were listening to Ganjo narrate a battle from *The Tale of the Heike*. "Uemon killed Sanza with one cut of the sword, but it took a troop of soldiers to kill Uemon. My, Uemon was a brave samurai. Wasn't he, Sankuro?" She turned to him, speaking vivaciously.

As might be expected, Sankuro refused to get involved in Okiku's attack on Okuni. He didn't reply.

Okuni merely frowned and said, "It's all foolishness."

It's true, Okuni thought, a warrior's life is fleeting and sad. Because Sanza believed in the pride of a samurai, he couldn't remain with the best woman in the world. He became a provincial bureaucrat. He was killed over a trifling incident and with a single blow of a sword. What a waste, she thought. For all his grand plans, what a disappointing end. Okuni could not help resenting it when Sanza deserted her. Now the oppressive feeling was gone. In its place a deep longing for his return began to grow. She did not shed one tear. Sanza's death purged Okuni of her bad memories. From this time on Okuni believed Sanza had left her side so that he might die.

Sarujiro joined the troupe that day. He was surprised to see the many prostitutes' theaters in the riverbed. There had been only one when he left Kyoto to join Sanza hardly three months before. He worried about the competition they would give their troupe in midsummer, when the rainy season was over. In spite of the rain, Sarujiro went for long walks to various parts of the city almost everyday. He went alone, and when asked, he said he was visiting places he had known before. He didn't mention what else was on his mind.

One afternoon Sarujiro stood quietly before Okuni and Densuke. "We should perform in the riding field of Kitano Shrine. It's crowded with people, even in the rain. I've just come from there."

"Kitano Shrine?" Okuni remembered how they hadn't been able to play at Kitano because they had been so afraid Baian would disapprove. Now they could perform any where they wanted. But Okuni was loath to leave Shijo Street.

"Someone might steal the theater," Densuke fretted.

Sarujiro had a confident reply. "Everyone in Kyoto knows this theater belongs to Okuni. Even the prostitutes can't challenge the banner of the woman who is Best in the World."

Somewhat reassured by Sarujiro, Densuke nodded. Okuni instantly made up her mind. "We'll set up a stage and dance at Kitano Shrine."

With these few words the gloomy atmosphere in the theater was transformed; troupe members were excited by the new challenge. The men immediately went to the riding field, found a good site on the broad grassy area in front of the shrine, and began to set up a small temporary stage that was gay and attractive. The women brought out all their kimonos. After spreading them out, they tried to decide which to wear at Kitano.

Turning to Sankuro, Okiku spoke out forcefully, "I'm going to play the *jabisen* on the stage at Kitano. I'm going to sing. I've learned three popular songs that men will like."

Okuni cut her off sharply. "No you won't, Okiku."

"What?"

"I'm not going to put a trained monkey on stage to beg for coins. I'll never use the *jabisen* in Okuni's Kabuki. Never."

"Did you call me a monkey, Okuni?"

"You're a talented dancer, Okiku. But when you play the *jabisen*, you're not any better than a trained monkey."

"What?" The blood rushed to Okiku's face. She leaped to her feet and struck Okuni, knocking her to the floor.

"Stop it! Stop!" Sankuro seized Okiku's hand and pulled her away.

Okuni calmly straightened her clothes. She looked at Okiku, who was panting and trembling in anger. "I don't care what you say, Okiku, Okuni's Kabuki doesn't need the *jabisen*."

As the pain began to spread from her eye, Okuni sat down and took out a mirror. Two long red scratches made by Okiku's nails ran down her cheek. Okuni laughed inwardly. She had remained cool while Okiku had lost her temper. That was the way she would win, she knew.

It was as if Okiku's blow had decided the matter for Okuni. From that moment on she planned every detail of the Kitano production herself. She borrowed nothing from the prostitutes' show. She relied on nothing Sankuro had taught her. Instead, she followed her instincts and relied on her own stage experience. She recalled old songs they had once done, and by rearranging them, she created interesting variations. She taught the girls the words they were to sing at Kitano; she set the gestures and steps they were to dance there. Densuke was astonished at Okuni's directing skill. When she was choreographing one of the dance scenes, Okuni assigned a small part to Okiku.

"I'm not going to Kitano," Okiku said through pouting lips.

"If you're not going, stay here and watch the theater," Okuni replied brusquely, showing no concern. With that decision, one more problem within the small company was resolved; Okiku would remain in Shijo where she could practice the *jabisen,* and Sankuro would stay with her.

Every morning Okuni rehearsed the girls in their dances. Densuke became more and more agitated as he watched, until at last he asked Okuni with an anguished expression, "Okuni, aren't you going to dance?"

Okuni stared open-eyed at Densuke. "Do you think I could bear it if I didn't dance? I'm not like Okiku."

"But you're not in any scene."

"Well, that's what I'm considering. When do you think I'll make my entrance, Densuke?" Okuni laughed delightedly. "If I can surprise you, think how exciting it will be for the audience. I'm not even going to tell you, Densuke, before we open at Kitano Shrine." She laughed again. Densuke had not seen such a dazzling smile in a long time.

The truth was that Okuni had become a different person as the rehearsals progressed. The apathetic, aged woman that she had been for the past half year magically disappeared. Okuni was the oldest woman in the troupe, yet Densuke could see that she was the most fascinating and vivacious among them.

The Kitano area, famous for its plum and cherry trees, was a far more beautiful place than the riverbed at Shijo Street. It was long past the season now for plum or even cherry blossoms, and the trees' lacy branches were pale green with young leaves. As its name indicates, Kitano, or North Field, was located in the upper part of town, not far from the Imperial Palace. Whereas customers along Shijo Street were predominantly men, Kitano's visitors were mostly women, including many court ladies. Ah, this is the audience that will like my Kabuki, Okuni thought to herself, when she saw the constant parade of women through the shrine area.

That morning people strolled through the grassy area of the riding field under a deep, blue sky, drawn out by the warmth of early summer. Kanji set out the troupe's two white banners that read Okuni's Kabuki and Best in the World, on either side of the theater entrance.

"The Best in the World?"

"It's Okuni's Kabuki."

"Have they come up from Shijo Street?"

"Let's go in."

When the first few spectators had gathered, every member of the troupe began singing in unison, following Okuni's plan:

> Viewed from afar
> Willow and cherry mingle,
> Adorning Kyoto
> In the springtime.

Some beat the drum while they were singing, while others struck the bell. Sarujiro played the melody on the flute. They repeated the verse again and again, until the sounds floating over the riding field drew enough curious spectators to fill the open ground in front of the stage.

It was midmorning when the girls came dancing onstage to a lively song. In spite of the hour, a few of the men in the audience were already, or perhaps still, drunk. Some clapped along with the girls' leaping steps. Some pranced in front of the stage—mimicking the girls—drinking from flasks of rice wine as they danced. When Densuke appeared as an old woman, several court ladies in the audience brought their sleeves to their mouths to stifle laughter, and the men howled and held their sides. Still Okuni did not appear onstage.

"Which is the number one woman?"

"Hasn't Okuni come out yet?"

Just as the audience was growing restless, Okane entered dressed in a flowered kimono, the crystal rosary encircling her neck. She began a long dance, fluttering the sleeves of her kimono and skillfully manipulating her trailing skirt.

> In Kyoto's flowery spring,
> In Kyoto's flowery spring,
> Let's go see the Kabuki dance.
> The plover cries, spring is gone,
> But the heart of Kabuki remains the same.
> Pilgrims in colorful clothes,
> People high and low,
> Are drawn to Kitano
> To worship
> And to cheer,
> God's gift to mankind!
> This is God's gift to man!

The audience listened raptly to the lyrics that, in a form reminiscent of Noh plays, cleverly brought together references to Kabuki and to Kitano Shrine. When the dance was over loud whispers arose in the audience.

"Wait a minute, something's wrong."

"Hm, I don't think it's Okuni."

"Is she the Best in the World?"

"Never. That's not her."

"Where's Okuni? We want Okuni."

"Come out, Okuni!"

Perhaps it was part of Okuni's plan not to enter until the audience clamored for her to appear. In any case, while everyone was looking at the stage, waiting for Okuni to come out dancing, a figure rose in the middle of the audience and addressed Okane in a silvery voice.

"I come to speak with Okuni. Do you not remember me? Cherished memories from the past draw me here."

Okane was as surprised as everyone else in the theater. She couldn't see the face beneath the man's large hat, but she noticed two gold swords in his sash. She quickly recalled the dialogue Okuni had taught her.

"How should I know you, appearing unexpectedly in the midst of a crowd? Yet you seem familiar. Tell me your name."

Loosening the cords of the hat, the man spoke in a ringing voice.

"In times past you and I played Kabuki together. I cannot forget the memory, and so I appear before you."

"Are you the spirit of a dead man returned to earth?"

The man came up to the stage and took off his hat. The audience gasped with a single breath: the man was Okuni. The two danced, singing in unison.

> I have as many words to speak,
> As there are needles on the pine.
> The scent of your sleeve leads me
> To the riding field at Kitano.
> Do you not know who I am?

Okane resumed the dialogue. "I cannot forget your parting words. Were you not the *kabuki* dandy, Nagoya Sanza, who dressed like the Southern Barbarians?"

"I am ashamed to hear my name. An enemy killed me in a foolish quarrel. I regret departing this world, leaving behind only my name, Nagoya Sanza."

As the dialogue continued, murmurs rose in the audience.

"That's Okuni."

"It's Nagoya Sanza."

"No one's seen Sanza in a long time. He was murdered, they say."

"She just said he was killed."

Okuni seized the moment to return to one of their old melodies. Okane's clear voice joined in the chorus and soon she and Okuni were ardently dancing in the center of the stage, as if in the throes of passion. The audience watched, enthralled. Okuni and Okane danced off the bridgeway to loud and cheerful applause.

"Nagoya Sanza's come back!"

"Okuni's playing Sanza!"

Word spread through the riding field, and indeed throughout the city, that the ghost of Nagoya Sanza had appeared at Okuni's theater to sing and dance in a new Kabuki play. It seemed that everyone in the city wanted to see Okuni's new performance, including many patrons of the prostitutes' shows at Shijo Street.

Okuni immersed herself in Sanza's memory. Gradually she added to her costume his plum-colored underkimono, red cap worn beneath the straw hat, Buddhist rosary, purple velvet sash, and red tassels at the waist—all the objects he had left behind. It was terrifying for Densuke to watch the tranformation; Okuni emptied her soul and welcomed the spirit of the man she loved so that she might become him. She was giving herself, and her life, to this dance. What would she do when the people tired of it? In time they would.

Dearest Okuni, how long can you dance?

Nineteen

Okuni's troupe danced every day that summer of 1604 in their small theater on the riding field beside Kitano Shrine. Perhaps it was the oppressive heat that year. Perhaps the prostitutes' shows improved. Or perhaps, as Densuke had predicted, people's interest in Okuni's portrayal of Sanza naturally flagged after a time. Whatever the reason, when the fierce dog days of late summer arrived in Kyoto, even Okuni, who rarely worried about the size of the audience, realized something had to be done. They discussed the situation off and on for several days without deciding what to do. Okuni didn't really want to leave Kitano, and, other than Shijo Street, where else could they successfully play? Two events occurred in quick succession that resolved the matter. When the decision came it was sudden but not, in hindsight, strange.

First, they were peremptorily summoned in the middle of August to give a private performance at the residence of Okubo Nagayasu, a very unusual retainer of Ieyasu. Nagayasu had been a Noh actor in the Kanze troupe before he had impressed Ieyasu with his remarkable administrative abilities. He brilliantly organized a system to supply and feed Ieyasu's army during the Battle of Sekigahara. He urged Ieyasu to shorten the official land measurement rod by four inches, with the result that the Shogun's income from the rice tax immediately increased. Perhaps most important, within months after Ieyasu appointed him supervisor of the new gold mines on Sado Island, Nagayasu increased productivity ten-fold. Ieyasu valued him highly and as a result, Nagayasu amassed a huge personal fortune from the business matters entrusted to him. He was a burly, aggressive man, used to having his own way. When he heard about Okuni in the midst of a drunken party, he decided to have her perform there and then. He sent servants and low-ranking samurai in his employ straight to the theater, and without even waiting for a reply, they put the troupe's instruments and costumes into chests and began to carry them away. Not even the emperor had treated them so arrogantly. Okuni was indignant, but they had no choice but to cut the performance short, apologize to the audience, and run after the servants. Soon they reached Nagayasu's large residence in the upper part of the city. Nagayasu was already drunk when they arrived, but he sobered instantly when Okuni began to perform. He liked her immediately. With growing admiration, he watched her strong, direct movements. Later, he was impressed by the confident way she answered the many questions he asked her about the troupe. He presented Okuni with valuable gifts, including a small gold case that a man would hang from his sash. Finally, he laughed expansively and said he wanted Okuni to perform Kabuki on Sado Island. Okuni didn't know what to say. She scarcely had heard the name Sado, let alone know where the island was. But Nagayasu didn't give her time to demur. He looked out at his guests gathered in the room and announced in a booming voice, as if the matter was settled, "I tell you, Okuni is the Best in the World. Two days from now, when I leave for Sado, Okuni's coming with me."

The following morning Okuni got up as the sun was rising. She woke everyone and told them to be ready for the day's performance.

"What performance, Okuni? We have to go to Sado tomorrow," Mame grumbled, opening his eyes.

"I know that. Tomorrow is tomorrow. And today is today: we have our audience to think of today." Not one person in the troupe wanted to go to far-off Sado Island. They were all extremely worried because no one knew how to refuse such an influential man as Nagayasu. But it was in Okuni's nature to set aside tomorrow's problems in order to focus on the needs of today. When the audience gathered, she danced with all her soul, as she always did. But Mame and Densuke and the others were too distracted to perform well.

Backstage afterward, Okuni showed her irritation. "There's no point yelling about Sado Island. You sang terribly today. And you danced terribly, too."

"We're not yelling, Okuni," Mame sulked, looking out the door. "It's Kanji in front, with a blind singer."

"What are you talking about? I said the performance was bad."

"He's looking for Okiku."

Okuni looked out of the door at the thin old man in a dirty linen kimono groveling in the dust and clinging to Densuke. "Why do you want Okiku?"

"We two are husband and wife. I seek my beloved." He spoke in exaggerated phrases, as if he were still chanting *The Tale of the Heike*.

The idea was preposterous but Okuni replied, "She's not here. Go to the theater at Shijo Street."

But Okiku was not at Shijo Street, the man insisted. He had just been at the riverbed searching for her. Okuni's theater and Okiku were gone. Kanji and Okuni ran the whole way to Shijo Street to see for themselves if it was true. Densuke started to go, too, but the blind old man clung to his legs and begged pitiably for Okiku.

Densuke hadn't the heart to leave him. "How did you happen to meet Okiku?"

"She came to me. Teach me to play the *jabisen,* she begged."

"You were her teacher? Are you Ganjo?" Densuke remembered the name from Okiku's conversation.

"She said I couldn't touch her body until after I taught her everything."

"What?"

"She learned quickly. I gave her all my secrets. And then, she and I..."

"She slept with you?"

"I can't forget it!"

Densuke shuddered as he looked down at the trembling old man, spittle dripping from his mouth, his limbs jerking grotesquely in the dirt. The memory of Okiku's warm, young body was imprisoned in Ganjo's withered flesh. His milky white, sightless eyes rolled up beseechingly.

"Okiku, can't you hear me? It's your Ganjo. I've come to find you. Okiku! Don't leave me!"

Densuke held Ganjo's hand and tried to soothe him. "Ganjo, Okiku's gone. You know yourself she isn't at Shijo Street. Well, she isn't here, either. Who knows where she's gone?"

Ganjo clasped the *jabisen* tightly in his arms and rocked back and forth on the ground, mumbling over and over, "Okiku. Okiku."

Okuni ran up to their site in the riverbed, shouting to everyone within hearing, "This is my place! This is where Okuni's Kabuki is performed! What are you doing here!" Kanji arrived a few steps behind her, panting heavily. They stared at a large new theater that stood where Okuni's stage once had been.

A deep, hard voice came from inside the theater. "What do you mean this place belongs to you, Okuni? My master, the owner of the Court Maidens, paid a man named Sankuro good money for this land." The implacable figure of Kyuzo came out from behind the lattice fence of freshly cut bamboo that surrounded the theater, followed by his dog, Black. Kyuzo's attitude was overbearing, as if he had been waiting for Okuni to arrive.

"Kyuzo! Sankuro sold you my theater?"

"He got a damned good price." He pulled a document from his breast and held it out contemptuously, saying, "The land is ours and we've got a license from the city magistrate to perform Courtesans' Kabuki on this spot. If you could read, Okuni, you'd understand." Okuni, seeing the look of dejection on Kanji's face as he scanned the paper, knew Kyuzo was telling the truth. There wasn't anything Okuni or Kanji could say. "Master, do you want to see the dancer who says she's best in the world?"

A fat, well-dressed man came out of the new theater. "So, you're Okuni, are you?" The owner of the house of prostitution then inspected Okuni as if she were some kind of rare animal and said with a slight smile, "Okuni, how would you like to dance for me? I'll gladly add you to my wares. And I'll buy your Best in the World banner, too."

"Master, that's a good idea. If Okuni's on our stage and her banner's in front, people will line up to see the Best Prostitutes' Kabuki in the World!" The two men roared at Kyuzo's cruel joke.

The agony that Sanza had endured when Uemon's sword entered his chest was surely no fiercer than the pain that now impaled Okuni's breast. It was as if her heart were being cut open. Without replying to either man, she turned away from Shijo Street and began walking north at a deliberate pace along the river's broad bank. She tried to imagine why Sankuro and Kyuzo so hated the Kabuki performance she had created at Shijo Street. She tried to think clearly, to understand; perhaps the theater in the riverbed was her castle, and the men had to destroy it and her reputation as Best in the World. She tried to forget the unctuous face of the Court Maidens' whoremaster, but his leering smile kept returning to her mind. Kyuzo, who had loved her in Izumo more than twenty years ago, could be forgotten. His deliberate, malicious revenge grew from a heart that was so dark she could not comprehend it.

Okuni was still locked away in her thoughts when she walked into the theater in Kitano. Kanji followed a few minutes later. It was left to Kanji to tell the others that Sankuro had sold their theater and that he and Okiku had disappeared. They sat in silent groups. With Sankuro gone and Okuni withdrawn into herself, no one knew what to do.

Suddenly, Ganjo lifted his face to the sky and cried out, "Edo! It's Edo!"

"Why are you still here, old man?" Okuni glanced with annoyance at Ganjo's wrinkled face. She hated the *jabisen* he clutched in his knobby hands. "What about Edo?"

"That's where Okiku is! I know it. She talked about it all the time. I'm going to Edo!" Ganjo scrambled to his feet and scuttled this way and that, as if searching for his bearings.

Okuni slowly stood and, looking around her, said, "I'm going to Edo, too."

"To look for Sankuro?" Kanji asked without thinking.

"No!" Okuni violently shook her head. "I'm not looking for Sankuro. I'm going to Edo to find myself." She continued, as if to convince herself, "I'm tired of dancing in Kyoto. I'm going to Edo."

So they all agreed, without more discussion, to set out for Edo. They left Kyoto that afternoon, carrying only their costumes, properties, musical instruments, and a few personal possessions. They didn't worry too much about what Nagayasu would do when he discovered they were gone. They were departing a day before Nagayasu and were traveling in the opposite direction from Sado Island, so they wouldn't meet him. After a few days the troupe settled into a leisurely pace, walking along the tree-shaded and heavily traveled Tokaido post road to Edo. They reached Mikawa Province, Tokugawa Ieyasu's birthplace, on the fifth day. On the eleventh day they passed Odawara Castle, which Ieyasu had helped capture for Hideyoshi in 1590. Several times along the way, they performed at post towns. It was pleasant to hear the country audiences laugh openly and lustily applaud at the end. They felt refreshed, though physically tired, when they arrived at the boundary of Ieyasu's new capital city after traveling for two weeks.

Edo is a new city with new ideas, Okuni reflected. I can make a new start here.

Tokugawa Ieyasu had been given rule over the six extensive provinces of the Kanto flood plain as a reward for his services in the Battle of Odawara Castle. The lands produced a staggering two-and-a-half-million bushels of rice annually, making Ieyasu the richest provincial lord serving Hideyoshi. Ieyasu deliberately selected the small village of Edo to be the site of his castle, a choice much criticized by his retainers, until Ieyasu became shogun in 1603. Then his wisdom in placing his government in an accessible place, at the edge of Edo Bay, became apparent. The period of internal wars had ended, and Ieyasu's task was to govern the country from his new city. Edo had the further advantage of being far from Kyoto. The emperor and his courtiers would not be able to continue their tiresome meddling in state affairs. And the austere code of discipline which Ieyasu tirelessly inculcated in his samurai would not be corrupted by the decadent values of the court.

One month after becoming shogun in 1603, Ieyasu set forth a strict conscripted labor requirement for each of his seventy vassal lords. Based on the size of their land holdings, each was responsible for providing not only an assigned number of workers and their food, but the tools and construction materials needed to build the new capital. At the city's center was Ieyasu's castle. Eventually it would be large and impressive, but even in the beginning it struck the observer as unusual. Unlike Osaka Castle situated on a high hill of rock or Fushimi Castle located on a mountainside, Edo Castle sat squatly on the flat plain.

When Okuni and her troupe arrived at Shinagawa in the southern outskirts of the city, already 40,000 laborers had been at work for two years altering the surrounding landscape. Earth taken from the former Kanda Hill filled Hibiya's swamps and reclaimed several miles of Edo Bay for docks and warehouses. Deeply dredged canals walled by high dikes were ready to contain the heavy flood waters that would pour through the Kanto plain when spring came. Everywhere they looked, construction projects were underway. Houses, stores, workshops, and government offices were going up at a furious pace, consuming uncounted quantities of lumber, paper for windows, and tiles for roofs, all of which were carried through the city by a ceaseless river of people. As the members of the troupe made their way into the city, they confronted traffic congestion greater than anything they had experienced in Kyoto or Osaka. The confusion, jostling, and fierce arguments they encountered every few blocks unsettled Okuni and the others.

Nonetheless, that first morning they began looking for a site for their theater. It was a complicated matter because they didn't know the city. Also, the city's wards and districts were just now being built and it was difficult to figure out where one could go. For several days they followed a routine: in the morning troupe members fanned out into the city and in the afternoon they met to discuss places they had seen. Thousands of laborers were living in Kanda, jammed like sardines into hovels that took up every inch of land. From Nihonbashi in the center of the city to Shinbashi in the south, the streets were taken up by stores of all kinds. There was open space in the hilly Yamanote area to the north, but this was reserved for residences of lords and retainers of the shogun. Kanji eagerly reported that in Dosanbori there was a brand-new prostitutes' quarter. It carried the familiar name Yanagi Ward to suggest the hedonistic aura of Kyoto's famous licensed quarter. Groups of singers and dancers who gathered there, Kanji said, performed in the streets and on small temporary stages. None of the places they had seen would do, but Okuni refused to go near the prostitutes' area. As it happened, they settled on a plot of vacant land in Shibai Ward. Many people passed through the area, and it was far from the houses of government officials or samurai.

The choice was not wholly deliberate, however. While they were inspecting the Shibai Ward plot, Densuke collapsed, exhausted by the strain of walking three hundred miles in the August heat. He had a raging fever and a harsh, rasping cough. Because Densuke was too sick to move, the next morning Kanji and Mame built a shed around him. By default the plot of land in Shibai Ward became their home. Over time, the shed grew into the troupe's regular living quarters.

"I'm sorry, Okuni." It was terribly painful for Densuke to speak. For several years he had known he was ill. Increasingly, a dull tiredness had pervaded his body, leaving him only when he was on the stage performing. He had not mentioned it to anyone, even to his wife, Omatsu. It was hard for him to breathe between deep, shuddering coughs. "Sorry," he whispered.

"Never mind. Do you want to dance, Densuke?" Okuni asked, smiling to cheer him up.

"Of course. . .I do."

"Then you have to get well soon. I can't dance without you."

They had come to Edo to perform, but since Densuke was confined to bed, they cheerfully settled into a pattern of life none of them had foreseen. Every day Okuni nursed Densuke. Periodically she changed the wet cloth that cooled his hot, red cheeks and dry forehead. Many times a day she trickled water into his mouth a few drops at a time in an attempt to relieve his thirst. Because he had no appetite and his throat was so raw, it was painful to swallow, so she would boil fish and vegetables until they were soft. She mashed them smooth and placed tiny bites in his mouth, coaxing him gently to get some food into his shrunken stomach. While Okuni stayed behind in the hut the others went out to work, for it was easy to get a job in this city. The young men from Izumo unloaded fishing boats that arrived in the harbor each evening, and Kanji hawked fish at the Uo-ichi morning market. Mame became a day laborer, carrying lumber from the bustling lumberyards in Zaimoku Ward to building sites around the city. Omatsu got a job drawing and carrying water for laborers in the lumberyards, while Onei and the younger women did domestic work in the homes of well-to-do merchants in nearby wards. Even Yata, who was eight years old, proudly earned his food money running errands for a wholesale cloth dealer.

Winter passed, each day following the next without incident, except that Densuke did not improve. When the spring rains began, his condition worsened.

"I'm sorry, Okuni. I know you want to dance," he managed to whisper.

"Never mind. You saved my life in Moriguchi village long, long ago. Do you think I could ever forget that? What else can I do but take care of you?" She smiled teasingly at him. Inside she felt deep sadness knowing how much he suffered.

The fact that Okuni took care of him brought Densuke unexpected happiness, even when he most strongly sensed that he would not recover.

Ganjo was the third person who remained in the hut all day. Okuni had been able to bear Ganjo during the trip to Edo, but while she didn't dislike him, she was annoyed that he showed no signs of leaving. It was some consolation that he went out most evenings.

Had she known he was going to prostitutes' houses to sing and play the *jabisen*, she certainly would have driven him away.

Days passed when Densuke slept as if he would never awaken. Other days he would wake, eat a bite or two, and return to sleeping. Even while he was sleeping, however, the dry, hard coughing never stopped. He was not getting better.

One day Ganjo cocked his head, listening to Densuke's laborious breathing. "You know, that might be worker's cough."

"Worker's cough? What's that? Tell me how it's cured."

"I heard it's usually fatal. Once, in Kyoto, some doctors talked about it when I was playing for them. They used the word consumption. The Southern Barbarians have a medicine, but it's expensive." Consumption was to spread rapidly in fetid urban slums in later years, but in the spring of 1605 Okuni had never heard of the disease. Doctors called it worker's cough because most victims of the disease were poor urban laborers. Ganjo rummaged around in his sash and came up with a few copper coins. "I can't do more than this, but I want to help."

Okuni didn't even thank Ganjo. Her mind was already searching for a way to buy the medicine Densuke needed. Ganjo's coppers weren't enough but she couldn't let Densuke die. She realized now that her dance hadn't depended on Sankuro's drum or on Sanza's flute. Her Kabuki came from Densuke's open nature, which flowered in his comic impersonation of a woman. He gave her the courage to dress as a man. When she put the damp cloth on Densuke's forehead it steamed. She touched his chest with her hand; it burned like a hot rock. She would not let this man die.

Without thinking it over twice, Okuni decided to sell her short gold-decorated sword. She sent Kanji, knowing the pawnshop dealer would try to take advantage of a woman. Kanji bargained well and got a good price. With the money Okuni went to an herb store, described Densuke's coughing and high fever, and was able to buy the prescribed medicine. She received the bark of an unnamed foreign tree, which she boiled into a dark tea that Densuke drank once a day. The small pieces of precious bark medicine lasted some four months. When the medicine was gone, she had Kanji sell her theater properties and costumes one by one: her long gold-encrusted sword, her crystal rosary, her coral rosary, and her brocaded kimonos. Every morning for eighteen months Okuni carefully boiled a small piece of the foul-smelling black bark in water and made certain that Densuke drank each drop of the hot, bitter liquid. In that time Okuni changed back into an ordinary woman, a woman who cooked and washed clothes and cared for a sick man. Her hair grew out and she lost the mannerisms of a fashionable *kabuki* dandy strutting at Shijo Street. Omatsu watched Okuni nurse her husband without saying, or showing, what she was thinking. Eventually the medicine took effect. Densuke's coughing subsided, his fever gradually fell, and his appetite returned.

"I'm sorry, Okuni." When Densuke was able to sit up, the first thing he said was, "I'm sorry you had to sell everything. How will you dance?"

"What a ridiculous thing to ask, Densuke! As long as I have my body and someone to play music I can dance, can't I? I don't need anything else." Okuni truly believed this. She hadn't danced in a year and a half. She didn't regret a moment of the time she had cared for Densuke, but now she wanted, more than anything, to dance.

During the months in which Okuni was absorbed by Densuke's illness, Edo had rapidly changed. Ieyasu relinquished the title of shogun to his third son, Hidetada, in 1605, and he now enjoyed the enviable status of Shogun-in-Retirement. The new shogun turned his attention to finishing Edo Castle. Hidetada ordered each vassal to contribute rocks to build its massive walls. Lords competed for his favor by trying to provide the largest stones. Some were immense, as much as twenty feet long and seven to eight feet wide. They were hewn from the living rock of distant mountains and valleys and transported on specially built ships into Edo's new harbor. Winds and currents sank scores of the unwieldy vessels, and it is recorded that in one hurricane more than 100 ships plunged to the bottom of the ocean bearing their rocky cargo. Altogether, 385 ships of various sizes were pressed into the shogun's service. The great rocks that reached Edo harbor were rolled on logs to the castle site. They were too immense to be weighed; they were classified according to the number of men required to pull them through the streets—hundred-man stones, five-hundred-man stones, and even thousand-man stones. It was backbreaking work, but people were excited to be part of a gigantic procession of men straining to roll one of the great stones. Volunteers were never lacking to pick up the thick hawsers of woven straw fastened to the stone. Onlookers cheered the pullers on, and dancers and singers performed on top of the stones as they rolled ponderously through the streets. It might be said that the sweating, raucous, physical "stone pulling" processions in Edo were Hidetada's rough answer to the elegant parades that Hideyoshi had staged in Kyoto during his rule.

"Okuni, they say there's a huge stone from Izumo in the harbor."

"Really? From Izumo?"

"Let's go and watch them pull it to the castle."

Two days earlier, a great stone from the south had been pulled through the streets, and yesterday it was a stone from the western provinces. Today, a stone from the land of their birth would be paraded into the new capital. Everyone except Densuke and Omatsu ran down to the harbor to see the Izumo stone.

"It's red!"

"So it is. A red stone."

Many people stood admiring the great cut stone that had floated down a river and across the sea and now glowed brick red in the rays of the morning sun. Workmen from Izumo were perched proudly on the stone. They shouted out, "It's from Iron Mountain. That's why it's red."

Iron Mountain. Red with iron. Red with fire and blood. This stone, like the sand that drowns the fields at home, has been borne down on the water of the Hii River. The same water that swept my parents away when I was a child. Okuni's childhood memories came rushing back to her, and she felt her heart pounding with joy and with sorrow at the same time.

After the stone from Iron Mountain in Izumo was unloaded from the ship, it was placed on rollers, and wrapped in ropes braided ten- and twentyfold. Slowly it began its journey, pulled by the straining backs of more men than Okuni could count. The workmen from Izumo began to sing a folk song that Okuni knew well.

> In the morning,
> See them working,
> Piling coal, piling ore.
> In the morning,
> Light the hearth,
> Flicker, flicker,
> Blooming flower of flame.

It was the Hearth Song and it described lighting an Iron Mountain blast furnace. Iron Mountain, where Okuni's father had crushed red rocks like the one in front of her to feed the hungry mouth of the hearth. Iron Mountain, where Okuni's mother had fallen in love with a man who had steel in his veins. The red of this great stone flows in my blood, too, Okuni thought as she gazed at it, soaking in its powerful color: the red stone that had sailed north out of Uryo Harbor, westward along the San'in Coast, south through the Straits of Shimonoseki into the Seto Sea; avoiding the Naruto Whirlpool, sailing eastward past Osaka and around Kumano to reach the harbor of Edo.

Stone of Iron Mountain, Iron Mountain stone, Okuni sang at the top of her lungs. She danced as the rhythm of the Hearth Song entered her body. She danced, making up for the months in which her voice and her limbs had been stilled. Okuni sang and danced without effort, in the midst of the straining, sweating men. Her voice blended with those around her and her movements followed the rhythmic pulling of the creaking ropes. People along the route sang lustily with Okuni and the men from Izumo, though they didn't know what the words meant. Slower than the music of the emperor's procession, more powerful than the music of the Gion Festival parade, the massed sound of hundreds upon hundreds of voices rolled in a wave across Edo.

This is Edo, Okuni rejoiced. Unlike the old capital, the new capital has a powerful young spirit. The strong, warm light of the stone from Iron Mountain cleared the shadow of Densuke's illness from her mind. Drawing the energy of the vital city into herself, Okuni danced beside the moving red stone.

Twenty

Omatsu ran into the hut, red-faced and out of breath. She had grown thick in the waist from working as a water carrier and her short arms and legs were heavy. Altogether, Omatsu looked very much like a crab.

"There's a Courtesans' Kabuki theater in Kobiki Ward. With a flag, Best in the World."

"Our flag?"

"I was so surprised to see Best in the World, I didn't go inside. I ran straight back."

"In Kobiki?" Okuni wanted to be sure. When Omatsu nodded, Okuni replied, "Then Kobiki is where we're going to put our theater."

The others read the challenge in Okuni's words and were quick to agree.

"You're right, Okuni. Let the audience decide who's Best in the World. They won't dare fly their banner beside Okuni's. Let's do it." Densuke spoke for everyone. It had been so long since they had performed. Without any more discussion they set to work.

It is easy to imagine the excitement they felt while preparing for their first performance in the city of Edo. They built a square, roofed stage with wood they were able to buy cheaply through Mame's friends in the lumber business. They surrounded the audience area with a board fence and added a small hut at the rear of the stage as a dressing room. Okuni's theater was much finer than the tumbledown rival next to them. Kobiki Ward was a working class district not far from the harbor, housing lumber dealers, sailors' inns and drinking stalls, ships' chandlers, stables, and blacksmiths. Their theater was in an excellent location; it was set at one end of a small field where draft horses grazed, and next to the ward's busiest street.

For the first time since leaving Kyoto, they had their own theater with the banners Best in the World and Okuni's Kabuki waving beside the entrance gate. After two years of not performing, Kanji struck the bell and Mame beat the drum with two thick sticks. The strong rhythm lifted their spirits. The young men from Izumo played flute melodies that wove in and around the girls' voices rising in unison. The melody was a familiar Kyoto song that aroused pleasant memories and brought radiant smiles to their faces. Their bodies and voices were charged with pent-up energy. Okuni danced as if floating on a cloud of joy. Her feet stamped loudly on the stage floor. She leapt lightly into the air. As Okuni had done so many times in the past, she abandoned herself to the spirit of the moment and moved as if entranced. They had done uninteresting work for so long, the euphoria of being on the stage again did not diminish even as the weeks passed. They didn't even notice when the little troupe of four or five entertainers next door took down its flag and disappeared.

Their old dances and songs were new to the people of Edo. Spectators were fascinated to see the black-robed monk metamorphose into a beautifully kimonoed woman. They were intrigued when Okuni stood up in the audience dressed like a man. The girls' light dancing steps as well suited the active temperament of residents of the new capital. Okuni's reputation matched the banner in front of their theater; word soon spread that the best dancer in the world was performing in Kobiki Ward. Edoites were curious to see the performer from Kyoto who had come to their city to dance. In a short time, Okuni's troupe began to receive invitations to perform at the homes of wealthy tradesmen and minor samurai.

At first Okuni and the other women had to appear onstage wearing ragged and patched kimonos. Their most beautiful clothes had been gifts from Kanbei and other patrons, and those had all been sold to buy Densuke's precious bark medicine.

"I'm sorry, Okuni," Densuke said again. "Little by little we can replace them. We'll be getting beautiful kimonos from your private patrons soon."

Okuni was irritated and worried, but not about their costumes. "Densuke, dancing in Edo isn't the way I thought it would be. I don't feel like I'm dancing when I'm on the stage here. When I stand up in the audience and say, 'I'm Nagoya Sanza,' no one shouts or claps."

"People in Edo haven't heard of Sanza, that's true. And they've never seen *kabuki* dandies wearing Southern Barbarian clothes."

"Why are we repeating what we already know? We can dance in new kimonos, but shouldn't the dances be new, too? Densuke, I came to Edo because it was a different place. I know I've got to dance differently, but how? Here they only like the *jabisen*."

Densuke knew that Okuni was right. Men in Edo got wildly drunk and the noisy, raucous music of the *jabisen* fit right into their drunken parties. You heard the *jabisen* everywhere, especially in the houses of prostitution in Yanagi Ward. It was a natural sound for this rambunctious city.

" I felt truly happy dancing alongside the Iron Mountain stone."

"I didn't see the Iron Mountain stone."

"It was cut from deep inside a mountain and carried down the Hii River and over the Japan Sea to Edo. There was the sight and sound of hundreds of feet stamping on the ground, pulling the stone. Many voices were singing. I could hear the mountain and the river speaking. Densuke, the ocean was speaking. Oh, I wanted to dance in a frenzy!" Remembering it, Okuni's face flushed and her eyes sparkled excitedly.

Watching Okuni's expressive body, Densuke was able to picture the stone from Izumo being pulled through the streets. Her body had absorbed Edo's new vitality and strength, and she wanted to express this in dance. Dance is what her life is for, he thought. But how? After lying in bed for so many months, Densuke couldn't imagine what style of performance people in Edo would like. Densuke had to say what was on his mind. "If you're going to dance in Edo, Okuni, you can't ignore the *jabisen*."

"Never. Never. The *jabisen* is for whores. It's for Okiku. Okuni's Kabuki doesn't need the *jabisen*. I hate it! I hate it!" Tears fell from Okuni's bright, staring eyes. "Okuni's Kabuki won't use the *jabisen*! I'll tell Kanji to put up another banner, 'No *Jabisen* Played Here'!" It was foolish to cry, Okuni knew. Still, the tears continued to fall. She longed for Okiku. Did she hate the *jabisen* because it had stolen Okiku from her?

Densuke worried because he had upset Okuni. She was so stubborn, even after all these years, he thought. But he didn't regret bringing the matter into the open. They had to change their performance. He sighed. He was very tired.

In the morning, one of the young men from Izumo came running back to the theater to report that three prostitutes' Kabuki troupes had moved into Yanagi Ward and a banner in front of each theater read, "Best Courtesans' Kabuki in the World." Okuni laughed gaily when she heard this. "Can more than one troupe be best in the world? I think it's funny."

Later that day Kanji and Mame went to Yanagi Ward and when they returned their faces were the color of ashes. Mame described in a low voice what they had seen. "We couldn't believe it. A whore dressed up like a man had Okuni's crystal rosary around her neck. And she wore Sanza's two gold swords in her sash."

"It's my fault. I sold Okuni's things in Yanagi Ward. I never imagined prostitutes would use them in Kabuki." Kanji looked beseechingly at Okuni.

Mame went on, "The prostitute who was dressed as a man flirted with a prostitute who wore Okuni's coral rosary. They sang a love song while the *jabisen* played."

Okuni laughed cheerfully. "Fine, the coral rosary is best in the world. But their dance isn't. It's only an imitation of mine."

Densuke listened incredulously. "You don't care if they copy you, Okuni?"

"I don't care. Before, in Kyoto, prostitutes set up their theaters alongside ours, and they copied my dance. Who cares if prostitutes in Edo do the same thing? It doesn't matter."

"Even if they steal our audience?"

Densuke watched with surprise as Okuni haughtily lifted her eyebrows and retorted, "If some people like prostitutes, let them go. Why should I care?"

During the next few days, Kanji went to Yanagi Ward several times to check on the banners. He felt a special pride, for he had written the very first one.

"Well, Kanji, tomorrow where will the next banner reading Best in the World sprout up?" Okuni asked, joking.

Okuni's words proved to be prophetic; troupes of prostitutes set up theaters, one after the other, in Sakai Ward, Fukiya Ward, Hirokoji Alley in Nakabashi Ward, and in other parts of Edo. Each theater flew a flag proclaiming itself Best in the World. In one sense, Okuni was right. The phrase Best in the World had lost its original meaning, so why be troubled if others borrowed it? Most of the theater audience was uneducated and could not read; the white flag in front of a theater simply meant "Kabuki is performed here." The universal use of the phrase signified the important fact that Kabuki no longer belonged to Okuni personally. What she had created as a private artistic expression now belonged to the public. In the future, Okuni would be only one of many dancers and performers shaping the direction of Kabuki's artistic growth.

The crisp air of autumn gave way to winter's cold evenings and clear days, and each day Okuni's audience diminished in size. More theaters were staging prostitutes' Kabuki in Edo than there had been in Kyoto when Okuni and the troupe left Kitano Shrine three years before. Many troupe members were discouraged. Okane and Onei quarreled endlessly over how to earn more money. Okane wanted to keep dancing no matter how few people paid to see them. Why else did we come to Edo, she asked? Onei retorted that they were already short of food. If we want to get through the winter alive, she said, we have to get jobs. Kanji and Mame tried to slip away to avoid their wives' acrimonious arguments. Densuke especially suffered through

Onei's repeated demands that they stop dancing and go out to work. During the autumn he had recovered enough to start dancing with the group again, and he didn't want to stop.

In the midst of a snow and sleet storm on New Year's Day, a young woman from Izumo who had joined the troupe three years before abruptly spoke out, "I want to go home to Izumo." No one contradicted her, for almost everyone that winter had thought of the possibility of disbanding.

The day after New Year's, they were standing behind the theater in the freezing snow, burning pieces of scrap lumber to warm themselves, when a message arrived from Okubo Nagayasu commanding them to come instantly to his residence to perform. Six months before, Nagayasu had left Sado Island to be close to the shogun in Edo. He also intended, in the sixty-third year of his life, to enjoy some of his immense wealth by buying the city's lively pleasures. He hadn't blamed Okuni for wanting to avoid faraway Sado Island, and when he heard she had a theater in Kobiki Ward, he sent a samurai in his employ to bring the troupe without a moment's delay. Nagayasu was in a jovial mood when they arrived at the large, rambling mansion lying in the shadow of the West Tower of Edo Castle. He warmly welcomed Okuni and asked her to begin dancing at once. As the afternoon wore on, his admiration for her grew. He sang for Okuni and danced with her as well. When he discovered that Okuni still kept the golden case he had given her in Kyoto, Nagayasu was deeply touched. He knew from the troupe's clothes that they were very poor, yet she had cherished his gift.

"Okuni."

"Yes."

"That gold case contains rare medicine from China. The pills will cure any illness." Nagayasu then laughed delightedly and said, "I want you to dance with this Noh fan, Okuni. It's heavier than the one you use. Let's see what you can do with it." The surface of the large fan was painted in gold designs, and a solid gold pin secured its thick bamboo ribs. Nagayasu marveled when Okuni, responding to the challenge, invented new movements for the large fan. Her gestures were free and instinctive. If you put Okuni among twenty professional dancers, he thought, the shogun would see only her. This woman is truly the best in the world. I will send her, beautifully attired, into the heart of Edo Castle. I will show Ieyasu's ministers what I am made of, he thought. His heart was beating as excitedly as if he had just discovered a new vein of gold ore deep in the mines of Sado Island.

In places other than Nagayasu's residence, however, the first days of 1607 were not auspicious. In Kyoto, the emperor was so ill the ceremonial New Year's Banquet had to be canceled, while in Edo Castle, Ieyasu lay in bed nursing a painful attack of gonorrhea. When the shogun-in-retirement did not appear during the ritual Noh performance that ushered in the New Year, gossips immediately spread a rumor through the city that he was dead. Yes, the new shogun, Hidetada, was firmly in command, but even so the Council of Ministers was gravely concerned. The rice harvest had been disastrous the preceding year, and *ronin* loyal to Hideyoshi continued to foment unrest in some areas of the country. A rumor of Ieyasu's death would encourage dissidents to resist the new government. The council decided that Ieyasu must show himself to the public, whatever the cost to his personal comfort. It announced a special series of Noh performances in the outer courtyard of Edo Castle that would be open to the public. Beginning on March 8, and continuing for four days, Ieyasu, his samurai retainers, and the citizens of Edo would all view Noh drama together. Billboards placed at Nihonbashi, Asakusabashi, Kanda Myojin Shrine, Yotsuya Crossroads, and elsewhere in the city announced that all commoners could freely enter. There was no precedent for such an event.

On a soft spring morning, the former and the present shoguns, Ieyasu and Hidetada, sat in open boxes before the public and watched a program of five Noh dance-dramas interspersed with four short Kyogen comedies. They sat for four days, usually from morning until late afternoon. Each day the open grassy area in front of the stage was crammed with laborers, tradesmen, servants, housemaids, farmers, and artisans. The grassy area was enclosed on three sides by a solid line of boxes, each paid for and occupied by an official of the shogun's government or a provincial samurai lord. This section of the castle courtyard was relatively open and close to the Great Main Gate. Thousands of people were able to come and go as they pleased. The news that Ieyasu was alive spread through Edo and eventually to all parts of the country.

Three days later Okuni and fifteen members of her company went to Edo Castle to perform Kabuki. They were escorted from Nagayasu's mansion past his towering storehouse abutting the Great Main Gate, as if its wealth could challenge the might of the samurai, across the castle moat, and into the courtyard between the Citadel and the West Tower. The beautiful Noh stage was gone, removed, at the insistence of the Kanze master, to prevent its contamination by riverbed beggars. Straw mats had been spread on the grass to serve as a stage in front of the large audience boxes. Handsome new banners, put up by Nagayasu, announced Okuni's Kabuki and Best in the World. So this is Edo Castle, Okuni thought. Towering white-plaster walls rose to meet gray-tiled, massive roofs. She had seen many castles but this was the largest. She was not intimidated. She smiled radiantly at Densuke and said, "If this is the inside of the shogun's castle, I can dance freely here."

"Um." Densuke could hardly reply to Okuni's cheerful remark. His forehead was beaded with sweat and it was difficult for him to breathe. He had to make an effort to stand because his head was whirling. He could not be carefree, like Okuni. His body was turning numb. He dug his fingers into his palms, looked at Kanji and Mame, and finally said, in a strained voice, "All right, everyone."

Flute. Bell. Drum. Sixteen voices echoed brightly in unison.

> In the capital's flowery spring,
> In the capital's flowery spring,
> Let's go see the Kabuki dance.
> The plover cries, spring is gone,
> But the heart of Kabuki remains the same.
> People in colorful clothes,

Men high and low,
Are drawn to cheer.

The Council of Ministers had not posted signs advertising Okuni's performance, so only a few people were present when the performance began. But when the sound of drums and bells and the women's voices reached nearby samurai mansions and the living quarters of the castle, flustered officials and samurai rushed into their boxes, not wanting to offend the shogun by being late for a performance he had arranged. When they saw Okuni dancing, they had no idea who she was, but they stayed, first out of fear, then from curiosity. Ordinary people who were walking past the castle gate heard the music and came in to watch. Okuni was pleased to see workers like themselves in front, even more than she was to see the elegantly dressed officials lounging in the boxes.

The Buddhist Prayer Dance was not on the program that day. Okuni did not dress like a man, nor decorate herself in Southern Barbarian style. The costumes from Nagayasu were certainly beautiful but they were displayed in a plain way that did not attract attention. Okuni had the women wear one kimono over the other, with the hems trailing behind and an attractive row of collars showing at the breast. The only accessory was Nagayasu's heavy gold fan, which Okuni carried in her right hand. Of course, Sanza's magnificent swords were gone as well as the rosaries. Nine women, with Okuni in the lead, entered in a line. Dancing as they sang, they circled the edge of the straw mat stage. Then the five younger girls from Izumo danced a set of three Short Songs that had been popular three years ago in Kyoto. When they withdrew, Okane and two of the women danced forward. Finally, Okuni reappeared alone and advanced to the center of the wide matted stage, singing sonorously.

Forgetting worldly cares,
People high and low,
Are drawn to worship,
And to cheer,

God's gift to mankind.
This is God's gift to man.

The serene attitude and rich voice of the large-bodied Okuni seemed to take the audience by surprise. They watched, scarcely breathing. Suddenly, Okuni tossed the opened fan over her head and switched to a completely different style of song.

Come, come,
The crow caws.
Come, come,
It caws, because,
It caws,
Come, come.

It was a children's song, traditional in Izumo. Okuni had not thought about it for years. But when she heard the men from Izumo singing the Hearth Song while they pulled the stone from Iron Mountain, its bright rhythm recalled the Crow Song to her mind. She and her playmates used to sing it when they were little girls. On the spur of the moment she decided to do the Crow Song in Edo Castle. The girls from Izumo, who knew the song as well as Okuni, beamed happily and hurried onstage to join her. Densuke and Kanji quickly picked up the catchy words. They sang the simple verse over and over with the young men from Izumo. Mame played brightly on the drum. The girls leaped in the air and fluttered their kimono sleeves as lightly as butterflies frolicking over the sands of the Hii River.

Densuke, sitting at the rear of the dancing area, caught the golden fan that Okuni had tossed in a perfect arc over her head. Now Densuke was supposed to fold the fan, push it in his sash, and dance his "Spinning Song" female impersonation with Okuni. He took a deep breath to focus his mind. Suddenly Densuke felt his insides heave and a wrenching cough exploded from deep in his lungs. He put both hands to his mouth. His chest was being crushed with pain. His vision went black. I mustn't let the audience see this, Densuke thought. He lurched to his feet and managed, with great effort, to stumble through the curtain that separated the dressing area from the mat stage. When he was out of sight he doubled over. A mixture of blood and phlegm poured from his throat. He fell forward and his face sank into a pool of blood and mucus.

> Who hung the curved bridge,
> Curved bridge?
> God of Izumo,
> God of Izumo,
> He hung the curved bridge.

Densuke was supposed to be onstage now. Where was he? When he didn't appear, Okuni began to dance his role. Soon she forgot that Densuke was not there. She was absorbed by the challenge of being a woman playing a man playing a woman. She did not copy Densuke's female impersonation exactly. Instead, she strove to suggest a man acting as a woman. She tried to suggest the three levels of character and of self that the situation contained. Could she ever be a man in her heart, she wondered?

No one in the audience laughed. Watching in fascinated silence, spectators could not imagine what Okuni was attempting to do. Nonetheless, people were enthralled. They could not take their eyes from Okuni's subtle finger movements, the twisting of her hips, her feet striking the ground. Wrapped in the echoing sounds of drum, bell, and the women's voices, Okuni wove a brilliant tapestry with her body in the space surrounding her.

That day the clear sky extended to infinity. Blue sky. Endless sky. I am liberated in a limitless universe. On this earth I am free to be a man, free to be a woman. Nothing hinders me, Okuni thought. Another folk song from Izumo echoed in her ears. She responded by singing out strongly.

> Flower here,
> Flower there,
> Blossoming flowers everywhere.

Around your waist,
Thinner than thread,
Twine gracefully,
Lovely flower.
Come back, come back,
Swaying my love.

Okuni floated across the stage, neither as a man nor as a woman. With her face lifted to the sky, her body responded joyfully to the open universe.

The varied members of the audience assembled in Edo Castle could not fail to be impressed by what they saw. Spectators who were familiar with the complicated music of the *jabisen* were at a loss to know what to make of the simple folk music that accompanied Okuni's dance. Eyes accustomed to the flamboyant performances touted as Courtesans' Kabuki, now found in every part of Edo, saw nothing outstanding in Okuni's neat dress; Okuni's dance, however, left no room for boredom. Court ladies were inexplicably attracted to Okuni's large, masculine movements when she imitated Densuke. The common people in front were mesmerized by the light yet powerful rhythm of feet beating on the matted ground. Samurai who were acquainted with the slow, monotonous movements of Noh were charmed at the unexpected sight of Okuni's flashing feet.

Nagayasu was the one person sitting in the audience who was not pleased. He scarcely glanced at Okuni the whole day. Instead, his attention was inexorably drawn to the empty boxes where Ieyasu and Hidetada were supposed to be seated. Where are they, he fumed. Why haven't they come? Nagayasu had arranged that day's performance as a way to assert himself against the Council of Ministers who jealously surrounded Ieyasu. In spite of the fact that Nagayasu was richer than most samurai lords and had served Ieyasu with unquestioned distinction for years, the ministers treated him with polite contempt. Members of the governing class looked on entertainers as pet animals: they were amusing to have around the house but should not be confused with human beings. The ministers never let Nagayasu forget that he came from a family of lowly Noh actors.

Nagayasu had suggested to the ministers that Ieyasu attend four days of Okuni's Kabuki performances. Others urged that he watch Noh. Nagayasu reasoned logically that if the government wanted Ieyasu to be seen by as many common people as possible, Okuni would draw a larger audience than the Kanze Noh troupe. Naturally, Nagayasu was not present when the ministers made their decision. He was pleased when he was told that both Noh and Kabuki would be performed, assuming Ieyasu would attend both types of entertainment. The ministers, however, deliberately misled Nagayasu. They allowed him to sponsor Okuni's performance, but they informed neither Ieyasu nor Hidetada about it. Nagayasu had no way of knowing this. He could excuse Ieyasu for not coming—everyone knew he was in agony with gonorrhea. But when Shogun Hidetada did not appear, he thought it was an unendurable insult. Nagayasu had gone to great expense and trouble in arranging this performance to help Hidetada consolidate his regime. He sat with folded arms, glaring darkly at the boxes of the ministers.

A servant of Minister Tadachika bowed obsequiously before Nagayasu. "Lord Hidetada could not attend because he heard the story about Lord Hideyasu."

"What story is that?"

"They say the woman Okuni once danced in Fushimi Castle. When she finished, Lord Hideyasu said, 'This woman is the best in the world, but I cannot become the best man in the world,' and he wept."

"What of it?"

"Lord Hidetada feels compassion for his elder brother. How could he watch the Kabuki woman who caused his brother such unhappiness?"

Nagayasu knew the story, and he didn't appreciate this twisted interpretation of it. The ministers were toying with him. What did it matter that Okuni was dancing magnificently? What did it matter that many boxes were occupied by the shogun's officials? The guests who counted were not there. I've been made a fool of, he fumed. I've been tricked. While Okuni was still dancing, he rose and said, "I'm going home." At his home Nagayasu ordered prostitutes to sing and play the *jabisen* while he got morosely drunk.

When Okuni came offstage and saw Densuke, she rushed to him and lifted his face out of the blood and phlegm on the floor.

"Densuke." She wiped blood from his pale face. His eyelids fluttered. "Densuke. Don't die," she sobbed.

Densuke's lips trembled and a faint voice emerged. "No, not yet." He smiled weakly. Then his chest convulsed and he lost consciousness.

When they arrived at the side gate of Nagayasu's mansion, a fisheyed servant informed them that Nagayasu would not see them now or ever. Nagayasu had turned them away without explanation, just as Kanbei had done at Fushimi. Sankuro believed in patrons, but the popular audience was more dependable, Okuni thought. It did not matter why Nagayasu had turned them out; they had to take care of Densuke. Without further words, they turned away from Nagayasu's house and went home to their theater in Kobiki Ward. In the three months they had been staying at Nagayasu's mansion, most of the stage flooring and fence boards had been stolen, but the stage pillars and the roof remained. They made a wall around Densuke's bed with the beautiful new banners that had flown at Edo Castle.

"Omatsu, bring lots of water," Okuni ordered the flustered Omatsu as soon as Densuke had been placed on a pallet. Without even nodding, Omatsu picked up a pail and ran outside.

Okuni reached into the bottom of the wicker chest that held the troupe's props. She took out the small gold case Nagayasu had given her more than three years before. Now she was thankful she hadn't known then about the precious Chinese medicine it contained. Surely this will save Densuke's life, she thought.

As soon as Omatsu returned with water, Okuni cradled Densuke in her arms and helped him sit up. "Densuke, drink, it's medicine."

She shook Densuke and called his name, but still he did not stir. Okuni became desperate. She feared he would die from loss of blood if she didn't act soon. She filled her mouth with water, slipped three of the pills between her lips, and pressed her mouth against his. At the same time she tightly embraced his chest. Densuke groaned and writhed as his breath was squeezed from him, and then water and medicine poured down his throat.

"Ahhh," he sighed.

"Can you hear me, Densuke?"

"Um."

"I've given you special Chinese medicine. You'll be well soon. Don't worry about the blood you lost, Densuke."

Whether Densuke heard or not, his head bobbed slightly. Okuni drew a deep breath and left Densuke's side. Silently she changed from her dance kimono into everyday clothes, noticing the large blood smears on the silk breast and sleeves for the first time. Was it a sign the consumption had returned, she wondered. Was Densuke's sickness really incurable? As she folded the bloody kimono, she felt eyes boring into her. She was certain it was Omatsu but when she turned, Omatsu was kneeling by Densuke's pillow, looking at his sleeping face. Perhaps she had quickly looked away. Okuni unconsciously lifted the back of her hand to her lips, dismayed. Just a few moments ago, I put my lips against his, she realized. She felt her face blushing red.

When she became calm again, Okuni spoke brusquely to Omatsu. "Starting tomorrow see that Densuke takes the medicine. Give him one pill each morning and another pill in the afternoon. Be careful. Do you understand?"

Omatsu raised her head and stared flatly at Okuni. She remained silent for some time. She nodded. Finally she spoke. "I understand."

Okuni saw sweat bathing Densuke's forehead. She did not wipe it off. She hurried from the theater as if driven out by Omatsu's reply. It's Omatsu's place to take care of Densuke. They are husband and wife. I have nothing to do with it, she persuaded herself as she walked out into the chill night air moving in from Edo Bay.

Twenty-One

On the day in late summer that Sankuro and Okiku arrived in Yanagi Ward in Edo, they heard the gossip that in March, a woman named Okuni who was Best in the World had performed Kabuki in Edo Castle. Sankuro was given a detailed account by a servant in the house of prostitution where they were staying. The man had been at the castle himself and witnessed the performance. Sankuro's face turned rigid. "Could that be Okuni?"

"Well," Okiku stopped wiping the bridge of the *jabisen*, "we saw Kabuki troupes in almost every town we passed through. They all had banners saying Okuni's Kabuki and Best in the World. Who knows if that was really Okuni or not?"

Okiku laughed, as if she didn't want to take the report seriously. Sankuro thought it must have been Okuni. The house servant admiringly described a beautiful, plump dancer whose flashing feet moved so quickly they didn't seem to touch the ground. There was no *jabisen* but it wasn't missed. If you once saw the woman you couldn't forget her. She really was the best dancer in the world.

"I was told some of the whores here in Yanagi Ward wear Oku-ni's rosaries and swords on stage," Okiku countered.

"Oh?"

"I'll bet she was hard up and had to sell them. Okuni, play at Edo Castle? Not a chance."

"Hm. This fellow said Okuni didn't wear Southern Barbarian clothes or carry a man's swords."

"And I didn't hear anything about a man impersonating a woman. It couldn't be Okuni, Sankuro. Someone's using her name. In any case, Okuni wouldn't be popular in Edo. No one knows Sanza here. Even if she played his ghost, who in Edo would care?"

Okiku piled on the excuses, trying hard to shut Okuni out of their lives. Sankuro was shocked by the possibility that Okuni and the Kanze Noh troupe had performed in the same place. Even so, Okiku's attitude was irksome and he looked coldly at her. "You've gotten fat," he said, changing the topic.

"Because I'm not dancing," Okiku retorted, resentfully. She had been proud of her slim arms and legs and her good figure, but for the past three years she had played the *jabisen* while others danced. Ugly fat creases appeared on her arms when she plucked the strings. She complained to Sankuro about it all the time.

"It's my punishment for playing the *jabisen*. I don't have a chance to dance anymore because I'm glued to the horrid thing. I was cursed the day I started playing it."

Sankuro grimaced. "Stop if you hate it so much. I didn't make you start."

"You did too. You said we'd fall behind the times because Okuni wouldn't use the *jabisen*."

"Yes, I said that. But you wanted to learn. No one forced you, Okiku."

"Don't pull that innocent act on me!"

Nowadays, they often quarreled over this point.

After Sankuro had sold their theater at Shijo Street to the Court Maidens, he and Okiku traveled north and east from Kyoto with no particular destination. Along the way they sought out invitations to stay at homes of local officials and provincial samurai lords. When they said they were from Kyoto, and that they had played Kabuki at Shijo Street, they were welcomed almost everywhere. Sankuro's Noh drumming proved popular in towns where samurai customs were strong. Merchants and samurai wives who fancied themselves up-to-date eagerly hired Okiku to teach them how to play the new and rare *jabisen*. Passing through Kusatsu and Mino Barrier they traveled leisurely along the Nakasendo post road up the center of the country, in time reaching the Japan Sea. They stayed two winters in the remote snowcountry, teaching drum and *jabisen* to the samurai of Echigo Province. They earned enough to live on, but Sankuro was aware that two years had passed without real success. Then they turned south toward Edo, still stopping at towns and castles along the way. At last they descended the mountain passes out of Kozuke and entered Edo from the north. They immediately went to the licensed quarter in Yanagi Ward. Two people alone couldn't open a theater by themselves. But they thought Okiku could easily find work playing the *jabisen* in a house of prostitution. This proved to be true, and she was hired at the first house they approached.

"Is Edo always this hot?" Grumbling, Okiku rested one hand on Sankuro's thigh and with the other daubed at beads of sweat dripping down her neck. It felt unbearably hot because she had become used to the colder climate along the northeast sea coast. When Okiku shook her head a rank smell from her hair assailed Sankuro's nostrils. He made a sour face. It was their third day in Edo, and already Okiku was complaining. Recently, everything about Okiku annoyed Sankuro. He couldn't stand being with her every minute. It was worse than when he had lived with Okuni. In the past, he simply went off for a day or two whenever he wanted to get away from Okuni. He didn't have that freedom with Okiku.

"Stay away. It's too hot," he said harshly, getting to his feet.

Edo was even more energetic and lively than Sankuro had imagined. However, when he went around to the samurai residences in the Yamanote hills west and north of the castle his first two days in town, he was turned away from every gate. No lord or official wanted them to teach or perform. It was widely known that Hidetada had not attended the Kabuki performance in Edo Castle. To stay in the shogun's favor, all his retainers were shunning popular entertainments. Even the powerful provincial samurai of the Horio, Sakai, and Okudaira clans, whom Sankuro and Okiku had taught during their travels, would not invite them into their Edo residences. And of course, he couldn't play the drum in prostitutes' houses either.

Sankuro realized on his third day in Edo that he couldn't find work. This unforeseen circumstance made him extremely irritable.

Okiku took the situation in stride. She was used to Sankuro's bad moods, and she had a job in the licensed quarter. Edo's Yanagi Ward was smaller and less organized than Rokujo Street in Kyoto, but at night it came to riotous life. Customers piled into the houses every which way and their parties were drunken and licentious. She played the *jabisen* while prostitutes sang. People liked her *jabisen* and already men had noticed her. She didn't see what was so bad about being beautifully dressed, singing, drinking, and having men. In three days she felt at home in Yanagi Ward.

Doors and windows in the licensed quarter were opened wide in the attempt to catch some small breeze. The hot afternoon streets were empty of customers. Women casually sat in open windows, stripped to the waist, putting on makeup and singeing unwanted hair from their arms and legs. Okiku was quietly playing the *jabisen* in the small room the house of prostitution had given them to use. Sankuro was somewhere outside. He had felt stifled, shut up with Okiku in their hot, smelly back room.

The blind monk moved slowly through Yanagi Ward in the blazing sun, his tongue lolling like an animal's from slack jaws. Suddenly he stopped, cocked his head, and listened. Then he gasped, opening and closing his mouth like a fish on land. Words he tried to speak came out as gurgling sounds. He rushed forward, stumbled, and broke his cane. On his hands and knees, he crawled to the door of the whorehouse, listening to the sound of the *jabisen* coming from inside.

"Okiku!" A grating cry rose from his chest. "Okiku!"

It was too early for a customer to show up on such a hot day. A servant of the house stuck his head out the door. "Oh, it's you, Ganjo. Haven't seen you in a while. What're you up to, old man?" Ganjo was a familiar sight in Yanagi Ward. After finally leaving Okuni's troupe, he had moved from house to house in the quarter, playing the *jabisen*. All the servants knew him.

"That's Okiku's *jabisen*. It is, I know it!" Ganjo shouted, pointing toward the sound of the *jabisen*.

"Ah, Okiku. She's a *jabisen* player, came just three days ago. She's better than you, Ganjo. Your stuff is old fashioned compared to hers."

"I taught her to play. Call her down here. Okiku, Okiku!"

"Simmer down, Ganjo. You taught Okiku to play? I think you're crazy." The servant hooted merrily and blocked Ganjo's way. Another servant, who heard Ganjo shout Okiku's name, went upstairs to tell Okiku.

"Ganjo, you say?" Okiku tried to recall the name. Surely it wasn't the old skin-and-bones who had taught her *jabisen* back in Kyoto. A blind man couldn't make it to Edo. Trying to imagine who it was, she came downstairs to find out. Her face paled when she saw Ganjo.

"Ah, Okiku. Do you know him? He says he's your teacher."

Quickly shaking her head, Okiku answered sharply, "Never. Never." She drew back.

Okiku's voice was unmistakable to Ganjo, who cried out, "It's you, Okiku!" Ganjo edged forward on his knees and wrapped his arms around her thighs.

"Let me go!"

"No. I'll never let you go. It's me, Okiku. It's Ganjo. Oh, I missed you. I longed for you. I couldn't forget you."

"I forgot you long ago. I never once thought about you."

"No."

"Let go of me. Ganjo, will you let me go!"

"Okiku!" His eyes opened wide, showing ugly red and milky flesh beneath his eyelids. "I knew you'd run away."

"Run away?" Her laugh was deliberately loud and derisive. Men and women watched from neighboring houses of prostitution and people had stopped in the street as well. She would not let a blind beggar humiliate her in front of these people. She would not be laughed out of town three days after arriving in Edo. "Me? Run away from a blind man? I go where I please and I go with the man that pleases me."

"Man? Who is it?"

"You should know. Sankuro and I were husband and wife years before you met me."

"You promised to be my wife if I'd teach you to play the *jabisen*, Okiku."

"You think I said that?"

"You said it. The time you made love to me, I know you said it."

"You're out of your head, Ganjo."

Okiku's laughter was forced. Inwardly she was on the verge of panic. It was also painful to admit, even to herself, that she had ever turned over her body to this ugly, stinking bag of bones. She had to make people believe her, not Ganjo's ravings. She dismissed him with a bright laugh.

"You're sad. Do you think anyone in Edo is mad enough to believe I would give myself to you? Don't bawl and whine because I once made the mistake of showing a bit of sympathy. Take your hands off me."

"Don't say cruel things, Okiku. Just say 'Ganjo' once, tenderly. I'm your master, but I won't force you, Okiku. I'll beg Sankuro."

"Beg for what?"

"One more time and I'll be content. Love me one more time. I've prayed for this. I've stayed alive, searching for you just so I could feel your body again."

As he spoke he clutched higher on Okiku's body, rubbing his hands amorously over her hips and thighs.

Okiku shuddered. "Please help me. Won't someone pry this blind creature off me! I don't know him, I never saw him before!"

Suddenly Okiku was shouting, but the people watching from windows and doorways of the prostitutes' houses and gathered in the street were enjoying the erotic quarrel. They merely laughed and smirked.

"Sankuro, where are you? Sankuro!"

Okiku struggled hard to escape, but Ganjo's grip on her legs threw her off balance and she fell to the ground. Ganjo took advantage of this chance to reach into her kimono and clasp Okiku's breasts. He rubbed his fingertips over her soft nipples. His body shook with excitement. He was aroused even more when Okiku called the name of her lover.

"Sankuro, help me!" Okiku was screaming desperately now.

"Do you yearn for a man, Okiku? I'm a man, too."

"Sankuro!"

"Oh, it's you, Okiku! I know this body!"

If Okiku had been a prostitute, servants would have stopped the blind beggar before he got near their precious house merchandise. And if Ganjo had been a stranger, people would surely have broken up the quarrel. But everybody in the quarter knew skinny, weak old Ganjo. Okiku, though small boned, was vigorous, plump, and young enough. No one doubted she could send the old fellow flying through the air if she wanted to. In the middle of a hot afternoon, the spectacle of blind old Ganjo pawing a shrewish woman in the street was appreciated as a ribald, comic show. It was the kind of lighthearted amusement that might well have come from a cheap comic novel.

Ganjo went berserk. He had finally found Okiku, and already she was rejecting and ridiculing him. At this moment he enclosed in his arms the soft body that he had made love to once and could never forget. But Okiku had a man. She said so herself. She continued to call his name. If he released her now, he would never touch her flesh again. In a frenzy, he made a decision. With his left hand he groped for her smooth throat. When he located the point at the base of Okiku's jaw, he cocked the black iron spike that was fixed to his right forefinger and slashed with all his strength.

"Help!"

A crimson jet of blood pierced the air together with Okiku's scream of agony. Horrified, at last the onlookers pulled the two apart.

"Okiku, Okiku."

"Ganjo. She's bleeding terribly. The woman will die."

"Yes, let her. I want you to die in my arms, Okiku."

Over the last few years, Ganjo had lacked the strength to pluck the strings of the *jabisen* with his weak and broken fingernails, so he had fixed a sharply pointed iron spike onto his right forefinger. It was stronger than an animal's claw, sharper than the talon of a hawk. Okiku's soft throat fell easy victim to this iron spike, driven into her flesh with desperate strength. Okiku died, her exposed neck and breasts bathed in blood, surrounded by stunned spectators. Servants removed her body, carrying it into a back room of the house of prostitution where she worked. The servants returned with cloths and water and soon all traces of the incident were erased.

When customers began to pour into Yanagi Ward a few hours later, the quarter showed a lively and gay face as if nothing had occurred. Edo's licensed quarters were not as carefully policed as those in Kyoto and violence often went unreported. Edo's daily gossip was of riots and brawls, so not many ears perked up at the mention of an unknown woman's murder.

The next morning, beggars and outcasts living along the banks of the Hira River saw the body of an old man floating toward the sea. No person who saw the derelict's body connected it to the murder of a *jabisen* player in Yanagi Ward. The two deaths were soon forgotten.

Sankuro felt no particular shock when he returned to Yanagi Ward and learned about Okiku's death. He was impassive when servants said Okiku had called his name repeatedly as she was being murdered.

"After how many years? I'm alone," Sankuro murmured to himself in the suddenly chill night air. In 1585 he had left the Kanze Noh troupe, carrying only his drum. From the time he met Okuni at Hoshi Temple in Osaka three years after that, his plans for success had been blocked and his fate eclipsed by two women, one plump and one greedy. This is what he thought. He realized he had spent nearly twenty years of his life with these two women, first Okuni and then Okiku, and now he was over forty. When he considered this, the prospect of being alone pierced him to the quick, more than regret over the passing of twenty years.

He had abandoned the Noh troupe he had been born into in order to achieve success. At the time he left, the Noh master's son had been eight years old. Now, at the age of thirty, he was the leader of the Kanze Noh troupe and Ieyasu's favorite actor. If Sankuro had not left the troupe he would be the troupe's senior drummer today. He would be a respected artist. He would be playing in Edo Castle, instead of Okuni. He groaned with vexation.

"There's nothing good in Edo."

Okiku had been killed on their third day in Edo. Was it a sign he should not stay in the city long? Would he be remembered if he ran into a member of the Kanze troupe on the street? After twenty years, it wasn't likely. But it was possible. He shied even more at the unpleasant chance of meeting Okuni or Kanji or Mame. If they laughed at him, or even worse if they showed pity, it would be unbearable.

That day he decided to return to the remote northern provinces he had passed through on the way to Edo. Snow lay deep in the winter, and the people loved to sing where the mountains face the Japan Sea. He could earn a living, alone, there with his drum. With good luck he would find service teaching the Lord of Echigo or Lord Maeda Toshinaga in Kanazawa. Sankuro thought it would be a suitable place for him to spend the last years of his life, putting aside the ambitions of younger days. Sankuro realized he didn't feel sad over Okiku's death. He felt released from a burden.

At the same time Sankuro was speaking the words, "There's nothing good in Edo," Okuni's troupe was leaving the southern outskirts of Edo with their Best in the World banner furled. Through the summer they had performed in Kobiki Ward for audiences who wanted to see the woman who had danced Kabuki in Edo Castle. But Okuni's fame lasted a mere three months, and by the last days of summer they were playing to very small houses. The fickleness of Edo people dismayed them. They all were upset that they had had to dance on straw mats at the castle instead of on a stage. Nagayasu had turned them away. From the time the troupe arrived in Edo, Densuke had been sick and could rarely perform. One of the younger girls remarked in passing that even playing in post towns along the road was more enjoyable that being in Edo. They nodded heads in general agreement. When summer ended, the troupe concurred without dissent that they would leave Edo and return to Kyoto.

Densuke was feeling well again. Over the summer, the Chinese pills had worked magic. Densuke's appetite returned and he was his fat, smiling self again. As far as anyone could tell he was fully recovered. As they were packing to leave, he laughed, "I miss Kyoto. Even if we can't perform at Shijo Street, we can get a big audience at Kitano Shrine. Who knows, maybe prostitutes' Kabuki isn't popular in Kyoto any more." The idea lodged in their minds. Everyone in the troupe was anxious to leave.

The first evening of their journey they stopped in Shinagawa, the first town on the Tokaido post road leading to Kyoto. A sand beach on Edo Bay was just a block away. Densuke ran on in a cheerful mood. "Now I'm well and must pay you back, Okuni. You were such a good nurse. I'll dance like a woman all the way to Kyoto. I'll bring in money, you'll see."

"Of course you will, Densuke," Okuni said, smiling happily.

It was late, and they were preparing for an early morning departure. Densuke's joking around amused everyone except Omatsu. She blankly watched the affectionate conversation between Densuke and Okuni. When Okuni noticed Omatsu, who was incapable of expressing joy or hatred, she felt guilty and defensive. You've no reason to dislike me, she thought. The first time Densuke fell sick, Okuni had kept Omatsu from her husband's side for nearly two years, while she coaxed him back to health. When it seemed Densuke would die of bleeding, yes, she had put her lips to his. To give him medicine. She had cared for him, that's all. I'm not an Oan or an Okiku, she cried out silently to Omatsu. I've done nothing to be ashamed of, I don't love your husband. When that thought leapt into her consciousness, she caught her breath. She had always thought Densuke was the last person in the world she could love.

Late in the night Okuni wandered like a fugitive along the shore, looking out at the flickering fire lures on the fishing boats in Edo Bay.

"I'm alone now," she murmured.

Sankuro had left her. Sanza had left her and died. She didn't know Sankuro's destiny and she didn't care. She didn't know that Ganjo and Okiku had died only yesterday, nor that Suekichi Kanbei in Fushimi and Hideyasu in Echizen had died one after the other that spring. Tiny waves rippled softly on the shore. From across the silent water of the bay the first chill wind of autumn began to blow.

"No," she corrected herself in a whisper, "I've been alone since long ago." She gazed at the distant fishing fires on the bay.

From the time she had left Nakamura village in Izumo until today she had lived only for herself. She existed in her dance alone. Sankuro and Sanza had been but shadows passing across that dance. Densuke is no different, she said to herself.

The boundary between the stars twinkling in the sky and the fires reflected on the water blurred in Okuni's vision. Tears came to her eyes and streamed silently down her cheeks. Densuke is Omatsu's, she told herself. You've always known that. It's stupid to cry about being alone now, when you've been alone forever. Then why am I crying, she asked herself. She stood motionless and silent, making no effort to wipe away the falling tears.

The night sky was enormous. In the moonless darkness the stars glimmered brightly. Instinctively, Okuni stood watch over the fishermen's fires, each far-off flame as brave as a separate star.

"Okuni." Densuke's voice came from behind Okuni.

"Why did you get up and come out here at this time of night?" Okuni spoke without turning around. Densuke was surprised by the sharp, accusing tone of her words.

"You're the one who's wandering around, Okuni. I was worried, so I came to look for you."

"Don't worry about me, Densuke. Worry about the cold night wind. It's not good for an invalid. Go back. Go back to Omatsu."

For a moment, a dark, weighty silence seemed to rebuke them.

"Are you saying I must go back to Omatsu?" Densuke's voice was husky.

Okuni altered her tone. "Omatsu will be anxious. The night wind isn't healthy. Go back. We've a long walk tomorrow."

"You, too, Okuni. Come back and get some rest."

"I'm going to dance."

"Dance?"

"I want to discover what it's like to dance under the night sky. Go back and don't interfere with my dance."

At last Okuni heard Densuke returning to Omatsu. The sand of the beach crunched under his feet as he walked away.

> Leave a corner in your heart
> For my secret love.
> I who know you,
> Can only weep and weep.

After she had sung the lyric several times, Okuni stretched out her arms and legs and began to dance under the stars. She felt the firm sand beneath her feet. She nostalgically remembered the sands of the Hii River. She remembered drawing water from the river. She remembered leaping lightly from one foot to the other in the brief moment before water, seeping up through the warm sand, could reach and dampen a white, childish sole. Now Okuni danced facing the sea. She danced and sang as if in a trance, making spectators of the distant fishing fires on the bay, and hearing a murmuring audience in the stars. The shore was a stage, limitlessly wide. The night sky, too, seemed to her as broad as infinity, broader than the sky over Edo Castle, into which she had gazed. Okuni danced and sang in a blackness that obliterated the boundary between earth and sky. Except for the single point where her foot touched the earth, Okuni's entire body reached out to fill the firmament around her.

Twenty-Two

Even before laborers finished the Citadel of Edo Castle, the shogun sent thousands of workmen to Sumpu to start building another castle. Long ago Ieyasu had chosen this site, famous for its views of Mount Fuji and the pine-clad shores of the Pacific Ocean, for his retirement. The retired shogun and all of his personal attendants transferred to this pleasant spot, a journey of five or six days south and west of Edo, in August of 1607, even while the castle was being completed.

It was now September. Okuni and her troupe had passed through Totsuka and Odawara. Just as Sumpu Castle came into view, they met a large procession moving out of the city. Ieyasu was returning to Edo accompanied by many vassals. They watched a column of drably dressed soldiers march by. It couldn't hold a candle to the gorgeous parades of the emperor and the former Lord of the Realm they had seen in Kyoto. The procession was long and contained squads of heavily armed soldiers, but that didn't lessen Okuni's disappointment. Ieyasu was a plain man, both by policy and nature. Nothing in his procession was bright or showy. Neither did Ieyasu advertise himself by emblazoning huge family crests on personal objects, as most samurai lords were fond of doing. Of course, everyone in the country knew the Tokugawa family crest, made up of three hollyhock leaves. But you had to look closely to see the tri-form crest of the retired shogun, painted small and in restrained colors, on lanterns, boxes, and implements carried by his servants. What *was* noticeable about the procession was the troop of a hundred heavily loaded pack horses. Clearly, Ieyasu was taking something important to Edo.

That night, servants at the inn in Sumpu openly bragged about the 30,000 sheets of gold and 92,000 ounces of silver in the horses' packs. The treasure would rest deep within the vaults of Edo castle.

"Thirty thousand sheets of gold! Hehh! So much gold in that ordinary parade?" Kanji made a show of surprise.

The owner of the inn was proud because Ieyasu had spent most of his early life in Sumpu; he was a local boy. The owner boasted, "Well now, this past spring Lord Ieyasu had all the gold and silver in Fushimi Castle brought here, and it took 500 horses to carry it. Just a dab of that went to Edo Castle today."

"Gold and silver from Fushimi Castle?"

"That's right. Everything valuable at Fushimi was brought here. Now that was something to see. Five hundred fifty horses and each carrying 600 sheets of gold. So they say. That's 300,000 gold sheets. My heart thumps when I think about it. Who do you think had to bring that big treasure here? Vassals of Hideyori. It shows our shogun and retired shogun outshine the young Lord of the Realm."

Merchants as well as farmers in this quiet part of the country were honest, unlike the sophisticated people of Kyoto. The owner of the inn boasted, but he told the truth. Ieyasu had ordered the lords of Hideyori's five provinces to supply bearers and horses. And with much grumbling, the lords complied. In April 150 horses and in May 500 horses had moved Fushimi's treasure to Ieyasu's unfinished castle in Sumpu.

"The treasure of Fushimi Castle?"

From that single event, Okuni grasped that a transfer of political power had taken place. When the owner of the inn left them alone, she said to no one in particular, "So, Osaka will move to Edo and Kyoto will move to Sumpu?"

"Yes, and the Abe River will become Yanagi Ward," Kanji said laughing at his own joke. Sumpu was originally a small post town. Now that it was booming, whores were streaming in from the Kyoto and Osaka licensed quarters to service the laborers, artisans, and merchants who filled the city. They congregated along the Abe River that ran through the center of Sumpu.

"Yes, Yanagi Ward will move to the Abe River!" Kanji added seriously, "And Shijo Street may be deserted."

Mame cocked his head skeptically. "Now wait, Kyoto's been a capital for ages. As long as the emperor lives there, it can't change. No, Kyoto won't be deserted."

Okuni nodded and spoke simply. "The gold and silver in Fushimi Castle belonged to Lord Hideyoshi, didn't it? What difference does it make if Lord Ieyasu moves it somewhere else? Most people who live in Kyoto don't have anything to do with gold and silver."

"Even if they say the capital is going to move here, it can't happen for a long time. A backwater country town like this isn't going to turn into a capital overnight. That's what I think."

Okuni laughed at Densuke's words, and added, "In the meantime a new Lord of the Realm is sure to pop up somewhere. The new lord will tear down Sumpu Castle and he'll tear down Edo Castle, too, won't he?"

She said this lightheartedly. But people of Sumpu would not have laughed had they heard Okuni's remarks. Soon after arriving, Densuke noticed that the common people fanatically supported Ieyasu, who had been their provincial lord for many years. They were proud that their lord had become shogun, ruling the sixty-six provinces of Japan. His tax system treated them fairly, and their lives had improved under his positive, energetic rule.

The same conversation continued sporadically over several days. In the meantime, the troupe set up a small stage on a grassy spot beside the Abe River. They performed for small audiences, earning enough to get by from day to day. One morning Densuke said thoughtfully to Okuni, "Perhaps it's not as cut and dried as you say, Okuni. Lord Hideyoshi and Lord Ieyasu aren't the same. The Lord of the Realm lived extravagantly, spent gold like water, built castles right and left, and died. But the retired shogun lives plainly. He's not impulsive or foolish. I think he's stopped the fighting between clans."

Since they might be staying in Sumpu for a while, Densuke thought Okuni should have a better impression of Ieyasu.

"You can call him plain or sober, but if both Lord Hideyoshi and Lord Ieyasu love gold and silver and both like to build castles, I don't see that they're different. And if the samurai stop fighting, does that matter to us, Densuke? Whoever's the lord, nothing changes for us."

"Well, Okuni, if you put it that way, I suppose you're right."

"I don't like people who build castles. And I don't like this place, where people brag about their wonderful old shogun-in-retirement every time they open their mouths. I'm sick of it."

For his solicitude Densuke had brought a hornet's nest buzzing around his ears.

Ieyasu's personal preference for simplicity did not prevent Sumpu from profiting tremendously from the retired shogun's presence. People came from different parts of Japan in great numbers to share in the prosperity. After Edo, Sumpu was now the busiest city in the country. Men in the town wanted to drink and enjoy themselves with prostitutes. The prostitutes gathered musicians and singers into troupes. By now, any street performance, dance, or even puppet play was indiscriminately called Kabuki. Banners reading Best in the World waved in the air all along the Abe River. From early in the morning crowds of men wandered from theater to theater, drinking rice wine from flasks until they were drunk. Even when they staggered and fell stupefied in the dirt, they continued to sing Kabuki songs in slurred, drunken voices.

"How can this be the retired shogun's capital? They can't tell the difference between whores and Kabuki dancers. It's an immoral city. I don't like it."

Okuni frowned, venting her dislike of the city. The streets clamored with the *jabisen*'s depraved sound. It was a noisy city, right down to the pigeons swarming around the new castle walls. If a lord can't control his own city, how can he rule a country, Okuni wondered to herself.

"Densuke, this isn't a place for us. Customers leer and treat us like whores in our own theater. I won't dance here anymore."

Okuni spoke out vehemently, expressing the shock they all felt at the treatment they had received in this city. From the night they opened, customers in the theater openly propositioned the women for a night's sex. Even Okane and Onei could not avoid those propositions, which horrified their husbands, Kanji and Mame. Men lacked all sense of discipline, and if one took the time to look about, everywhere one found an atmosphere of total dissipation. Women of the town, samurai, and commoners alike spread thick makeup on their faces day and night. Men who vied to learn the latest current songs and dances didn't care if their teachers were whores or Kabuki artists.

In June of the following year, Ieyasu finally addressed the situation. He banned both unlicensed prostitution and performers of Courtesans' Kabuki from the city. At the same time, he parceled out the area beside the Abe River to create a licensed quarter, organized under strict laws, laws that in time would govern the famous Yoshiwara pleasure quarter in Edo as well. Yet June of 1608 found Okuni far away. Disgusted by Ieyasu's city, she had left his domains before the new laws went into effect.

Because of Densuke's delicate health, the troupe traveled at a leisurely pace south and west along the Tokaido post road. They had endured Edo's harsh winter winds and the bitter cold of Kyoto winters, so it was a luxury to bask in the mild weather along the Pacific coast. When they felt like it, they performed at post towns, usually for several days. In Mikawa Province, at Goyu and again at Chiryu, they crossed paths with Courtesans' Kabuki troupes traveling to Edo, each proud of its banner reading Best in the World. Performers from those troupes proudly boasted that they had performed on Shijo Street in the capital. They sneered derisively at Okuni's small troupe, saying, "Country bumpkins going up to the capital, eh!" Densuke and Okuni couldn't help but smile wryly to each other.

As the journey continued, the troupe fell into a pleasant, peaceful routine. Only two events of note occurred. To rest from walking, they took the ferry across Ise Bay, starting from the port of Atsuta on the bay's east side. On board ship they met a group of merchants from Osaka who told them that Suekichi Kanbei had died quietly in his home the previous spring. The merchants went on to marvel that Kanbei's son, Magozaemon, had blossomed into a flamboyant personality after his father's death. He now loved to captain a luxuriously appointed trading ship to the Philippine Islands in the company of *jabisen*-playing courtesans. Okuni felt inexplicably sad. As they approached Kuwana, on the west shore of Ise Bay, she sang one of the songs Kanbei had enjoyed, as much to still her disquiet as to repay the hospitality of the merchants.

The second incident occurred as they were crossing Suzuka Pass, just a few days' walk out of Kyoto. They spent the whole night listening to locals berate Ieyasu. According to them, the old wolf had taken more to Sumpu than Fushimi's gold and silver. Ieyasu had stolen every movable object in the castle—clothing, furniture, cooking utensils, and even the straw matting on the floors. A disgusting fellow, Ieyasu. Tight and miserly. They remarked contemptuously that people raised in the backwoods of Mikawa even stole rubbish. When Ieyasu had commanded Hideyori's vassals to provide horses and men, it didn't prove his greatness. It only confirmed what they all knew: that Ieyasu was an ill-mannered, insolent wretch. The troupe was now near Osaka and Kyoto and it was clear that Ieyasu would never be popular here. Okuni had chuckled to hear the stories, telling Densuke it made her eager to be back at the riding field of Kitano Shrine, where she would dance, and dance, and dance for the rest of her days. Okuni told Densuke that Edo and Sumpu were rude, rustic places. She never wanted to see them again. They arrived in Kyoto as spring blossoms were bursting from the still leafless branches of the plum trees.

They immediately hurried to the riding field west of Kitano Shrine, pushing their way through the milling throngs of people and shouting happily to each other.

"Kyoto! It's Kyoto!"

"We're back in Kyoto, Yata. Do you remember?" Mame asked his son.

"Look at the people. It's even more crowded than I imagined."

"It's spring and it's Kyoto. How foolish I was ever to leave this beautiful place." Okuni looked around, her heart racing with joy. Where there are flowers and people, I can dance. I don't need more, she thought to herself. She looked around and saw the haze of fragrant blossoms that covered the ancient plum trees. Some trees were thick with double-petaled blossoms. There were pale pink blossoms, flowers that cascaded in arcs like weeping willows, and even rare red plum blossoms. The petals were stirred by the spring breeze and by the sighs of pilgrims visiting the shrine. In Kyoto, I can always dance, she exulted.

The riding field was filled with worshipers because that past winter the eight buildings of Kitano Shrine had been rebuilt and dedicated anew to Tenjin, or Sugawara Michizane, the god of knowledge and literature. Hideyori and his mother had borne the enormous expense. Hideyori was naturally anxious about Ieyasu's intentions toward him and he hoped that if he made lavish donations to shrines and temples, the gods and Buddhas would intervene on his behalf. Ieyasu could not yet conquer Osaka Castle and carry off the gold and silver Hideyoshi had hoarded there. But he could encourage Hideyori to squander this fortune, thus weakening the only family that had the power and the will to oppose Tokugawa dominance. Ieyasu had strongly urged Hideyori and his mother to give generously to religious works, with the result that the interconnected buildings of the shrine were magnificent. Gleaming cypress wood pillars and walls of the Hall of Worship, the Dance Pavilion, and the Inner Sanctuary contrasted with the dark, rough bark shingles of their roofs. A large earthen embankment was raised to separate the riding field from the shrine proper. In past centuries, courtiers had left their horses in the field when they called at the adjacent Imperial Palace. Centuries later the palace was relocated several blocks to the south, but the field was left unchanged. It was Kyoto's largest public gathering place. It was here that Hideyoshi had held his extraordinary public tea ceremony in 1587, at which, it was said, he personally served a thousand guests. It was a fabled event, still talked about as one of the Lord's happiest and most bizarre gestures. People noted that one generation later

Hideyori was forced to come here out of fear for his life. The irony of the situation was not lost on the people.

Worshipers, pilgrims, and sightseers congregated in the riding field each day from dawn through the evening, as they came to pay homage to the deity Tenjin in the new shrine buildings. Naturally troupes of all kinds set up stalls and theaters to attract the festive audience.

"I just saw a troupe called Okuni's Kabuki," Kanji ran up to them shouting.

"What?"

"They've got three flags out front. Best in the World. Okuni's Kabuki. And a flag that says Izumo."

"Where?"

"In the middle of the riding field."

"Why, that's one of the fenced-in prostitutes' theaters, isn't it?"

"Yes, Okuni."

Large theaters in the riverbed at Shijo Street that performed Courtesans' Kabuki had become an important Kyoto landmark and tourist attraction. But so far only one of those troupes of prostitutes had pushed north to Kitano Shrine. It infuriated the young men from Izumo that a troupe of whores had appropriated Okuni's name, her reputation, and even their home province of Izumo.

But Okuni clapped her hands and spoke cheerfully. "That's fine. We'll set up our theater right beside them."

Four years ago that spring Okuni had had her great success playing Sanza in the riding field at Kitano Shrine. It seemed to Okuni that Kyoto hadn't changed at all. She optimistically believed that people would remember her when she performed again. Mame set out the two white banners and the men started pounding posts into the ground to support the stage. However, people passing by did not stop to look at the banners. They didn't seem to be anything special.

On the same day Okuni's troupe opened its theater in the riding field at Kitano, Kyuzo was questioning one of his servants. "What? Okuni's Kabuki has set up right under my nose?"

Skillfully managed by Kyuzo, the Court Maidens had become

one of the largest and most prosperous houses of prostitution in Rokujo Street. The theater Kyuzo ran at Shijo Street, too, was considered the best in the riverbed. He made a point of searching out the most beautiful young prostitutes to put on stage, which in turn ensured the house in Rokujo a fanatical following. Business was so good that Kyuzo was able to purchase land adjacent to the Court Maidens and expand the original building several times over. Still not satisfied, he opened a second theater on the riding field when he heard that Hideyori was rebuilding Kitano Shrine. He knew that for the next several years Kitano would be the liveliest place in the city. Had Okuni come back to Kitano to spite him? Many troupes boasting that they were Okuni's Kabuki had passed through Kyoto, but Kyuzo's sixth sense told him that this time the challenger at Kitano was the true Okuni.

"All right." He frowned thoughtfully as he spoke to his servant. "Take half the riverbed girls up to Kitano Shrine. Send more drummers and flute players. Add *jabisen* players, too. Beat the drum in the tower so loudly no one will go near the other theater."

"Master, it's a second-rate troupe. It doesn't have fifteen members. We have twice that many dancers at Kitano now."

"No. I won't let them set their banners next to mine. I'm going to kick them out. We have legal control over the riverbed at Shijo. But Kitano Shrine is open to any troupe. That new troupe is asking for a fight. Add ten more *jabisen* at Kitano."

"Master, the other troupe doesn't have a single *jabisen*. I don't think we have to send up more."

"Are you arguing? Can't you obey an order?"

"Yes, Master. At once."

The former owner of the Court Maidens had retired, leaving Kyuzo in full charge of the business. People called him "Master" and respected him as one of the wise men of the quarter. He had gotten quite fat. With his potbelly, thick black eyebrows, sharp eyes, and lined face, he seemed at home wearing the sober silk kimono of a wealthy merchant.

"Here, Black. Come here." Black had become old, and was so fat he could hardly move. To stay on Kyuzo's good side, the girls fed him constantly. Black raised his head and looked through dim eyes in the direction of his master's voice. Kyuzo lifted Black in his arms. "Black, they say Okuni has come back from Edo. It's hard to believe she danced at Edo Castle, but they say she did. She's back. Up at Kitano. Let's go see for ourselves. All right?"

Kyuzo put Black down on the ground in front of Okuni's theater. He noted sourly that many people were buying tickets to see Okuni but no one was going into the Court Maidens theater. He went backstage and spoke crossly to his stage manager and everyone else within hearing. "Come on, why aren't you singing louder? The flute's weak. Hit the drums harder." He continued to rail at them as they tried to outdo Okuni's group next door. Although they played as loudly as they could, no new spectators came in. The audience was half its usual size.

Okuni's sonorous voice rising over the racket in his theater irritated Kyuzo. When he poked his head out of the entrance to look across at Okuni's theater, he noticed that Black was gone.

"Black, Black! Where are you?"

A violent change came over Kyuzo, alarming the doorman. Frightened, he said he didn't know.

"Well, aren't you supposed to know? I raised him from the time he was a pup. He's old. He can't take care of himself. Who stole him?" He raged at the doorman. Kyuzo's corrosive resentment toward Okuni erupted. He seized the trembling doorman by the collar and shook him like a child.

"Master, the truth is. . ."

"Yes?"

"He's next door."

"In the theater?"

Kyuzo believed someone in Okuni's theater had lured Black away. Cursing, he stormed into the entrance of the theater, yelling, "You bastards! Do you have to steal a dog to get a customer?"

"A dog?" Hoping to quiet the angry man, the youngster from Izumo who was taking tickets said good-naturedly that he was sorry if a dog had slipped past him, he'd look for it and bring it out. Impatient to find Black, Kyuzo pulled a handful of coins from his purse and threw them down.

"A ticket for me. Use the change for my dog."

He vividly remembered that he had bought a ticket for Black when he entered Okuni's theater at Shijo Street years ago. Black soon scented his master and came tottering over to Kyuzo. Somewhat calmer, Kyuzo settled himself at the back of the nearly full theater, where he had a good view of the stage. Omatsu was dancing with the four young girls from Izumo. "Young" in Okuni's troupe meant twenty-three or twenty-four years old. Kyuzo scratched the tip of his nose with satisfaction. Men who bought prostitutes wanted youth above all. As whores, these "girls" would be decrepit has-beens, he thought. Soon the five went offstage and four other women entered dancing. Kyuzo knew them all: they had come from Izumo with Okuni. Kyuzo clucked his tongue as he he considered the fact that the little girls he had known in Nakamura village were now old women in their thirties. They had been dancing for twenty years. Their leader, Okane, was thirty-three. Okane had been the prettiest of the girls, after Okuni and Okaga, and some of that beauty remained. But her neck was thick and her body had gotten heavy in spite of the years spent dancing. Inescapable crows' feet of age showed around her eyes. Kyuzo laughed out loud.

The sound of many *jabisen* playing in unison welled up from the Court Maidens theater. The singing next door became so loud you couldn't hear the flute and bells coming from Okuni's stage. Kyuzo smiled confidently and cuddled Black in his arms. The next moment, however, he froze, transfixed by what he saw.

Okuni had entered onto the stage.

Her remarkable appearance destroyed every expectation that Kyuzo, or anyone in the audience, may have held. Her forelock was parted in the middle and dark strands were tied back at each temple with a scarlet silken cord. Long hair streamed abundantly down her back. A white linen cloth was folded in neat creases on the top of her head.

"It's a candy seller."

"You're right. That's what she is."

The spectators murmured and nodded to each other. Okuni was dressed as a candy store waitress who sold confections made of sweetened seaweed. Her unusual costume went back to the middle ages. Of course it had been theatricalized: the underkimono was dyed a luxurious indigo blue, the red-spotted sash was of the kind usually worn by men, and her skirt trailed on the floor. Those details were not to be found in real life. Still, the audience could easily identify Okuni as a candy store waitress.

> When we love another,
> Is our love for another?
>
> Loving the wrong person,
> We forget our dear homeland.
>
> Thinking of one's love,
> Is thinking of oneself.

While Okuni was singing short aphorisms about love, Densuke entered the stage. He was dressed as a pottery maker, balancing a shoulder pole with a basket dangling at each end. Kyotoites knew at a glance that he was supposed to be a potter from Fushimi. Okuni and Densuke had been gone from Kyoto for four years. Returning in the spring, their art flowered in a wholly new direction. The story they created was this: on his way home from business a potter stops to rest at a candy store; a pretty waitress serves him sweets and tea; the potter is smitten and she falls in love with him; dancing together, they show the joy of being in love.

The audience was moved by the ordinary story's simple truth. They cheered and applauded. Okuni was bringing to the Kabuki stage a gentle and pure drama that wholly rejected the eroticism of Courtesans' Kabuki. The audience was charmed.

Next, the others reappeared dressed as working women. Each wore the special costume of her trade: the vegetable seller, the fish peddler, the wet nurse, the flower vendor from nearby Ohara village. Yata leaped onto the stage swinging baskets from a green bamboo pole on his shoulder. The dozen troupe members, each dressed as a Kyoto commoner, danced in unison, circling around Okuni in the center. Their feet stamped a joyful rhythm on the wooden floor. The sound of the music coming from the Court Maidens theater appeared to be accompanying them. The truth was that Kanji and Mame had realized they were hopelessly outnumbered. So they deliberately fit their bell, drum, and flute music into the louder *jabisen* music coming from next door. The louder the *jabisen* music sounded from Kyuzo's Courtesans' Kabuki, the more festive the atmosphere in Okuni's theater became. Together actors and spectators were carried away by the joyful spirit of their group dance. The custom of ending a Kabuki performance with a cheerful group dance was to continue for two hundred years.

Irritated beyond reason, Kyuzo rose and quickly left the theater. Black tottered after his master as fast as his old legs and heavy body would allow. Outside, Kyuzo scooped the dog up in his arms and started home. He didn't stop at the theater at Shijo Street as he usually did but kept on walking. A smoldering anger filled his chest as he recalled the scene. He heard again the lilt in Okuni's voice as she sang the song of the candy seller. He saw Densuke's joyful leaping steps as the young pottery vendor. Most painful for Kyuzo, he pictured Okuni and Densuke openly showing their love for each other. Their affection was clear to anyone who had eyes to see. Kyuzo had laughed because the man Okuni married was a buffoon. When he recalled Densuke tenderly touching Okuni in the theater today, his resentment was unbearable. Bastards, he thought.

Kyuzo was a strong man, but when he arrived at Rokujo Street he was out of breath and sweating heavily from the effort of carrying Black. He put Black down, petting the dog's thick coat to calm himself.

"Damn her. She's not going to do this to me," he growled to himself. He was amazed that he felt so much anger. Okuni had found the one thing the whores could not imitate. If a prostitute played a common working woman onstage, she would not draw customers after the show. Kyuzo marveled that Okuni had come up with such an original and brilliant idea. In the next moment, he cursed himself for admiring Okuni. He hated her. His eyes glittered vindictively in his heavy face. It had been a long time since they had shone with such hostility and malice.

Twenty-Three

After the last flower of spring had fallen to the earth, the mountains north of Kitano were blanketed in pale green stretching from east to west as far as the eye could see. The cuckoo's call heralded a fragrant breeze and the morning air was clear and crisp. After four years away from the city, Kanji walked through the streets of upper Kyoto, nostalgically revisiting places he had known since he was a child. Kanji thought some of the time spent on the road and living in Edo had been enjoyable. But no place was as good as Kyoto. He had been born in this city, and he never wanted to leave Kyoto again.

"Kanji? Is that you?"

Kanji turned to see who was calling him. "Oh, Sarujiro. Well, hello."

Kanji was surprised at the change he saw in Sanza's former servant. In those earlier days, Sarujiro had been black from working in the sun and wore simple clothes. Now his face was powdered a creamy white, and he was dressed in an expensive dark kimono and cloak. The overall impression was of a soft person. Kanji could not help asking, "What sort of work are you doing, Sarujiro?"

"We can talk about it over food. Let's have a bite."

Sarujiro led the way up a narrow street to a discreetly furnished shop. From the way the proprietress greeted Sarujiro it was obvious he was a regular customer. She brought out tea and delicate cakes for two. Kanji looked around at the other customers. They were exceptionally well dressed and prosperous looking, not like the audience they played for. Kanji could not help blurting out again, "What kind of work are you in, Sarujiro?"

"Just like my master Sanza, I'm interested in Kabuki."

"Oh?" Kanji didn't know what he meant. "I'm still with Okuni's troupe. We came back to Kyoto this spring. We've put up a theater at Kitano Shrine."

"I heard. You're famous. You must be making a lot of money."

"Well, not really." Kanji spoke openly to Sarujiro, as he would to an old friend. Sarujiro listened politely. "At first we had a big audience. They cheered Okuni's new play. But from the start of this month things haven't been going so well."

"Oh? I heard the Courtesans' Kabuki troupe next to you folded and ran away."

"Yes, but the interesting thing is that when they were there, we danced to their *jabisen* playing, and the audience liked the lively atmosphere. Now that they're gone people are bored with our flute and drum music. I thought the audience in Edo was fickle, but Kyoto audiences are fickle, too."

"No, people in Kyoto aren't fickle, Kanji. I've been doing the same work for four years and people aren't tired of it."

"What work do you do, Sarujiro?"

Sarujiro did not reply. They ate the confections on their plates. Kanji had never tasted anything more delicious. He couldn't help comparing their luxurious sweetness to the plain food they ate at the theater.

"When I served Master Sanza, I lived proudly, because he was a samurai. But I was poor. I couldn't dream of eating food like this. I admired him, but I wasn't free to do as I liked."

"So what do you do?"

"I get up in the middle of the day and no one says boo. Like Master Sanza, I'm surrounded by women."

"Sarujiro, what are you talking about?" Kanji couldn't hold back his irritation.

Instead of answering, Sarujiro called the woman over to pay the bill. Kanji's eyes bulged when he saw how much money Sarujiro casually took from his fat purse. Envy mingled with curiosity in Kanji's confused mind.

"Well, Kanji, why don't you come to my place and see for yourself. Seeing's better than words."

"All right. Where is it?"

"Shijo Street," Sarujiro said grinning, and walked out of the shop. On the way to Shijo Street he didn't once look back, as if he knew that Kanji would be following him. When they reached Shijo Bridge, Kanji rubbed his eyes. He thought he'd been bewitched by a fox. There was the same prostitutes' theater with its waving banners and green bamboo fence they had just driven from Kitano. Sarujiro spoke to the ticket taker at the entrance and they were waved in.

"You play the flute here, Sarujiro?"

"Relax and look around. You'll be surprised by many things." Sarujiro smiled mysteriously. Leaving instructions with some women to take care of Kanji, he disappeared backstage.

Kanji was astonished by what he saw. Whores were laughing familiarly and drinking with spectators who had arrived early. In the past, performers were not allowed to leave the stage and mingle with the audience, but this regulation was clearly not being observed.

The women Sarujiro had spoken to sat beside him. "Will you drink something?"

"No, I don't drink."

"Oh, such a serious face."

"Really, I don't drink and I haven't got money with me today."

"Who said you had to pay?"

"What? Drinks are free?"

The women laughed at Kanji's naivete. One whore gave him a cup and another poured it full of clear rice wine. The *jabisen* played a lively tune. More spectators entered the theater. Men and women laughed cheerfully. Kanji got drunk on a single cup of wine. His body was numb and his head felt light. He couldn't help reaching out to take the hand of the woman next to him. She caressed his hand, smiling.

"What's your name?" Kanji finally had courage to ask.

"Me? Come to the Court Maidens in Rokujo and look for me."

Her words had the easy flow of a well-rehearsed speech, Kanji thought. This was how passersby were snared, netted like fish out of the flowing river. A spectator could drink and enjoy the company of young girls while watching the show. Then he could spend the night with the girl he liked. Okuni's theater couldn't compete. This was big business. Kanji didn't say these things out loud, but even in his intoxicated state he knew they were true.

Whores moved coquettishly onto the stage in groups of fifteen and twenty. Their kimonos clung to the curves of their lithe bodies and their hair was piled and twisted high on their heads, making them seem tall and alluring. When one of the group dances ended, Kanji saw a single beautiful woman enter the stage.

"Who is that? A prostitute from the Court Maidens?"

"That's Okuni." The woman beside Kanji nudged his shoulder, suppressing a giggle.

Shrill notes of a flute were heard. A man dressed like Sanza swaggered on stage. He and the woman danced together.

"Why, isn't that Sarujiro?"

"It's Nagoya Sanza."

So that was what Sarujiro did. He made a living acting the role of his master in a whores' show. Kanji wasn't drunk now. He stared at the stage, listening intently. Sarujiro, as Sanza, spoke amorously to the prostitute playing Okuni. After that a comic character came on and moved between the two lovers, separating them.

"It's Shikazo," Kanji blurted out. Shikazo was a good friend of Sarujiro's. He had been a servant in Sanza's house, too. "He's playing Densuke?"

"It's Okuni's friend. Isn't he funny?" The women around him laughed gaily.

Kanji was in a daze when, after the performance, he was led backstage to see Sarujiro.

"Did you see it, Kanji?"

"I don't know what I saw, Sarujiro."

Sarujiro chuckled, wiping off his thick makeup. "Well, what about it? Will you join us, Kanji? If I talk to the master, he'll pay good money. Our orchestra is big but, you know, it lacks something. You're just what we need. Please join us."

"Who's the owner?"

"The master of the Court Maidens runs this theater. You'll see, he's kind and generous."

Kanji could easily imagine the scene if he told Okuni he was leaving to play for prostitutes' Kabuki. But Kanji, who was born in the capital, wasn't happy with Okuni's new dances that portrayed working women on the stage. He had discovered, when they were traveling to Edo and back, that he disliked everything that smelled of the country. Would Okuni put farmers onstage next, he fretted? But Kanji worried about money most of all. Everyone had been optimistic when they arrived in Kyoto, but then they saw their audiences get smaller and smaller. Kanji felt uncertain about the future.

"Kanji, our master is coming."

Kanji did not have time to wonder if this was part of a plan. Kyuzo immediately began telling Kanji how good his situation would be and how much money he would earn, as if he had already decided to join the troupe. He offered a salary that made Kanji's eyes pop. To judge from Sarujiro's expression it must have been at least as much as Sarujiro was paid.

"Please, Master," Kanji protested, stammering, "I can't decide by myself. Can I have some time to talk it over?"

"Oh? Are there others?"

"Yes. Seven or eight young people from Izumo. And my wife."

"Well, I see," Kyuzo replied, as if he knew nothing about it. "I can use experienced musicians. And more dancers. In that case, I'll pay a commission for each person you bring with you."

"Eh? Pay me?"

"My theater features players from Izumo. The more Izumo people we have the better. Let's see then, how much money will that be? First there's you, your wife, and. . ."

Kanji didn't discern that Kyuzo's motive in harping on salaries and commissions was to hire away all of Okuni's troupe. He was simply dazzled by the sums Kyuzo was offering him.

At about that time, the members of Okuni's company were wondering where Kanji was but when he didn't come, they struck the bell, they beat the large drum, and they began to dance and sing without him. Okuni had worked tirelessly to drive away the competing prostitutes' theater. But now that it was gone, her small theater in the middle of the field seemed lonely. Because Kanji, usually the gayest person in the group, was gone, others lost their spirit. The few spectators who were in the theater looked bored.

Okuni sang out impatiently:

> You cannot know another's heart,
> You cannot know the truth,
> That lies in another's heart.

While Okuni was singing, she came to realize the meaning of the words she had sung so many times. Where has the audience's heart gone, she wondered, distractedly. She glanced at Densuke, who was dancing with her. His face was blank and drained of color.

> Leave a corner in your heart
> For my secret love.
> I who know you
> Can only weep and weep.

He sang lifelessly, looking straight ahead.

Remembering the night she had danced under the stars at Edo Bay, Okuni's heart ached. She realized that after twenty years of dancing, only Densuke was left. And he was Omatsu's husband.

Kanji did not show up for the performance the next day either. When he did appear, late in the evening, Okuni spoke sharply, "Kanji, where were you? We worried about you."

"Do I have to tell you everything I do, Okuni?" Kanji defied Okuni, looking directly into her eyes. Without giving any explanation, he left the theater, taking Okane him. The next day the younger members of the troupe furtively passed in and out of the theater. Okuni did not know what was going on but she felt a foreboding so strong that she was afraid to speak. Over the next several days, most of the young people disappeared. Kanji and Okane were gone. In desperation Okuni decided to ask Densuke, but he too was gone.

"Omatsu, where's Densuke?"

"Shijo Street, he said. He'll be back by noon."

"He went to Shijo Street? Why?"

"To see what's happening."

"Happening? What do you mean?" Omatsu clamped her lips tight. Everyone else knew, except Okuni. Okuni could not stand the suspense any longer. "I'll see for myself." As she turned to leave, Omatsu seized the sleeve of her kimono.

"Omatsu, why are you stopping me?"

"Densuke told me I must."

"He did?"

"Watch Okuni, he said."

"What a strange thing to say." Although Okuni tried to laugh, her throat was dry and her voice caught. "Omatsu, is there any water left? I'm thirsty. Summer is coming. Kyoto will be steaming hot."

"Some of Densuke's water is left, but he said you shouldn't drink it. You might get his consumption."

"Is Densuke's water so precious, Omatsu, that I can't have some?"

"No. But Densuke's sickness. . ."

"What are you talking about? Densuke's well. He was cured by the Chinese medicine."

The tenor of Omatsu's remarks disturbed Okuni, especially since Omatsu so rarely spoke. Okuni went to Densuke's water jar and drank deeply from the wooden ladle. The cool water immediately refreshed her, soothing her parched throat. Just then Mame and Densuke returned running, for it was time to begin the day's performance. "The audience is coming," Densuke said, his face drawn. "All right. Let's sing." The others nodded. They went onstage and let the words of the song rise from their throats.

Okuni entered dancing. When she looked back she saw only Densuke, Mame, and Yata sitting at the rear of the stage, singing and playing the drum and bell. Onei and Omatsu, plus two girls from

Izumo, were dancing. Even Okuni was not dancing well. During the first number, one by one the handful of spectators in the theater rose and walked out.

"Tell me what's happening!" Looking like a fierce temple guardian, Okuni hurled her words into the empty theater. "Densuke! Mame!" she begged as she turned to them, "Why don't you answer me? Where did everyone go? Why haven't they come back? What are you hiding from me?"

Densuke averted his grief-stricken face. Mame tightly clutched the drumsticks and he appeared to be weeping. Moving beside Yata, Onei looked straight at Okuni. "Sister Okuni, it's time to go back to Izumo." She continued resolutely, as if she had worked out the words in her mind before speaking. "I've wanted to go back to Nakamura village for a long time. I don't want Yata to end his life singing and dancing. I want to go home to Izumo so Yata will know its rivers and mountains, and so they will be his. Yata is eleven. I want to see him grow to be a man in the fields of Izumo."

Okuni asked, in a calmer tone, "What do you think, Mame?"

Mame was encouraged by his wife's words. "To tell you the truth, I was a runaway farmer when I joined the troupe. I miss the earth. Now I'm getting old, Okuni, and have a son. I think about the future. I want to live in one place with my family. If we go to Izumo, Onei's family has land. Even if it's wasteland, in time we can make something good of it. I want to eat food we've planted and harvested ourselves."

"And you, Omatsu?"

"I'll dance. I don't care where." Omatsu was obstinate, implacable.

It was bewildering to Okuni. Her least-talented performer was insisting on dancing while Mame and Onei, two pillars of the troupe, wanted to go home. How could they throw away twenty years of dancing? And the others? Where have they gone?

Okuni turned to Densuke. "Where did everyone go? Densuke, I've asked and asked. Why won't you tell me? I can't stand this!"

At last Onei spoke out. "They went to Shijo Street, Sister Okuni."

"What?"

"Kanji told them the prostitutes' troupe would pay them a lot to join the orchestra."

"They're playing for prostitutes?"

"They're making two, three times more money than here."

"You're telling me the whorehouses bought and stole them away?" Okuni persisted.

"It's not just the money, Okuni. Prostitutes' Kabuki is a big success. Maybe they want to stay in Kyoto and have a settled future," Onei replied.

"Can't they feel settled with us?" Okuni demanded. More quietly, Okuni asked, "And Okane?"

"She went with Kanji. She'll sing or help Kanji." Onei nodded toward the two younger women who had stayed behind. "The reason they didn't go was that they were afraid the owner might sell them as prostitutes. They want to go back to Izumo."

Okuni was uncharacteristically sardonic. "Is that so? Okane followed Kanji into a whorehouse? I suppose a woman's happiness is just being with the man she loves." Okuni was determined she would not go back to Izumo at the head of this tiny troupe, as if in defeat. "Anyone who wants to can go home. I won't stop you. I'm going to dance. No matter what anyone says, I'm dancing. If I have to wander over the country to do it, I'll keep dancing. How can I not sing! How can I not dance!"

And so they stayed and they danced. Densuke and Okuni had to double up, doing five or six numbers in each performance. Mame beat the drum, often with tears in his eyes, and Yata did his childish best to play the flute. Omatsu stolidly danced behind Okuni. Often only three or four people paid to see them, but as long as even one person appeared, Okuni insisted that they dance. Okuni danced and sang with the energy of three. She was dancing, she knew, to remain sane. She did not notice the dark circles beneath Densuke's exhausted eyes.

Around the time the cool air of autumn could be felt at dusk and dawn, Onei brought familiar news: "Prostitutes' Kabuki is setting up in front of us again." The banners went up opposite their small theater. Court Maidens. Best in the World. Okuni's Kabuki. The inviting sounds of many *jabisen* called out across the riding field. Instead of being discouraged, the challenge rejuvenated the few members who were left in Okuni's troupe. In the crisp fall weather, the conch shell at the Court Maidens theater blew loudly to draw in spectators. Suddenly Onei, who had said she wanted to go back to Izumo, leaped on the stage, eager to add her footsteps to those of Omatsu and the other girls. The drums beat loudly, and Densuke appeared carrying two baskets of pottery on the end of a stout pole. He dropped the baskets to the ground, twirling the pole in a bravura display of strength. His virile, masculine movements were so new and unexpected the audience was jolted into excited applause. The number of spectators in the theater grew. Okuni felt relieved. A new dance piece assured them of good crowds for some weeks to come. And she was excited by the challenge of dancing against Densuke's twirling pole. She leaped over and beneath it. She avoided and parried the pole as if defending against a spear-wielding soldier. Densuke's powerful gestures were the start of *aragoto*, the "rough" acting style for which Kabuki would later become famous. Okuni twisted her waist and hips and stamped lightly with her feet on the stage floor. When Densuke's and Okuni's eyes happened to meet, they smiled spontaneously at each other. Omatsu watched them stolidly from the wings. The audience was delighted. Okuni thought no pleasure was greater than dancing with Densuke.

> Together let us cross
> The slippery bridge of life.
> Shallow or deep,
> Should we fall,
> Let us fall together.

Kyuzo's stomach knotted in rage. Was Okuni laughing at him? He had hired half of her company. His theater had taken most of her audience. In spite of it, she continued to perform for a handful of spectators, as if nothing mattered. He would find another way.

One day Okuni was dancing leisurely in the cool fall air, as naturally as a fish swimming in water. She noticed a large man walk into the theater, holding a fat, black dog in his arms. The audience consisted of just three people that day, so Okuni immediately became aware that a fourth person had appeared. She stopped dancing so abruptly that Densuke's pole almost struck her. The pole fell to the stage floor with a clatter. The singing of the women trailed off. Mame's drumsticks were suspended in the air. Kyuzo gazed at their small stage, a mocking smile flickering across his face.

"Kyuzo. What do you want?" Okuni's voice was powerful, for she had been interrupted while singing. It surprised the spectators, who thought perhaps it was a new scene Okuni had invented. Kyuzo laughed lightly, as if Okuni's discomfort amused him. He sat down, holding Black in his lap.

"I've come to see the dance of Okuni, who calls herself the best in the world. Well, don't stop. You're offending your audience."

"If you don't want the audience offended, Kyuzo, you should leave."

"What a thing to say. I'm part of the audience. I bought a ticket and one for my dog. Black's a connoisseur, you know, and he doesn't like clumsy dancing."

"Of course. Is that why the dog hates whores' Kabuki so much?" Although Okuni laughed brightly, her eyes were fixed on Kyuzo.

"Ha, ha, ha." Kyuzo returned the laugh. "Since a dog can't buy a whore, I felt sorry for him and brought him along to see you dance."

"I refuse. Take your money back. Get out, Kyuzo."

"But I'm a customer. Money that's once paid can't be returned. Just like a grudge that's once earned can't ever be repaid."

"You're spiteful, Kyuzo. Aren't you satisfied that you bought my theater at Shijo Street? Are you set on destroying this theater, too?"

Kyuzo looked around at the three spectators. He nodded to them politely. "Okuni, I do think you should dance. Your fine audience is bored. If you don't dance, just as you say, your theater will be ruined."

"I want you to get out, Kyuzo. I'll never dance in front of you. Never."

"I've come to see you dance, Okuni. I paid my money and I'm not leaving until you do." Kyuzo took tickets out of his kimono breast and nodded politely to the spectators sitting beside him. "She is very discourteous to you. Here are tickets to see Okuni's Kabuki next door. Use them any time. Eat and drink all you want while you watch the show at the Court Maidens." Kyuzo turned smoothly back to Okuni. "I see you don't have many customers. You must be hard up. I could pay ten times the money you've taken in today, Okuni." He continued to grin broadly as he shifted his gaze to Densuke. "I owe that one a lot. You were kind to me when Okuni wasn't. You said she was your wife. Well, I heard Okuni loved someone called Sanza after that. Who's Okuni loving now? You must worry about it all the time. You know, even in my whorehouse we don't have women as loose as Okuni. If she weren't so old, I can tell you I'd snap her up for a whore."

Before Okuni could answer, Densuke leaped off the stage and struck Kyuzo with the pole he was carrying. Black tried to guard his master, but he was too old to help. Kyuzo fell backwards, blood oozing from a gash along one side of his face. Mame pulled Densuke back onto the stage. The other spectators fled out the door shouting. In another instant several roustabouts from the Court Maidens theater rushed in through the entrance.

"Master, Master! Are you all right?"

"Get me out of here. Quick."

Densuke did not regret his violent outburst, even though his stomach turned when he saw Kyuzo's bloody face. Probably more blood streamed from Densuke's wounded heart than from Kyuzo's face during the fight. Densuke felt a terrible fatigue. His head whirled. He couldn't stand.

Because Kyuzo was the master of an important house of prostitution, the case was referred to the city magistrate's office, which was charged with keeping order in the licensed quarter in Kyoto. The magistrate announced his decision the following afternoon: Okuni's troupe was expelled from the riding field at Kitano Shrine. As a matter of course, Kyuzo had bribed the magistrate but even if he hadn't it was an open-and-shut case. Witnesses had seen Densuke strike

Kyuzo and Densuke did not deny his guilt. The troupe had no grounds on which to contest the ruling.

"Another journey?" Densuke coughed. Looking over his shoulder, he asked Omatsu how many pills of medicine remained in Nagayasu's gold case. Omatsu didn't ask why he wanted to know. She replied that three pills were left.

"Just three?" Densuke coughed weakly and his gaze drifted far away.

Twenty-Four

One month later, in midautumn 1608, the troupe turned off from the coastal highway at the castle town of Himeji and took the branch road leading northwest toward Izumo. Walking under a cloudless sky, after a few days they reached the province of Mimasaka, where Sanza had been killed five years earlier. Farmers were reaping a rich harvest of grain in the rice fields that stretched in rolling, yellow waves to the horizon. It was hard work to cut each stalk by hand, as was the custom. When the troupe was still a day away from the site of Lord Tadamasa's castle on Tsuru Hill, Densuke became too ill to walk. A sympathetic farmer allowed them to stay in his barn in exchange for help with the harvest. They were welcome because, as the saying goes, a farmer will borrow even a cat's hands to get in the harvest. Each day Okuni, Onei, and the others cut the ripe stalks of rice and carried the sheaves in from the fields while Omatsu cared for Densuke. The women easily adapted to the demanding labor, for their bodies had been hardened by many years of dancing.

A few evenings later, drums and flutes sounded from the neighboring village of Nagi. The villagers were joyfully celebrating the bountiful harvest with a shrine festival. Each night Okuni joined the dancing, praying to the gods that Densuke would recover so that they could dance together again. The last evening of the festival, Okuni returned to the barn and showed Densuke how she had folded her hands to pray while dancing.

"Densuke, tonight I danced exactly like a shrine priestess."

"Yes. As Baian said, a shrine priestess." Densuke closed his eyes, too exhausted to say more.

Densuke's racking cough and whistling breath gradually worsened, until finally he couldn't eat the smallest morsel of food. Okuni showed Omatsu how to massage his body to relieve some of the agonizing pain in his chest and limbs. Okuni was shocked when she felt Densuke's emaciated bones beneath her fingers. On the advice of a local doctor, Mame and Yata searched out and killed a snake for its fresh blood. As Densuke was trying to drink the blood, he began to choke. He gasped for breath, writhing in agony. In desperation, Okuni put her mouth to Densuke's and sucked thick plugs of phlegm, mucus, and blood from his throat and lungs, enough to fill three bowls. When the choking subsided, Densuke weakly smiled at Okuni and reached for her hand.

"How long are you going to dance, Okuni?"

"Until the day I die. Get well quickly, Densuke, so we can dance together at the Grand Shrine in Izumo."

That night Densuke seemed to breathe easier, but in the morning he was dead. He was buried in the hard, dry earth of autumn with autumn flowers on his grave.

Everyone except Okuni and Omatsu wept when Densuke died. For the next several days Okuni moved in a daze. Although Onei cried hard, she did not lose her presence of mind. "It's time to go home, Okuni," she said quietly.

"Home?" Okuni stared vacantly.

"To Izumo. Home to Izumo."

"Well, Yata, will you dance with me in Izumo?" Okuni asked the boy.

"I'm going to be a farmer. I'll dance in Izumo's festival, like everyone."

Okuni turned to Omatsu. "Will you come to Izumo, Omatsu? It's far from Moriguchi village."

Omatsu, who had been drained of life in the days after Densuke's death, answered Okuni strongly, "I'm going where Okuni goes. That's what Densuke would do if he were alive."

They left for Izumo in the night. As the small group walked

beside lush fields of rice waiting to be harvested, the moon rose in the clear, cold sky. Sanza was dead. Densuke, too, was dead. Only Okuni was left. She stopped walking. Although it was the full moon of autumn, Okuni's vision was blurred so it looked like a hazy spring moon. Tears that burned her eyes froze running down her cheeks. Okuni set her lips and tried hard not to weep. She tried to keep her body from shaking in the cold. She lifted her face to the heavens, and looked at the misted full moon with unblinking eyes.

Okuni returned to Izumo in 1608 in the middle of winter, twenty-one years after she had left to dance in the capital. On the heels of a rich harvest, unusually fierce winter winds swept the farmhouses of Nakamura village, nestled close to Izumo Grand Shrine. But people in their heavily-roofed houses ignored the intense cold because they were occupied with an all-consuming, sacred task. They were rebuilding the Grand Shrine. Every thirty years the Deity required a new residence and the time had come for workmen to construct a duplicate of the main shrine building. In the spring, the Deity would move into his new dwelling in a divine ceremony. According to Shinto belief, the community's health and prosperity depended upon expelling ritual impurities. Defilement increased with age. Hence, constructing a new shrine building to house the God was a symbolic act of regeneration.

The winter mountains were as Okuni remembered them from her childhood, already white with advancing snow. The Hii River, the Eight-Legged Dragon, was totally changed, however. Where streams once flowed there were now sandy rice fields, and where houses and fields had stood Okuni saw steep frozen banks of the river's meandering branches. Okuni showed Omatsu around the village. They visited Sanemon's old home. He had died some years before, but his family prospered by running a smithy in his large home. Near a fiery-red forge, men were hammering out iron nails, clamps, and metal decorations for the new shrine building.

"Sanemon's dead," one of the men said. "He had two daughters. The youngest went off to the city. She danced Kabuki with Okuni."

"You mean Okiku?"

"Um. The oldest, Okaga, became a nun."

"I heard that. Where does she live?"

"Renga Hermitage." He pointed the way to a grove of trees across the fields.

Okuni saw a bent and wrinkled old woman reading Buddhist prayers inside the tiny hut. Okuni and Omatsu stood outside in the snowy garden waiting for her to finish so they could ask about Okaga.

When the nun put her books away and looked up, she called out, "Okuni? Is it you, Okuni?"

"Okaga?"

"Yes, it's me." Okaga smiled and waved Okuni and Omatsu into the small room.

"Okaga, you've changed."

"You haven't, Okuni." Okaga laughed and showed a toothless mouth. It didn't seem possible that Okaga had become this nut-brown, shriveled-up woman. Okaga was younger than Okuni by several years. But Okuni had danced without stopping, while Okaga had let the months and years slip past, scarcely living.

"Make yourselves at home," Okaga said warmly. "I'm penniless but you can live here. I guard our Lord Buddha of Mercy and have an easy life." She laughed again, her creased face so wrinkled that Okuni could scarcely recognize her.

"People in Izumo seem prosperous. I didn't expect that."

Okaga put some rice gruel over the wood fire to warm. "They're getting good wages to rebuild the shrine. But in half a year, when that's done, we'll be poor again. Unless the new shrine tames the Dragon this time."

"Is the river that bad?"

"The sand from Iron Mountain keeps coming down the river. It's burying Izumo."

In the days that followed, Okaga often asked Okuni to tell her everything that had happened in the troupe after she left. Okuni recounted some events but often she did not feel like talking. One day after Omatsu had gone outside, Okaga said in a low voice, "I heard that Okiku did a foolish thing with Sankuro. I wonder where she is in this cold weather?"

"Omatsu told you?"

"I pried it out of her. Okiku's my sister. I wanted to know. You wouldn't say anything."

"Okiku wasn't foolish, Okaga. When a man and woman love each other, they find happiness living together."

"You've always said that, Okuni. Oh, I suppose the one who goes off to a new lover is happy. But when you're left behind, it's misery. I never got over losing Yokichi. I haven't been alive since he died. You know, when I came back to Izumo, Kyuzo asked about you so many times I felt sorry for him."

"I don't want to talk about it."

"Yes. It's old history." Okaga laughed understandingly. Omatsu returned to the room, and then went out again to get water. "I can't believe Densuke married that dull Omatsu. I thought Densuke loved you, Okuni." Okaga chuckled.

"Omatsu nursed Densuke when he was sick, and then. . ."

"Oh, I see." Okaga continued to chuckle and wrinkle her face in a toothless, knowing smile.

"It's true."

And then Okuni began to tell Okaga the story of her love affair with Sanza. Wasn't it strange, she thought, that she was talking eloquently about Sanza as if he were a character in a novel or a play? Okaga wept when Okuni described Sanza leaving her and his death.

"When you passed through Mimasaka did you visit his grave?"

"Whose grave?"

"Why, Sanza's. Did you go there?"

"No. I didn't look for it."

"Being the lord's brother-in-law, he would have a big grave. Even if you didn't look. . ."

"I didn't think about Sanza in Mimasaka."

"You're merciless, Okuni. I think you left Kyuzo and Sankuro because thay didn't suit you." Okaga's face crinkled up as she laughed again.

As the winter grew colder, Okuni began to feel strange. She was restless. She knew she couldn't live with Okaga much longer, but her limbs were so heavy she could hardly move. She was tired all the time. Omatsu did the housework around the hermitage while Okaga went out each morning begging in the village for their food. Okuni did not go out.

"Omatsu, would you lay out my bedding now?"

When Omatsu was helping Okuni into bed, she found that Okuni's skin was burning hot. She wet a towel and placed it on Okuni's forehead. Okaga was terrified when steam began to rise from the towel. She pulled Omatsu away from the bed. "What a terrible fever. What is it?"

"Consumption, most likely."

"Do you know what consumption is, Omatsu?"

"Densuke died of it. In the beginning he had a fever, too," Omatsu replied matter-of-factly.

"Then, Okuni got it from Densuke?"

Omatsu didn't answer. She went back to the bed and replaced the steaming cloth on Okuni's forehead with a cold one.

Okuni's fever lasted ten days. As it progressed, she groaned in agony but she did not cough. The New Year came and went. Okaga brought home rice offerings that had been placed on the altar at the Grand Shrine. She cooked the excellent rice, and Omatsu fed it to Okuni in tiny mouthfuls. Okuni gradually got better.

"I'm sorry I was so much trouble, Okaga, Omatsu. People get sick when they move from one place to another." Okuni spoke in a leaden voice. She had eaten little, and her large body had become thin.

"A message came while you were sick. The blast furnace workers at Iron Mountain want you to dance for them."

"What? At Iron Mountain?" Okuni sat up, her eyes suddenly alive and sparkling.

Okaga gently pushed her down on the pallet. "You were in the middle of your fever. I told them you were sick. I sent them away," she said soothingly.

"I'm going to dance, Okaga. I'm going where they make molten steel, and I'm going to dance."

"Get well and then you can dance. The people in Nakamura are expecting you to dance at the festival when the new shrine is opened in April. You can dance then."

"No. I'll dance for the steelworkers at Iron Mountain first."

"Calm down. First you have to be cured."

"I'll get well if I dance. The reason I had the fever is that I'm not singing and I'm not dancing." Okuni believed this, or at least she wanted to believe it. "I'm sick because all I do is talk about depressing things with you, Okaga."

"How can you say such a dreadful thing? Well, it shows that you're getting better." Okaga laughed and said, "You'll end up doing what you want to do no matter what I say." She didn't try to stop Okuni after that.

Staring into the space above her head, Okuni could feel strength coming into her body again. The furnaces where molten steel was forged were calling her. The people of Iron Mountain who gave birth to her father and mother had sent for her. I will dance. I will dance at the blazing furnaces of steel.

"Omatsu, tell Mame to bring the banners. Go to the houses of all the girls. We won't be a large troupe, but we'll dance at Iron Mountain exactly as we danced in Kyoto."

Omatsu did what Okuni told her to do. Late in the evening she returned to the hermitage alone. She was carrying the two banners herself. With Okaga's help Okuni had been laying out all the costumes and was trying to decide who should wear which kimono. She looked up as she heard Omatsu enter. "What happened?"

"They're not coming."

"Why not?"

"Mame and Yata have to work at the shrine. Onei doesn't want to leave her family. She's just settling in, she said."

"And the girls?"

"The same as Onei."

"They said they wouldn't come, eh?" Okuni glared fiercely at her.

Okuni understood what Onei and the others were feeling. The people in Nakamura village feared and hated the steelworkers from Iron Mountain. It was the steelworkers who filled the river with sand that flooded their rice fields. At the same time, those steelworkers made the iron that Sanemon's family forged into hoes and plows for the farmers to use. The steel to decorate Izumo's Grand Shrine came from Iron Mountain, too. There was a long-standing relationship between the people of the plains and the people of the mountains, but it wasn't friendly. Okuni knew perfectly well that the farmers had protected her mother and father partly out of spite toward the iron-workers, as well as in sympathy for the young couple.

"I'll go alone."

Omatsu looked reproachfully at Okuni. "If you go, you know I'll go with you."

"That's right, Omatsu, we'll go together."

Okuni nodded firmly, but then felt completely lost. Who will sing? Who will beat the drum? Who will strike the bell?

"We have to rehearse, Omatsu."

Not just rehearse. The entire performance had to be changed. Could Okuni's Kabuki be done by only two women? Okuni lay with her head on the pillow. She closed her eyes to think. Okaga motioned to Omatsu to put away the costumes that were scattered about.

For several days Okuni arranged the program in her mind. Then she and Omatsu began to rehearse. Often she felt exhausted but she did not stop practicing. Omatsu is as bad a dancer as ever, Okuni thought. As in the old days, Okuni scolded Omatsu, and Omatsu made no response. They continued rehearsing.

Okaga visited Sanemon's family at the smithy to ask them to pass on Okuni's message to the steelworkers. A reply quickly came back from Iron Mountain: Okuni was to come immediately.

Okuni set out for Iron Mountain that day, brushing aside Okaga's objections that it was snowing and Okuni was too ill to travel. Okuni cut off her hair to look like a man, put a heavy hemp robe over several layers of dancing costumes, and hung the Buddhist rosary and prayer bell around her neck. She turned to Omatsu. "All right, Omatsu, let's go."

The banners, Best in the World and Okuni's Kabuki, were wrapped around two freshly cut bamboo poles, and Omatsu fastened the poles to her back. Okuni and Omatsu silently left the hermitage. Dawn was just breaking and the wind was strong. Large snowflakes scattered before them. The two women walked without speaking beside the Hii River. By afternoon the curves in the river became sharper as the path climbed the foothills of Iron Mountain. Okuni looked back. Omatsu was following with the two poles strapped on her back.

"Are they heavy, Omatsu?"

"Yes."

"I should have asked Mame myself. He would have come."

"I don't mind. I'll carry them."

The path got narrower and steeper. Okuni took up the front of the poles, so that with Omatsu plodding steadily behind her, she had no chance to stop and rest. She laughed to think how willing she had been to enter the mountains in midwinter on this steep, difficult path. Where the poles rested on her shoulder she could feel Omatsu's steady strength supporting her. How strange, she thought, that only we two women are left. The woman whom Densuke had loved but had never made love to, and the woman to whom he had made love and had never loved. Okuni's eyes filled with tears as she acknowledged that it was Densuke who bound Omatsu to her. She stopped, and pushed from behind by the poles, Okuni fell to her knees.

Each ate a rice ball in the late afternoon. When they began to feel the cold they started walking again. The path became steeper and slippery with ice and hard snow. They continued walking in the dark, now with Omatsu in the lead.

Okuni staggered and fell. She could see a fire up ahead.

"We can rest. You look tired." Omatsu showed no expression.

Okuni shook her head. "No, that must be Iron Mountain village. We'll go on."

They continued to walk for what seemed a very long time without the fire coming any closer. The waning moon was setting when they arrived at the house where the small fire burned. They knocked, exhausted and cold. The man who opened the door brightened when he heard Okuni's name. Everyone was waiting for her. He clucked sympathetically, "Have you women been walking since morning? That's awful. Sit by the fire while I get you something hot. It's another day's walk to the furnaces at Iron Mountain. You can sleep here tonight."

Okuni and Omatsu devoured a full pot of steaming rice gruel before they fell into a deep sleep. Okuni was much too exhausted to dream.

Tanabe Michikuni sat upright in his study with his arms folded. "Hm. So the woman Okuni has arrived from Izumo?" Michikuni was the sixth generation of his family to be headman of Iron Mountain village. His brisk, hearty commands showed that he was in an ebullient mood, proud to be Okuni's sponsor. They also made clear that his authority was absolute and unquestioned in Iron Mountain.

"Have Okuni describe the stage she used in Kyoto. Build a stage exactly like it. Pass word that the performance will begin two hours after noon today."

It was the morning after Okuni and Omatsu had arrived at Iron Mountain. Okuni felt wonderfully refreshed after sleeping for ten uninterrupted hours. After she and Omatsu prepared for the performance, one of Michikuni's officials led her through the village to the tall, heavy gate that opened onto the Tanabe family compound. When several servants pushed the gate back, a large crowd of people swarmed through the open entryway into the compound. They were the workers of Iron Mountain, miners who dug iron-bearing rocks from the mountainside, crushers who smashed the rocks into ore, and coolies who hauled the ore to the furnace. Some were laborers who dumped the slag and sand into the river and packers who carried the finished steel on their backs down the mountain. Most important were the smelters, who managed the intricate process of making molten steel. This steel-smelting village and others like it were deep in the mountains. It wasn't strange that desperate men came to work here—*ronin*, samurai deserters, peasants cast out of their villages, derelicts, tramps, and even thieves and murderers. When farmers' crops failed, they too came to the furnaces to work. Men who came into the mountains had to be strong and resourceful to survive. They were a formidable group, existing outside of samurai control. The Lord of Izumo worried about their power constantly. What if they descended from their mountain stronghold to attack him in his castle at Matsue?

"What is this?" Okuni stopped in the street, looking at the thick whitewashed walls of many buildings.

"This is the residence of the village head, Tanabe Michikuni."

"All these huge, square buildings? It looks like a castle."

"You won't see a turret or citadel," the official said, smiling. "They're storehouses."

"Really? What do you keep in them?"

"Many things. Rice. Tools. Finished steel before it's carried out. There are forty-eight storehouses."

Reaching Michikuni's residence, Okuni looked around and saw that it was surrounded on all sides by towering storehouses, just like the inner keep of a castle. Only a provincial lord could build a castle, but the Tanabe family of commoners had planned this castlelike complex of buildings as strong as any samurai fortress. Do all men, she wondered, want to build castles?

The official took her into the inner courtyard, now solidly filled with men. She had never imagined that so many people lived in Iron Mountain. There were thousands upon thousands. Men were perched on storehouse roofs like pigeons. The acrid smell of workmen's sweat filled the air, almost overpowering Okuni. Then she saw the stage set up in the garden. It was much finer than she had expected. In fact, it was better than any stage she had danced on in Kyoto. The aroma of its freshly sawn cypress planks still rose in smoking tendrils in the cold air. Skilled workmen had built the splendid stage and entry ramp in less than three hours. The stage faced the open, main room of the Michikuni's residence, just as the stage at the Imperial Palace had faced the open-sided audience hall when Okuni danced for Lady Sakiko six years before.

Omatsu was already backstage. She was wearing a bright woman's kimono of gold-colored silk brocade. Her hair flowed down her back and a broad scarlet sash was tied around her waist. In contrast, Okuni put on a man's plain blue-green kimono that she secured low on the hips with a man's narrow sash. She tied her short hair up in a masculine style. As a single touch of femininity, Okuni slipped a sprig of plum blossoms in her hair. A Buddhist prayer bell rested on the breast of each woman.

"It's time, Omatsu."

"Yes."

Okuni raised a red-tasseled mallet in her right hand. She struck the bell on her breast, at the same time singing out in a clear voice. She danced along the rampway and onto the stage.

> In Kyoto's flowery spring,
> In Kyoto's flowery spring,
> Let's go see the Kabuki Dance.
> Birds' songs change each year,
> But the heart of Kabuki remains the same.
> People high and low
> Come to worship
> And to cheer,
> God's gift to mankind!
> This is God's gift to man!

Okuni saw the dignified man sitting on a luxurious cushion placed in the center of the main reception room. It was Michikuni, her host. Okuni moved to the front of the stage, where she introduced herself in the formal manner of the protagonist in a Noh drama. Her voice rang out clearly in the cold winter air. The men, packed together in the garden and looking down from the roofs of the storehouses, gradually became silent.

"First of all, know that I am a Priestess who serves the Grand Shrine at Izumo. My name is Okuni. On this occasion, I have come from the Capital to present myself to the residents of Iron Mountain where my parents were born. Now, I will begin the Kabuki Dance."

The rough steelworkers yelled their approval when they heard Okuni's skillful introduction. They clapped loudly and called out for her to go on. Many of the workers were slightly tense because their master was present, but Okuni's confident manner put them at ease. Although it was midwinter, the day was cheerfully bright. Michikuni had placed scores of servants in the audience who now began to pour hot rice wine freely. Michikuni had carefully prepared this treat for his followers. The audience of working men began to drink and enjoy themselves.

> Each year passes and men age
> In this uncertain world,
> But the color and the scent of the flowers
> At my lodging never change.

Omatsu did not add her rough voice. Okuni continued to sing alone. And she continued to dance.

> Sadness lasts a short moment,
> Happiness, too, when we reflect,
> Is a dream.
>
> Vows of love are transient,
> Sash of flowers, half untied.
> Great names rise,
> But the body decays.
> The heart of man,
> Changeable as the water's flow.
> On what can man depend?
>
> Put the moon in a flower basket,
> Never let it go.
> Hold it as a treasure,
> Never let it dim.

Okuni continued to sing without reservation the songs she had cherished most during her twenty years of dancing. She went on dancing, sometimes dreamily with tears in her eyes, sometimes leaping high in the air as she kicked up the hems of her skirt. She did not even hold a fan in her hand. She danced with her arms and her chest, with her hips and feet. Stimulated by many cups of wine, the workmen packed together at Michikuni's residence were also intoxicated by Okuni's dance, drawn in by each gesture of her hands, mesmerized by the rhythm of her feet. No one saw Omatsu, though she was dressed in a gorgeous kimono. Okuni's singing captured the men's hearts, whatever she sang entranced them. Okuni's soaring voice, passing over the tops of the storehouses, seemed to echo in the surrounding mountains, reaching into every valley. Seen against the plain costume, the one splash of bright red from the silk cord around her neck made Okuni seem like an incarnation of a plum tree in first bloom.

After the last song, there was a stir among the men, and calls rang out: "Beautiful!" "Sing it again!" Pleased that the workers liked the song, without pausing Okuni sang it again.

> Put the moon in a flower basket,
> Never let it go.
> Hold it as a treasure,
> Never let it dim.

The men applauded and some took up the lyrics, so that Okuni repeated the song a third time. By the end of the short verse, it seemed that everyone in the compound was lustily singing along with Okuni.

> Put the moon in a flower basket,
> Never let it go.
> Hold it as a treasure,
> Never let it dim.

The steelworkers were so moved, and they had had so much to drink, that they wouldn't quiet down after Okuni had sung her last song. Some groups of men tried to remember the lyrics and continued to sing. Others urged their friends to mimic Okuni's dance movements. Men gulped down whole cups of wine until they were half crazy with excitement. They howled and yelled. The courtyard was in such an uproar it resembled a disturbed hive of mountain bees. Michikuni, too, was strangely aroused, and he wanted to talk with this woman. But first he had to assert control over his workers. He spoke to Okuni in a loud voice, as much to quiet his tumultuous men as to address her.

"Okuni from Izumo, you danced very well." His bearing was as refined and commanding as a samurai lord. "Name your reward! I will grant it!"

Okuni had intended to approach Michikuni at the end of her performance, but workers in front of the stage were packed together so tightly an ant could not squeeze through. So Okuni knelt where she was, on the fresh-scented boards of the stage, and bowed to Michikuni. "Since you command it, I request three favors." Although she modestly lowered her gaze, Okuni drew on twenty years of stage experience to project her voice into the farthest corners of the compound.

"Three? Very well. Make three requests. I shall grant them all."

The men quieted in order to hear the remarkable exchange between their master and Okuni. Keeping her fingertips respectfully on the floor, Okuni lifted her head. She gazed at Michikuni, a man not much older than herself.

"My father and my mother were Iron Mountain people," she announced.

"So you said onstage. Is it true?"

"My father was an ore crusher and my mother's family were smelters. Because she was higher in rank than he, they could not live as husband and wife in Iron Mountain village, for that was against your custom. They ran away and lived at Nakamura village in the plains. A few months after I was born, they were drowned in the great flood of 1573."

The men stirred. They had not imagined that Okuni was connected to Iron Mountain. What Okuni did not say was that the elders of Iron Mountain had driven her parents from their home in the middle of the winter. Or that Iron Mountain men had pursued them down the river, hoping to capture and kill them. She did not describe the terror her mother felt or the poverty her father endured. When Okuni was a tiny girl, her granny recounted those terrible stories to her again and again. Instead, Okuni looked at Michikuni and continued her carefully prepared narration.

"When my parents died, I was brought up by one Sanemon, a farmer and blacksmith in Nakamura village. His house is in the shadow of the Grand Shrine. Therefore, I announce myself as Okuni from Izumo."

"Very well. Tell me what you want." Michikuni was not interested in the details of Okuni's life. He impatiently waited for Okuni to answer his question.

"First, I want to be buried a woman of Iron Mountain when I die."

"That's easily done."

"So that no one will ever know where I lie, I ask to be buried in an unmarked grave."

"Oh, and why do you want that?" It was a bizarre and amusing request, Michikuni thought, edging forward. She was young and very famous. Why would she want to be buried anonymously?

"After a flower blooms on a tree, its seed melts into the earth and disappears. It is nature's law. I, Okuni, planted the seed of Kabuki on the riverbank in the capital. Now blossoms of Kabuki are found in Edo and in every part of the country. Their color and scent will change according to people's taste, which includes even the brightness of *jabisen* music, which I so dislike. As long as my name lives, I want Okuni from Izumo to be remembered as the seed that vanished into the eternal earth and not compared to the full-blooming flower."

"Agreed. And second?"

"Second, please allow me to see the blast furnace fire."

"Ahh, the fire that has burned for six generations? It's not like your Kabuki seed, Okuni. The fire in my family will burn forever.

Agreed, you can see the fire." He laughed disdainfully, in a loud tone, so everyone would hear. "Well, well, so this is what the best woman in the world wants? There isn't a more powerful family in western Japan than the Tanabes of Iron Mountain! The Lord of Izumo has bad dreams at night when he considers what my ten thousand men might do to his castle! Yet Okuni can only ask that I guard her grave and let her see fire! Ha, ha, ha!"

"And third," Okuni broke in, stopping his mocking laugh, "please build barriers in the Hii River against the sand."

"Do what?" The confident smile on Michikuni's face instantly vanished.

Okuni continued smoothly, "I was born a child of Iron Mountain, and so I have the fire of steel in my veins. But I was raised on a farm in Izumo, by compassionate foster parents. If my dancing pleased you, make barriers in the river to hold back the sand. In this way I will repay the debt I owe to the farmers of Izumo." She bowed deeply.

Michikuni stared pale-faced at the prostrated Okuni. His clenched hands were trembling. The work would take hundreds of men and horses. It would never end. He was not even certain it could be done. He had been careless to goad the woman who was, truly, the Best in the World. What should he do? He had given his promise before thousands of his men. They had heard Okuni's request. Michikuni swallowed and sat erect.

"Okuni!" He called out, so that everyone could hear.

"Yes."

"You've asked me to stop the sand in the Hii River. I will do it!" In the end, it might be good to be seen as a benefactor of the farmers in Izumo.

"Thank you."

"Show her the fire." Michikuni threw his words at the manager sitting at his side. Michikuni had intended to ask Okuni to dance for several more days on the large new stage. But now he had no desire ever to see her again. His mind was deep into the problem of how to build the barriers he had promised. Michikuni rose and hurriedly strode out of the reception room.

Omatsu remained behind when Okuni was led to the site of the blast furnaces by an old man wearing dark blue work clothes. Immense wooden buildings stood in a row along the base of a hill. "Women aren't usually allowed to see the fire. But it's our master's order, so follow me," the old man said. He stopped at the door to one of the buildings. "This will protect you from the fire." He helped her put on special clothes of thick indigo-dyed cotton. Her whole body was covered, except for her eyes.

During the seventy-seven-day process of making molten steel, the only way into or out of the building was through a tiny crawl hole. Okuni stooped and went through that entrance. A pillar of fire rose before her eyes. Four men, stripped almost naked, trod on poles that worked a huge bellows. Each time they put their weight on the poles, flames shot into the air. Black figures moved in the darkness. The boss smelter intently monitored the flame, determining from its color when to have men add coal to the fire or spread more iron ore on the flame. The open fire was beautiful. Its splendor overwhelmed Okuni. More than twenty men shouted as they worked, but the furnace, roaring like a giant animal, obliterated their sounds. Okuni felt sweat pour from her skin and in an instant disappear in the terrible heat. Her mother and father had put this fire in her body. Now she understood their pain at leaving it. She felt she was being consumed by it. She had a burning thirst. All the moisture in her body was being sucked out by the terrifying heat.

The old man plucked at her sleeve and pointed to the tiny door. Okuni nodded. She thought it was right that this fire was kept secret and sacred. Outside, the biting cold air refreshed her. They started down the slope, leaving the furnaces behind.

"Could you show me where my father crushed rock into ore?"

"It's up the stream. It's easy to find, but you'll be cold."

"I don't feel cold."

"It's where the water turns red."

"I can go alone."

"I'll show you if you want." Reluctantly, the old man started along the river. He was tired, and he was missing out on the free wine being served back at his master's. "It's snowing. Look." He stopped. Clearly, he didn't want to go on.

"I'll go along the river as you said. And I'll come back the same way. Don't worry, I won't get lost. Thank you for your trouble."

Okuni waved gaily to the old man, who had already turned and was hurrying away. She climbed alongside the narrowing stream. It was not a tenth as wide as the river in the plains where she had drawn water as a child, Okuni thought. The stream became swifter, tumbling in steep falls and cascades. It was violent, sharp.

"Ahh!"

In an instant the flowing water had turned red. She cried out but the sound caught in her dry throat. The Hii River is red. Exactly the color of blood. It's red with iron mineral crushed out of the rocks above. She climbed beside the ever-steeper, swiftly flowing stream, now so narrow she could step across it. She bent over and scooped up a handful of the water, swirling with grains of the fine red mineral and white sand. She ran and crawled over the rocks, climbing higher and higher toward the red rocks that her father had quarried and smashed in the flowing stream. The snow was falling harder, melting in the water but piling up on the ground and rocks. She got handholds on rocks and kept climbing the slippery path.

A dull thud came out of the earth. Okuni looked up and saw a boulder rushing down the hillside. She tried to get out of its path. She slipped and the rock struck her. Searing heat flashed through her right leg, as if it had been thrust into the fire of the blast furnace. Had she been struck by a ball of fire, not a falling rock? She lay prostrate in the snow, slowly savoring the heat in her leg. Snow fell heavily with a faint rustling sound. She had no sensation of pain, only of an intense heat.

After a time Okuni lifted her head. She twisted upright, trying to see what had happened. One leg was crushed. She saw the white snow turn crimson where it was falling on smashed flesh and bones. Blood oozed and then poured from the pulverized leg. Her first thought was that she would never be able to dance again. Her legs were her life. As she watched quietly, she saw blood spurt from severed veins and arteries. The thought revolved slowly through her mind, I cannot dance again, I will never dance again.

She looked around and saw the boulder a few steps away. She decided to walk to it. When she tried to stand, a terrible pain shot through her leg, or through her mind, or both, she couldn't tell. Biting her lips, she slid through the snow and pulled herself onto the rock. Where her body brushed off the newly fallen snow the rock's beautiful red grain appeared. Black stars of crystal glittered in the deep red base. Where had she seen that before? Of course, the rock from Iron Mountain that lay at the base of Ieyasu's castle in Edo. Okuni placed her cheek affectionately on the boulder's blood-red surface.

"How long are you going to dance?"

"Until the day I die." She had danced until that day. She was content.

Peacefully, she closed her eyes. The pain in her leg gradually faded under the deepening snow. But the red of the plum blossoms in her hair would not ever fade.

When all around her was sheltered beneath the white, pure snow, a vision drifted through Okuni's mind. Densuke beckoned to her with a half-opened fan. She walked with light steps toward him. She buried her face in his bosom. Densuke began to sing in a voice that sounded to Okuni like her own. Or did it sound like the men of Iron Mountain?

> Put the moon in a flower basket,
> Never let it go.
> Hold it as a treasure,
> Never let it dim.

The snow swirled down and down as if it would never stop.

Epilogue

The soft breeze of early summer rustled the heads of rice that grew thickly in the paddies. Many days after Izumo's new shrine had been joyfully dedicated, puzzled farmers met and whispered among themselves.

"The Dragon isn't moving."

Each spring and summer the farmers of Nakamura village dreaded to watch the Hii River roll its ever-moving coils out of the mountains, through numerous clefts and valleys, and over Torigami Waterfall. Reaching the Izumo rice plain, it relentlessly scoured new channels through their fields. But this year the Eight-Legged Dragon slept. Its eight twisting legs did not bring sand down from the mountains, nor did the river channels change their course. Perhaps the farmers should have been pleased, but they wondered uneasily what it portended.

Later in summer people heard the news that barriers were blocking the upper course of the Hii River. According to the story going around, Okuni, the Best Woman in the World, had it done. People recalled that Okuni hadn't performed that spring when Izumo Shrine was rededicated, although many other Kabuki troupes from around the country had brought their songs and dances.

Curious neighbors in Nakamura village called on the old nun Okaga at Renga Hermitage. "It's too late to make a fuss about Okuni now. She died on Iron Mountain." Okaga spoke out bitterly. That winter, she had told many people of her fears for Okuni when she didn't come back from the mountains. But the neighbors hadn't listened to the old nun. They were preoccupied with the coming shrine ceremony.

"Okuni, dead?" The inquiring farmers were genuinely surprised. "Why? What happened?"

"I don't know," Okaga said, scowling. She had gone to the smithy to ask travelers from Iron Mountain. All they could say was that Okuni had died in the snow. Beyond that, they were evasive and unhelpful.

Spurred by curiosity, a party of farmers from Nakamura village set out to learn what had happened. They followed the same steep path Okuni had taken to Iron Mountain. Was it true that sand barriers had been built in Iron Mountain? Was it true that Okuni had ordered it? Where and how had Okuni died?

"The old nun says Okuni's folks came from Iron Mountain."

"An ironworker's kid? Raised in our village?"

"I don't know. She jabbered on and on. I couldn't make head nor tail of what she was saying."

"She said she danced in Okuni's troupe herself."

"Ah, she's lying."

"Well, I didn't believe her."

"Can you picture that old nun dancing?"

"It's nonsense. Could be the whole story about Okuni's a lie."

"Well, that's why we're going to Iron Mountain, isn't it? To find out."

"Right, that's right."

One man pointed ahead to the river and they all ran forward shouting. Looking down, they saw a row of closely spaced bamboo posts crossing the river from side to side. Fresh pine boughs lashed between the posts completely blocked the river's flow, except for a narrow channel that enabled fish to pass through.

"So it's true. There *is* a sand barrier."

"From the looks of the wood, it hasn't been up long."

"It must catch a lot of sand. What do they do with it?"

They continued their climb up the river, coming across more dams of the same type. They were impressed by the care with which the dams had been made: every last grain of sand was being settled out of the descending stream.

"The Dragon hasn't a chance of moving now."

"This was an enormous job."

They stood in awe, looking at each other and wondering who was responsible. Regardless of whose idea it was to capture the river's sand, one thing was clear: the dams would end the long history of antipathy between the farmers of Izumo and the steelworkers of Iron Mountain. The farmers bowed respectfully toward the sand barriers. They clapped their hands in prayer, thanking the gods for this favor. No one laughed for a long time after that.

When the farmers were nearing Iron Mountain village on the upper reaches of the river, they came across a party of workers dredging sand from the base of a dam and carrying it away in wicker baskets. The travelers bowed politely. "Hello. We're farmers from Nakamura village by Izumo Shrine."

Perhaps because the dialect and behavior of lowlanders was strange to them, the mountain men stood mute. They glared suspiciously at the farmers.

"We heard that a Kabuki actress named Okuni came to Iron Mountain to dance. We came to find out about her."

"Don't know."

The workmen inhospitably turned back to scooping up sand.

After a few moments, one of the farmers got up the courage to ask, "Who ordered the sand barriers to be built?"

"Our boss in Iron Mountain, Tanabe Michikuni."

"So it's true. Then it's really true." The farmers nodded to each other and then called down, "We're deeply grateful." The men from Iron Mountain didn't reply.

"We heard that Okuni danced in front of your master. Is it true?"

"Um. We saw it."

"You did? Really? We also heard that Okuni died."

"Yes. She died."

"How did it happen?"

"Don't know."

The workmen, who had appeared to be loosening up, now clamped their mouths shut. Swinging baskets of sand onto their shoulders, they bore their heavy loads out of the riverbed and down a mountain trail until they were out of sight.

The farmers from Izumo asked many people in Iron Mountain village about Okuni. They learned that Okuni had requested the sand barriers. They also learned that she had died in the snow with her cheek on a red boulder, and that the people of Iron Mountain gave her a proper burial. But they were not told about Okuni's conversation with the master of Iron Mountain, nor how she died, nor where she was buried.

The farmers from Izumo asked to have the red granite rock that Okuni lay beside in the snow. They lashed the rock to a pole and bore it home to Nakamura village on their shoulders, alternating carriers along the way.

The red rock was placed in the center of Nakamura Sanemon's family plot in the graveyard of Renga Hermitage. After a time, people in Izumo began to call it Okuni's gravestone. Indeed, Okuni's long hair, shorn off before her trip to Iron Mountain, rests beneath the rock, placed there in a Buddhist ceremony by the old nun, Okaga. Okaga cared for Okuni's grave the remaining years of her life. Her sudden aging, which had so surprised Okuni, ceased and she seemed to grow no older until the day she died fifty years later at the age of eighty-seven. While Okaga was living, she plied visitors with stories about Okuni, woven of fragments she had heard from Okuni, her own memories, and her imagination, so that after a while people in Nakamura started calling the hermitage Okuni Temple. A few people even worshiped a painting of Okuni for a time after the nun died. Eventually, the people who remembered Okaga's tales were all gone. But Okuni's granite stone remains. Its gleaming red form stands today, as it has for more than three hundred years, in the center of the Nakamura family plot, surrounded by the dark stones of Sanemon's family.

One other woman spent her life guarding Okuni's grave. Like the nun Okaga she, too, was long-lived.

Every month on the twenty-fifth day, which was about the time the nun Okaga had died, a stooped old woman from Iron Mountain village would appear beside a narrow channel of the Hii River. She would scoop up water in a wooden ladle and disappear through the trees in the direction of the red granite stone. Her forehead was deeply wrinkled, her head thrust forward, her face the exact image of the old woman from Moriguchi village who had died cursing Okuni. It was Omatsu. Okuni's death day was the twenty-fifth of February, the same day and month that she had danced at the Plum Blossom Festival at Tenmangu Shrine when she was seventeen years old.